RULES

of

ARRANGEMENT

MAREN MACKENZIE

ONE

"I'll write the paper for you, but ten pages on the decline of the USSR is going to cost you."

The gangly, acne-ridden boy sitting in front of her was Garrett Jacobsen, a sophomore having his third consultation of the year. He fidgeted and twisted his clammy hands as he spoke, his voice cracking every few words. In their two previous meetings, Garrett had never once forked over any cash—the victim of a guilty conscience, fear of getting caught, or both.

"Whatever you want. I just need some help this time, Addie. Really."

"Three hundred then. Four if I have to dig out any dusty, old textbooks at the library."

Garrett swallowed hard. "Okay. Deal."

Adelaide sighed and pulled out her trusty green notebook, which contained the signatures of all her paying customers. Her version of a binding contract. "Sign here and give me the prompt."

Garrett stared at the lined paper so hard that a vein in his forehead bulged. His pen shook over the paper as sweat beaded on his face. She waited for him to work up the courage, but after nearly a minute, she swiped the notebook back and closed the cover.

"Garrett, why do you torture yourself? Get to the library and write your damn paper."

"No!" he cried, motioning for her to open it back up. "I want you to do it."

They were sitting in a bustling coffee shop on the outer perimeter of campus, both because it was more discreet and because they gave discounted refills. The essay-writing business was good, but it wasn't *that* good.

Adelaide wasn't worried about anyone seeing them, but she knew better than to tempt fate. The longer she sat there, watching Garrett waffle, the greater the chances that someone would glance over and question what she did here every Sunday morning, meeting with an eclectic blend of university students that ranged from sports players and sorority princesses to STEM majors and drama kids.

Garrett was a double major in history and physics, a minor in engineering. He had more brain power than she could imagine, and yet even he'd ended up in front of her, asking for help. It wasn't good business to send him away—and it wasn't like her to say no to anyone who could pay—but Garrett was clearly a kid with morals, and she'd rather not see him compromise them. Not the way she had.

"Believe me, Garrett, you'll write this paper so much better than I can. You'll only feel like crap if you let me do it, and you know it."

His face fell into a grim line of acceptance. At their first meeting, he'd chickened out three minutes in. The second had gone only slightly longer. This time, he'd actually brought the money with him, but she was relieved to find him as reluctant as ever. People like Garrett reminded her that unlike many of her clients, there were actually some decent students left at this college, ones who valued hard work and originality instead of the easy way out. Garrett's fear—and ultimate reneging—was a refreshing change from the jaded peers she normally dealt with, who handed over whatever sum of cash she requested as long as it meant they could party as hard as they wanted, without the hassle of academics getting in the way.

"Here," Adelaide said, rummaging in her beat-up, oversized satchel. She pushed past Agnes Ritter's four-pager on Gaugin's *Vision After the Sermon* and Joe Hachoo's midterm analyzing the diverging economies of Argentina and the United States, and ripped a piece of paper out of a notebook. On it, she scribbled the name of a textbook she'd used for a similar paper last semester. "Forget the first four chapters; they're totally pointless. But the rest will give you all the information you need to get started."

Garrett accepted the slip of paper like it was a bar of gold, and she forced down a laugh. His appreciation was endearing.

"Thank you, Addie."

"No problem." She waved as he half-tripped and half-climbed out from his side of the table. "When you finish, send it my way. I'll give you a proofread, free of charge."

His grateful smile made her smile too. The book wasn't anything he couldn't have found on his own, but Garrett walked away, thinking he'd gotten the leg up he wanted, and she'd saved what felt like the last good person at Cranst University from a taste of corruption.

Tim Acker was her next client of the day, a star basketball player who'd been the buzz of campus since he arrived freshman year. Unfortunately, she'd offered her services to him while intoxicated, and even more unfortunately, it had been after they made out in a darkened corner of Cranst's local dive bar. She'd thought perhaps he wouldn't show—after all, they hadn't spoken since that night a week ago—but he burst through the doors a few minutes after Garrett left, as muscled and tan and blond as she recalled.

When he sat down, he kept his sunglasses on, as if they were in bright daylight, not an indoor café. "Hey, Addie."

"Hey," she greeted, trying to keep her posture cool and aloof.

The morning after she'd met Tim, she'd woken up cursing herself for revealing her side gig. She usually stayed away from the college's party scene for reasons like the one sitting in front of her. They presented too many opportunities for things to get out of control. She'd thought Tim was cute, and she'd been a little drunk, so she'd bragged a bit to make him interested in her. A completely brainless move on her part—if anyone at the university found out she wrote other people's papers for money, she'd be expelled immediately.

"So, how does this work? I pay you, and you bang it out?"

"Not so fast. First, we should talk about your assignment and go over dates and pricing."

Tim surreptitiously glanced around before he muttered, "It's an Economics paper, and I don't care what it costs."

Adelaide frowned. "No one is going to know what we're doing here unless you act like we're doing something illegal."

"We *are* doing something illegal."

"Debatable." Adelaide had become immune to worrying about that on a day-to-day basis. If she hadn't, she'd never get to sleep at night. "It's been three years and I haven't gotten caught yet."

"So you mentioned."

She had? Parts of their conversation were fuzzy, and she winced, wondering what else she wasn't remembering. She was *never* drinking again.

"Tell me about your paper."

"I have a girlfriend, you know."

Adelaide's stomach dropped.

Surprise must have shown on her face because Tim shrugged, like *my bad*, and uncomfortably ran a hand through his hair. "Just in case you were thinking me showing up here meant … I can't, like, be in a relationship with you or anything, just so you write my papers."

She wrinkled her nose in disgust. She'd never thought to ask him if he was in a relationship the other night—she hadn't thought she needed to. Which was another reason she stayed away from the party scene—most of her male peers were interested in quick hook-ups, followed by easy getaways. Sure, a drunken encounter was exciting every once in a while, but she never made it a habit. Guys her age usually disappointed her.

Tim was no different.

"One, you are seriously delusional if you think I accept *that* as a form of payment, and two, are you telling me that you had a *girlfriend* the other night when your tongue was halfway down my throat?"

Tim cringed. "I was drunk. I don't even remember what I was doing."

"Except you remembered enough to show up here?"

He gave her a blank look, completely missing her point.

She threw her hands up. "Forget it. Just tell me the assignment, please."

"It's ten pages on China's economic growth over the past twenty years."

"Due?"

"Tuesday."

"That's in two days."

"Yeah ..." He gave her another casual shrug. "I guess I forgot about it until now."

To ensure her fist didn't collide directly with his jaw, Adelaide flipped open her notebook and consulted her schedule instead. She was pretty booked for the next two days since three weeks into the semester was prime paper-writing season, but if she pushed some things around and worked through the night, she could get it done.

"With the rush charge, that's five hundred."

"Isn't that a little steep?"

She would have charged anyone else three fifty, but since Tim was higher on the douche scale than usual, she gave herself some cushion.

Adelaide snapped the notebook closed. "I'm sure you'll manage to get it done."

"No, no, wait! Okay. Five hundred. But it'd better be good."

"I'm assuming that means you want an A?"

"What else would I ask for?"

She shrugged. One of the most important parts of her business was agreeing upon the grade her customer wanted to receive—she'd learned that early on. It kept her customers happy and her workload down since most people only asked for a grade they themselves thought they could get, which was infrequently better than a B-plus. The really desperate ones were always willing to shell out more for a higher grade. That was where she made a nice bonus.

"One A on China's economic growth over the past twenty years. Give me the prompt."

"I needed to bring that?"

Adelaide rolled her eyes. "Get it to me by six, or the price goes up. I only take cash."

Tim snuck a glance around the coffee shop before holding out the bills under the table, forcing her to grab them there. She scowled but stuffed the money in her purse before he could change his mind.

"Sign here."

Unlike Garrett, Tim scribbled his name in her notebook without hesitation. She could see the relief in his posture once he had.

"Thanks, Addie. I knew you'd get it."

"I definitely got it," she responded dryly, shooting a dirty look at his back as he looped out of the coffee shop and into the sunny September day.

Tim Acker had had an easy life at a private high school, gotten a full ride to college, and would undoubtedly be sleeping with all sorts of adoring fans and cheerleaders once he hit the NBA. People like that didn't deserve any more lucky breaks. Still, Adelaide wasn't in a position to turn down five hundred dollars, not by a long shot.

She tried to shake off any lingering bitterness as she made her way back to her dorm, winding through the pathways and overpasses of the Connecticut campus she knew well now that she was in her senior year of college.

Home to seven thousand undergraduate students, Cranst University was a three-hundred-year-old New England institution that prided itself on its academics, culture, and a few celebrity alumni. At an hour and a half north of New York City, the location couldn't be beat. Adelaide had cried tears of actual joy when she was accepted because it meant she got to move back to Connecticut after being abruptly displaced by her sister six months prior.

But with that acceptance had come a hefty price tag. Cranst was an elite private school that didn't do merit scholarships, so tuition alone sucked her dry—not to mention, rent, food, and all the other expenses that went along with being a living, breathing human being. She'd been on her own financially since her parents died three and a half years ago, leaving her and her two older siblings orphans.

At least they'd be proud of Samantha and Michael, Adelaide thought wistfully.

Her brother and sister had plenty of money, didn't kiss other people's boyfriends, and would never even *dream* of writing someone else's paper for them. Her parents' deaths had fractured their relationships deeply, but even if it hadn't, she'd never tell her older siblings how she managed to afford her life here.

In her reverie, it took her a moment to realize someone had called her name. She looked to the left and right, but not until the voice shouted, "Addie!" a second time did she realize it was coming from behind her.

Adelaide squinted, trying to place the slim figure jogging toward her, whose face was covered with wiry sunglasses. He was wearing linen pants and a blue button-down shirt, looking more like he belonged on a yacht in the south of France than a historic college campus in Connecticut.

"I knew it was you," he exhaled, slowing to a walk and pushing his glasses into carefully styled dirty-blond hair.

She blinked in surprise. "Declan?"

"Adelaide Wright, I was worried you'd forgotten me."

Declan Jones had grown into his looks since they'd been neighbors, back when she lived in her childhood home in Hamden, Connecticut, before her parents died. His face was still long with little lines around his mouth, but now, he had a squared-off jaw and narrowed eyes, no longer the thin, knobby eighteen-year-old who had made her gasp in excitement, pain, and curiosity that summer night six years ago. She'd been sixteen at the time, but she could still remember the sweet taste of peach on his lips when he kissed her.

She'd never forget him—what girl ever forgot the boy she'd lost her virginity to?

Adelaide slowly shook her head. "What are you doing at Cranst?"

Declan's tongue snaked out of his own mouth, like he was remembering the taste of her too. She noticed he'd gotten his teeth fixed—they'd always been a little crooked, one overlapping the other.

"I'm here for an art class. My parents told me you had moved to California right after …" He trailed off. "I'm sorry, Addie. About your parents."

"Thank you," she responded automatically and hoped he didn't try to hug her or anything weird like that. There were many ways to live with grief, but the one she chose most often was to flat-out ignore its existence. "I'm a senior here now."

He gave her an unabashed once-over. "I can see that."

As a teenager, her brother, Michael, used to call him Declomania because he was convinced Declan had some sort of hidden serial-killer streak. She thought the way her mother had described him was more apt.

"He's just off-center," she'd correct, which was a polite way of saying his ultra-creativity made him someone others found it hard to relate to.

That air of awkwardness still clung to him now, despite the obviously expensive clothes and coiffed hair, but it had morphed into something brazen. "You've grown in all the right places."

Blood rushed to her face. When she had been a teenager and Declan was the shy, creative boy next door, she always found him more endearing than off-putting. They'd never been friends, more like acquaintances, so at the time, it was easy to invent her own ideas about the painting prodigy next door. He was quiet, mysterious, and people used to buy his artwork out of his parents' garage. It had been the perfect recipe for an adolescent crush.

"An art class?" she repeated, trying not to seem like his words made her fidget. "I thought you went to school in London."

"Not school exactly. Though I certainly got an education."

Whatever that meant. He was two years her senior; he would've graduated by now.

"We should catch up one day, Addie. Talk about old times."

"Sure. Maybe I'll see you around." She forced a smile and started to turn. "Good luck with your class."

She barely continued two steps down the path when he grabbed her wrist.

"Hang on, wait." His touch was alarmingly hard at first and then loosened. When she spun around, she found him looking guilty. "I wasn't completely honest with you just now."

"Excuse me?"

"Thing is …" He laughed awkwardly, running a practiced hand through his hair, almost like he was posing. Paint was embedded in the cuticles of his fingernails. "Shit, this is hard to say. I was actually going to meet you at the coffee shop, but I sort of chickened out."

Adelaide narrowed her eyes. "You saw me at the coffee shop?"

"No. I mean, yes. Yes, I saw you there. What I'm saying is, I was going to *meet you* at the coffee shop."

She stared at him, trying to figure out if he meant what she thought he did. All her customers knew about her Sundays at the coffee shop—those were her officially unofficial office hours. Clients came to pay, give her new work. New prospects would seek her out there, too, but her regulars always gave

Adelaide a heads-up when they sent someone to her. It was how she knew they were legit. Since no one had said anything, she felt her hackles rise. How the hell had Declan found out?

She shrugged, feigning innocence. "I have no idea what you're talking about."

He squinted at her, like he was debating something, and then pointed to a bench up ahead, along the path. "Can we sit down? It's so weird, running into you and then asking you about this, out in the open."

Adelaide wasn't wild about the idea, but curiosity got the better of her.

Once they were on the bench, Declan took a deep breath and faced her. "I'm taking History of Painting this semester— it's an art lecture, basically, pretty dry stuff. It's not hard, but I am inundated with work right now. Someone told me you could help me with that. I mean, not *you* specifically, but they said if I showed up at the coffee shop on Sunday morning, I'd find a girl who could."

"Who told you that exactly?"

One rule of her business: *if you get caught, never give anything up unless you absolutely have to.*

Declan folded his arms and smirked, like he was a parent, impressed with something their child had just said. "Agnes Ritter. She said you were helping her with a paper on Gaugin for Professor Hargrove. He teaches History of Painting."

Adelaide made no sudden moves. Agnes Ritter and her big mouth. When she'd agreed to that essay, something told her Agnes was going to blab to someone, but she needed the cash too much to refuse. She had explained to Agnes very clearly that this was a delicate business and that if Adelaide got in trouble, she would surely face punishment as well.

Agnes must have missed the memo.

"I'm taking History of Painting too," she said lamely, trying to buy herself a few seconds to think.

"Really? I haven't seen you."

"I haven't been yet. It's for my arts and humanities requirement. Why are *you* in that class? You already know all about painting."

Declan's lips twitched. "You remember?"

"Of course I remember. Four hours, sitting still for you? I don't think my spine has ever been the same."

His eyes darkened, heavy with memories. She instantly regretted bringing up the portrait he'd painted of her for reasons that had nothing to do with her spine curvature. "Then, I guess you remember what happened after too."

"Declan," she warned, waving him off even though she was still blushing. She did not want to talk to him about *that*. Ever. "Look, I really don't know anything about art. I'm barely a page into my own paper."

He leaned forward, his face conspicuously close to hers. "Not according to Agnes."

Adelaide considered him. She didn't like being approached this way, and it confused her that Declan was even *at* Cranst—especially for art. He could paint like a real artist, like the kind someone ended up studying in school.

Then again, her life had gotten derailed in ways she never imagined. Maybe something had happened to Declan too. She knew firsthand how surprising life's curveballs could be.

Declan raised his eyebrows. "I can pay whatever it costs."

She wasn't in a financial position to say no to that. Adelaide blew out a long breath. "Did you pick which painting you'd like me to write about?"

He smiled and settled back onto the bench. "Delacroix's *Liberty Leading the People*. Four pages, due this Wednesday, as you already know."

"Two hundred."

"Is that the former neighbor's discount?"

"There are no discounts," she said evenly without batting an eyelash.

Declan stuck out a hand. "Fair enough."

She hesitantly shook on it, unable to return his smile. "I only take cash."

"Of course. I assume I can pick it up in the same spot?" He pulled out his wallet and handed over two crisp hundred-dollar bills. "It really *was* nice to see you again, Addie. Weird circumstances, but you turned out just like I'd thought you would."

"Sure," she murmured, staring after him as he sauntered away.

Declan wasn't the way she remembered at all. She tried to shake it off, but as she gathered her things, an uneasy feeling descended on her, making the hair on the back of her neck stand at attention.

Halfway home, she realized that in all her surprise and fluster, she had forgotten to have him sign the book.

It had started as proofreading for her friends. A paper here, a cover letter there, a quick idea or two during the outline phase. She was a good writer, and she didn't mind helping.

The first time she wrote a paper for someone—first to last sentence, title to works cited—was freshman year. A girl in her dorm had broken her ankle and spent the entire night before the paper was due in the hospital. A mutual friend suggested she give Adelaide twenty dollars for six pages, double-spaced, one-inch margins—an analysis of a Malcolm Gladwell book covered in her Expository Writing class.

"You should consider doing this professionally," the girl joked when she got an A.

So Adelaide did.

Some of those initial essays were shaky, but once she learned standard formats and what each professor liked and didn't like, the work became better, more polished. She didn't advertise her services, of course, but six months into her sophomore year, she found she didn't need to. Word had gotten around. And it paid more than nannying bratty kids every weekend.

The risk was high, but her clients were happy to keep her services a secret. And just in case, she had them sign the notebook. Mutually assured destruction was a concept everyone seemed to understand in this line of work—if one went down, they all did.

There were only two people besides those listed in the book who knew how she made her money. They were sprawled out on their apartment's futon, eating Chinese food and watching television.

"Garrett finally pay up?" Katy, her roommate, asked without taking her eyes off the screen. "Imogen and I made a bet."

Imogen laughed around a mouthful of noodles. "I bet no, but only because she bet yes first."

Adelaide tugged her coat off and picked noodles right out of the container with her fingers. Their apartment was a typical college duplex with peeling paint and loud radiators. The whole place had seen better days, but it had a certain charm that worked for them. Plus, it was the only apartment they could afford.

"Sorry, Katy. Human decency lives to fight another day."

"Hell yes!" Imogen clapped, sticking her tongue out at Katy, who rolled her eyes and tugged apart her blonde topknot.

The three had lived together for two years now, though it felt like they'd been best friends a lot longer than that. Katy had been Adelaide's freshman roommate, and they had bonded over the generally deplorable conditions of their dorm. Imogen had lived down the hall with the same girl Adelaide had written her first paper for—Imogen was the one who had suggested it.

If they hadn't been there since the beginning, she doubted she'd have told them her secret. But she didn't regret that they knew. They were the two people she had never written papers for, the same two people who would never ask her. It was an unspoken agreement that what she did was about business, not friendship. Plus, moral or not, sometimes, you just had to come home and bitch about work.

"Katy owes me a drink."

Adelaide laughed. "That wasn't even the most interesting part of the morning. Do you guys remember the story about the peach schnapps?"

Katy's eyes went wide. "You mean about the artist guy?"

She nodded and told them all about bumping into Declan, which was juicy enough to make them pause the movie they'd been engrossed in.

"He *painted* a picture of you before you had sex," Katy reminded her, as if she could forget. "That rates as, like, one of the greatest first times of *all time.*"

"It was way less romantic than you're imagining. Sitting still hurt. Having sex hurt. And he seems to have grown up to be a stone-cold weirdo." She shrugged. "Still cute though. In a funny-looking way."

"Maybe it's your chance for a do-over," Imogen suggested with a wink.

Adelaide wiped her mouth and stood. If she didn't get behind a closed door, she'd get sucked into their hangover vortex of greasy noodles and happy-sad movies. "No sleeping with the clientele," she told them, making the rule up on the spot. She felt another twist in her stomach about Tim Acker's girlfriend. As if her karma wasn't shitty enough.

She wouldn't have blamed Katy and Imogen if they wanted nothing to do with her. By most people's standards, what she did was wrong—*really* wrong. In the beginning, a knot in her stomach would form every time she handed over a paper, but that, like the fear of getting caught, had faded over time. It wasn't her problem that kids were cheating themselves out of an expensive education at one of the nation's best universities. Like her, they had made their choices.

Plus, it gave her the chance at an education most people only dreamed about. If her work had been turned in legitimately, she'd have degrees in at least three more subjects than English by now.

Settled at her desk, she switched on her MacBook—a purchase made possible by one particularly difficult philosophy professor—when her phone rang.

She debated letting it go to voice mail. Adelaide loved her brother, but sometimes, it was easier to love him from a distance.

After their parents died, her sister, Samantha, promptly sold their childhood home in Hamden and moved them to California, where they took up residence with her new, NFL-player boyfriend. Michael had gone back to Notre Dame to finish his degree, leaving Adelaide stuck until she turned eighteen.

They were the hardest six months of her life. Samantha had always been uptight and slightly controlling, but becoming Adelaide's guardian made her unbearable. They fought constantly, and the words they'd hurled at each other during those dark days *still* cut deep enough to hurt.

Cranst had been her chance to get away from her sister and back to the last place she felt like she had a home. Or at least it *was*—until Samantha told Adelaide that if she left California, left their "family," she'd never see a dime of the inheritance her parents had left behind.

It was amazing—up until her parents died, Adelaide always felt defensive when people called Samantha a bitch. But once they were gone and her sister became her guardian, she had started to call her far worse. To her face.

"Ads!" Michael said when she gave in and answered. "I miss you."

"You saw me two weeks ago, Michael."

Whenever her brother came to the East Coast for work, he always made it a point to see her.

"Two weeks too long. How's school?"

"School is … the same as it always is. Busy semester. Lots of electives to finish up before graduation."

Straitlaced, hardworking Michael would be furious if he knew about the paper writing. And he'd no doubt go running to tell their sister too. Out of everyone, Samantha could *never* know about her little side hustle. If she had to choose between the university finding out and her sister, she'd take the university. The satisfaction Samantha would get, knowing that Adelaide had been forced to turn to a life of—if not crime—then extreme misconduct, made her twitch.

"The big G!" Michael cheered. "Take a left here, please. Sorry, Ads, I'm in an Uber."

Most of her calls with her brother happened while he was in transit. Michael worked for a big public relations firm in Los Angeles and spent most of his time traveling from meeting to meeting, lunch to drinks, drinks to dinner. Hobnobbing seemed to be a part of his job description.

"You sound busy," she noted, hoping it would prompt him to hang up.

"Never too busy for my baby sister. Tell me more about your classes."

"They're fine, Michael, I just told you. Hey, guess who I bumped into today?"

"Waiting on you."

"Declan Jones. From next door."

"Declomania?" Michael confirmed. "The nerdy art kid?"

"He's not really a nerd anymore. He's, like, suave and intense." She wound her pen through her fingers, thinking back over that morning's encounter. The more she thought about it, the more she became convinced Declan had been trying to overcompensate for his awkwardness as a teenager. He hadn't been a complete nerd anyway. He'd just been artistic, deep in his own head.

Her brother barked a few more directions at the driver before he returned his focus to her. "That kid always had a crush on you. I could never tell if it was cute or creepy."

Adelaide scoffed. She'd never told anyone besides her roommates about The Night of the Peach Schnapps, and she wasn't about to tell her brother. "He was just off—"

"'Off-center.' Yeah, I got it, Mom."

Adelaide knew he meant it as a joke, but for some reason, the comment sent a tight pain through her chest. She had no idea how he could bring her up so casually, like their mother was still there somehow, like their whole world hadn't completely imploded when she left it. It was only in the past year that she could say *Mom* or *Dad* without the words feeling like lead weights on her tongue.

"Well," she reset, "now, he's just, like, smirky."

"Smirky? Don't you take some sort of complicated English classes at Cranst? Listen, Ads, I do have to talk to you. The reason I'm really calling is—"

"No," she said before he even started.

"You didn't let me finish— Wait, don't take this exit!"

"I know the tone. And I don't want to talk about it."

"Just call her, Ads, please. Call her for five minutes."

She could read Michael's thoughts through the phone—*poor little Addie, the baby of the family, orphaned and angry at the world.*

And that wasn't how she felt at all, not really. She was just angry that her sister had turned into such a tyrant after their parents' deaths. Making them haul ass to California only weeks after their parents were lowered into the ground. Spending more time being wined and dined by her boyfriend than grieving, though Samantha had barely known the guy for six weeks when they moved. Refusing to sign over Adelaide's inheritance if she left the West Coast and went to Cranst, thereby forcing her sister into a life of fraudulent paper writing.

Your everyday family drama.

"Mom and Dad would have been devastated to know how it is between you two," Michael pleaded.

Dammit, this was exactly why she hadn't wanted to answer the phone. He always brought up the shit she didn't want to talk about.

"It's been three years since you've spoken to her, Ads."

"Tell it to Samantha, okay? I'm not the one who turned into a dictator."

Michael was just too sensitive, the torn middle child. He was always playing peacekeeper, no matter how many times she told him she and Samantha would never have a relationship again. That was why she kept her distance with him, too, to a lesser extent—she knew he ran back and reported everything to Samantha. He would never be mad at her, not like Adelaide was—Samantha had given him *his* part of the inheritance because he agreed to go back to California after he graduated.

"They wanted me to have that money, Michael. It's not her call to make. End of story."

He sighed. "Look, you know Samantha doesn't always know how to show she cares. She does it in fucked up ways sometimes."

"Refusing to give me the money my parents willed to me in the event of their deaths, because of where I wanted to go to college, is a little more than fucked up."

They had this conversation at least three times a year. But the divide between sisters was too great, and the longer it went on, the less she cared about repairing the damage. Graduation was in sight, and she'd managed to get here on her own. She certainly wasn't going to try and fix things now, just because Michael wanted to pretend he had one big, happy family.

Now it was Adelaide who sighed. "You should get to your meeting."

"Yeah," he agreed, though he sounded sorry about it. "Hey, I'll be back in New York in a few weeks for a business trip."

Her voice was flat when she murmured, "Great."

"Ads, I love you." Michael's voice was gruff. "I'm sorry it's like this. It's not fair."

Not fair for who? she wanted to ask as she ended the call. Him because he insisted on bouncing back and forth between sisters, trying to convince one that the other wasn't Satan incarnate? Or her because she'd been forced into scraping by every damn day? Or their parents, who weren't here to make sure their children were provided for equally, the way they'd always intended?

When she set her phone down, she sat in silence, looking around her bedroom. Just when she thought she'd moved on, something like this happened, and it felt like her parents had died all over again. She could feel the tears gathering, her face cracking open, but before the sob broke free from her chest, a text made her jump.

An A just like you promised, you little wizard, Olivia Rhys, a junior, had texted her. *I have a Spanish History paper due Saturday. LMK details. THANKS!!!*

Adelaide swallowed the rising tears, forcing the meltdown back into her chest. She hated Olivia, hated Samantha, hated the fucking cycle that she had started and couldn't get out of if she wanted to. But she needed the money. There was no crying when you needed the money.

In her world, for the foreseeable future, money was the only thing that mattered.

TWO

Adelaide's own History of Painting paper was a B at best. She'd written it halfheartedly, in the midst of outlining other people's essays. One of her rules was to always do her best work for herself, but she could barely focus after her call with Michael, and eventually, she had given up on doing more than getting the required number of words on paper.

The class had already met four times, but the professor didn't take attendance, and Adelaide had been strategic about skipping. Those were often prime essay-writing hours she couldn't afford to waste. She had to show today to turn in the paper, but she planned to make good use of her time by recording the lecture on her laptop, which she'd listen to later, and creating a study guide for her calculus test instead.

She absently followed the stream of students pouring into the lecture hall, head down. She didn't realize she was about to bump into the person in front of her until it happened.

"Oh, sorry—"

A strong hand shot out and steadied her by the elbow. "Careful, Addie. Wouldn't want to draw attention to yourself if you don't plan to come back again."

She ripped her arm away from Declan faster than she'd meant to. There was his same smirk, the one he'd worn the last time she ran into him.

Earlier that week, she'd hunted down his email address and sent him the paper on Delacroix, even though she preferred to keep her activities offline. Exceptions, like discounts, were given to no one. That was another one of her rules. But the rounds of silent arguments she'd been going through in her head ever since her conversation with her brother had exhausted her. It always took a few days to get out of the sticky spiral of emotions the Samantha conversation produced. That was why she preferred when they stuck to neutral topics that didn't dredge up all the awfulness of the past.

Adelaide forced a tight smile. "Sorry. Distracted."

"No harm done." He pressed a hand to his chest in some weird gesture that she thought he meant as chivalrous and sidestepped her.

Michael's words rang in her ears. *I could never tell if it was cute or creepy.*

The answer today: creepy.

Adelaide found an empty seat in the back. Professor Hargrove was an unfriendly older man who docked points for small things, like word choice and formatting. She'd written at least a dozen papers for his classes, but she'd never actually been a student of his until now. Walking the stage at the front of the lecture hall, he directed the students to hand their papers to the TA and launched into a spiel about trauma's relationship to shape that was totally devoid of flair. She opened her laptop and hit Record.

At least Declan hadn't tried to sit next to her. She craned her neck to see where he was, but couldn't find him. Maybe he'd bailed after handing in his paper. Just as well, she decided. She had enough to worry about without The Night of the Peach Schnapps on her mind too.

She was reaching for her calculus notes when the TA came to take her paper, stopping squarely in front of her, so she was looking at the tips of his leather loafers. When her head snapped up, her breath left her in one hard *whoosh*.

No.

No, not possible. It couldn't be because he'd come to her just a few days ago and asked—

Horror washed over Adelaide as the full extent of her misunderstanding sank in.

Declan *was* the TA.

That smirk pressed in the corner of his mouth suddenly made a lot more sense.

"You …" she started, but he coyly shook his head, leaning down to pry the paper from her clammy hand.

"Be at my office hours," he whispered and started moving down the row, away from her, gathering the rest of the papers without looking back.

A jolt ran through her, making her entire body feel fiery and chilled at the same time. She was almost feverish, dizzy with mounting terror as she realized in wave after crashing wave that she was going to be expelled. That her entire college career was over. Everything she'd worked for, everything she'd risked … it was all for nothing.

At some point during the class, her mind went into shock. She merely sat there, staring straight ahead but not seeing anything, aware of sound but not hearing, breathing but barely alive. When class ended and the room started to empty out, she waited until all the other students were gone before she pushed herself out of the chair, rising slowly in case her knees gave out.

When she stood, the knot in her chest finally unfurled. Adelaide barely made it to the restroom before vomiting up the meager contents of her stomach. She hadn't eaten lunch, and her abdomen contracted uselessly, over and over, until finally she sagged against the wall of the stall, shaky and weak.

This can't be happening.

She had been so careful, so discreet. For years. Until…

She was going to wring Agnes Ritter's neck. Sweet, big-mouthed Agnes and her stupid paper on Gaugin that she'd insisted she get an A on. Adelaide's instinct from the beginning was that it was a mistake to let Agnes become a customer, but she hadn't thought the girl would be stupid enough to talk to a TA about it. Unless Declan had tricked her, which, even if he had, Agnes should have figured it out by now and come straight to Adelaide so that she could do damage control. Whatever kind of damage control she could possibly do in a situation like this.

Adelaide sank to the cold, sticky tiles of the restroom floor, frantically considering her options. Approach the professor, plead her case, say it was a onetime thing? Proactively go to the dean and beg on her hands and knees to keep her place at the school? Call her roommates and ask them to smuggle her out of the country? Call Michael and ask his PR advice on how to manage a crisis? Bash her brains against the wall of the building until she lost all her faculties?

Declan had said to come to his office hours. Pushing out of the stall, she threw her bag next to the sink and began rummaging for the class syllabus, stuck in one of her notebooks. His office hours were held in the clock tower, Room 230. Right now.

Her stomach twisted again, but she swallowed over the rising nausea. She'd go there and convince him that this was all a misunderstanding, that she had never done anything like this before. She'd make him understand.

She had to.

Declan was wearing thick-rimmed glasses and poring over what looked like a 1970s coffee table book when she tapped open the door of his office. He looked up at the noise and, to her complete surprise, smiled.

"Hi, Addie."

"Hi," she said, clearing her throat when her voice cracked. "Listen, I can explain."

"I'm sure you can." He nodded at a chair in front of his desk. "Sit down."

His office, like most of the offices they gave to the TAs at Cranst, was actually a converted closet in the university's clock tower, the oldest building on campus. During orientation week, all freshmen were taken for a walking ghost tour by their resident advisor—a strange, collegiate version of an icebreaker. She recalled this building was said to be haunted by the founder of the college, who had tragically fallen from the roof in a freak accident.

"Or was it?" Katy had whispered in her ear dramatically.

They'd barely known each other, but started laughing and become fast friends.

As she sat, she wished she could rewind to that moment and rethink every decision she'd ever made, all of which seemed to have led her here, to the nightmare at hand.

Before she could speak, Declan rose to flip the latch on the door behind her. It made the stuffy office, which he'd filled with books, sketches, papers, and magazines, even more claustrophobic.

If he asked her to give him a blow job for his silence, the answer would be unequivocally no. *Fuck no*, to be exact.

Right?

"Okay," he said, sitting behind the small desk again.

He was wearing dark jeans and a blue blazer with a perfectly pressed white button-down underneath. She wondered how he afforded the snazzy wardrobe on a teaching assistant's salary.

"The first thing I should tell you is that what you're doing is basically grounds for expulsion. More than expulsion maybe. But by the look on your face, you already know that. So, the second thing I should tell you is that I haven't gone to Professor Hargrove with this … yet."

That brought her no relief because she sensed a big *but* hovering. "Why?" she croaked.

Declan raised an eyebrow. "Why do you think, Addie?"

She turned her palms up.

"Oh, come on. Play along for me." He was gloating. Proud of himself.

"Sex?" she guessed.

"Tried that already."

"Something sex adjacent?"

"Tried that too."

"Then, I'm out of ideas."

Declan smirked. "I think we can help each other out."

When she didn't react, he leaned in to fold his hands across his desk. She moved back in her seat, as if whatever he was going to say next would physically harm her.

"I'd like your help in getting back something that belonged to me. Something very, very important."

"Help you," she repeated slowly, trying to wrap her mind around what that could mean. "What did you lose?"

Declan's face went from haughty to angry in a flash. "My *pride*, Addie!" he cried, slapping his palm on the desk like she should have known this already. "My goddamn pride."

Adelaide flinched at the sudden outburst.

He turned in his swivel chair to stare out a small window, so she could only see him in profile. "The short story," he said in a purposefully monotone voice, "is that someone who promised me a bright future reneged on their word. And I want you to help me make it right."

Her eyes went wide, but she forced herself to keep her breathing measured. Calm.

"I just liked painting, Addie," he insisted, slowly spinning back around to face her. "That's it. *Just* painting. You remember."

She remembered he liked painting *her* at least.

"And I thought that was all I needed to do to be successful. That if I was true to the art, the rest would fall into place." He folded his hands again, hunching over his desk. "Do you remember when I told you I was going to London?"

She nodded.

"An art dealer had approached me—a highly successful one at that—and said he wanted to represent me. That he was going to make me enormously successful. And I'd been painting for so long that it just felt like … destiny. He told me that if I came to London, he'd make me the next big thing." Declan's eyes glazed over, far off in a memory. "When I got there, he put me up in the best hotels and set me up in a studio in his gallery. Introduced me to all these amazing buyers. Praised my work *constantly*." His lips curled. "I mean, can you imagine someone telling you that your line was on par with Picasso when you were barely nineteen? Can you *imagine* that, Addie?"

Of course she couldn't imagine it. She wasn't an artist, and she also wasn't a sucker. If someone had told her that, she'd have regarded it the way she regarded everything—with a healthy dose of skepticism. When something sounded too good to be true, it usually was.

Then again, people had always fawned over his art, labeled him great from early on. By the time The Night of the Peach Schnapps had happened, Declan Jones, the artist, had amassed a large online following and been profiled in several small art magazines. She could see how someone swooping in and promising him even more had probably felt like the next natural step.

Declan didn't wait for her response. "A week before exhibit, his secretary called me up and said that, unfortunately, the market was going in another direction and he was closing down his gallery. Just like that. Prick hadn't even had the decency to call me himself. I had to call my parents and beg them to send me money for a plane ticket home when he turned me out two days later."

He shook his head, jaw working. "I mean, the people you write papers for, they're just grabbing at what's easy, right? They want the simplest way to the greatest success. Hell, I bet you could write all sorts of nonsense in your essays, and they'd never even notice. It was the same for me with London. I took the easiest path available to me and never once checked the fucking fine print."

"I don't see what that has to do with me," she interjected, sensing that the story was veering off course.

Declan didn't hear her. He was still in the memory, one she could tell he'd relived many, many times. "And now, six years later, I'm sitting here, in this shithole office, grading papers on the history of painting. I can't live with that, Addie. I have to make it right."

The nerves making her skin tingle had faded considerably while she was focused on his rambling, but now, they returned with a fierce intensity. She wished she had a bottle of water, either to moisten her lips or drown herself with. "And you want my help?"

Their gazes met and held.

"Exactly right, Addie." He pushed a folder across the table to her.

With slightly trembling fingers, she opened it to find a stack of papers, stapled together. The first was a photograph.

"Jack Nolan, said art dealer," Declan informed her.

During his story, she had pictured a crotchety old man with white hair and a sleazy mustache, in a crinkly suit and delicate glasses. Instead, Jack Nolan was a man in his late thirties—dark-haired, blue-eyed, and cuttingly handsome—with a faintly rugged sort of look that somehow both softened and enhanced his strong features. In this picture, his mouth was half-pursed, making it impossible to tell if he was a moment from a smile or a frown. He looked intimidating. Arrogant.

Next was an article from an art magazine that had profiled him two years ago, when his gallery hosted a retrospective of some dead artist's work whose name she didn't recognize. The next was a ranking from the internet of the most successful art dealers in the world, which listed him in the top five. The final item was a list of the paintings Declan had ostensibly entrusted Jack Nolan with and their last known whereabouts.

When she was done perusing, she stuffed the papers back in the folder and looked up at him blankly. "What am I supposed to do with this?"

"It was one thing for him not to want to work with me. That was damaging, but I could have lived with it. But when he returned my artwork to me after the falling-out, he didn't return it all. He said he did, but that was a lie. He kept one of my collections."

"Why would he keep it if he didn't intend to … sell it?" She thought that was what art dealers did at least—she'd never given a single thought to one before.

"Because he's a greedy son of a bitch. Jack Nolan is the most vindictive man I've ever known. He didn't want my paintings, but he didn't want anyone else to have them either. They were my best work—he knew it, and so did I. They were going to put me on the fucking map."

"Again, Declan, what do you want *me* to do about it?"

Declan steepled his fingers and leaned back in his chair, studying her for a moment before responding. "If you help me get my paintings back, I won't go to the professor."

For a second, she didn't speak, trying to process the information. "But I wouldn't know how to even begin helping you—"

"Don't worry; I've thought of that." He took a deep breath, like he was gearing up to read off lottery numbers. She could see now that the whole story had merely been a buildup to this, like a conductor leading the orchestra to a crescendo. "Jack Nolan pays women to date him."

"*Date* him?" she repeated.

"I don't know if he fucks them all—I assume he does. They aren't real relationships though; he keeps them on his payroll and trots them out to his events for a few months before finding a new one. Makes it look like he has arm candy all the time."

"Okay, so he's gross. I still don't see what that has to do with me."

Declan arched a blond eyebrow.

"You're kidding." She chuckled despite the direness of the situation. Realization was dawning on her, but it was too ludicrous to consider.

"Have you seen me laugh yet?"

"I can't do that," she blurted quickly. "I'm sorry he screwed you over, Declan, but I'm not a"—her nose wrinkled—"hooker." As she said it, an even darker thought presented itself. "Did you, like, seek me out here?"

Declan rolled his eyes, as if to say, *Don't flatter yourself.* "You weren't plan A, Addie, if that's what you're asking. You're plan D at the very least. Having an inside girl is something I've been thinking about for a long time." She must have looked unsure because he made a frustrated noise in the back of his throat. "Jack Nolan is the biggest donor to Cranst's art department. Working here gives me the chance to keep tabs on him. That's the only reason I'm at the university."

"Then, why were you talking to Agnes Ritter about me?"

"I already told you. I didn't *know* it was going to be you. I was just keeping my ear to the ground with the students. Agnes thought I was her classmate, and I didn't correct her. Imagine my shock when she let it slip that someone was writing her paper for her. Someone who wrote *loads* of papers." He shrugged. "I had to see what was going on before I reported it."

She opened her mouth to respond, but she was speechless again.

"Have you ever heard the saying, Addie," Declan continued, "'*luck is when preparation meets opportunity*?' I just never found the right opportunity. Until you."

Adelaide gaped. "This is blackmail."

He shot her a patronizing frown. "If you didn't want to get dirty, Addie, you shouldn't have been lying in the mud." When she didn't react, he lifted his old desk phone out of its cradle and punched in an extension. "Hi, Professor Hargrove, please?"

Adelaide leaped out of her chair and slammed the switch hook down, not letting up until she was sure the line went dead.

Eyes victorious, Declan replaced the receiver.

She huffed and indelicately fell back into her seat, the sudden spike of adrenaline making her weak. "How would me dating him help get your artwork back?"

"You'll have *access*, Addie. Access is everything. Once you're in his life, you'll be able to find the paintings for me. Or at least where he's keeping them."

She pressed the heels of her hands into her eyes. "This is far-fetched."

"Not as far-fetched as you'd think. Surely, you've heard the term *sugar daddy*."

Her face twisted in horror. "I meant, finding the paintings."

"He'll make you an offer. If you do what I tell you." When she didn't answer, his eyebrow rose. "Or I'll call Professor Hargrove. I can't very well let you continue writing papers for other students, Addie. If anyone finds out I know about your side gig, I'll lose my job."

Humor flipped easily back to fear. She swallowed over a fresh wave of nausea.

"Give me some time to think." *Think of a way out of this.*

"There's no thinking, Addie. You've had plenty of time to consider the implications of your actions while you've been writing papers and profiting off them. It's now or never. Expulsion or Jack Nolan?"

"I'm—" she started, but words failed her. She had no idea what she was trying to say. "I don't think this will work. Seriously. He's not going to want to date someone like me."

"Please," Declan scoffed, waving the thought away. "I'll *make you* into someone he's interested in."

When she didn't respond, Declan stood. He slowly moved toward her, stopping next to her chair and crouching down in front of her. Even his body language had changed since they'd been teenagers—where he had once been stiff and a little clumsy, he was now graceful, assured. He pinched her chin in his fingers, nudging her to look down at him. His touch was dry and made her face burn. She wanted to pull away from him, even as she found herself drawn into his suddenly sympathetic eyes.

When he spoke, his voice was low, pleading. "He deserves this, Addie. Jack Nolan is a bastard who doesn't care about anyone or anything. He crushed my future in the palm of his hand without batting an eyelash. I can't stand by and watch while he does it to someone else. He doesn't deserve wealth, or power, or accolades, or anything like that, and I want you to help me make sure he doesn't get it." He stroked her chin lightly. Intimately. "And if you won't do it for that, do it for the money. He's rich. He'll pay you well. You'd be able to buy yourself new things, pay your bills. Enjoy life instead of just getting by." His eyes fell to her mouth. "You'd never have to write another paper again, Addie. That's *real* freedom."

"I can't," she whispered, an edge of begging in her own voice. "I can't do this." Whatever *this* was. Being a paid escort? Having sex with a man for money? Writing papers was sleazy, but this was crossing an entirely different kind of line.

He sighed and shook his head, and for the first time since she had encountered him again, he looked like the Declan she remembered. The one who had asked her if she was sure fifteen times during The Night of the Peach Schnapps.

"Don't you want a life better than this one?"

Of course she did.

Declan couldn't know about Samantha, about the constant struggle to make ends meet, about the skipped lunches, the ratty clothes she wore year after year because new ones were an extravagance she couldn't afford. About feeling more disgusted with herself with every new paper she wrote or keeping her distance from new acquaintances because she couldn't even be honest about her own life.

But somehow, staring into his eyes, she felt like he could see right into her past, right into *her*, where all that heartache and struggle simmered right under the surface.

He could probably even see that a small part of her wondered if this really *was* a way out, even as her stomach turned at the thought of it.

"Yes," she whispered.

Declan's smile was slow, triumphant. He took her hands in his, and she let him. Somehow, she let him.

"You'll be fine. You'll have so much money that you won't even care. Like I said, I don't even know if he fucks them."

"I'm not going to—"

"There's an auction on campus in a week, at the Claremont. Fundraising for the new art library. Jack is a huge donor, so he'll be there for it. And so will you."

"And I'm going to do *what* there exactly?"

"Woo him. Use your female wiles. Make him *have* to have you."

No one *had* to have her—even her own family.

"My female *what*—"

He stopped her with a thumb on her mouth. "You're smart. I trust you'll find a way. But here's the thing, Addie." He stood and dusted off his pants, though they remained pristine. "You're going to need some sprucing up."

THREE

The Night of the Peach Schnapps had gone like this:

Adelaide's family was away for the weekend. She had to stay behind to take her PSATs, and it was the first time she'd ever spent more than one night home alone.

The first night went fine. She studied late, woke up early, spent most of the next day at the test. But when she returned home, the house was silent, almost eerie. More than a little creeped out by the quiet, she decided to head out on her deck for some sun.

And that was where she found Declan Jones, sitting on a lounge chair with a sketchbook in his lap. It looked like he was trying to capture a set of weeping willows in his neighboring backyard, though he was drawing them upside down. She and Declan weren't friends, but they'd been neighbors their entire lives and therefore always had a vague idea of what was going on with the other. She'd been nursing a slight crush on him for the past two years—she liked that he was quiet and a little brooding, that he had something he was committed to. All the boys in her grade were lame in comparison.

Eighteen to her sixteen, he never seemed as old as the other seniors she knew, which was probably because his parents homeschooled him so he could focus on painting. Adelaide guessed that was what made him shy.

"The angle is better from here," he explained, motioning to his bordering backyard. His pale skin was getting red in the sun. "You mind?"

"No," she lied. She had on a bikini top and felt self-conscious wearing it around him. She wished she'd remembered a T-shirt, but she didn't want to show her hand and go back in for one. Instead, she casually crossed her arms over her midsection, hoping it hid her.

"Why are you drawing?" she asked after watching him sketch for a while. His pencil strokes seemed to make no sense for the longest time, only to miraculously form an object with a single slash. "I thought you painted."

Declan's hand never faltered. "I can't get the trees right in the painting. Not like how I see them in real life at least."

"You see them upside down?"

His face was angled away from her, but she was almost sure he smiled.

When they didn't speak for several minutes, she tried to break the awkwardness again. "My mom said you were going away for some sort of program?"

"I'm moving to London."

"What? Why?"

Her mother hadn't told her this. She wasn't disappointed exactly, but she'd been flirting with the idea of asking him to come to her junior prom.

"To improve my painting. Get my name out there. Someone saw my artwork online and thinks they can help me break into the industry."

"When will you come back?"

Declan peeked behind him, his gaze quickly dropping to her chest, his skin going even redder than before. He turned back to his sketch. "I won't, if all goes according to plan."

"Oh." That feeling—not quite disappointment, but something like it—intensified.

Samantha was off, starting her own life in New York, and Michael was at college, having too much fun to want to come home to his family, except for holidays. Lately, she'd been feeling the sting of everyone moving on, leaving her behind, and Declan felt like another tally mark on an invisible scoreboard.

After a beat, he turned back to look at her again, though this time, his gaze lingered. Recalibrated. She was about to ask him if a bug was on her when he folded his sketchbook and turned all the way around.

"Addie?" he called. "Can I paint you?"

"Can I paint you?" There hadn't been—and would never be—anything asked of her that was more romantic than that.

They went down to his basement, which contained an easel and several canvases, a couch splattered with paint, and a bottle of peach schnapps hidden in a cupboard, which he pulled out almost as if it were a magic wand.

"Here." He grinned shyly, handing it over. "It can get kind of boring up there."

"Up there" turned out to be a stool in a bare corner of the room, which forced her spine unnaturally straight and made her butt go numb. Five minutes in, she was cracking the seal on the bottle and taking a swig just for something to do. It was syrupy and surprisingly delicious, like drinking candy. She'd drunk a few times before, mostly something dark and bitter from someone's parents' liquor cabinet, but this was tasty, fun. She felt herself getting a little tipsy.

Declan had angled the easel away, so she had nothing to do but watch as his focus went from the canvas to her face and back to the canvas again. All the eye contact made her blush, especially because she never knew when he'd look up and meet her eyes. For an hour, it was pure teenage swooning.

Until the stiffness set in. By hour two, she was sore and aching. Relief came only when Declan would get up and stand next to her, taking a few small sips from the bottle as she stretched her arms over her head, embarrassed and flattered when his eyes trailed over her torso.

Two more hours, and it was finally done.

She stood up and unattractively cracked her back. "Well?"

"I've never done anything quite like it." He cast a worried glance in her direction. "I'm not sure you should look."

"Looking is the whole point," she chided.

Adelaide moved to walk around the easel, but he awkwardly tripped in front of her, blocking her path. She blinked up at him, surprised by the proximity, and tried to step around him again. He stepped with her.

"Declan," she muttered, darting the other way, annoyed, only to have him follow her. They bobbed like this a few times until she stopped and demanded, "What are you doing?"

And then he kissed her. She'd fooled around with a few boys in her grade, nothing that had gone too far, but this felt different. None of them had watched her for hours through strange eyes; none had tried to capture her likeness on paper. He saw the world through a different lens, and it made this feel serious, urgent.

She knew what would happen the second they kissed. He was leaving. She'd had a crush on him for years. Three-quarters of the bottle of schnapps was gone, and she didn't even feel self-conscious about her bikini top anymore.

It occurred to her later, after the deed was done and she was pulling her shorts back up, that she didn't know if it was his first time too. He'd brought her to the paint-flecked couch confidently enough, but she'd felt his hands shaking when he moved over her, and he'd kept asking if she was sure, over and over until she wished he'd just shut up. Adelaide wanted to ask him, but he was trying hard to seem nonchalant, and she thought she might embarrass him.

And then she saw the painting.

Adelaide was thinking about that now as Declan slid into the booth across from her at an off-campus diner, pushing designer sunglasses into his hair and ordering a wedge salad.

She'd spent two sleepless nights trying to figure a way out of her bargain, but she had come up short at every turn. Every path ended with the university finding out about the papers. Even if she went to them with Declan's ultimatum, she knew it would pale in comparison to what she'd been doing. And for *years*, no less.

She, quite simply, was fucked.

"So," Declan told her, downing half a mug of coffee in one gulp, "the first thing we're doing is cutting your hair." He'd brought a pen with him, and he wrote down *hair* on a napkin.

Adelaide pulled it out of her messy bun and touched the ends, which were almost to the dip in her waist. "What's wrong with my hair?"

"Too straggly, too blah. We have an appointment in an hour."

"An hour?"

"I told you to clear your whole day. We also need to get you some clothes that don't resemble … grunge."

She gazed down at her jeans and old Cranst fleece. "What *should* I be wearing?"

He snorted. "Nothing with a zipper." He wrote down *appropriate wardrobe* next. "Third … a tan."

Fourth was a manicure. Fifth was elocution—"You say *like* so much"—and sixth was perfume.

"Are you going to Eliza Doolittle me until I'm a Barbie doll?" she snapped, wondering if these things were for the art dealer or if Declan himself wanted them.

"I'm going to Eliza Doolittle you until Jack Nolan can't physically stand to have you out of his line of sight."

She shook her head at his confidence. "This is *not* going to work. How can you know what type of woman he even goes for?"

Declan gave her a look like *you have got to be kidding*. "Research, Addie. You don't have a monopoly on doing it well. I spent six months straight with him in London. I've kept close tabs on him ever since. I know what he wants. *Who* he wants."

"Which is?"

"Beautiful. Posh. Smart. Mature." He raised an eyebrow. "You've got two out of four right now."

Her mouth dropped, and though he didn't elaborate on which two boxes she ticked, she narrowed it down to *smart* and *mature* since she *definitely* wasn't the other two.

"Jack is a snob and gravitates toward other snobs. He wants—he *needs*—someone who knows the world he operates in. The best restaurants, the right people. Someone well-read but not offensive. Likable but not the center of attention. Sexy but … sweet."

"Sexy but sweet?" She laughed. "Hate to break it to you, but that woman doesn't exist. Anywhere. I don't care how pretty or rich she is."

Declan drained his coffee and threw a twenty on the table. "But she *can* be created. Let's go."

He drove her to the salon in a sleek Audi she had no idea how he afforded, snapping at her rudely when she hiked her foot up on the seat. Another thing that had changed about him: he'd become materialistic in a way she didn't remember him—or his parents—being. The clothes, the car, the way he catalogued her flaws—image had become important to him. A very specific kind of image. Was that Jack Nolan's doing?

The salon was one of those posh, swanky places where everyone knew each other and people stopped in for blowouts and deep conditionings once a week. The women inside clomped around in stilettos and fur vests, which made her beat-up sneakers stick out like sore thumbs.

She was assigned to Hallie, who stationed Adelaide in a swivel chair and began mixing bowls of white and purple substances, looking at Declan with a mix of amusement and confusion when he took the chair next to her.

"All right." He clapped. "Class is in session." He began rattling off facts about Jack Nolan. "He's thirty-eight, originally from Boston, but he's lived in Manhattan for most of his adult life. Did his undergrad at UCLA for business and then went on to get his master's in art history while he worked for—Addie, are you paying attention?"

Her gaze had wandered to Hallie, who was now folding her hair into strips of tinfoil. "He went to school, got a job. Wait, you want me to *dye* my hair?"

"Highlights will do you wonders," Declan told her dismissively.

"What color?" Adelaide balked.

"Come off it already. You think I'd dye your hair green?"

"It's just a little bit of blonde," Hallie reassured her kindly. Then frowned at Declan. "It's her hair, no?"

"You'll look better when it's done, and that's all you need to worry about. Like I was saying, while Jack was in college, he worked for Rene Saegner, the biggest art dealer in the world. You'll need to know who that is, so don't forget. I'll send over some books to your apartment, and I'd like you to read them before next week."

Books? As in multiple?

Adelaide scowled. "You know, I do have classes to get through this semester if I want to get my degree."

He ignored her. "Relationships are important in art, Addie. It's what the whole industry is built on. You need to know the key people in Jack's world if we're going to have a shot at him." He leaned forward and flicked her arm. "And there will be no degree if you don't. Besides"—he settled back in the chair and added something unspoken to the napkin of to-dos— "relationships are important in *any* industry. This might teach you even more than your classes."

She snorted. Right now, all she was learning was that deceit and dishonesty weren't limited to the Cranst student body.

"Fine, don't take it seriously," Declan sighed, yanking his phone out of his pocket and making like he was going to start pressing buttons. "It's your funeral."

That shut her up, fast.

When the appointment was finally done, she had to admit, her hair looked nice. Now, it fell just past her collarbone and shimmered with subtle blonde highlights. She tried to admire it in the mirror, but Declan ripped her out of the place before she could even thank her hairstylist.

They went to another salon that took care of her hands and toes. And another that Declan sent her into without joining her, which she quickly realized was full of women getting every patch of hair on their body waxed off.

She stormed out and demanded he take her home.

Declan hid a laugh behind his hand, like he'd expected this reaction. "Okay, Addie. We'll save that for another time."

When he pulled up at her apartment, she stepped out and faced him through the window, hands on her hips. "You know, you're way more of an asshole than you used to be."

The insult didn't seem to faze him in the least. In fact, he grinned. "Or were you too distracted by my good looks back then to notice?" He pushed his sunglasses onto his nose even though the sun had nearly set. "By the way, I would have given the paper you wrote for me a B."

She gave him the finger as he drove off, laughing, though she wasn't sure if he even looked in his rearview mirror.

Over the next week, Declan treated her like his very own piece of living art. At least, that was how she felt when he dragged her to salon after salon, store after store, yelling at her for countless little habits she hadn't even realized she had.

"Stand up straight," he would chide when she slouched in her chair.

"Don't touch your hair so much," if she twirled it absently.

"Stop leaving the house without mascara," after a long day of classes.

"Chew delicately and never eat everything on your plate, no matter how small," when they stopped for breakfast.

"Declan," she groused, shaking off his hand when he helped her out of his car—an annoying habit of *his*. "I'm not a gorilla. I know how to behave in public."

"Not this kind of public. You can't just walk around and talk about binge-drinking with these people, Adelaide. They're educated."

She faux gasped. "And here I was, thinking my degree was only good enough for slinging burgers."

He rolled his eyes, unamused. As usual, Declan was dressed impeccably, today in a white sweater and dark pants, his hair perfectly flopped. Meanwhile, she had rolled out of bed and struggled into loose jeans with holes in the knees, hair scraped lazily back.

"It's not that you aren't pretty," he said as she lay face up on a table in a back room of a quiet, shadowy spa.

They'd ventured into one of the ritzy neighborhoods surrounding Cranst today, so she could have extensions added to her eyelashes—a procedure she hadn't been aware existed prior to this morning.

Declan flopped in a chair beside her. "You're a beautiful girl, Adelaide. You just aren't the kind of beautiful Jack Nolan wants. He likes polished, sexy, immaculate. Not young, casual, and comfortable."

Adelaide stiffened as the woman sitting near her head put a cold pad under her eyes, effectively sealing them shut. She took a deep breath and tried to focus on talking to Declan, annoying as it was. "For the record, I like the way I look."

He ignored her. Clearly, the record made little difference to him. "Have you had a chance to read those books and articles I sent you?"

No, of course she hadn't. She had been too busy with all this grooming nonsense, plus her schoolwork, to even consider looking at the dozens of magazine articles he had emailed her about Jack Nolan. Half of them were from snooty art magazines that barely made any sense to her anyway.

"Can you just give me the bullet points? I've been kind of strapped for time."

He must have leaned forward because his voice was closer now, tenser. "Addie, I get the feeling you're not taking this seriously. Need I remind you that I have Professor Hargrove on speed dial? All it would take is one phone call ..."

Adelaide tried to crack her eyes open to see if the technician applying her eyelashes was paying attention to the douche bag footing the bill, but the woman simply admonished her, "Eyes closed. You'll get a burn."

"Sorry. I'm just not used to this." To Declan, she said, "Fine. I'll read them. I had a Chaucer paper due."

"Yours?"

She pressed her lips together. "Yes, mine." Something poked against her closed eyelid like a persistent insect. She fought the instinct to swat it. "And you still feel confident this will work?"

"Like I said, I *know* Jack Nolan. He's an expert in pretty things." He fell quiet for a second. "And you, Adelaide, are now a very pretty thing."

It was a good thing something pointy was weaving around her eyelids. Otherwise, they would have flown open in surprise.

Awkwardly, she shifted against the table, searching for something to change the subject. She came up with a question that had been turning over in her mind this week. "Have you tried talking to Jack?"

Declan's laugh was bitter. "Are you kidding? He won't let me anywhere near him."

"But—"

"You don't think I've already exhausted every option available to me, Adelaide? The guy's a megalomaniac. All he cares about is himself and his own success. He's calculating, vengeful, and ice cold."

"I *know*," she insisted, though she had a hard time summoning the degree of anger Declan had. Maybe once she met Jack, she'd see what he meant. Since she'd first heard his name, the man had been looming over her like a phantom. She'd even begun to *dream* about him. "But you're so talented. You could start over. I'm sure another dealer would jump at the chance to represent you."

"Addie, don't you get it yet? Jack ruined me. No other art dealers would touch me after he turned me out. He's ruthless whenever someone poaches—or even *tries* to poach—one of his clients. Another dealer would have been too scared to try and work with me after he had." Her palms were resting flat at her sides, and abruptly, she felt his fingers brush against hers. "And they'll still be too scared if Jack has my best work stored away. If they think he'll go after them for trying."

Adelaide quickly moved her hand out from under his. Mentally, she added another line item to the increasingly long list of things she was learning about Jack Nolan.

He didn't play fair.

FOUR

"**I** don't know if I can do this."

Declan frowned as he looked her up and down. "I'm starting to have my doubts too."

They were waiting in the valet line outside of the Claremont Hotel, the only hotel in the vicinity of the Cranst campus. It was a large building made out of stately brick, with a golden revolving door and attendants outside, waiting to cater to their guests' every need. It was where the wealthy sorority girls hosted their swanky formal nights and occasionally even a wedding reception, and it was booked for graduations three years out.

It was very far from Adelaide's scene. If Declan hadn't insisted they get a room for the night, she would probably never have stepped foot inside. He said it was so she could slip into the fundraiser more easily, but she had a sickening feeling it was because he hoped she might end up in Jack's room.

She watched as the door to a limousine just ahead of them opened, and a well-dressed woman in sunglasses popped out. "Well, if you don't think it's the right time, we can—"

"No rescheduling. You know the alternative."

She blew out a breath of air and hoped it would calm her down. "Fine. Let's do this."

Though she'd gone through enough sprucing up to make her into Miss America, she still felt like an imposter when the valet opened her door and extended a hand to her. She'd toned her look down today, so she wouldn't arouse the suspicions of Katy and Imogen when she slipped out of the apartment. She'd tell them—maybe—but later. *Much* later. Luckily, they had been busy with their own schedules, so she hadn't seen much of them lately.

Instead of taking the hand offered, Adelaide stepped out on her own and hugged herself. When she looked up at the building's intricately carved cornices and bright bay windows overlooking the grounds, she felt her stomach sour.

"Luggage in the trunk, ma'am?"

Adelaide blinked when she realized the young valet was talking to her. "Uh, I've got it," she mumbled. It was only an overnight bag after all. "Thank—"

"Yes, luggage is in the trunk," Declan said over her, stepping to the curb and handing over his keys. "We're checking in. Room is under Jones."

He looped an arm through Adelaide's and led her inside. She looked up at the several-stories-high foyer, at shimmering chandeliers and crown moldings. The furnishings inside the massive space were unabashedly expensive—dark leather chairs situated around a fireplace, decadent floral arrangements, uniformed staff looking stiff and impeccable. It reeked of class and privilege, screaming at her, *We are better than you.*

But Declan marched across the thick Oriental rugs as if he belonged there. She trailed slightly behind him, like his tail.

As they waited to check in, he took her hand and squeezed it hard, which gave her the impression that he wasn't happy with her. "Stop looking like you're going to throw up."

When he gathered the key cards and turned her around to face the gleaming elevator doors, she took one look at her reflection and saw what he meant. She needed to get control of herself. Jack was never going to strike up a conversation with her if she looked like she was going to hurl on his shoes.

She dragged in calming breaths and checked her phone. Two hours until showtime. Plenty of time to transform herself.

Adelaide was relieved to find their room had two beds. When their luggage arrived shortly after they did, Declan threw himself on one and pointed to a garment bag. "You'd better get ready."

"What is that?"

"Your dress. What do you think?"

She pulled open the material and gaped. "You call that a dress? There's barely any material to it! It's going to cling to every—"

"It's hot. Wear it. Trust me, he likes that stuff. And it'll make you look, you know …"

She let the bag fall back down, appalled. "Is that seriously what he likes? Why doesn't he just hire someone off one of those paid-escort websites then?"

Declan tented his hands behind his head and crossed his legs at the ankles. "You won't look like a paid escort, no matter what you wear. Get dressed."

She wasn't sure if that was a compliment. She decided she didn't want to know. He was staring at her, so she grabbed the dress and marched for the bathroom door.

"Wait."

She whirled.

He reached into a suitcase and pulled out a small bag, tossing it over to her. "Cotton undies aren't going to cut it tonight."

She gawked at him. "I don't even want to know how you guessed my sizes."

"You can model those for me too, if you want."

"Thanks, but I'd rather chew on rusted nails."

"It's nothing I haven't seen before," he called after her.

"Don't remind me!" she growled and slammed the bathroom door behind her.

That didn't mean she didn't look at herself in the undergarments though.

Before she put the dress on, she made herself do a careful three-hundred-and-sixty-degree rotation in front of the mirror, clocking the way her body looked at different angles. She was by no means in shape, but all the stress of the past week had helped her shave off a few pounds, which gave her a surprising hit of confidence.

She tried to imagine being like this in front of a stranger tonight.

I can't sleep with him, she decided in one second. *Do I have a choice?* she wondered in another.

It had been easy to push sex out of her mind while she focused on everything else Declan wanted her to do, but now, the scenario loomed like a thundercloud. Adelaide wasn't a prude, and as a college student living in a microcosm of hormones, she certainly wasn't immune to the occasional one-night stand. But this person was someone she was pretty sure she was going to hate. And the stakes were much higher than a one-off encounter—if she slept with him and it went badly, she could kiss her degree good-bye.

She suddenly wished she'd done research of a different kind.

Declan had chosen a slinky violet dress that was so tight she'd have to modify her walk to accommodate it. And it was much shorter than the loose T-shirt dresses she usually gravitated toward. After doing whatever she could to stretch it so that it covered more of her thighs, she finally gave up and stepped outside, bracing herself for Declan's inspection.

The moment his eyes drifted to her, they widened with appreciation. He shoved up off the bed and stalked toward her. "Not bad. Not bad at all."

"I look like a whore," she muttered even before her eyes fell upon the black heels on the night table. They looked like lethal weapons. She pointed. "With *those*? You're not serious."

Of course he was. He grabbed them and placed them on the ground, dragging her hand to his shoulder for balance as he coaxed her feet in. Her ankles wobbled when he stepped away.

He twirled a finger, motioning for her to spin.

When she did a full turn, he made a *hmm* noise in the back of his throat. "Your breasts."

She crossed her arms over them. "What?"

He motioned upward with both hands. "You need more cleavage."

Scowling, she turned away slightly, dug her hands into the lace bra he'd picked out, and rearranged herself. Then, she adjusted the top of the dress and turned back to the mirror. Now, her cleavage popped, almost obscenely.

"Better," he murmured, gazing at her reflection.

She shivered when he stepped behind her and boldly dragged the clip pinning her hair out, causing it to spill down the nape of her neck.

"Down. Definitely wear it down."

She bit her lower lip. "I never wear my hair down."

"You just started," he whispered, their eyes locked in the mirror.

His hands went to her shoulders, his fingertips gently skimming along their curve. She tried and failed to fight the goose bumps popping up along her skin.

For a moment, she braced like he might lean in and kiss her.

For a moment, she *wanted* him to.

She thought of his peach schnapps–scented breath, the way his lips had felt on her skin all those years ago. Her first time hadn't been the stuff of romance novels, but really, none of the subsequent times with frat boys and Tim Acker types had been much better. They'd all been fumbling, alcohol-fueled hook-ups. She wondered if Declan's technique had become more sophisticated, just like his wardrobe.

When he opened his mouth, she thought he might call her beautiful or say something sweet.

Instead, he broke her gaze and said, "It's time. You should get down there."

She looked away from her reflection and found a small evening bag in his hand. Was there anything Declan hadn't thought of? "Where are you going to be?"

"I'll be around. But you probably won't see me."

"Why not?"

"Because you're going to put yourself everywhere Jack is. And I'm going to be where Jack *isn't*. If he sees me, I'm done."

She nodded, nervously tucked a lock of hair behind her ear, and headed for the door.

"Wait."

She stopped. Turned.

This time, he seemed to absorb her as a full picture instead of clocking things to fix. He took in each part of her, but it wasn't with the critical eye from before. He was looking at her like … a man.

"What?" she finally demanded.

Declan slowly shook his head, eyes trailing up her legs, her waist. When they rose to her face, he flexed his hand at her like he was casting a spell. "You are not you."

No, she wasn't.

She'd had no warning when her parents' car crashed and ended her known world. Her life had changed—*she* had changed—entirely without her permission.

Standing in the hotel room doorway, she knew in an elemental way that once she stepped over the threshold, her life would change again. But this time, she wasn't sure if she had somehow consented to it—if this was Declan's choice or hers, or if her choice had been made long ago, the day she had written that first paper—and something in her broke.

She vowed right then to find Declan's paintings and get out of this godforsaken arrangement. Once it was done, she'd never be pushed into anything again. The choices would solely be her own.

Adelaide lifted her chin and stared at Declan head-on. "You could have just said I looked nice."

Then, she closed the door on his rather stupefied expression and headed for the elevators.

You are not you.

She didn't know what he'd meant by that, but as she wandered through the carpeted hallway, she wondered if that might be a good thing. Maybe the way to get through tonight was to pretend she wasn't herself, that she was a different girl—woman—one who was confident, worldly. She was already playing dress-up. The rest would just be theater.

Maybe, just for tonight, she'd leave the real Adelaide Wright behind.

The looks she got during her descent to the lobby were plentiful—from men and women alike. From the men, there was no mistaking the lust, the intention in them. From the women, she sensed judgment and occasionally disgust, but she kept her head held high, deliberately avoiding eye contact as she did her best to balance on her heels while making sure her dress didn't ride up. Jack Nolan definitely didn't date women who mooned a ballroom full of people.

The thought made her laugh. It felt good to smile, so she didn't entirely let go of it, and she put a swing in her hips, too, letting her hair fall in her eyes, the way that always earned her an extra-long glance from Declan.

After all, this was just a performance. And she was here to put on a show.

She flashed her room key at the attendant waiting at the entrance to the ballroom, where a long set of stairs would lead her down into the party. He waved her through without a second glance.

The fundraiser was a blatantly expensive affair—tuxedo-clad men and finely dressed women, round tables with ornate flower centerpieces glowing under crystal chandeliers. A string quartet played Vivaldi. In front of mirrored walls around the perimeter of the room stood easels with various pieces of art, waiting to receive their bids.

She fixed the idea that she could afford whichever one she wanted in her mind, straightened her shoulders, and descended the staircase.

The first thing she did was search for the bar because both the fake and real versions of herself were desperate for a drink. As she scanned the area, something caught her attention.

Though most of the crowd was pushing fifty, a throng of predominantly younger women seemed to be congregating in one area in particular. At first, Adelaide thought they must be looking at a painting, but then one stepped away and revealed a quick flash of a dark male head.

Just like that, her veneer slipped.

Jack Nolan.

She'd built him up in her head to be one way, but the second she saw him in person, she realized she'd been completely wrong. She didn't know how she could be so sure, but she was. Like a lightning bolt had hit her, she sensed he was warmer than she'd imagined, than Declan had said. But he was a little meaner too—not just cold or detached, but more short-tempered, sharp. She could tell that by the way his gaze seemed bored and a little annoyed, even as he shot one of the women a charming smile.

His eyes, she thought abruptly. She'd been so wrong about his eyes.

"You are not you," she whispered under her breath.

And then someone tripped into her, and she had to move, and whatever weird feeling had come over her was wiped away.

Back to the task at hand.

She rolled her shoulders and tugged down her dress one last time. Jack was clearly the man of the hour. How the hell was she going to get his attention, short of waving frantically, faking a medical emergency, or dropping her top?

If this were a movie, now would be the part where he'd catch her eye all on his own, struggle to break free of his many admirers, and rush to her side, taking her hand and planting a gentle kiss on her knuckles.

But this wasn't a scene from Cinderella. Cinderella didn't have to manipulate the prince. And she had a fairy godmother to rely on.

All Adelaide had was Declan, who was more like one of the evil stepsisters.

Of course, in the original story, the stepsisters sliced off parts of their own feet to try and make the glass slipper fit. They wanted to be chosen so badly that they'd maimed themselves for life.

Kristy Wertz had only gotten a B-plus on that paper. It still pissed Adelaide off.

Spotting the bar a few yards from Jack, she took the sultriest walk of her life past the gaggle of women, hoping that she'd somehow catch his eye. No luck. He'd been obscured by the women again, who were all trying to look innocent and refined.

Adelaide did, however, catch the eye of a man waiting at the bar.

Bald, bow tie askew, beer belly popping, he leaned into her before she realized he was there and whispered a wet, "Buy you a drink?"

She regarded him with all the distaste of a piece of gum on the bottom of her sneaker.

The bartender leaned over and said, "It's open bar, miss."

The man guffawed.

Adelaide slid away to the opposite side of the bar. "I'll take a beer—vodka soda," she corrected, worried Declan would appear from behind the bar and scold her for drinking anything that was served in a bottle.

She got another chance to look at Jack as she waited, and it became obvious he'd chosen the person he was most interested in speaking with at the moment.

And it wasn't a woman; it was an older man, nodding at a framed sketch. Jack was standing slightly apart from him, motioning to the piece, his hands gently tracing the lines as he spoke.

Even though Jack's head was partially turned, she found things to admire about him. He had a strong profile, one she was sure Declan would've loved to draw, if he didn't hate the man so much. His tuxedo was immaculate, like a second skin, and he was obviously comfortable in it, moving as if he spent most of his time in one. Though he was over a decade older than her, his hair was thicker than some of her peers. It tumbled on his head like silken waves. Would she get the chance to run her hands through it? Did she want to?

"I wouldn't bother, if I were you."

She blinked and realized that it was the bartender speaking to her over the array of liquor bottles. "What do you mean?"

"When he comes to these things, he's a rock star. He spends most of the night in the center of crowds that thick." He ran an appreciative eye over her. "You don't look to me like the kind of girl who should be kept waiting."

She sipped her drink. "Thanks, but I don't know what you're talking about. I was just trying to see what all the fuss was about."

The bartender nodded ruefully, filling a glass for another guest. "Jack Nolan. He has his charm with the ladies."

Adelaide took her glass and decided to check out the other paintings around the perimeter of the room. She found a Mystic harbor scene done by a local artist and absently stared at it, trying to figure out how to penetrate the group and make an introduction to Jack. But at the same time, her mind wandered to her parents and how they'd walk her around downtown Mystic and she'd collect seashells from the shore.

Lost in that thought, she only noticed the crowd around Jack had dispersed when a strong, self-assured voice said, "Excuse me."

She spun, just in time to see Jack Nolan coming toward her, blue eyes catching on something just over her head.

This was it. Time to work her magic. Just as he stepped near her, she opened her mouth to speak and—

"Tommy," he greeted, nodding at a smiling blond man who had stepped out from the crowd. "Excuse me," he murmured in a dismissive, businesslike fashion, sliding around her so he could shake the other guest's hand.

They continued back through the ballroom, ascending the stairs and disappearing out the double doors.

She felt like someone had blown her up like a balloon, only to pop her before the party got started.

He hadn't even looked at her. Not once.

She was so incredibly fucked.

FIVE

"What do you want me to say, Declan? I couldn't just sit on the guy's lap and force him to make out with me!" Adelaide complained, throwing her heels from last night into a tartan duffel that was one of her mother's final Christmas gifts to her. She was sure this was not the way her mom had envisioned her using it.

"You certainly didn't have to let him walk out of the room without saying more than two words to him the whole night!" Declan barked, throwing a few final items into his own suitcase before roughly zipping it.

When she'd returned to the room last night, full of excuses and repudiations, he'd held his hand up and asked her to not speak to him. That had made sleeping—in separate beds but close enough to hear every disappointed grunt from him—almost impossible.

"Maybe he just isn't interested in me. You said it yourself—I'm not exactly his type." Adelaide went into the bathroom to collect her toothbrush and swipe the extra soaps. Her curled hair was still bouncing, and her eyelashes were still superglued to her face. Last night, she had taken off whatever makeup she could and left the rest.

"I don't accept that." It was such a Declan thing to say. He was acting like it was a huge personal insult that his training hadn't been enough to make Jack Nolan get on his hands and knees in front of her.

"It was a long shot."

"Long shot, my ass. You didn't try hard enough."

She didn't dignify that with a response. She had done exactly as he'd instructed, but Jack Nolan was in his own world. And there was no substitute for real chemistry—you either had it or you didn't. Declan had made it sound like Jack would be actively looking for a new piece of arm candy to show off, but in her eyes, he couldn't have been less interested in that last night. He had been all business.

Declan rubbed his forehead. "There's a new exhibit opening at his gallery in New York in one week. You'll try again then."

She dragged her suitcase over her shoulder. "I don't see how it's going to work in New York if it didn't work here."

His eyes were cold when they met hers. "If that's the attitude you have, I'll go see the dean right now." It shut her up, just as his threats usually did. "I'm going to pay the bill," he muttered as he stalked out, slamming the door behind him.

Leaving her to struggle with the bags.

She bumbled down the blessedly empty hallway, grateful no one was around to see what a fool she was making of herself. Maybe she had looked like she was someone special last night, but right now, in her jeans and old cardigan, beat-up sneakers on, wisps of hair escaping her ponytail, she looked exactly like what she was—a broke college student who needed a bellhop.

She accidentally stepped off the elevator at the top level of the two-tiered lobby and had to rearrange the bags again, winding the long strap of her duffel around her shoulder and fitting Declan's into the crook of her forearm. As she descended the grand staircase she had been so impressed with yesterday, she shot a dirty look at his back, where he was handing over a credit card to a woman working the front desk.

When she reached the bottom, Declan's suitcase collapsed into her own and dragged half her body to the floor. She moved to disentangle herself, her shoulder feeling half out of its socket, when someone grabbed the strap, taking it right off of her back like it was stuffed full of cotton. She looked up, startled, and nearly toppled over.

Jack Nolan tilted his head impassively, dangling her duffel from his hand. His eyes were the same navy blue they had been last night, but when they latched on to hers, no amount of preparation could have gotten her ready for it. His rich, careful gaze took her in, sized her up. It was even more intense than she'd expected, making her throat dry and her heart pound.

"They should really have more bellhops here," he offered politely, ignoring her disbelieving stare.

Adelaide fumbled for her words, like she'd just run into a celebrity. "Totally—I mean, thank you. I thought I could handle more than I could."

Jack had on a dark gray suit and tie, looking only slightly less casual than he had in his tuxedo last night, but still without a hair out of place.

And she looked like this. *Shit*.

It appeared Jack Nolan wasn't the only one who'd noticed her struggling, because a bellhop finally jogged over to take her bags. She gratefully passed them off to him and told him they went to the black Audi. He lingered, eyeing the bag in Jack's hand.

"Can I have that back?" she asked awkwardly, motioning to her duffel.

Jack's gaze didn't waver as he passed it off. His jaw was smooth and freshly shaven, and her eyes got stuck on the clean, hard line of it. It was strange to know so much about a person and yet never have met them in real life. It reminded her of how she felt when she took a class with a professor she'd already written papers for. Like meeting someone but already keeping a secret from them. She certainly had a few to hide from him.

"Have we met?" Jack ventured, narrowing his eyes at her.

She'd didn't know the meaning of his expression, but it felt important she figure it out.

"Maybe we passed each other at the hotel?" She shrugged imperiously, looking everywhere but at his face. Definitely not over his shoulder, where Declan was staring, openmouthed, waving his arms like a psycho to egg her on. She hadn't known he was capable of exhibiting glee.

"I'm sure I would have remembered." He didn't smile, just kept looking at her like he could stare her into divulging something.

It was probably easy for him to break people under that look. Not only was he incredibly attractive, but she could also sense something aggressive about him, almost impatient. He was someone who was used to getting what he wanted.

Okay, come on, Addie. Flirt back, she commanded herself. *He pays women to date him. Good-looking or not, he isn't someone who deserves your awe.*

She raised her eyebrows. "I'm sure you would have."

Finally, a smile. It just touched the corners of his mouth, giving him a rueful sort of look, but it was enough that she'd gained, if not the upper hand, then at least a leg up.

"Have a drink with me before you check out," he suggested boldly, motioning toward the hotel bar.

"It's ten in the morning."

"Coffee then?"

Out of the corner of her eye, she saw Declan furiously pointing in the same direction, looking like a funny cross between a stern parent and a fledgling rock star.

Adelaide contemplated. Yes, that was exactly what she should do. Sit at the bar and be charming and take her hair down in some sort of sexy way that would sell the shit out of whatever crap Declan had fed her over the past week.

Except if she was thinking that was how this would play out, Jack probably was too. It was too easy. Forced. Call it instinct or foolishness, but something told her Jack knew exactly how she'd take down her ponytail. If Declan was right, he had done this many times, had the act down pat. With a face and body like that, Jack Nolan could have any woman he wanted, and she assumed most wanted him back.

Quite simply, if she had a drink with him, she would cede the power to him. Become ordinary.

So, she did the only thing that she thought might maintain the very slight hold she had now. "I'm sorry, but I can't really spare the time. Thank you for the help, Mr. …"

"Nolan," he said politely, leaning in to take her hand. If he was disappointed by the rejection, he didn't let on. "Jack Nolan." His grip was warm and very firm, covering her whole hand with his. "And you are …"

"Adelaide," she said, leaving off her last name on purpose. No reason for him to try and Google her, not that she had any social media presence to speak of. The less information that existed about her, the better. The last thing she needed was for a client to pass her profile around, putting a face to her name.

"What were you doing here at the hotel, Adelaide?"

"I'm affiliated with the university," she answered smoothly. Who the hell was she, speaking with such confidence? She felt like she'd slipped back into her makeup and jewelry from last night, morphing into someone older, wiser. Someone unruffled by daily life. Someone wearing shitty clothes because she had so much money that she had nothing to prove sartorially.

She began moving toward the door, ignoring Declan silently mouthing, *What the fuck are you doing?*

Jack followed, eyes still all over her. If only he'd been this attentive last night. "You really won't stay for a drink?"

This time, she sensed it. An unease. Maybe he was used to being turned down occasionally, but persistence usually won out. Women didn't turn him down a second time.

She smiled, ignoring the question as the valet approached. "Thanks for the help, Jack."

And just like that, she intercepted the keys to the Audi, slid inside, and drove away.

When she picked Declan up at the back of the hotel ten minutes later, she thought he might actually throttle her.

"What the fuck, Adelaide?!" he screeched, slamming into the passenger seat. The anger hummed around his body, filling up all the air. That was why she stayed in the driver's seat. He wouldn't hurt her if it would hurt his precious car.

"I did what you wanted!" she fired back. "Just not exactly *how* you wanted. That doesn't make us adversaries." When she saw the whites of his eyes, she huffed impatiently. "Declan, it was the right thing to do."

"No, it absolutely was not!"

She shook her head and pulled smoothly away from the curb. If he cared that she was driving his car, he didn't give any sign. Probably because he was too busy trying to burn holes through her with his eyes.

"I'll go to the exhibit in one week, like we discussed. I will interact *for real* with him there. Declan, the element of surprise is our friend here. What are you always telling me? Jack Nolan wants a certain kind of girl. Well, maybe giving him what he wants isn't the right way to … ensnare him. I bet he could have any woman he wants, and men like him want the chase. I bet a woman he *can't* have will be much more attractive."

"Bullshit."

"Come on. If I'd slept with him last night, it'd be over. He'd lose interest. Women were crawling all over him, and any one of them would have gladly gone back to his hotel room. If I was like everyone else, why would he ever let me get close enough to find out where your paintings are?" She hoped that sounded reasonable. She was purely going off instinct here; she had no real idea how to handle a man like Jack Nolan. "If I let him pursue me, think he's won me … then he'll be more likely to let me in. Trust me."

She glanced over at Declan for a second to find him still staring at her with wide eyes and a hanging jaw.

"I think it will work," she added quietly, not sure if it would help or dig her even deeper into the pile of shit she'd stepped in.

He flopped back against the seat, running a hand through his blond hair, pushing most of it over his right eye. "You'd better make it work, Addie. Or so help me, I'll march into that professor's office in the middle of the night and raise hell."

She couldn't help but grin a little. Finally, she seemed to have gained some semblance of control over the situation. Or as much as she'd had since the day she showed up to History of Painting. She was willing to test just how much—at least for as long as she remained in the driver's seat.

"Declan?" she asked, tugging her hair out of its ponytail. "Do you still paint?"

He didn't turn from his window, but she saw his shoulders rise and fall in a heavy sigh. "Sometimes. It feels different now."

"Can I see?"

"If you want."

"Can I see *now*?"

Another sigh. "If you want."

At his apartment, Declan led her up a spiral staircase she had previously not been allowed to climb. She'd been in the living room for a few minutes before, but it was a bland, sparsely furnished place without much to notice. The staircase led to a loft that acted as a makeshift studio with the floor covered by drop cloths and shelves of supplies on the walls. There was an easel in the far-right corner and paintings, mostly incomplete ones, lining the walls.

"This looks like more than sometimes," she noted with a raised eyebrow.

He dismally surveyed the room. "Creativity comes in bursts."

"What's this one?" she asked, walking up to contemplate the painting currently on the easel, paint filling only a quarter of the canvas.

Declan had mixed varying shades of red, thick and oily, but not in a particular shape.

"Not sure yet. I started it after we ran into each other again."

Adelaide dropped to the stool in front of it and faced him. "That gave you a burst of creativity?"

"Yes."

"Creep."

He laughed and sheepishly rubbed the back of his head. "What can I say? You're good for my art."

She wanted to ask to see the painting he had done of her, but she wasn't sure if it was an awkward subject. He'd probably painted over it long ago or destroyed it. She would rather not know.

"What will you do with all of these?"

"Nothing. They're not good."

She tilted her head. "No, they're not so—"

"They're not finished, and I can't figure out how to finish them. They're flat. Everything I paint is flat as hell. No substance. No spark."

"You ever think you might just be too hard on yourself?" she asked, picking up a paintbrush. "I mean, I'm doomed to stick figures."

He dug his hands into the back pockets of his pants and let out an abrupt laugh. "It's not that hard to re-create what you see. But elevating reality, making something that people can relate to, that speaks of a universal truth. Good art should transport you. That's what I'm missing—the soul."

She went to an empty canvas and picked up a tube of purple paint. "May I?"

"Knock yourself out."

She dabbed paint on the brush and made a circle on the canvas, and then a line extending from the bottom of it.

"Nice stick figure."

"Ah, but you're wrong!" she said, wildly marking out lines, radiating from the circle's perimeter. "Bet you didn't see that coming. A sun! Or … a virus."

He smirked. "Incredible."

"What are you talking about? Can't you feel the *soul* in it?"

"Oh, yeah," he assured her dryly. "It's bursting."

Their eyes met and held, and Adelaide could sense something fall away from between them. Declan wasn't being as frosty and weird as usual, and she liked that. Maybe he was just happy that she had interacted with Jack. Or maybe it was because, for a moment, he saw they were more alike than different—both struggling to find their way in a painful, unforgiving world.

"I should drive you home now."

Before he led her out, he took the canvas off the easel and set it down to dry. "One down," he remarked, winking at her when her mouth parted in surprise.

SIX

Adelaide's leg had been bobbing under the table for most of lunch with her brother.

It wasn't because she'd spent an entire two hours stuck in traffic on 95 with Declan as they headed to New York City for Jack's gallery opening tonight or because he'd checked the two of them into a fleabag hotel since he wasn't able to get anything decent on such short notice. Or because of the butt-ugly dress he wanted her to wear later, which featured a tiny flower print that made her look like a whorish Laura Ingalls Wilder.

It was all that. And more.

"What's eating you?" Michael mumbled as he worked to pry the meat from a lobster tail, tapping her calf under the table with his shoe.

"Sorry," she murmured, crossing her legs to still them. There wasn't a single item on that list she could tell him about. "Big test coming up that I really need to pass."

"What class is the test in?"

"Art," she responded absently, pushing roasted vegetables around her plate with her fork. She'd wanted to dive right into a big bowl of spaghetti, but true to form, the prairie-by-way-of-a-strip-club dress Declan was going to make her wear clung unforgivingly to every inch of her body.

Michael raised a dark eyebrow. He and Adelaide looked the most alike of the three Wright siblings with the same brown hair and hazel eyes, features similar enough that there was no mistaking them as relatives. Thanks to his life in Los Angeles though, Michael had a permanent tan and glaringly white teeth, and he'd turned his body into one that was hyper-fit but a little too lean, the way all the people she'd met in California seemed to be.

When Samantha had hauled them out west, Michael was twenty, a sophomore at Notre Dame, but once he graduated, he was all too happy to make LA his permanent home. Bear, her sister's boyfriend, got Michael a job at his publicity firm, and thanks to that connection, Michael climbed right up the corporate ladder, set to make partner by thirty.

How her siblings had chameleoned so easily in these new lives still dumbfounded her. Didn't they miss their cozy, old house on Walnut Drive? Didn't they want to be close to the last place they'd been a family?

"Why are you taking art? I thought you wanted to go to law school."

"I'm *thinking* about law school," she corrected him. "And it's an elective to fill my arts and humanities requirement. Trust me, I regret it daily."

Hourly, if she was being honest.

"Why'd you come into town then?" he asked, nodding at the waitress as she topped off his glass of wine. "Sounds to me like you should've stayed back on campus and studied."

"And miss the chance to see my big brother? Never." He was staring at her doubtfully, so she quickly covered up with, "I told you, my friends wanted to come into town for a show, so I tagged along."

"What show?"

"I can't remember. It's some off-Broadway thing," she said dismissively before changing the subject. "When do you go back to LA?"

"Monday morning for Bear's game. He got me and a date seats in the family box."

"Samantha's letting you bring someone besides her? That's shocking."

She'd meant it as a joke, but it wasn't all that funny.

As the oldest, Samantha had always felt like she had some sort of say over the two of them. When they were young, it felt like Adelaide had a third parent. When she got older, it felt like she had a warden.

Michael had played by her rules and was rewarded. The same could not be said for Adelaide.

Her brother wiped his mouth with a napkin and said, "Speaking of Samantha, I have news."

News. The way he'd said it indicated it wasn't the good kind. If it *were* good, Michael would've told her the second they sat down to eat.

Adelaide dropped her fork. "What?"

"Samantha and Bear are engaged."

Her stomach coiled up like a wire. It wasn't that she didn't like Bear. He was big and kind of oafish, the way most tight ends were. Always smiling, about as uncomplicated as a person could get. But though he had the brawn, it was clear Samantha wore the pants in their relationship. Adelaide hated to see a nice guy like him being taken advantage of, especially by her own flesh and blood. "When?"

"Last weekend. In Italy."

Another crossed-off item on the list of Samantha's steps to a perfect life.

Adelaide said the only word that came to mind, "Ugh."

"What do you mean, *ugh*?" He gave her a pleading big-brother look. "Don't you think congratulations are in order?"

"Okay. I'll call Bear and congratulate him."

Michael rolled his eyes to the ceiling. "This has been going on far too long, Ads. You've got to get over it. One of you just needs to be the bigger person and—"

"Not me. She's the one holding on to my money, Michael. I don't owe *her* anything." Adelaide felt her temper start to rise. "I don't know how you can be so delusional about her. She is the one who vacated our house like she couldn't wait to go! She was the one who wanted to wipe all memory of Mom and Dad away. And look, now, she's even dropping the last thing she has that ties her to them. Their last name. *Perfect.*"

Her brother tiredly slumped in his chair. "Well, I thought you should know. Samantha's planning the wedding for May."

"I'm sure you'll have a lovely time," she assured him, saccharine sweet.

"Ads …"

She waved him off. "You know, Michael, I should go. I said I'd meet my friends."

He reached for his phone. "Let me call you a—"

"No. I'm fine." She leaned toward him and kissed the top of his head. "I'll see you soon, okay?"

"Love you," he called after her, a little disappointed.

She could feel his eyes on her, even when she went outside, staring at her through the window. She broke into a jog, so she didn't have to bear the weight of his gaze anymore and only slowed down when she reached Fifth Avenue.

Fists clenched, hands shaking, she tried to calm down. She had no idea why the news of Samantha's engagement—which had taken longer than she'd thought, all things considered—had worked her up so much. She'd known it would come eventually.

But now that it was real, it felt like another example of Samantha's life unfolding in easy, blessed steps while she floundered, pushed around by person after person, trying desperately to claw her way out.

Why was it that everyone seemed to think they could just lead her around, like she was a dog on a leash? She remembered her promise to herself last week—that after she found Declan his artwork, she'd never let someone push her around again.

Maybe she should start now. None of the choices Declan had made concerning Jack had helped her as far as she could tell. She'd caught his eye on her own, intrigued him enough to ask her to drinks on her own, and tonight, she was going to reel him in on her own too. Until he wanted her. *Needed* her.

Declan had been right about one thing. She'd written the papers; she'd known the risk. And same as that, it was time to stop playing the victim and take matters into her own hands.

She'd start with her outfit.

She stopped suddenly in front of a window of a low-end boutique with mannequins wearing party dresses. In the very center, she saw it.

Yes, in many ways, she was trapped. But she wasn't entirely powerless.

She pulled out her phone and typed in a text to Declan.

Burn the farm-girl dress. I'm getting my own.

Then, smiling, she walked to the door of the boutique and yanked it open.

Ten minutes and counting. Adelaide sat in front of the mirror, trying to psych herself up. She'd hoped that meeting Jack in the lobby of the Claremont would have eased tensions, but instead, she felt a bigger weight on her shoulders than before. She'd promised Declan that not accepting Jack's offer of a drink was the way to get him interested, and she couldn't afford to be wrong.

Hours ago, he'd responded to her text with four words of his own.

Don't fuck this up.

And she planned not to. But that didn't mean everything would go without a hitch. Her resoluteness from earlier had been leeched away by doubts. What if Jack was similarly occupied by his female admirers tonight? What if he didn't notice her? What if he got a stomach bug and didn't show?

Not possible, she thought, screwing the back of a drop earring into her lobe as she inspected herself. *It's the man's own gallery.*

The dress she'd chosen wasn't painted on and slutty, but it wasn't that of an innocent schoolmarm either. Scarlet red, it ended mid-thigh and clung enough to show her body but not enough to reveal her exact outline, leaving something to the imagination. She shouldn't have spent her own money on it, but as soon as she'd tried it on, she had known it was so much better. More refined. A man with Jack's tastes couldn't ignore it. In front, she wore her mother's gold chain, and on her feet were the pumps she had spent the past week breaking in. In this outfit, she felt more like herself. More confident.

When Declan burst in the room, clearly ready for a fight, he skidded to a stop and whistled as his eyes fell upon her. "I take it back. This is better."

She smiled at him from her place at the vanity. "I know."

When she stood, his eyes followed her every move. He was wearing a jacket, his tie loose, and looked as though he'd spent a long, hard day at work.

He ran a hand through his sandy hair as she neared him. "Don't forget to—"

"I won't," she said, effectively silencing him as she went to the door. She stopped as she opened it. "Are you going to tell me where the gallery is, or do I have to guess?"

He seemed to break from whatever trance he had been in and dug in his pockets for his keys. "It's in Chelsea, on East 23rd. Across from the School of Visual Arts. I'll drive—"

"No need. I'll take a cab. The car will take forever to get pulled from the garage."

She closed the door on his hanging jaw, knowing he'd get it together and follow eventually. She might even see him this time, peeking in the windows of the gallery to make sure she wasn't royally fucking things up.

When Adelaide's taxi pulled up to a sign that said *J. Nolan—New York*, she knew she had found the right place. The front windows of the narrow building were awash in light, the double doors open to a steady stream of well-dressed patrons.

Stepping onto the sidewalk, she looked up at the artwork in the window—jagged edges of a mirror glued to canvas but broken into sections, as if to look like stained glass. According to the placard beside it, the artist was Hiroko Ishimi, and it was part of a collection called Mirror, Mirror. The piece showed Adelaide's face in a frighteningly warped way, like a fun-house mirror.

Inside, the bright gallery practically shone because of all the mirrors reflecting strategically placed lights. The place was grand and immaculate with a shining, lacquered wood floor and spotless white walls to draw attention to the artwork. Groups of people milled about, contemplating the various pieces. After taking a glass of champagne from a waiter, she absently signed her name in the gallery's guest book, trying to blend in while scanning the area. No sign of Jack.

Adelaide walked behind a couple sipping champagne and discussing how the piece in front of them was a pastiche of some other artist she had never heard of. Another woman studied a diamond-shaped mirror with an awestruck look and remarked to no one in particular that its optical clarity was *stunning*.

She tried to catch a bit of the excitement that the other patrons had. She found a space at another mirror and stared into it. A placard beside it called it *Light in Bloom*. Tilting her head, she admired the lines of it, trying to decide what about it "elevated reality," like Declan claimed art should do.

It was only when she was about to turn away that she looked beyond her own reflection and noticed a tall figure behind her, two surprised eyes watching her through the mirror.

Jack.

Their eyes caught, and one corner of his mouth lifted in a smile.

She sent up a quick, silent prayer as she spun.

Adelaide wrinkled her brow, pretending to take a moment to place him as he crossed the floor to meet her. He was wearing an entirely black suit, which made him look even more devastating than she remembered. As he neared her, she caught the woodsy, leathery scent of aftershave, which sent her senses spinning, almost making her lose her nerve. But she managed to force a polite smile.

Jack stopped in front of her, eyes a dark blue, thanks to the gallery's spotlights. "You."

He was so good-looking that she grew intimidated as she met his eyes. "Hi," she breathed. "I'm—"

"Adelaide," he interrupted, her name instantly in his mouth. "The woman who was too busy for me at the Claremont."

Her smiled turned up a bit. He remembered—that was a good sign.

"And you're …" She pretended to think for a moment, cheering silently at the small burst of hope, and then chagrin, behind his eyes. He wasn't used to being forgotten. "Jack."

He raised a dark eyebrow. "What brings you here? Are you an art collector?"

"That's right. I see you are too?" she said lightly. She knew the question made her sound silly, but that was the point. The last thing she wanted to do was make it seem as though she'd sought him out, and she definitely didn't want him to know that she knew exactly who he was. So, she'd decided long before to feign ignorance.

His lips twitched. "You could say that. Are you here alone?"

She nodded.

Something like approval slid into his expression. "What do you think of the artist?"

She thought of all the gushing compliments she'd overheard the many enthusiasts give and parroted, "The optical clarity is stunning."

"Hmm. Very astute observation. I'd love to hear more of your thoughts on the work."

She demurely batted her eyes. Flirting with him like this was easier than she'd thought. "Is that an invitation?"

He drained the flute of champagne he was holding and motioned to a waiter, who obediently came to him. He took the empty flute from her hand—*when had she finished it?*—placed both on the tray, and then grabbed two more.

"I do seem to remember you turned me down once before for a drink."

She gratefully accepted the glass from him. "Well, I'm not turning you down now."

He opened his mouth to respond, but just then someone called his name. He looked over Adelaide's head, his charming smile fading a bit. Whatever spell had fallen upon him seemed to break, and he cleared his throat.

"Not here though." He brushed his hand down her arm, and his eyes fell on hers, the slightest shard of an apology in them. "Too much to take care of tonight." He cocked his head, like he was suddenly suspicious she was playing a joke on him. "This is my gallery, Adelaide. *I'm* J. Nolan."

She gasped in insincere surprise. "Are you?"

"Yes. I *did* tell you my name the other day."

She tapped the side of her head, as if to say, *Must've slipped my mind.*

He nodded at her like he understood, but she caught his hand tightening at his side. The subtle way he was suddenly thrown off by it. "I'm occupied until the exhibit ends. But there's a bar on the corner."

Adelaide curled her hand around the glass, hoping it would keep her fingers from trembling. "I'll meet you after."

"Good. Now, if you'll excuse me," he said, striding away, leaving her woozy with nerves and anticipation.

She wandered about the place for a while, casually stealing glances at Jack, but his eyes were never on her. He was good at his job—she could see it, even from afar. Focused and intentional, just the way he'd been described.

Eventually, she went outside, half-expecting to see Declan hiding in the shadows of a nearby alley. But it was New York City on a Friday night, and the streets were crowded with people. She was swept into the flow of foot-traffic almost immediately.

When she arrived at the dive on the corner—an unremarkable tavern called Winston's—she wondered if this was the right place. She'd expected velvet couches and fancy cocktails, but this bar was dark and a little old-fashioned, full of glowing lights and casually dressed people. An old Led Zeppelin tune wafted from the jukebox, and unlike the gallery, the patrons here seemed to favor clothing more Adelaide's style—jeans and T-shirts. People watched her as she walked in and slipped onto the nearest barstool, probably thinking she'd made a wrong turn on the way to a wedding.

"A beer—" she started but stopped. Time to graduate. "Scratch that. Dirty martini." It was Michael's go-to.

She sipped her drink, practicing witty things to say when Jack finally arrived. Would he expect to "test the merchandise" before offering her a contract? And if he wanted that tonight, should she let him? As much of a pull as she felt toward him, she wasn't sure she could take this sexy act into the bedroom.

One martini later, she felt brazen enough that she didn't entirely care.

That was just when Jack Nolan sidled up beside her, motioning to the bartender. "Another for her, and I'll have the same."

She spun on her stool to face him. His eyes searched her face, a wolfish look in his eye, like he'd just spotted his next meal. There was no doubt about his intention now.

Oh, he definitely wants to fuck.

She hugged herself to keep from shivering because right then, with all the liquid courage in her, it didn't seem like a terrible idea. "How did the exhibit go?"

"Perfect." He shrugged, as if that was how all of them went. "We'll sell most of it in a week or so."

"You seemed very focused."

"I told you"—he nodded at the bartender when his drink was presented—"I don't mix business and pleasure. When I'm working, that's what I need to be concentrating on. No matter how beautiful the patrons are."

Adelaide took a demure sip of her martini, hoping she seemed impassive instead of awkward. She'd never been complimented so openly by someone as old as him, and it felt wrong and good simultaneously. "How long have you represented the artist?"

"Frances Thayer used to," he explained, as if she was supposed to know who that was. "Hiroko was languishing though. He needed to be nurtured. Grown."

Jack gave her a rundown of his own career, which she already knew most of from Declan. When he wasn't exhibiting at his own galleries or recruiting new artists, he was buying and selling art for private collectors and advising some of the most renowned museums in the world. Jack didn't just spot amazing art; he decided what amazing art *was*.

"You must be very good at what you do to be so successful," she murmured, surprised that she'd already made it to the bottom of another drink when he was barely through half.

"I'm more interested in hearing about you." He turned to stare at her intently, eyes trailing over her dress, her bare legs. "You came alone tonight."

"Is that a question?"

"Only if there's something I need to know."

"You're very forward," she surmised. Then, she whispered in a voice that was hushed for so many reasons, "There's nothing you need to know."

For the first time, Jack smiled at her full-on. And it made her want to run very far away and close the distance between them at the same damn time. She'd drunk too much. Didn't trust herself anymore. Not when his eyes had gone hooded and her toes were curling in her shoes.

"I really can't stay any longer," Adelaide announced. "You've kept me out past my bedtime."

"That's a shame. Can I walk you home?"

She shook her head and slipped from the stool. "Maybe I'll see you again sometime."

She knew he'd get up to follow her, so she wasn't startled when his voice snapped from behind her, "Wait."

Adelaide didn't. When she neared the exit, the door swung open. Cool night air whipped against her bare legs, but before she could even think to feel cold, he wrapped his arm around her and pulled her sideways, into a narrow hallway near the door. She was tipsy, and it felt pleasant to be easily turned around by him, pulled into his chest. She wrapped her arms around his neck and was intrigued to find it was a perfect fit.

His eyes scanned the empty hallway and then landed possessively on her. "Do you know how hard it was for me to work tonight after I saw you? I couldn't stop worrying about you being here, praying you would show. I could barely get the names of the damn pieces right."

She felt herself blushing. Surely, that couldn't be true. Not about her—or at least, not the *real* Adelaide Wright.

She teasingly pushed against his chest, surprised when he grabbed her hand and held it there. "I bet you say that to all the girls. You seemed just fine to me."

Jack's grip tightened on her hand, even as a playful, sensual smile covered his mouth. "I don't say that to anyone—*ever.* Weakness is not how you get to be where I am."

"Where's that exactly?"

"Wondering if you know every man you've passed tonight wants you or if you're really that unaware of how gorgeous you are."

She summoned the courage to ask, "Do *you* want me?"

He chuckled darkly as he raised her hand to his mouth and lightly kissed her knuckles. "Isn't that obvious, Adelaide?"

Then he pushed her back against the wall.

She sucked in a breath as he dragged a finger down her cheek, moving closer until her breasts pressed up against his chest. His eyes had gone a shade of blue-black that made her pulse race. A single dull bulb overhead cast an orange light down upon his strong jawline, illuminating the stubble there, and she instinctively wanted to touch him.

In a voice that wasn't fake at all, she whispered, "Show me."

His eyes scanned her face—from her eyes to her nose to her lips, as if trying to commit it to memory. When he was satisfied, he leaned in, covering her mouth with his. Something passed between them that was unlike anything she'd experienced before and unlike anything she expected to feel again. It was like sparks crackled in her toes, and the shocks went all the way up to her eyebrows. Like she'd been stung and soothed in the same sublime moment.

Her lips opened slowly, accepting him, and he just as gently slid his tongue inside.

It felt so incredible that Adelaide let out a small moan of pleasure.

When he realized she liked it, he pressed closer, one arm braced over her head, the other pinning her arm behind her back.

She was in control and not in control. Jack kept her where he wanted, yet when she parted her lips further, he deepened the kiss immediately, his tongue moving more forcefully into her mouth. She tasted the champagne, the salty martini, the sweetness of something uniquely him that she hadn't expected.

His hands strayed to her shoulders, her hips, sliding them down the contours of her body and groaning when she hitched a leg up around his waist. There was nothing diabolical behind it; she'd just moved on instinct. On need.

Jack hauled her up, dragging both of her legs around his waist but never taking his mouth off hers, not even when she gasped at the contact.

Adelaide was thrilled and scared in equal measure. She wanted him and thrived off of him wanting her back. How could she not? He kissed her savagely but ran his hands over her like she was breakable, whispering her name into her mouth when she shifted against him and felt how hard he was, right there against her stomach.

Emboldened, she threaded her hands tighter around his neck, breaking off to trail her lips across the jaw she'd been so intrigued by, breathing in the smell of him.

"Uh, excuse me?" a flat voice asked.

Their heads shot up at the same time.

Two glassy-eyed girls were glaring at them and pointing over Adelaide's shoulder. "You're in the way."

She followed the finger and realized their bodies were blocking the narrow hallway, which she now saw led to the restrooms.

Jack slowly let her down, his eyes pained with the effort, like he was debating on telling the drunk girls to go away. But Adelaide thanked God for the interruption. The effect Jack had on her just now wasn't normal. Made her lose control instead of keeping it. She'd felt powerful before, but now, her knees were so weak that she had to grab the wall to steady herself.

It was only then that she felt her phone buzzing inside her bag.

She opened it a crack and glanced at the single message from Declan.

Where the hell are you? The exhibit ended an hour ago.

"I should go. I have to …"

Jack licked his lips, his eyes heavy, lecherous even. He pushed her shoulders flush against the wall again, but instead of bringing his demanding lips back down to hers, he only bent forward to kiss the side of her throat, where her pulse thrummed. "Come to the gallery tomorrow afternoon. It's not open to the public. I want to show you the exhibit properly."

She had no doubt that wasn't *all* he planned to show her. "All right."

She escaped out into the chill of the night and hurried to the hotel. When she got to the room, there was a single light on, but she could barely see Declan among the haze of cigarette smoke trickling in from the small balcony. He was slumped in the chair out there, suit rumpled, staring at nothing. She'd never seen a melancholier sight.

"This isn't a smoking room," she warned him, yanking the sliding door closed as she stepped out. "You want to get us—"

"What the fuck happened to you?" he snapped, still not looking at her.

Adelaide fisted her hands on her hips. "What do you mean? I was exactly where you wanted me to be."

"Funny. Because I went there and I didn't see you."

"You went inside?"

Declan fed the cigarette into a beer bottle. "No. Of course not."

"Well, you must've just missed—"

The words caught in her throat as he grabbed her wrist, unexpectedly pulling her down onto his lap. When she tumbled on top of him, she could smell perfume that wasn't his. And was that lipstick on his shirt?

"Tell me what I want to hear."

It was only then that she noticed the wet slur to his words. His eyes were unfocused. He was drunk. Sloppy. Whatever alarm she'd felt upon being pulled toward him quickly faded to disgust. She pried his fingers off her wrist, shoving away from him, and he let her without a fight.

"We had drinks together." There was a hard edge to her voice as she added, "And I'm seeing him again. Tomorrow. At his gallery. And this time, I want to be alone."

For the first time, those wild eyes met hers. "Yeah?"

She didn't know what part he was referring to, but she nodded at it all.

"Good." He sank deeper into the chair and closed his eyes, the momentary triumph dissolving once again into sullenness.

She decided not to tell him about the kiss. He didn't need to know, and with the way he was acting, she wasn't so sure he'd be happy about it.

And she sure as hell wasn't going to tell him the most surprising thing of all—that she'd liked it. And wanted desperately to do it again.

SEVEN

Adelaide spent most of the following morning overthinking everything.

She'd been primed to hate Jack Nolan—to find him intolerable, repulsive—and yet her lived experience with the man was directly opposite to what she'd expected. Instead of lewd and lascivious, he'd been all heat and flirtation, desire and demand. Her mind kept trailing back to the kiss—the way his finger had stroked her cheek, the way he'd bitten at her mouth like he couldn't get enough, the way he'd gazed at her like he'd never get the chance to look again.

No boy had ever looked at her like she was the only woman in the world. But perhaps that was because Jack wasn't a boy; he was a man, and she was beginning to see there was a huge difference between the two.

Stop it, she told herself as she swiped on lipstick. *Don't even think about enjoying it. Jack Nolan looks at you like something to be bought and then used. There is nothing romantic about that.*

Of course, the more she willed herself not to think of it, the more she did—until the entire encounter was playing through her head on a loop, like some terrible earworm.

Luckily, Declan was too hungover to rouse himself from bed, so she had the luxury of getting ready without his nagging. She was also free to dress how she wanted, and this afternoon, she chose a pair of dark jeans and a white shirt, along with her mother's locket and a pair of chunky boots. Declan probably would have said she wasn't sexy enough, had he been conscious to survey her, but Jack had noticed her when she was dressed down. She felt like she should remind him of that today.

On the ride to the gallery, she felt nervous—too nervous—and she wasn't sure she'd be able to hide it from Jack. Her entire body prickled at the thought of being alone with him. Desperately, she tried to psych herself up. She could do this. All she had to do was step into the role she'd already cast for herself. What would that Adelaide do?

For one thing, run fashionably late.

When the cab pulled up to the sidewalk, it was two twenty—twenty minutes after she was due to arrive.

Taking a deep breath, she went to open the car door, startled when it opened for her. She looked up, surprised to find Jack standing there, staring down at her.

"You're late." It felt like an admonishment, though he'd said it blankly, like an observation.

One look. That was all it took. One second's view of those startlingly blue eyes, and all the confidence she'd drummed up drained away.

"Am I?" She'd wanted her voice to be sexy, seductive, but it came out mouselike.

He held out a hand, which she took, hoping hers wasn't slick with perspiration. His was warm as he helped her to her feet and guided her to the door of the gallery, his hand grazing the small of her back. "I don't like waiting," he informed her in a cool, distant tone she couldn't read the meaning of.

Is he pissed at me for twenty measly minutes?

"Um. Sorry?"

"That's all right. It gave me a chance to decide what we should devote our time to."

She stepped inside and shivered with the feeling of aloneness. The space was freezing and so much more expansive without bodies to fill it. The mirrored artwork she'd seen last night intimidated her with its reflections, her own distorted image staring back at her from every angle.

"I thought we should start over here, at the chiaroscuro. It's one of the artist's most celebrated pieces. Did you get a chance to look at it last night?"

Chiaroscuro. Declan had lectured her on that, but damned if she could remember what the word meant.

They walked deeper into the gallery, her heels echoing loudly and hollowly on the lacquered wood floor, but nowhere near as loud as her madly thudding heart. Adelaide felt jumpier than she had last night, hyperaware of everything around her.

"Only in passing." She'd tried once again to put a seductive lilt in her voice, but again, it wobbled.

"Here," Jack said, extending an arm toward a footlong mirrored cube on a pedestal. "No doubt, you've seen it before in various publications. But they don't ever quite do justice to the real thing, do they? I wanted you to see it in the daytime. It's a totally different experience in natural light."

She tilted her head, mind racing as she scanned through the things Declan had told her. It was just a damn cube—how much was there to say?

"Hmm," she said, tapping her chin, trying not to tense up when Jack slid an arm around her waist. She lost her train of thought completely. "It's stunning in its optical ..."

Shit. She cringed.

He pulled away and stared at her, his gaze penetrating, making her feel as though he could read her mind. One of his eyebrows arched significantly higher than the other. "Clarity? Yes, you said that before, about a different piece."

Could he read her mind? If so, she was certain he wouldn't like the things he found there.

Quickly, she tried to backpedal. "Well, I—"

"Adelaide, are you trying to spare me my feelings?"

"Of course not. I love art, but—"

"Not all art is for everyone," he assured her. "What do you *really* think? I want you to be completely honest with me."

His gaze, smoldering and demanding, was too much. And though she couldn't be *completely* honest, there was no sense in playacting. She'd done that before, under Declan's tutelage, to disastrous results.

She exhaled a long breath. "I get the artist has a thing for mirrors, but this one is kind of dull, don't you think?"

He laughed aloud and looked around the room, pursing his lips, as if he was trying to decide if she was right. "You're not going to just tell me what I want to hear, are you?"

Oh, Jack, she thought sarcastically, even as she pasted on a small, innocent smile. *You have no idea.* "Maybe I just don't understand it." She forced herself to look right into his eyes. "Can you explain it to me?"

Something shifted in his gaze, almost imperceptibly. He lightly touched her elbow, guiding her over to the nearest installation, a hanging mirrored sculpture made to look like an evergreen tree.

He stationed her in front of it with his hands on her shoulders and spoke quietly, into her ear alone, his voice spilling out in a low, velvety register. "Mirrors often depict the fragility of the viewer. You've heard that beauty is in the eye of the beholder? Well, so are many other things. Our pain is there. Our joy. Our art is a reflection of ourselves."

"It looks like a Christmas tree–shaped disco ball," she blurted.

He made a thoughtful noise and led her to the next piece. She managed a glance up at him, her skin flushed by his nearness.

"What do you think of this one?"

This one—four small mirrors placed at the corners of a bright, paint-spattered canvas—was even less impressive.

She read the placard and snorted. *Loneliness.* "It depicts the viewer's own loneliness."

"Actually, it does. It conveys the feeling of being separated from your tribe, the people who really know and care about you, by the noise and chaos of the everyday world."

"Hmm," she murmured, closing her eyes for a moment and then opening them to look again.

With his words in mind, she saw how the mirrors were actually all slightly glazed, so none would show the viewer's reflection clearly. Because of their size and separation, you'd never see your whole face at once, even if you went close.

"There's something so … compartmentalized about it. So"—she laughed, even before the word left her mouth—"lonely."

"It's my favorite," he murmured, almost to himself.

So, he was lonely. That was interesting.

Declan had said good art transported, and this must've qualified because she started imagining just what loneliness Jack had encountered in his life, even as she felt the familiar stab of emptiness for her parents. She thought about them and how much she'd relied upon them, how the hole inside her had only widened since their deaths. She was going through her life, but there were always other pieces of her separated, across time and space and wherever her parents were now.

When tears began to prick at her eyes, she snapped back to reality and realized that Jack was no longer looking at the artwork.

He was staring at her, mouth pursed. "Adelaide. You went somewhere else?"

"Oh," she sniffed, shaking her head to clear out her thoughts. "I'm sorry. This one is …" she trailed off, at a loss for the right word.

His expression didn't change, but a look of approval slid into his eyes. He tapped her nose knowingly. "I think you just saw your own reflection."

Her mouth parted, but no sound came out. She felt abruptly exposed, scared at how easily he'd intuited her thoughts. Both times they'd met, Jack sent her too deep into her own feelings. And that was not what she was here for.

He seemed to realize he caught her off guard and shot her a wink, effortlessly breaking the tension. "I find it interesting that you don't care for this artist or the exhibit. That means you must've come back for another reason."

Adelaide made herself smile shyly. An answer all on its own.

Jack took her face in his hands and swept his lips across hers gently. A wistful sigh escaped her throat. Both of their eyes were open, and his asked silently for permission to proceed.

She fisted his shirt in response, and the next time their lips met, there was no tentativeness. He claimed her mouth and she let him, arching back, allowing herself to be taken away.

When they pulled apart after an eternity, his lips were red. A little breathlessly, he said, "Believe it or not, this isn't what I asked you here for."

Heart beating like a drum, she managed a coy smile. "Then, why am I here?"

But Jack wasn't playing. Not anymore. His smile faded to something infinitely more serious and with what seemed like a great deal of effort, he backed away from her, so they were no longer touching. "Come with me, please."

He led her through the gallery, down a narrow hallway, then up a staircase. She knew what was coming next. Jack would offer to pay her—after a kiss like that, how could she expect him not to?

By the time they stepped into the small office, adorned with gloomy, muted artwork, his mood shifted again. Whereas he'd been intense and curious downstairs, once the door closed behind them, he grew emotionless, curt.

Jack stepped behind a sleek, modern desk that was a bit of an art piece itself with a gleaming white surface and brushed nickel fixtures. He motioned to an uncomfortable-looking chair in front of it. "Sit."

She slowly lowered herself down slowly, attempting a chuckle. She'd barely leveled out from the kiss downstairs, and now, her nerves were rattling in a different way. "Why do I feel like I'm in the middle of a job interview?"

He laced his fingers in front of him. "Actually, that's not what this is. You already have the job. That is, if you want it."

"I'm sorry?"

Jack leaned back into his chair. "I'm in a business where I need to focus on the artists I work with. I can't have anything getting in the way of that. And yet, whenever I show up to these events alone, inevitably, I'm surrounded by women attempting to take my concentration *off* my business. And I can't have that. Not for a single moment."

Adelaide waited.

"So, in the past, I've employed women to accompany me to my events with the understanding that it's not a relationship. It's a business arrangement." Jack spoke with the precise language of a doctor explaining a complicated medical procedure to a patient.

She'd been braced for what was coming, and yet it still shocked her to have him say it so directly. Hearing it from the mouth that had kissed her so dotingly downstairs, made is sound incredibly cold. Twisted. She had no reason to believe the feelings flickering between them were different than what he felt with any of his other women, yet it seemed impossible that things were always that magnetic. Maybe she was naive, but she couldn't see how he replicated that kind of spark time after time.

"Adelaide? Do you understand what I'm saying?"

Whatever she'd felt for him downstairs flooded out of her abruptly. She might as well be sitting across from a cardboard box. She nodded slowly. "You want to pay to date me. Like an escort."

"That's right. Although I don't think the term's connotations apply entirely."

"Would sex be a requirement?"

His dark eyebrows flew up, clearly surprised at her directness. "No. Completely optional. But I don't see a problem there. We're clearly attracted to each other. As long as you understand that it can't go further than that."

Her mouth opened, and she had a hard time closing it. His words struck her as presumptuous in the extreme. Last night, ten minutes ago, their flirting could've passed as romantic, but now it seemed seedy, crass.

In the span of just a few short minutes, the man in front of her had morphed drastically from the one she'd met in the bar last night. Now, she felt borderline ... disgusted. The attraction was still there, but it was tainted. Corrupted.

"You've done this with other women," she stated.

He nodded.

"Why? You know you could date any woman you want."

"Perhaps. But they would want something from me I'm not looking to give. The women I pay operate under an understanding."

She let out a breath. "No attachments."

"Precisely."

"And these other women, how many of them have you—"

She was silenced by his raised palm.

"Adelaide, that subject is off-limits. I won't discuss the other women I've entered into this arrangement with. It's irrelevant."

She felt like a recalcitrant child being scolded by a parent. "But—"

"No." He shut her down again. His voice was sharp. "I won't ask you why you're doing this, and you don't ask me. *Why* doesn't matter. As long as you understand that, we'll get along just fine. Here." Jack opened the drawer at his right, pulled out a clipped stack of paper, and slid it across his desk.

It was a contract. One her name was already on.

> *I, Adelaide Wright, hereafter known as Contractor ...*

"You already drew this up," she murmured. "Before I even got here?"

"I like to be prepared."

"How did you know my last name?"

His eyebrows knitted. "You signed the guestbook."

She blinked, thinking of how different last night must've been for them. To think, she'd gone to bed, dreamily playing over the kiss, hoping he was thinking of it too. But no. Jack

Nolan's mind had been on something a lot more unemotional. His method revealed itself to her with merciless truth: the kisses, the flirting—it was all just a means to get her here. Everything he'd said, everything he'd done—he had been priming her for this.

A sour feeling churned in her already-soured stomach.

She made like she was carefully reading the contract, but it was hard to focus. She could feel his eyes on her, and it was too disconcerting.

Among the legalese that made little sense to her, a few things jumped out. A period of three months. And, *Contractor is to make oneself available within twenty-four hours' notice.*

All of it, every word, rubbed her the wrong way, but she stifled her revulsion. Because Declan had been right—the number of zeros in this contract was startling.

"What's this?" she asked when she got to a section marked *Trial.* The contract read, *Hiring party is to furnish Contractor the first installment, plus expenses, following trial.* "A trial?"

When she looked up, he was studying her intently. "Yes, the first event is a bit of a test run. It's a birthday party for one of my associates this weekend. If all goes well, I'll wire you the first installment and weekly thereafter. You'll have to give me your bank account number."

A test run. Sort of like taking a new car out for a spin.

At that moment, Adelaide truly couldn't look at him. She'd met plenty of assholes before, but this guy was in the running to be the whole ass.

Good. She'd love to help Declan find his paintings and outsmart Jack Nolan. After spending this time with him, she thought it was the least he deserved.

She put out her hand. "You have a pen?"

"There's nothing you'd like to change?"

"Like what? Sleep with you *without* getting paid?"

Jack pursed his lips at the caustic tone bleeding into voice. "You tell me. The rules for this are whatever we say they are."

She couldn't think of a single one that would make this less horrifying. She motioned again for a pen.

Once he handed it over, she flipped to the end and signed her name quickly. "I'll wait for details on the party." Standing up, she stiffly moved to the door, avoiding his eyes.

"My assistant will be in touch for your banking information. Adelaide." He pushed up from his desk, giving her an unsure look. But he decided against whatever he was going to say. "I'll see you soon."

He didn't follow her out. Even before she hit the front door of the gallery, she was shaking, half-expecting someone to stop her on the street and shout about what she was doing. Jack had let her go like this was nothing. Like he did this all the time.

Which, obviously, he did.

When she reached their hotel again, she found Declan sitting in the exact same place she'd left him, looking hungover and miserable. He scowled when she entered.

"Oh no," he groused. "What's that look for? What happened?"

Adelaide kicked off her shoes. "You should be happy. The deal is done. I signed a contract, like you'd wanted."

His eyes lit up. "Seriously?"

She nodded and collapsed on the bed, exhausted. She wanted to bury herself in the blankets and sleep for days, then scrub her skin until she felt clean again. Something about this had her feeling sick inside and even more scared than she'd been before.

Her arrangement with Jack hadn't even begun, yet she already felt like writing papers was child's play compared to the dangers she was about to endure.

EIGHT

Jack forwarded the details of their first engagement to her email two days later. He'd been almost annoyingly curt and precise with his instructions.

> *Cocktail attire. No black. Arrive at 6:15 p.m. precisely. Tell the doorman you are here for Nolan and wait to be escorted upstairs.*

As if having Declan rule her life wasn't enough, now, she had Jack telling her what to do.

A middle-aged woman with a long blonde braid collected her from the lobby with a decidedly impersonal handshake. She doubled back to the elevators without checking to see if Adelaide was following. "I'm Gerta, Mr. Nolan's housekeeper," she said more to the space ahead of her than to Adelaide. "Mr. Nolan had an unexpected work emergency pop up, but he shouldn't be too long. I'll show you to a room where you can freshen up."

"A work emergency?"

She nodded. "He's very serious about his job. You'll see."

"I'm sure I will," she muttered, gazing at her reflection in the gleaming doors of the elevator.

Gerta pressed the button for the top floor and led her down a small hallway once they arrived. Jack undoubtedly lived in a lavish penthouse suite decorated like a museum, a cold and unwelcoming showplace for his priceless art.

Adelaide was surprised when the door opened to a space much warmer than she'd expected. When she stepped over the threshold, she found a sprawling great room with a large fieldstone fireplace, which opened to a modern yet intimate white kitchen on the other side. The walls were decorated with brightly colored artwork, and the sofas looked comfortable and homey. She could almost imagine snuggling up on the couch in front of a roaring fire with a cup of tea and a good book.

That feeling of relaxation only lasted about ten seconds.

Because at that moment, a voice down the hall yelled, "I don't care what you have to do. I told you, I need to get the Klee for Paris!" followed by a loud thump and then another one. Then loud footsteps.

A second later, Jack appeared, wearing dress pants and a button-down with the first two buttons undone. If he saw her there, he didn't care. He simply stalked toward Gerta and growled, "I need you to pack my suitcase tonight. I have to be ready to get to Rio on short notice."

"Yes, Mr. Nolan," she said as he swept past Adelaide and disappeared up a set of stairs just off the kitchen.

She suddenly felt a little afraid.

Gerta gave Adelaide a look like, *You see what I mean?* "Let me show you to your room."

It was enormous; she suspected her entire apartment at Cranst could fit inside. There was a plush bed, plenty of pillows, and large, decorated windows showing off the last streaks of the sunset.

Doesn't he live alone? How could he possibly need all this space?

Then again, she knew that when it came to wealthy people, bigger was always better. That was her sister, Samantha's, motto at least. Bigger husband, bigger house, bigger life. Why do anything unless you could *over*do it?

When Jack's housekeeper left her alone, she kicked off her shoes and sank her toes into the thick carpet. Tonight, she was wearing a silk dress with a gold belt around the waist, which the salesperson at the store had assured her was *very* trendy right now. Adelaide wouldn't have known to disagree with her.

She went to the mirror, fluffed her hair, fixed her makeup, and told herself that it was okay if Jack Nolan was an asshole to her. He was paying her, which was what mattered. Even better, he'd let her into his private domain. She'd have the money and the paintings in no time. This was just business.

That hadn't stopped her from wanting him to look at her downstairs though. Acknowledge her even if it was just a quick touch.

Moments later, he knocked on the door. "Ready?"

She opened it to find him already stalking down the hallway, wearing a black suit and tie, smelling of fresh aftershave.

As they made their way downstairs, he kept his eye on his phone, even as he barked information at her. "This is a birthday party for Franklin Watts, the chief curator at the Guggenheim. He's a friend and a very important business associate of mine, so I need to make sure I get face time with him. While I'm doing that, I want you to mingle. Look like you're enjoying yourself, but blend in."

"Blend in," she repeated with a nod. She felt awkward with him tonight in a way she hadn't at the gallery last week and decided it was better to speak when spoken to.

A town car idled at the curb. Jack waved to the driver to get in, opened the door for Adelaide, and slid next to her.

Once the driver took off, he started his instructions again. "Use good judgment. Don't talk about anything too heavy. Stick with the arts scene. If anyone asks about me, change the subject."

She didn't feel any better when they pulled up to a historic house on the Upper East Side, the streets peppered with arriving guests.

"Come," he ordered her when he stepped out of the car, crooking his finger at her like she was his pet.

He lightly put his arm around her, which was the touch she'd been wanting, yet now it gave her no reassurance whatsoever. In fact, it felt a lot more like *don't fuck this up* than *I'm right here if you get scared.*

As promised, the second they stepped inside, he nodded at her and went off to talk to some important-looking people. She gawked at the marble floor, the vaulted ceiling with stained-glass skylights, and the effortless elegance of the attendees. Nearby, a socialite prattled on to a group of other women, saying that she simply couldn't find a single good nanny to mind her son; she had to have a team of them. Another man showed off pictures of his new million-dollar yacht. It looked like a page out of a Gatsby party. All these people, bored with their wealth, trying to outdo one another.

And Jack wanted her to blend in?

Half-disgusted, half-curious, she wandered through the vast living area, taking an amber-colored cocktail presented to her on a sparkling silver tray. Tight groups of people stood about, deeply involved in conversation. She hoped one would take notice of her and readied her smile, but none did. Everyone seemed to already know each other. She'd never be able to make it seem like she belonged.

After a few moments of trying not to fidget, Adelaide meandered toward the back of the room, to the massive picture window overlooking the backyard. She took a few deep breaths, trying to recapture her Zen. Would it be totally out of line to hide in the ladies' room for a while?

Just as she was about to go search for it, a hand fastened around her upper arm. "What the hell are you doing?" Jack hissed, whipping her around roughly.

"Well, I—"

"You're supposed to be *mingling*, not standing around, looking like you confused the dosing on your antidepressants."

The acerbity of his words startled her.

He brought his face close to hers, every word brittle with disdain. "I *want* people to notice you, don't you understand? Everyone in this room should leave here either wanting to be your best friend or wanting to fuck you."

Adelaide glared at him. He hadn't exactly been nice before, but now, he was yelling at her. "You said to blend in," she asserted, trying to keep her voice even.

His face pinched even more, if that was possible. "Blend in doesn't mean hide. It means don't embarrass me. Haven't you ever been to a—" He cut off, shaking his head tiredly. "If you can't handle this …"

"I can handle it," she insisted, straightening her shoulders. Not handling it wasn't an option. She drained her cocktail glass. "I'm going to get another drink."

"Don't get drunk," he ordered after her in a low voice.

Yes, sir, she thought, stepping past the other guests.

Notice her? These people were too busy with their heads up their own spectacular asses to notice anything else.

When she finally found the bar among the maze of rooms, she slipped onto a stool and ordered a dirty martini. She sipped it quickly, wondering how many of them she'd have to imbibe before she was brave enough to approach a stranger. It wasn't like Jack could do her a favor and introduce her around.

"Don't you stick out like a sore thumb?"

Adelaide looked up to see a man, in his mid-forties, with thick black hair, looking at her from a few feet away. His face was blotchy, likely the result of too much drink, but he had a bit of a mysterious look to him. His glazed eyes traveled over her, stopping on her cleavage.

Nice to know I'm not totally invisible.

She shot him a rueful look. "Thank you for the reminder."

"What I mean is," he said, slipping from his own stool and taking the one right beside her, "all these people are the same. I see them time and time again at these things. But you're a new face here. That interests me."

He was leaning over to her, and though her instinct was to back away, she fought it. *If Jack wants people to notice me, fine. He wants every man to want me? I'll start with this one right here.*

She put on her imaginary mask and extended a hand. "I'm Adelaide. And you are?"

He took her hand and shook it but continued to hold on, refusing to relinquish her. "Franco," he said, licking his lips in a wolfish way. "Friend of the man of the hour, though I don't particularly enjoy his company."

Adelaide couldn't help but smile—she knew exactly how he felt.

He pitched forward a little as he spoke, close enough that she could smell the faint alcohol on his breath. "Are you here alone?"

"No. Yes."

He laughed. His warm eyes were brown, complementing his olive skin. Not her type, but nothing to balk at either. "A perfect answer for the most stunning woman in the room."

Why did it take a stranger to tell her she looked nice instead of the man who expected her to be at his beck and call for the next three months?

She was about to respond when Franco's eye caught on something over her shoulder. His grin fell from flirtatious to apologetic. "Adelaide," he murmured, "are you here with Jack Nolan?"

She was inching closer to him but stopped abruptly. "Um, why?"

"Because he's glaring at me like I just raised Satan himself." He grimaced at the same time she felt someone slide behind her.

She didn't need to turn around. She could feel him there, her own dark shadow.

Franco tilted his head. "Jack."

Jack wound a hand around her elbow. It didn't hurt, but it didn't try *not* to hurt either. "You met Adelaide," he answered, his voice low.

Franco held his hands up in surrender. "Only just. You have the most beautiful date here tonight." He winked at her. "It seemed like no one had mentioned that to her yet."

She loved this man. She hated this man.

Jack's fingers tensed. "Get your coat, Adelaide. We're going."

As before, she had to trip over herself to follow him, with the very keen sense that, once again, she'd done something wrong.

"What the fuck was that?" he demanded once she slid next to him in the town car.

"I was—"

"Don't ever, *ever* flirt with other men when you're out with me."

She gaped at him, feeling like she'd been tossed for yet another loop. "You're the one who said you wanted every man to leave there, wanting to fuck me. How exactly do you think that happens?" When he didn't respond, she defiantly folded her arms and stared out the window. Unable to resist, she added under her breath, "And it's not like you were paying attention to me."

Jack pulled her around by the shoulder, so he could see her face. "I told you, I had to work. These functions are not for entertainment. What did you miss when I said this was a *business* arrangement?" He huffed a little when she didn't answer. "What did you want me to do?"

She bit her lip because honestly, she didn't know. What she wanted from Jack had become a murky subject, like a canvas painted with too many colors. On one hand, his attention, and on the other, his distance. She wanted him to touch her the way he had in the dive bar and for him to keep his hands entirely to himself.

"I want—" Her voice gave out. Something thick had crawled up into her throat. "Nothing. There's nothing I want from you."

When the car pulled up to his apartment, she was unsure of what to do. Would he tell her to go home? That the deal was off? She didn't think tonight was supposed to end in an argument.

Instead, he stepped out, pointed toward the building, and said, "Inside."

She followed behind Jack like a chastised puppy. Or at least, that was what she felt like on the walk through the lobby as she tried to read the line of his shoulders, the way he loosened his tie, the violent way he jabbed at the elevator button.

It's over, she decided, bracing herself for the inevitable conversation. She was getting expelled—first from Jack's apartment and then from Cranst.

When they reached his apartment, Adelaide crossed the doorway a few paces after he did, steeling herself as she turned her back to him, to shut the door.

Jack was behind her before the dead bolt snapped into place.

One of his hands slammed her palm flat against the door, and the other gripped her hip, massaging her flesh. She felt two shocking things at once—the softness of his lips and the hardness of his erection, both competing for her attention. Jack's mouth was on her neck, moving steadily up to her jaw, giving her something between kisses and bites, cruel and kind in equal measure.

"Am I paying enough attention to you now?" he whispered, mouth hot against her ear.

"Jack," she breathed, surprise mangling her heartbeat. "I thought you were angry with me."

"I just wanted to punch that piece of shit, Franco," he murmured, moving his hand to her ass.

That wasn't what she'd meant, but when his lips touched the perfect spot under her ear, she forgot all about what she'd meant. Adelaide instinctively arched her back, giving him more access, which made his mouth feel like it was smiling.

"You think I didn't notice you, Adelaide? I couldn't stop noticing. You, in this dress, were making it so fucking hard for me to focus. I kept thinking about doing this."

Without warning, his hand slipped through her legs from behind.

"Holy shit," she choked as unexpected sparks of pleasure ignited in her. She checked out the darkened apartment, clinging to her last shred of dignity. "Where's Gerta?"

"Already went home."

With that, she completely surrendered. Her forehead fell against the cold door, next to where his hand covered hers. That hand was currently her only anchor to the earth. Her breath misted against the door as she let out hard, desperate breaths, biting her lip to keep from crying out.

He nipped at the back of her neck. "You want more?"

She couldn't respond. She had forgotten how to move her mouth and her head because all her attention, every nerve ending, was tuned to his hand on her, which was producing the most delicious sensations she had ever felt in her life.

"Adelaide," Jack prodded, low in her ear, his hard-on grinding into her butt, showing her just what he thought of her. Just what this version of her could do. "Tell me what you want."

"More," she gasped, reaching back to grab his head, to hold his mouth right there …

The hand under her dress disappeared abruptly, catching her wrist before she had time to get ahold of his thick hair. He slapped her palm against the door with his own, same as the other, boxing her in with two hands covering hers. She rocked forward, panting, shocked by the sudden absence of friction.

"Take off your clothes," he growled.

It was as simple as that, she realized, the moment that Jack's hot breath carried the words across her skin. In fact, there were no simpler four words in an arrangement like this. *Take off your clothes*. That was the agreement they'd really made.

Adelaide squeezed her eyes closed and asked for forgiveness. From whom, she didn't know. But she slowly slid her hands out from under Jack's, who didn't budge an inch, and listened.

First, she slipped her coat off, letting it pool on the floor around them. Jack warmed her goose bump–speckled shoulder with his mouth. She went for her belt next, looking down as she tried to remember how the hook clasped, shivering when he pressed his face into her hair, half-teasing, half-rushing.

"Keep going," he instructed as her belt landed with a clatter on the floor.

All that was left was her dress. He was really going to make her strip right there. She hadn't known it was possible to be this intimidated and this turned on at the same time.

She pulled the material over her head.

"Now, turn around."

Adelaide did slowly. Jack still had her in the circle of his arms, and they felt like boundary walls, keeping her mind from moving anywhere beyond this moment. His eyes were heavy-lidded, full of desire and heat, watching her like she had been created just for him. Which, she realized with a jolt, she had been. And even though it scared her, she found herself hungry to see what he did with the things that belonged to him. Because in all the awkward, fumbling sex she'd had with intoxicated college boys, none of them had ever looked at her like they were about to drop to their knees right there.

"Incredible," he whispered, running the back of his hand over her stomach, awe in his voice. "Your body is incredible."

She was on fire already, but when his skin met hers, it somehow singed her even deeper. She couldn't take the way he was looking at her, the way he was touching her. She wanted this. Him. Now. Everything about this situation was fucked up, and she didn't give a damn.

"Your turn," she croaked.

She forgot who she was talking to.

Jack's eyes latched on to hers for a brief thunderbolt of a moment. Then, he closed the space between them with one step, his palms swallowing her cheeks, his mouth prying hers open to slip his tongue inside. She swallowed his relieved groan and gave him one in return, losing absolutely all of her remaining sanity when he pressed his body over hers. She tried to wind her arms around his shoulders, but Jack pinned her wrists against the door, his mouth never relenting, not even for a moment. His teeth scraped her lips, his tongue licked into her mouth over and over again, and he pressed his thigh between her legs. It was rough, dirty. The kind of kiss that said who called the shots here. Who was doing the fucking and who was getting fucked.

"I need you in my bed," he breathed hoarsely. "I can't have you how I want you against the wall."

Has he given much thought to that? she wondered distantly as he spun her around and marched her through the kitchen, up the stairs, down the hallway to his bedroom.

He palmed her breasts while they walked, teasing her until she finally reached around and undid her bra clasp, desperate for his touch. The second the lace hit the ground, he filled his hands with her, stopping right there in the hall to roll her nipples with his fingers, kissing her neck between half-formed whispers of how beautiful she was, how much he wanted her, how hard he'd been all night.

"Jack, please," she begged.

He must have understood because he dropped one hand to steer her toward the door, brushing soothing strokes over her ribs with his thumb.

She had no idea what his bedroom looked like, and she didn't care. Jack smoothly lifted her onto the bed and then dragged off his shirt, so she could finally see his bare chest, muscles on his stomach stacked like bricks, veins pronounced on his arms. He was strong, tan everywhere, with a light dusting of hair dipping into his pants. She'd felt his body but not seen it, and they were two entirely different experiences.

At the bar, they'd barely separated long enough to look each other in the eye. But now, when he crawled toward her, something heavy dropped out of her chest and crash-landed in her stomach.

They were kissing again, like downstairs, except this time, they were horizontal and that made it so much better than before. Jack's breath was sweet, but his mouth was vicious. The kiss demanded honesty, and for all the things she was hiding from him, her desire wasn't going to be one of them.

"I can feel the heat coming off of you," he whispered, cupping her between her legs.

Adelaide's eyes fluttered shut. It was the single dirtiest thing anyone had ever said to her.

He moved down her body to trace his tongue across her stomach, over her belly button, along the waistband of her underwear.

Her eyes shot open. "Wait." She sat up and dug a hand into his broad shoulder. "No one has ever done that to me before."

"What?" He frowned, eyebrows drawing together. "Are you joking?"

Shit. She had reacted too quickly. Reacted like herself and not the person she was supposed to be. *Dammit, Adelaide,* she cursed. *This is not a moment for truth. There is nothing truthful about any of this.*

"It just ... never came up."

Jack was still looking at her like she'd sprouted feathers. "You never wanted to?"

"It just never seemed like a priority—actually, never mind." She attempted to pull him back up. "Forget I said anything."

He let out a very un-Jack-like laugh. "No."

Jack proceeded to gently kiss her through her underwear, sweet little pecks that made all the muscles in her stomach ripple. She had no idea how the person who had kissed her mouth so roughly a few moments ago could kiss her like this now, as if she were delicate, breakable. A desperate noise dissolved in the back of her throat as she watched him.

Jack's cheeks twitched. "Lie back. You'll be more comfortable."

The first touch of his tongue reminded Adelaide of the swirls of paint she'd seen at his gallery. Controlled, smooth, curving, spreading out in a slow circle that made her fist his sheets. The second was the same, but he pressed harder, leaving an impression behind. The third was her reward for the first two because this time, after his tongue swept over her, his lips closed, making her jolt so hard that her hips came off the bed.

"Don't come yet," he ordered in a low, smooth voice before dipping his head back down. "I want to feel you around me the first time I make you come, Adelaide."

He proceeded to test her in doing just that. She had no idea how he could bring her to the edge without jackknifing her over, but he did it again and again, like he was purposely giving her more time to enjoy the experience. She was desperate to get off, and yet she never wanted this to end—his silky hair against the inside of her legs, the roughness of his chin when he angled his head for more access, the thrill of threading her hands through his when the pleasure grew too intense and she started twisting against him. When he finally raised himself back up, dragging her panties off with him, she whimpered in protest.

"We'll return to this, I promise. Who the hell have you been sleeping with, Adelaide?"

Declan, she thought randomly, though that made no sense.

She felt drunk, wild with desire. She watched him take off his pants hungrily, biting her lip when he freed himself. Like everything with Jack, this part of him was also beautiful, intimidating, and powerful. Smooth and heavy at the same time. She wanted to feel him in her hands.

A condom appeared between his fingers. Adelaide lost her breath as he rolled it on, kneeling between her legs, eyes boring into hers. He gathered her hips in his hands, raising her lower half clear off the bed to position himself at her entrance.

A sharp hit of fear spiked—she'd reached the point of no return.

Jack lifted her onto him like she was weightless, sliding her over him inch by perfect inch. "Goddammit," he muttered halfway, squeezing his eyes shut.

But Adelaide couldn't wait for him, not anymore. His rules be damned. She rolled her hips once, twice, until he gave in and pushed the rest of the way inside her.

"Thank you," she breathed, eyes fluttering shut as she adjusted to him. It was a delicious and devastating feeling, and mixed in with her own anxiety, it made her head spin.

It took five strokes for her to detonate.

"Yes," Jack whispered, bringing his temple down to hers, smoothing her hair back from her forehead. "Let me feel you, Adelaide."

He brushed her lips with his as she shuddered through an orgasm, nibbling on her jaw, her chin, her mouth, encouraging her to keep going in whispers she could barely catch.

No one had ever watched her lose control like this before—she'd never trusted anyone half that much. It made no sense to trust Jack either, and yet she felt safe in his hands, knew instinctively that he wouldn't take her vulnerability for granted. He'd exploit her in other ways but not like this. Never like this.

She had barely returned to earth when he flipped her onto her stomach and then dragged her to her knees. She cried out when he thrust himself back inside her in one fluid motion.

"Jesus," he muttered, pressing his forehead into her skull. "You're so tight like this. You'll barely let me go."

When he started moving, she tipped forward into the pillows, losing her grip on herself, on everything that wasn't what he was giving to her. He rained openmouthed kisses over her back, using his tongue for some, his teeth for others, kneading her breast in one hand and teasing all the sensitive spots he'd discovered with his mouth before with the other.

"That's it," he urged, angling himself deeper still. "Good girl, Adelaide. Take me all the way in."

The way he touched her, the way he *talked*, sent her over the edge again. She wasn't even sure he realized it because he didn't stop the smooth rhythm he'd created, even as she reached a hand behind her, clawing at his stomach, pushing him away and begging for more at the very same time. She'd never had such a primal reaction to sex before; she was gasping, moaning, repeating his name like a mantra.

"I'm getting close," he warned her between clenched teeth.

"I want to see you," she pleaded, her voice foreign to her own ears. "Please, Jack. I want to watch you too."

Jack acquiesced, drawing out of her for one desperate moment while she flipped onto her back. She could tell he was close by how slowly he reentered, squeezing his eyes shut for more control, a line of concentration forming between his eyebrows.

She reached out to smooth the crease away, and when she did, Jack leaned in instinctively, letting his cheek fall into her palm.

Adelaide sucked in a surprised breath, and his eyes snapped wide open. Caught in a vulnerable moment. One he hadn't wanted her to see.

She brought her other hand up to his face.

"Adelaide," he started roughly, but her mouth captured his before he could finish.

He thrust inside her one last time, stilling, letting her kiss him unrelentingly and panting into her mouth, until his entire body went slack. He collapsed on top of her, breathing hard, pressing his head into her collarbone when she raked her nails through his hair.

His shoulder was so close that she could kiss it. She thought about leaning over to try—she wanted to taste his skin badly, wanted to explore him too—but abruptly, Jack said, "I'm crushing you," and rolled away.

He swung his legs to the floor, shaking his head like he was trying to clear his thoughts. Jack stayed like that for a moment, his sinewy, muscled back hunched as he tried to regain control of his breathing until he finally pulled off the condom, dragged his hands through his hair, and stood.

Adelaide was frozen with her hands clasped at her chest. Should she ask if that was okay for him? She was pretty sure it had been just fine. Say thank you? She'd already done that at one point, she thought.

Before she could try anything, Jack turned and headed into his bathroom, switching the shower on and climbing inside without a word.

He might as well have left a tip on the nightstand.

In that instant, she realized she'd been imagining this scenario all wrong.

The hard part would not be the sex, the amazing—*literally* amazing—sex she'd just had.

The hard part was going to be everything after.

NINE

S omewhere far away, Adelaide's phone buzzed.

Too early.

She rolled over in bed, expecting to feel the scratch of the sheets. She stuck her foot out, so it would hang off the edge of her twin mattress. She yawned and stretched her arms over her head, knowing her hands would hit the wall behind her.

When none of these things happened, she blinked and shot up.

Realization flooded in at once, and in the next second, she was wide awake, gazing around the vast, unfamiliar room. Morning sunlight was pouring through the windows, from which she could see the tops of Central Park's trees. Outside, Manhattan traffic raged.

But no Jack.

Of course not— she'd spent the night in the guest room.

Last night, after he'd raced away from her a millisecond after pulling out, she had decided she'd outstayed her usefulness and was no longer welcome in his bed. The thought left a sour taste in her mouth. She'd scrambled around the apartment to find her randomly scattered clothes before hightailing it to the guest room.

Wiping the sleep from her eyes, she finger-combed her hair and hurriedly pulled on some clothes. As she did, she checked her phone. There was a one-word message from Declan.

So?

She groaned under her breath.

The apartment was silent as she made her way downstairs, no housekeeper and no Jack in sight. Adelaide stood in the kitchen for a moment, overnight bag in hand, wondering what to do.

Should she just leave? Wait for him to come back? The event was over, but was she supposed to linger until he dismissed her?

Dismissed, she thought angrily. *Like a fucking child.*

She turned to get a water from the fridge and her eyes landed on a piece of paper—the only piece of paper—tacked to it. *Workout Schedule* was bolded on the top. The way his body had looked last night made more sense now—his exercise regimen was rigorous. Right now, for instance, he was with a trainer named Victor, working on abdominal supersets.

Which meant she was alone in his apartment.

Adelaide went right to work.

He wouldn't be back for at least half an hour, and she kept one eye on the clock as she went through his closets, digging through to the back to see what was inside. When those proved unfruitful, she moved on to the upstairs, where she found an office decorated with funky artwork that wasn't Declan's, a den, two more spare bedrooms, her room, and finally, his. She forced herself to enter brusquely, not stealing more than a glance at his already-made bed, where she'd writhed last night like an absolute imbecile.

The paintings weren't under his bed or stacked in his walk-in closet either. The apartment was big, but there were only so many spots Declan's paintings could have been stored without her finding them.

She shook her head and headed back for the hallway. Except when she opened the bedroom door, she ran straight into the wall that was Jack Nolan's chest. A wall she was very well acquainted with now. She backed up and took him in. He was bare-chested but wearing workout shorts, hair damp at the temples from sweat, a duffel in his hand.

And here she was, unshowered, makeup-free, rumpled, and smelling like sex. Smelling like *him*.

"Hi," she breathed, nerves rippling across her skin. "I was just, um, looking for my ... earring."

He looked behind her into his room and then lowered his eyes to hers. "Are you leaving?"

She nodded awkwardly, unable to meet his gaze. "Yeah, I've got to ..." She couldn't think of an excuse. "Unless you want me to stay?"

"No need. My office will email you." He stepped around her and into his bedroom, closing the door on her.

She glared after him. He couldn't even manage simple human decency, even after he'd been *inside* her?

Declan was right; Jack Nolan was a conniving prick. It was like he knew just how to reel her in, keep her wanting, so that he could do what he pleased with her.

Adelaide found herself stewing about it on the train back to Cranst. She had no right to feel blindsided by him, yet she did. He'd told her exactly what the relationship would be, and he was acting on it. But how had he faked what he obviously felt last night, in that brief moment when the shield around him had slipped? She was sure she'd seen something there—*someone* there.

Her anger had dulled only slightly by the time Declan picked her up from the train station. They went back to her apartment without speaking, where she showered and changed into leggings and a big sweatshirt. Meanwhile, Declan ordered them Chinese food and beer. When she reentered the kitchen, she felt like she'd climbed back into her own skin and the night before had been some weird fantasy.

He had a plate waiting for her.

"Thank God," she sighed gratefully as she grabbed a fork and dug in. "I don't care what they say about you, Declan. You're an okay guy."

He simply studied her, a question on his face.

Avoiding it, she twirled the noodles on her fork and stuck it in her mouth. "Well, other than the whole blackmail thing."

"Adelaide." He tapped a finger on the table. "Tell me what happened."

She shrugged. "What happened is that you're right. He is a dick."

"And?"

"And what?"

"Did you look for the paintings?"

She gave him an incredulous look. "It was our first real date. I looked around his apartment a little, but it's not like he had a sign on the wall that said, *Here are Declan's stolen paintings*. Besides, I didn't really get away from him for too long. We went to a party and then ..." She trailed off, the story taking a turn she wasn't entirely comfortable sharing with him.

Declan put his beer bottle down very slowly, working overtime to keep his eyes impassive. "Did you sleep with him?"

Adelaide faltered as she brought her fork to her mouth.

"You did."

She looked anywhere but his face, trying to gauge whether he was disappointed, disgusted, or pleased. He *should* be thrilled, considering how much access that gave her. "Yes," she admitted quietly. "But don't remind me. I'm trying to forget about it."

"Did you like it?"

The question made her cringe, especially as she remembered Jack's mouth between her legs. She brushed her hair behind her ear. "I really don't want to talk about it."

But she felt like she'd revealed her hand anyway.

The admission awkwardly sat between them for a few moments until Declan crossed his legs and picked his beer back up. "So, you got close enough to get into his bedroom but not to find out about my paintings."

"Give me some time! He hasn't even said if I passed the trial run yet."

"If you slept with him that quickly, you passed it."

She hated the way he talked about it. Hated the way he was probably right. "What's so special about these paintings anyway?"

"I told you already."

"Yes, but you didn't tell me what makes them so good."

Declan pushed his own plate away and looked off toward the door. She wondered if he was going to leave instead of answering. But he turned back to her.

"The collection is called Abscission." His voice grew softer now and a little wistful. He shut his eyes like he was seeing it in his head. "They're a set of six paintings, all which work off the other. I worked on them in stages, as I developed as an artist, and that's … that's how I wanted it to be shown." His eyes opened. "The collection was my best; it was obvious. After he took them, I tried to start other projects, keep myself going. I went to art school in Vermont, thinking the change would help. But everything there turned to shit. I was completely blocked. Miserable. It hasn't gone away since."

"Declan," she murmured with a sudden pang of sympathy.

"If I get Abscission back, I think it might unlock something. Get me back on track. Ever since he took those paintings, I haven't been the same artist. I've been … less."

She stared at him, surprised. At moments like this, it was easy to forget that he was blackmailing her. That he was just as big of a manipulator as Jack, twisting her up and using her easily.

But something about his words got to her. She'd been screwed over herself but by her own flesh and blood. She knew exactly what it felt like to be betrayed, to spend sleepless nights agonizing over her future after it was thrown into chaos by one selfish, arrogant person. In that way, she and Declan were kindred souls.

"I get it," she told him honestly. "I thought moving to California would be a fresh start too. I didn't want to do it, but I gave it the benefit of the doubt. And when I got there, I *hated* it. And I only got more resentful, the longer I stayed. My sister, Samantha, was … well, you remember Samantha."

He nodded.

"I isolated myself from everyone and everything out there. Nothing seemed to be working; nothing felt normal. In the end, I didn't even try to fit in. I just wanted to escape."

He gazed at her and said gently, "That's why you came back here?"

"I had it in my head that moving back would make everything better. That I would have my parents back somehow or feel them again or just be less sad than I was." She rested her hand on his forearm. "But it didn't, Declan. I still had the same old problems. Same old heartaches. Getting those paintings won't do it for you either."

The force with which he pulled away surprised her. His eyes shuttered up again; his face reformed into his usual scowl. "Save the parables for Philosophy 101, Addie. I don't need you to tell me what's right for me or for my art."

"Declan—"

"Your focus is on getting the paintings back. Other than that, keep your opinions to yourself." Declan leaned forward, narrowing his eyes at her. "And don't start thinking what you did in his bedroom this weekend means anything. Because it doesn't. You're there for *me*, Adelaide."

"What is your problem—" she started to ask just as the front door to the apartment swung open, and Imogen and Katy walked in, giggling about something.

When they saw Adelaide and Declan together, the laughter stopped.

Katy stared at them for a beat and then dropped a bag of groceries on the chipped Formica counter. "Sorry. Were we interrupting something?"

Declan set his bottle down, wiped his mouth with the back of his hand, and stood. "No. I was just leaving."

"Are you sure?" Imogen asked as Declan squeezed around her, headed for the door. The kitchen space was too cramped, even for just one body. "You don't need to—"

"It's all right. I've got work to do." The door slammed behind him, before Adelaide even had a chance to think about introductions.

The three of them stared after him until Imogen plopped down and motioned expectantly at Adelaide.

"Peach schnapps," she clarified, massaging her temples.

Katy opened the fridge and began to fill it with groceries. "He's pretty hot, girl. Are you guys, like, dating?"

"No, we're—"

"Sleeping together? Again?" Imogen pressed, excited now.

"No. Definitely not. We're just"—Adelaide let out a tired breath and lifted her hands—"friends. That's all."

Imogen and Katy exchanged a glance.

Then, Imogen said, "You can tell us if it's more. He's a little odd, but the hotness almost makes up for it."

She shook her head and stood. "I've got to go finish a paper."

That wasn't a lie. She might have cut back on the paper writing, but she still had her own schoolwork to concentrate on. But as she sat behind her laptop, trying to bullshit about Joseph Conrad, she found the words wouldn't come. Try as she did to force the thoughts away, her mind kept trailing back to Jack, hovering over her, moving deep inside her.

The most annoying part about it was that if Jack was thinking about her, it was probably not in a way that made his heart flutter the way hers did now. No, he was likely recalling the night in cold, clinical detail, deciding whether or not she was worth another round.

Judging by the way he'd chewed her out over her behavior at the party and the way he'd flown out of the room after having sex with her, the answer was likely a resounding no.

Yet that moment she'd held his face in her hands …

Her phone buzzed, pulling her from her thoughts. She lifted it up and saw a notification from her bank that she'd received a new deposit. She didn't have to check the amount to know what it meant.

She'd passed the test.

TEN

The email came in bright and early on Monday morning.

Ms. Wright,

By way of introduction, I'm Edith Smith, Jack Nolan's assistant. I write to let you know that Mr. Nolan requires your presence at a dinner this Thursday night. Donald Willis, an extremely important client of Mr. Nolan's, is arriving from Miami to discuss a potential sale. A car will pick you up at your apartment at five p.m. Dinner is at eight p.m. sharp.

A dossier on Donald Willis was attached, and a brief skim of it told her he was some corporate CEO of a tequila company, who had an interest in surrealism. She scanned the bio, detailing the pieces he'd acquired recently and the one which Jack was hoping to discuss with him.

On Thursday …

Why was that date sticking out to her?

Rummaging through the papers on her desk, she found her syllabus for her Modern Mysteries: From Doyle to Christie class. She had a test on Thursday from five to six thirty.

Immediately, her mind went into overdrive. Professor Linker was a humorless, unforgiving woman; there was no way she'd let her skip this final. She needed at least forty minutes to work on the test, and the train trip from Cranst to the city would take a little over an hour.

She quickly brought up the train schedule on her phone. If she banged out her final in thirty minutes instead of forty, she could get changed, take the six forty-five train, and make it to the restaurant on time. At least, that was the plan.

She replied:

> *Thank you, Ms. Smith. Please inform Mr. Nolan that due to a prior engagement, I will have to meet his party at the restaurant.*

As soon as she sent the email, she sat back and waited. And waited. Surely, Jack would have something to say about this. If her experience in his bedroom had told her anything, it was that he wanted things his way.

A few moments later, a response arrived from Jack's assistant.

> *Mr. Nolan says that is fine but stresses that you must not be late. He'll expect you there promptly at eight p.m.*

She could totally do this.
She had to.

Adelaide fisted her hands in her lap as she stared at the clock on the taxi's dashboard, willing it to stop advancing.

It was 8:27 p.m.

She had surpassed fashionably late and was edging closer to obnoxiously late. *Fire me* late. She leaned over to the driver and said, "How much longer?"

The driver looked over his shoulder at her, like she was an insect he needed to flick away. "Ask the cars in front of me."

She gnawed on her lip. She'd applied sexy red lipstick hours ago, but looking good had fallen by the wayside when she raced into the train station and realized that all trains were operating on a twenty-minute delay due to some power failure in New Haven. Her plans had gone completely awry when she found she couldn't hail a cab out of Penn Station to save her life.

"Do you know a shortcut?" she asked hopefully.

He rolled his eyes.

She glanced up the street. Traffic lined the road the rest of the way downtown. Grabbing her credit card, she said, "You know what? Pull over here. I can probably walk it faster."

He seemed glad to oblige.

After she paid for the ride, Adelaide raced down the sidewalk in her pumps, feeling sweat streaming down her rib cage. Exertion and the fear of what would be waiting for her at the restaurant made her nerves rattle in equal measure. Jack's assistant had called her five times already, but she'd been too scared to answer. She didn't need to talk to her to know Jack was freaking out.

She'd bombed her final, whipping together a half-baked essay comparing and contrasting the investigative styles of Sherlock to Poirot in about five minutes flat; she'd applied makeup on the train while scarfing down the only thing she could find in the kitchen, which happened to be a Pop-Tart; and thanks to the damp night, her hair had air-dried into a frizzy, untamable mess.

Even before she arrived at the restaurant, she knew this night had disaster written all over it.

When she finally reached the entrance, Jack was pacing the sidewalk. He locked eyes with her and bridged the distance between them so fast that she nearly ran headfirst into his chest.

"You're late," he snapped, gripping her arm.

"I know. I—"

"Let's go." He jerked her into the restaurant and dragged her coat off her, tossing it toward the coat check. "You aren't wearing that. Come this way. Hurry."

She looked down at her dress. It was stylish, professional, the dress she'd had on the first time she met him at his gallery. He'd liked it then. But tonight, he almost seemed to be gazing through her, as if she weren't really there.

Jack guided her toward the ladies' restroom, and when she looked back, she realized he had a blood-red piece of fabric draped over his forearm. Where had he gotten that? And surely, he wasn't going to accompany her into the ladies'—

Before she could fully think the thought, he shoved open the door and slipped inside.

There was a little vestibule between the door and the stalls—filled with vanities, sofas, and mirrors—which, luckily, appeared to be empty.

"Put this on."

"What's wrong with what I'm wearing?"

"Adelaide," he warned, his voice in a barely controlled clip. "This is not the night to argue with me."

She glared at him but said nothing as she shimmied out of her dress and let Jack pull the red one over her head. In another world, having him dress her would be kind of sexy. In this world, he was disdainful as he yanked the dress over her butt, muttering to himself.

She gaped down at her body without even looking in the mirror. It was skintight, showing plenty of cleavage, the outline of her skimpy underwear faintly visible. "You're not serious."

Jack stepped back to appraise her, squinted, and then shook his head. "Take off your panties."

Her mouth parted. "Are you seriously turned on by—"

"I can see them through the dress."

"Jack." She halted, eyes wide. "No, I can't."

"Didn't I say this was not the night to argue with me? You're half an hour late, your hair is a mess, and I don't want every person in this restaurant knowing my girlfriend wears lacy black thongs. Off."

And when she still didn't move, he started reaching for them himself.

"Okay, okay." She caved, slapping his hands away. Reaching under the dress, she slowly slid her underwear down, cringing with each uncomfortable inch.

"Come on, come on." He hustled, bending to pick the lace off the floor and stuffing it into his pocket.

Her face was burning when she turned toward the mirror. She felt angry. Degraded. "This dress is heinous," she remarked snidely as he came up behind her.

"When you're on my dime, Adelaide," Jack replied, finger-combing a knot out of her hair, "you'll wear whatever the hell I want you to wear."

His eyes fastened on hers through the mirror, giving her a possessive, primal gaze of pure male dominance. She sucked in a breath when he slid his hand up her side, but he simply snapped the tag off the dress and then jammed it into the trash.

"Let's go. I've kept them waiting long enough. And, Adelaide?" He had started for the door but unexpectedly whirled on her. He brought his mouth to her ear. "Keep those legs closed. No one sees you but me."

Goose bumps rose on every inch of her skin, which she told herself was just from his warm breath tickling her ear. "Yes, sir," she muttered sarcastically as he ushered her out, past the coat check and the hostess stand, into the main dining area. She followed him cautiously, walking as if on stilts.

He motioned with his chin to a table by the window. There, she saw a balding, sixty-something-year-old man who was far too tan and wearing far too small a shirt. It was open to mid-chest, baring a tuft of chest hair and a stacked gold chain, painfully tight over his rounded belly. Sleazy was an understatement. But what was perhaps sleaziest, was the way he was leaning over a blonde stick with boobs, coiling a lock of her hair around his fat finger. At least thirty years his junior, she was wearing a hot-pink Barbie-style dress, not very different from the one Adelaide had on.

So, *that* was why Jack had chosen this outfit.

"*He's* your client?" she hissed.

"I had Edith send over information. Didn't you read it?"

"I did, but—" She shook her head, giving up. Jack, she was learning, was pointless to argue with. "And her?"

"The girlfriend experience," he muttered, grabbing her hand and yanking her toward the table.

Ouch. She almost felt bad for the woman. That was, until she realized that Jack probably felt the same way about *her*.

The man popped a roll into his mouth just as they arrived.

Jack said, "Don. Here she is. This is Adelaide. Adelaide, this is Don Willis and his friend Kitty."

"Hello. Nice to meet you. I was stuck in traffic," Adelaide explained in a professional tone, reaching over to shake their hands.

Don swallowed and gave her boobs a leering smile. In fact, Adelaide was pretty sure his comment was directed entirely at them when he said, "Well, aren't you something, Adelaide? Gorgeous."

Kitty giggled. "We thought you'd never arrive!" She licked butter from her finger. "Now, we can eat! We're *starving!* We've barely had anything since smoothies at the airport in Miami."

"I'm sorry if I kept you waiting."

Jack pulled a chair out for her next to him. Ever the gentleman, he settled her in before sitting to her left. He checked out her tightly crossed legs as he did, shooting her a look that said, *You're on thin ice*, but also, *You're doing this*, and also, *Get over it.*

"Not at all," Don said, still speaking to her chest.

Kitty, if she noticed her date staring, didn't care. She simply checked out her manicure and then picked up a knife and tilted it, trying to catch her reflection. Adelaide had no idea how Jack had ended up with these two, who were radically different than the snobs she'd seen him with so far.

"So, Adelaide," Don continued, leaning forward, "you from around here? You're gorgeous, by the way. Did I say that already? Jackie here probably can't keep his hands to himself."

Jack's jaw clenched, but he didn't interject.

"Thank you. Uh, yes … I'm from the East Coast," she answered vaguely. "You're from Florida, right?"

Kitty giggled. "I'm from Iowa actually. But I moved to Miami because of Don. We met on a website!"

I bet you did, Adelaide thought wryly.

And it must have shown on her face because Jack gave her a wicked little pinch under the table.

"He saw my profile, messaged me, and two days later, he flew me out to Miami! I'd never been anywhere before that. But Don has taken me all over since." She counted off on her fingers. "Hawaii, Dominica, those little tiny islands in Thailand?"

"The Maldives," Don supplied.

"Right! Oh, they have nude beaches! It's super savage and fun. You feel like you're a native in the old days, before clothing. People have sex right on the beach. But as good as it is for my tan lines," she said, dipping her dress down to prove it, "the humidity was awful for my hair."

Ignoring her, Don said, "Adelaide, I bet you make a good travel companion, huh? You look like you're up for anything. Even nude beaches?"

Adelaide stiffened uncomfortably, casting a sideways glance at Jack, but his eyes were trained straight ahead, face emotionless. Was he really not going to shut this guy down? He'd had a coronary for less last weekend.

"I'm not much of a beach lover. But I hear that you're an art lover?"

He shook his head. "Nah. I need some pieces for the little shack I bought Kitty here."

"Shack?" Kitty balked and leaned in. "It's a six-million-dollar estate on the beach. But I can't live with him until the divorce is final."

Adelaide nodded, as if the whole thing wasn't completely appalling.

Throughout dinner, Don kept peppering Adelaide with personal questions, and Adelaide did her best to keep things professional. Whenever Jack tried to say something, he was met with a terse response, as if Don had no interest in interacting with him whatsoever. When he managed to swerve the conversation to art—and more specifically *Confluence*, the piece Don was interested in—Don seemed impassive. Jack's hands slowly balled into fists.

By dessert, Adelaide felt like she was sitting beside a volcano about to blow its top. She could tell Jack was an inch from exploding at this guy. He might have iron self-control, but even he was rapidly approaching his limit.

Without really thinking about what she was doing, she put her hand over Jack's, as if to say, *Please don't get upset with me*, and leaned intently toward Don. "Mr. Willis," she said breathily, matching Kitty's timbre, "have you had a chance to think more about *Confluence*? I've heard the way it evokes Egyptian hieroglyphics is sublime."

And she really had because true to her word, Adelaide *did* read the packet Jack's office had sent over. She wouldn't make that mistake twice.

It was the same question Jack had asked an hour before, but this time, Don actually seemed to hear it. "Not really, no. I've been too busy with the divorce to think about decorating. Nolan sent some pictures over, and Kitty liked it. She loves neon colors, don't you, Kitten?" He gave her a shrug. "She thought it would look good in the upstairs bathroom."

"Not only because it's neon," Kitty added seriously—or as serious as she could be with her high, whispery voice— "whenever I look at it, I feel like I have to pee!"

Adelaide covered her mouth to stifle a laugh. Jack pounced on the opening and started rattling off facts about the kind of investment the piece would be. He'd apparently decided Don had had long enough to flirt with her because he started using his *don't argue with me* voice that she was getting to know well.

Seeing Don's distraction, Kitty tiredly shook her head at Adelaide. "I don't know about you, but honestly, I don't give a rat's ass about the painting." Her voice had lost the wheezy little sound and dropped to a normal-sounding register.

Adelaide blinked at the sudden change in her. Kitty had gone from call girl to real girl, like she'd dropped a mask.

"Don just loves to buy me shit. It's important to let a man know you don't come cheap. I mean, we wouldn't be with them otherwise, right?" Kitty winked, like they were sharing a secret.

Adelaide forced a halfhearted nod. As she did, she caught the eye of another woman across the room, and it might have been innocent, but she suddenly had the feeling *all* the people in this exclusive restaurant were looking at them. Judging them. She'd been judging Kitty for most of the night. But why? She was no different. *They* were no different. Jack might have been hot, smart, and extremely good at sex, but there was very little to separate his intention from Don's.

Jack was to her what Don was to Kitty. She was bare-bottomed in a sleazy dress to prove it.

The thought twisted a knot in Adelaide's gut.

Jack pulled out a piece of paper and scribbled a number down. Before he folded it, Adelaide managed a glance at what he had written, which was either *$80,000* or *$800,000*. Did people really pay that much for art that didn't have a Picasso or Rembrandt signature? Or was Jack's eye really that good?

Don opened the slip of paper and didn't raise an eyebrow. He nodded. "Fine, fine. Send over the paperwork."

Inwardly, Adelaide let out a sigh of relief. Maybe now, Jack wouldn't lay into her for being late.

Wishful thinking.

When they were sealed in the back of a town car, he said, as if they'd never taken a break from arguing earlier, "If you're late like that again, I'll sever the arrangement."

She couldn't take it. Not now. Her mind was still turning over Kitty, disturbed by the way she'd lumped them into the same category. But they *were* in the same category. The money in her checking account, half of which she'd already spent, made that clear. She might not be as blatant as Kitty, but ultimately, it didn't matter. The arrangement mattered. That was who she really was.

And because the realization was making her depressed, all she wanted to do was get back to Cranst and forget the night had ever happened. "Fine."

His eyes snapped to hers. "What?"

She didn't respond.

Shooting her a dirty look, Jack directed the driver to take them to his apartment.

Adelaide leaned forward. "Take me to Penn Station first, please."

"No," Jack scoffed. "Good luck getting a train back at this hour of the night." He motioned to the driver. "My apartment is fine."

"*No.*" She scooted forward in the seat. "Trains are still running. And even if they're not, I'd rather wait there all night for the first train out. Please, take me to—"

"Give it up," he muttered, unruffled by her antics. "He's on *my* payroll."

She scowled at him and then peered out the window. Sure enough, the car was headed straight through Midtown, away from the train station. She slammed her body against the seat back.

"You know Don would never have bought that artwork from you if I hadn't been there," she snapped, aware of how childish she sounded. "*I* sealed the deal for you. I might have been late, but I brought him in."

Jack chuckled darkly and cast a withering glance in her direction. "Adelaide, I knew he was going to buy the piece before we even got our drinks. If you think I'm paying you to help me with my work, you are seriously overestimating your job description."

And it was reductive and dismissive and mean, and she hated him in that moment—*really* hated him. "I want to go home, Jack."

There was a pause.

Then, Jack said, "Scott, let's take her to Penn. I have work to do anyway."

The driver reversed course, but somehow, that didn't make Adelaide feel better. Jack could clearly see she was upset and didn't attempt to smooth things over. Because that was what she was to him. Expendable. A cost of doing business.

She held her hand out to him when the cab pulled up to the train station, tears hovering in her eyes, ready to spill the second she hit the sidewalk.

He looked confused.

"My underwear," she said flatly.

Jack's mouth parted, but he took them from his pocket and handed them over, watching her with an inscrutable expression as she slid them over her knees and up her thighs. She refused to look back at him as she got out, slamming the door as hard as she could.

She was sniffling as she boarded the train back to Cranst. She'd missed a series of texts from her roommates, detailing their increasingly drunken revelry.

> *I: We're going out to Willy's tonight. When you get back, come out!*
>
> *K: Girl, where you at?*
>
> *I: So bummed you're not here!*
>
> *K: We love you and miss you!*

Adelaide stared at the messages. She'd never had a normal college experience, but at that moment, she'd have given anything to be there with them, drinking and relaxing and enjoying some downtime. That had never been an option for her.

Maybe it never would be.

Because right now, she felt as far from "normal" as one could possibly get.

ELEVEN

The following week, she was back to the old college grind—classes, papers, studying. She was glad for it because after the humiliation of last week, she wasn't sure what more she could endure. Jack hadn't texted or called, and his assistant hadn't sent her any more emails. After a few days, she almost began to believe that what had happened the previous week was nothing but a bad dream.

That didn't mean Jack was totally off her mind though. Declan wanted updates, wanted to know why the hell she hadn't been back to his apartment since the night of the birthday party. By now, it had been three weeks since she'd met Jack Nolan, and their relationship was all stops and starts, burning hot and then ice cold. She had no leads on Declan's paintings—a fact that made him edgier by the day. Which made *her* edgy because if he got worked up enough, she could see him going to Progressor Hargrove—or worse, straight to the university's president—without so much as a warning.

So, she told him a little lie.

"There's a safe in his apartment," she fudged as she walked to her Nineteen-Century British Literature class, phone pressed against her ear.

"How big of a safe?" Declan asked suspiciously.

"Big. What sizes are the paintings?"

"I don't remember exactly. Maybe twenty-by-twenty."

"Oh yeah. They'd definitely fit."

"Get him to open it then. Or find the code."

"Duh, what do you think I've been trying to—oof!"

In her focus on the lie, she'd collided with someone walking the opposite way down the same path.

"Sorry," she mumbled, picking her head up to see a middle-aged man in an overcoat, frowning at her.

He was with two other men, dressed similarly, sticking out like sore thumbs among students wearing what could be described as glorified pajamas. She smiled apologetically and stepped around him, her eyes sliding over the other two men as she did.

Oh fuck.

She was hurrying away by the time she processed Jack's wide blue eyes and parted mouth, looking at her like she'd just morphed into an alien species.

"Adelaide."

She sped up when she felt him close behind, dodging into the shadows of an overpass.

"Dammit, Adelaide," Jack growled, gaining on her.

She was about to break into a run when she felt a hand clamp down on her wrist and roughly twist her around.

Jack wasted no time getting in her face, fuming. "What the hell are you doing here?"

"What are *you* doing here?" she fired back, legs shaky, attempting to pull away.

"I have a meeting for an art scholarship program I fund." He checked over his shoulder for anyone watching and then backed her up into the wall of the overpass. He was staring in horror at her outfit, at her satchel, at her lazy, lopsided ponytail. "Are you—are you a *student* here?"

She looked off, praying for any excuse whatsoever to come to her. When none did, she was left with no choice but to nod.

Even in the shadows, she could tell his skin went white.

"How *old* are you, Adelaide?"

"Oh my God," she whispered, wrenching away from him. "Old enough!"

He didn't move a muscle. "How. Old?"

She held out for ten seconds before relenting. "Twenty-two."

"Twenty-two?" he breathed, tilting his head back like she'd shot the words into his mouth. "But you seemed so—you never said you were still in fucking *college!*"

"I told you I was affiliated with the university."

"Affiliated is *not* attending!" His raised voice drew the notice of a passerby. He glared over his shoulder until they moved away and then brought his face close to hers. Unreal that a few weeks ago, those lips had kissed secret spots of her body that made her feel like she was in a fever dream. Now, they were slanted in a line of pure fury. "Show me your driver's license."

She barked a laugh. She was getting angry, offended even. She couldn't react to him though; she knew that would make things worse. What she had learned about Jack throughout their brief acquaintance was that he was a know-it-all, so if she rose to bickering with him, he'd never let this out of his teeth. And she had to salvage this. She had to play it cool. Things might have been bad last week, but everything could come crashing down *for real* if she didn't play this exactly right.

"Jack, I'm twenty-two, I promise. Now, come on. This really doesn't change anything."

"It changes *everything.* What were you thinking?"

"That you were going to pay me and didn't care what my reasons were. Or are you saying that, now, you do?"

Jack drew back like she'd punched him.

"I'm graduating in the spring," she continued evenly, pushing herself to her full height and tapping his chest to make him step back. "And I've been very much twenty-two the entire time you've known me, so there's nothing to get so dramatic about. Honestly."

She couldn't read his expression exactly. He seemed pissed but a little embarrassed too. Adelaide was pretty confident she knew why—he'd broken his own rules. He cared, however briefly, about why she'd agreed to this, though he'd been so clear that *why* didn't matter. And because of that, he'd stepped smack into the drama he claimed to avoid.

Interesting. Maybe there was a bit of a human underneath that cold exterior after all.

"You should have told me," he said finally. "I would have— you just should have told me, all right?"

"All right," she agreed, keeping an innocent and vaguely impatient expression on her face. "I'm very, very sorry."

He gave her a look like *don't even start* and checked his watch. "I've got to get to this meeting. We'll discuss this later. I'm not happy with you, Adelaide."

And that was what he left her with, which was annoying, but nowhere near as bad as *I'm firing you, Adelaide.*

"There's a shocker," she mumbled after him.

Men can be so stupid, she thought as she dusted herself off and continued to British Lit.

She was surprised she was hanging on to the resolve she'd shown Jack before, but for the first time in a long time, she felt like she had the upper hand. She'd backed him into a corner, using his own rules, which was something *he* normally did to *her.*

It seemed that Jack hadn't realized that having rules wasn't always an easy solution, as she herself had learned.

If you weren't vigilant, someone could come in and undermine them all.

Instructions for the weekend arrived in her inbox a few days after her run-in with Jack. She hadn't been concerned it would affect their arrangement, but she felt relieved nonetheless. Ever since they'd had sex, their relationship seemed to be slowly deteriorating. How had his others been able to pretend so easily? How had they justified it to themselves? Because ever since dinner, she had been having a hard time meeting her own eyes in the mirror.

Katy and Imogen went wild with another round of questioning when she told them she was leaving again—even Kyle Coral's senior thesis on European Hegemony in the 1800s hadn't kept her this busy. But her roommates still thought a rekindled romance with Declan was the reason, and since it gave her a good alibi, Adelaide didn't deny it.

Jack wanted her to join him at a private showing for a select group of VIPs at his gallery outpost on the Upper East Side. According to the email she'd received from his assistant, the artist was an eccentric, mostly reclusive man who wasn't fond of large, showy exhibits. That point was proven when she arrived and her name had to be compared with a predetermined guest list.

"Stay close today," Jack instructed her curtly, after she was waved through. He pressed her toward the coat check. "I've got collectors here from Madrid. You need to occupy the wives."

"Fine," she said dismissively, shrugging out of her jacket.

Once she handed it off, Jack grabbed her shoulder and drew her into him, so close that her chest brushed against his. He brought his mouth to her ear. "We'll talk about your little omission later. I do *not* want to hear about it during the exhibit. Understood?"

Her nerves flared, but she gave him one hard nod.

"Good girl." He casually pecked the corner of her mouth and stepped back. "Now, smile and stop looking like you want to fillet me open right here."

She turned her mouth up in a grin that felt as inhuman as it probably looked.

As if he was purposely messing with her, Jack returned it with a devastatingly sexy smile of his own. Linking her arm through his, he pulled her toward the first collector.

Adelaide did her best to make small talk with his wife, who was overall pretty boring. She wouldn't stop talking about the leather furniture she was importing from Italy and the hassle it had been to find accurate fabric swatches. On and on, until Jack finally bowed away, murmuring details to his assistant as he pulled Adelaide along with him.

They repeated this a few more times, and after an hour, Adelaide's mouth was parched, her jaw aching from fake smiling her way through small talk.

"I need water, or I'm going to pass out," she whispered to Jack between conversations.

"Don't you dare," he grumbled, unwinding her fingers from his arm one by one. "I have enough issues right now."

His frustration surprised her. "It's been fine, Jack."

"It's not *fine*. They're not excited. They don't trust these pieces are going to be worth what I'm telling them."

"How could you possibly know what they're thinking?"

Jack peered down at her. "Because I'm very good at what I do. I *make* the market trends, Adelaide. I don't wait for someone to tell me what they are. And I'm trying to do that today, but Javier is ..." His eyes shut for a moment. "It just doesn't help when the artist is a wallflower. Mysterious can be a selling tool but not when it makes buyers lose confidence that he'll keep producing great work."

Adelaide's eyes cut to where Javier Morales, the artist—a boyish-looking man in his late thirties—was fastened to a corner of the gallery. He'd spent the evening there, shoulders curving in, eyes on his phone. Twice, Jack had brought buyers over to make introductions, and twice, Javier had mumbled something too low to make out. The guests would turn back to Jack with confused looks on their faces, and he'd have to guide them somewhere else, all charm and smiles, but secretly seething underneath—she could tell things like that about him now.

Jack working overtime to keep the VIPs interested amused her. He'd pissed her off mightily in the past few weeks, and seeing him humbled felt like closure. He was human, just like everyone else, despite the impermeable wall that seemed to contain him.

Once Jack waved her off to the bar, Adelaide downed an entire bottle of water before coming up for air. Declan had given her a crash course on all things Jack Nolan, but he hadn't prepared her for the stamina she needed to keep conversations going with Jack's associates.

Speaking of Declan, Adelaide couldn't help but wonder why this artist rated so high to Jack when Declan hadn't. Javier was more established in the industry, but she knew from the dossier she'd read that Jack had gone all the way to South America to find him and traveled back frequently to review his work. That seemed like a lot of effort when all Declan had required was a hotel room and a few nights out on the town.

Adelaide tilted her head, inspecting Javier, who was giving Jack and his newest attempt a blank look. Was it possible he could shed some light on Jack Nolan and his methods of working with young artists? It was a long shot, but any information he could give her might be worth something. Declan was chomping at the bit; she needed to give him a kernel at least. And soon.

Avoiding Jack's eyes, Adelaide crossed the gallery floor to where Javier sat, eyes on his phone. "Hello," she said, dropping onto the opposite side of the bench from him. "Javier, right? I'm Adelaide. It's nice to meet you."

Javier grunted but didn't respond.

"The collection is amazing," she tried again, dipping her head when his eyes slid to look at her briefly. "It's about migration patterns, right? Did you interview many people for it?"

He bobbed his head once.

"I loved the way you embedded materials into the pictures. Anyone can depict what they see, but you captured the soul of the places, I think." She was cribbing from Declan, but she wasn't bullshitting. She liked his work and even felt like she half-understood it.

"Thank you." He slowly turned his head to look at her. He was youthful in the face, which was only enhanced by the shyness in his eyes. "Which one is he trying to sell you?"

"Oh." She sat back, surprised. "None actually. I'm Jack's, uh—Mr. Nolan's …" She paused before testing out the word. "Girlfriend."

"Hmm," he murmured. "I met the one before."

"Ha," she responded dryly.

"She never introduced herself."

Adelaide would have loved to ask for details, but she had more pressing matters, and she didn't trust him not to clam up on her. "Has Jack represented you long?"

"He's the only dealer I've ever worked with, so yes."

"He's quite good," she noted, watching as Jack made introductions between two groups of people.

He was wearing the same suit she'd seen him in the morning they first met at the Claremont, but now, she knew what was under it, and that made it look a thousand times better. She'd caught herself mentally peeling the articles of clothing away more than once today, remembering the warm feeling of his body over hers, the way he'd tossed her around in one instant and cradled her the next.

"You must trust him, if you've stayed with him this long."

"There are always other offers." Javier shrugged. "But Jack is loyal to my work, so I am loyal to him." His shoulders curled in again. "I just don't enjoy this part."

Jack? Loyal? Not that she'd seen. He'd been ready to fire her for running twenty minutes late.

"It would help sell the collection though."

"Make him money, you mean."

"Make it for you too." She was worried she was putting a foot out of place, speaking like this, but she hadn't seen him talk to anyone this much all night. She followed Javier's gaze, aimed somewhat spitefully at Jack. "Jack isn't always the most self-aware man."

"He's a jackass," Javier corrected. His bluntness made her laugh. "He's become jaded. Harsh. He needs to focus on the art, not just business." He angled toward her. "The first time Jack came to visit me, he stayed for a month, just to watch me work. Just watching, watching, watching. I was working with eggshells at the time, and he counted each one. How many I used exactly."

Adelaide furrowed her eyebrows, unable to imagine Jack dirtying his hands with something like that. "Why?"

"I don't know. But he repeated the number to every buyer in New York, and they loved it. We sold the entire collection in one night. So, you see"—he tapped his chest—"loyalty."

"Or a break with reality."

Javier laughed suddenly, a sound so loud and jarring that the result was like a record screeching off track. The low, pleasant murmur of conversation died off. People stopped what they were doing and turned to check out what was going on. Even Jack. He'd been conversing with two well-dressed men near the door, but at Javier's outburst, he swung around to look at him. Then, his eyes locked with Adelaide's.

She kept her face neutral, waiting to see if he was angry.

But after a long moment, he gave her the smallest of nods. She might have imagined it, but it almost looked like appreciation. Adelaide subtly turned up her palm, beckoning him closer. And Jack, despite everything simmering between them, came.

Javier didn't make a drastic change in demeanor after that, but he opened up a bit, answering questions tersely but *answering* when Jack introduced a fresh round of buyers to him. Adelaide stayed at his side until the crowd thinned, scared if she moved, he'd shut down again.

When the last buyer had been escorted out of the gallery, Javier stood to leave. He was going right to the airport, but before he left, he pulled Adelaide's hand into an unexpected shake. "Please don't misunderstand what I said." He nodded toward Jack. "He's a good representative. He protects me, does right by me financially. But his real gift is understanding those who create and helping them do it. He must return to that. Always, always return to that."

"I'll keep that in mind," she whispered, checking to see if Jack had heard.

He was too busy at the other end of the gallery, signing paperwork.

When Javier moved to the door though, Jack reached both hands forward to shake his, but Javier bypassed him with a grunt and headed outside, into a waiting taxi. Jack watched him go, shaking his head slightly. Then, he let out a great sigh of relief.

"He wasn't *that* bad," Adelaide pointed out.

"Well, maybe not to you. He clearly loved *you*." He twisted the lock on the gallery door and flipped off the lights.

Blinking to adjust her eyes to the dark, she found him halfway across the gallery floor, his shadow cast in moonlight streaming through the front window. She followed him up the stairs, to his office. He'd sent his staff home, and she didn't want to wait downstairs alone. "He was very sweet once we started talking. But, no, he doesn't like you much."

"I don't need my clients to like me in order for me to make them successful."

Adelaide slumped in a chair, feet hurting from the hours of standing. She thought of what Javier said about Jack downstairs, about his gift for understanding artists. "I don't think Javier cares about success as much as you think."

"Believe me, he'll care about the check I send him." Jack rifled through some papers, snagging the ones he needed. "What were you talking about that made him laugh like that?"

You, she thought but couldn't say as much. "Nothing important. He's pretty deep."

"I should've figured you two would get along."

"What does that mean?"

He gave her a meaningful look. "You come across as a bit of an old soul yourself."

"Oh." She pushed some hair behind her ear and sat up straighter. "That."

"Yes, that. You don't act twenty-two. Probably why I thought you were older."

"I really didn't think it mattered, Jack."

"It matters because this takes more than a little maturity. If I'd realized how old you were, I probably wouldn't have asked you to do it. But you act like …" He shook his head and met her gaze head-on. "Like somewhere along the line, you've seen some shit."

It was a surprisingly astute observation, since the only times he really seemed to notice her was when his hands were all over her body.

"I have," she admitted plainly, unsure why she chose that moment to go with honesty.

His eyes stayed on her, but she wasn't sure if he was waiting for more or trying to signal that he didn't care to know the details.

Struggling to think of some way to change the subject, she blurted, "How old were the others who … did this with you?"

"Adelaide. We've discussed this. You know that's a question I have no intention of answering." He pushed back from the desk and motioned for her to follow him out. "The truth is, I'm usually much more discreet about my arrangements. I run a background check at least. But with you, I was …"

"Desperate?" she guessed, only half-joking.

"Fascinated," he corrected, giving her a long, charged look.

Her face grew warm. Was *that* a compliment? It felt like one, but as usual, she could never be sure with Jack. People had been fascinated by the freak show at the circus once upon a time too.

He retrieved her coat and held it open when they got to the doorway. "Turn around." After she did, Jack slowly slid the fabric over her shoulders before smoothing it down her arms. Then, he spun her back to face him and began fastening the large buttons for her. His hands brushed against her stomach, higher to her chest, taking his time on purpose.

She stepped out of his reach.

Unruffled, he slipped on his own jacket. "Young is all right," he continued as they moved outside into the chilly night air. "But this is too young. I can't have anyone knowing you're still in college. I already have a reputation, Adelaide, and I'm not interested in adding to it. Do you understand?"

She nodded, wondering if that meant he wouldn't trust her again. Wouldn't *touch* her again.

No, she decided. He'd touch her again. He'd just tried. That had been all her, pulling away. She didn't like the way sex had twisted things up for her and wasn't ready to wade back into those dangerous waters just yet, if ever.

Jack stopped her before she got into the car, his hand still on the door. His lips were slightly pouted, making his mouth look full and delicious. "You really won't tell me how you got him to laugh?"

"Jack," she chided, a wave of annoyance rolling through her gut, "you're the expert here. I wouldn't want to overestimate my job description."

He scoffed at her sarcasm, but miraculously, he didn't get angry. In fact, as he leaned forward, he looked slightly amused. He tipped her chin up to his. Coming in to whisper something— or worse, to kiss her.

Before he could move another centimeter, she ducked in the car, keeping her eyes straight ahead.

For a moment, he said nothing, still holding the door. Then, "It's like that, is it?"

She didn't respond, and eventually, he had no choice but to climb in after her.

That night, they went to separate bedrooms without another word spoken between them.

TWELVE

When Adelaide woke up, the sun was bright, and the hour felt late, much later than the time she'd planned to get up and haul herself back to campus for a full day at the library. She paused outside the open door to the master bedroom and listened for any movement, but she heard nothing. It felt too late for Jack to be home anyway. She'd never been here on a weekday before—it was Monday morning, so he'd probably already left for his office.

Downstairs, Gerta was wiping down the counters.

"Hi," Adelaide said, surprised that Jack's housekeeper seemed unsurprised to see her.

Gerta nodded towards the stove. "I made eggs."

"Oh, thank you, but I'm actually just on my way out." She gestured to her overnight bag. "Woke up later than I meant to. I have to get back to school—" She bit her lip, remembering what Jack had said about keeping that quiet.

"It's only two eggs. Here."

Before Adelaide knew it, she was up at the counter, eating a veggie omelet and drinking orange juice, chatting with Gerta as she made up a new flower arrangement for the dining room.

"How long have you worked for Jack?" she asked around a mouthful of avocado.

"Almost ten years now. He's a good boss, except for when he tries to cut out carbs. That's usually when I ask for a day off."

Adelaide laughed, although Gerta didn't seem fazed. She couldn't help but wonder how many women she'd made omelets for like this. For all she knew, there was a new girl at this counter every morning. Just because Jack wanted her for all the public stuff didn't mean there wasn't a real girlfriend—or even several side pieces—who took her place the other nights of the week. Did Gerta know about the arrangements he made the same way his assistant did?

"Gerta," Adelaide started, pushing away her cleaned plate. Something in her voice must have given her away because Gerta waved the cluster of hydrangeas in her hand, as if to ward her off. "Can you just tell me if—"

"You should study here," she cut her off. "I'm going to do some errands, and then I'll be upstairs, cleaning the windows most of the day. Nice and quiet."

"Oh no," Adelaide started. "I couldn't. I shouldn't, honestly."

"You can," Gerta told her.

And just like with the omelet, somehow, Adelaide had a fresh cup of coffee in front of her and was setting her laptop up on the kitchen bar along with her textbooks and pens.

By the time the sun started to go down, Adelaide had made it through her own paper and half of Jodi Freeman's. The week before, Jodi had pleaded with Adelaide to write her essay, offered her any sum of money she wanted for it, and Adelaide couldn't bring herself to turn down it down. When you had scraped by as long as she had, it was hard not to constantly feel insecure about your finances, and even harder when your current source of income had an expiration date.

Anyway, Declan had already found out about the essays—what was he going to do to her now if she wrote a few more? Tim Acker kept badgering her too, as had several of her regulars. There was still money to be made. As long as Declan thought she might find his paintings, he wouldn't turn her in.

Yet.

It was a more productive day than she'd had in a long time. Whether it was Gerta's surprisingly strong coffee or the quiet, ensconced space of Jack's apartment, something made her fingers fly across the keyboard. Adelaide had every intention of leaving before Jack got home, since she had no idea if staying past her designated hours was allowed.

She almost made it, except as she was heading for the door, he was walking through it.

"Oh," Jack said, pausing in the doorway. He looked distracted and a little cranky, like he had been shut up in a dark room all day and was surprised to see light. "Hi."

"Sorry!" Adelaide exclaimed, face flaming. "I'm sorry."

"You're still here." His eyebrows drew together as he took her in.

She could see the wheels turning in his head as he put the pieces of her day together. She made a fair guess he was pissed she'd spent the day using his house as her own personal hangout. Eating his food, kicking her feet up on the couch. She should have left an hour ago when she was sure he was still at work.

"I'm leaving," she corrected, shouldering her bag and tucking her laptop under her arm. Her heart started beating in her ears. "I overslept, and then Gerta said I should study here. Then, I lost track of time and—sorry about that. I'll just get out of here."

"Adelaide," he called, following her as she slid her body and duffel bag around him to head down the hallway. He halfheartedly reached for her, but she was already at the elevator.

"Sorry!" she called over her shoulder as she stepped inside. "Sorry, won't happen again!"

Outside, she all but flung herself into traffic in pursuit of an empty cab. She knew she shouldn't be splurging on one, but her head was spinning, and she didn't trust herself to navigate the subway. She had put a serious foot out of place, and she knew it. Jack was probably going to freak out and tell her he was breaking their contract or something. Squatting wasn't part of the deal.

Her phone started ringing as she pulled up to the train station. *Jack.* She got horrified all over again—he was calling to end things. That was it for her; she had seen the discomfort all over his face when he walked in. The brief moments she could even look at him, that was. She ignored the call.

She ignored his next call too. But when he called a third time, after she collapsed into a seat on the train, she knew she couldn't run from it forever. Maybe she could grovel, make up a lie. Tell him her apartment had flooded or something.

"Hi," she answered, clearing her throat.

"Where are you?" He sounded a little surprised she had answered.

"I'm on the train. I didn't hear my phone, sorry."

"It's okay." He was quiet for an excruciatingly long moment. "That was weird."

"I know. I know, and I'm really sorry. I didn't mean for that to happen. It's your house, and I shouldn't have—"

"You didn't let me—"

"Overstepped like that. I'll just go next time—"

"Adelaide," he cut her off, exasperated. "Stop apologizing. I don't kick out the women I sleep with after we're done. That goes for my house *and* for my bed."

She wondered how long he'd been sitting on that. She fumbled over her response, making a few starts and stops that she hoped he thought was bad reception, until finally landing on, "I've never done this before, Jack. I don't know the rules."

"The rules are whatever we say they are. Didn't I tell you that at the beginning?"

She could sense he was frustrated with her. The little Declan on her shoulder was telling her to defuse this situation, but that patronizing tone Jack had was starting to piss her off.

Focus on the money, she told herself. *Just focus on the money.*

She gritted her teeth. "Yes, you did. Let's forget it. It's an adjustment for me still. Next time, I won't use the guest room."

"Christ, *Adelaide*," he said, and now, he sounded even more pissed than before. "I'm telling you that if you want to use the guest room, *use it.* Pick another one of the three bedrooms if you don't. But don't make me into some asshole who wants to fuck you and then get rid of you the second I've finished."

"Do you realize what an incredible *hypocrite* you sound like right now?" she snapped, regretting the words before she even finished the sentence. On the other end, she was met with dead silence. "Sorry. I meant—sorry."

After another long pause, Jack sighed. "It sounds like we have a lot to talk about the next time we see each other. I'm not sure this is the arrangement we both signed up for."

"Look, Jack—"

But he was already gone.

A two-hour train ride back to school was not the ideal way for her to digest the conversation. Part of her was tempted to call him back, grovel again, say she didn't mean it, that she'd spend every night in his bed, have sex with him until he didn't want to anymore. But she knew that would only make her sound more nuts. The whole unexpected encounter made her uncomfortable mostly because she'd been reckless, out of control. What she realized about this endeavor, without anyone having to tell her, was that controlling yourself and your emotions was of the utmost importance.

So, just before the train pulled in, she sent him a very thought-out, calm email.

Subject: Our conversation

Midterms have me high-strung. I'm just trying to figure out what we are both comfortable with. Of course I'm good with the arrangement. Thanks for the offer to use your pad. ☺

She hated the message and herself the second she pressed Send, but she'd be damned if the reason Declan turned her over to Professor Hargrove was because she'd had one indulgent afternoon. She could still walk it back; she just needed to get her shit together.

Except, deep in her gut, she knew she'd lost him. The exact reason he had contracted with her in the first place was for no drama, and here she was, stirring the pot.

When Jack responded a few minutes later, his reply gave no clue as to what he was thinking.

Subject: Re: Our conversation

Good luck on your midterms. Gerta says you forgot your hat.

The following day, Adelaide jolted when a text from Jack himself popped up on her phone. He'd never texted her before, preferring to contact her through his assistant.

Please meet me at the Cranst train station at seven p.m.

She paced, panicked, and finally responded:

Okay.

Declan, of course, had been calling her since the weekend, looking for updates. She told him she was close to finding Jack's nonexistent safe and would keep him apprised of any major developments. As far as he knew, everything was status quo. She'd nearly convinced herself she was as confident as she sounded.

Dressing in jeans and a plain black sweater, she made her way to the train station, steeling herself with every step. She had formulated a plan that afternoon and would launch into her spiel straightaway, and then she'd be back in her apartment in plenty of time to drink herself silly. She'd need to after this conversation.

But when the doors of the train opened and Jack stepped out, she did a double take.

First, because he'd actually taken the train up, and second, because he was dressed down in jeans and a light jacket, like he was anyone else in the crowd. She had grown so used to seeing him spiffed up that she realized she'd never actually seen him in everyday clothes, though she had to figure they existed.

When his eyes found hers, she felt a twist in her stomach. His mouth was a straight line, revealing nothing about what he might be thinking. Their last conversation floated through her mind. He was ending it. She could see it in his shoulders, his eyes.

She swallowed. Everything she'd planned on went flying out the window. "What brings you here?" she croaked, putting up a hand when he got closer to her. "Sorry I look so crappy. I was just going to—"

"Can you do me a favor tonight?" he said, stopping in front of her with his eyes narrowed. His cheeks were pink. "Please don't apologize to me again. I don't expect you to look like a supermodel at all times, and it makes me feel very uncomfortable when you act like I do."

"Sor—okay. Okay, I won't." *Of course he doesn't care,* she scolded herself. *He's breaking up with you.*

"Thank you. So," he said, rocking back on his heels, "what's good around here? I'm starving."

"You're here to … eat? With me?"

He raised an eyebrow. "Is that a problem?"

"No," she finally said, deciding it was a kind parting gesture. A last meal before the execution.

She took him to a small, homey-feeling restaurant a few blocks away, where they sat across from each other at a corner table. It was probably not up to his Michelin-star standards, but they wouldn't run into anyone she knew here. Plus, the food was impossible not to like, provided he was eating carbs. She had a flash of fear, staring at the menu.

"What?" he asked, catching her expression.

"Are you eating carbs?"

Jack's eyebrows pinched together for a millisecond. "Yes."

"Good," she sighed.

He eyed her carefully, one corner of his mouth quirking up in a smile.

Once they ordered—two beers in frosted glasses and two burgers, medium well—she reached in her bag for a copy of their contract. She'd thought long and hard about how she would work this, and now, it was time to play hardball. "I want the twenty-five thousand dollars."

Jack almost choked on his drink. "Excuse me?"

She pointed to a bookmarked page. "The fee if you end the contract prematurely is twenty-five thousand dollars, and I'll be holding you to it. And I'd like you to prorate this month too."

"Adelaide"—Jack frowned, taking the document out of her hand and scanning the pages—"you brought a copy of our contract with you?"

She crossed her arms. "I thought you wanted to talk."

"I do. I didn't mean talk about"—he motioned to the paperwork—"*this*. Well, not technically. I'm not trying to end the contract."

"Then, why did you say you wanted to talk about the arrangement?"

"Because we clearly need to figure out why we had insane, amazing sex one time and now seem to be unable to hold a normal conversation."

"Oh." *So, he thought it was amazing too?* She crumpled back into her seat. "I thought you were angry."

He opened his mouth like he was going to chastise her but then closed it, giving her a sad, frustrated little grin instead. "I *am* angry. But mostly because I can't figure out what I did to make you so disgusted with me. We slept together, and then you disappeared, so it had to be something. You've been circling me like a scared kitten for weeks."

"*You* disappeared into the shower actually."

The corners of his mouth curved. "I was thinking you'd join me."

She narrowed her eyes, debating whether she had really misread the interaction or if he was just trying to cover his own ass. "I'm not disgusted with you, Jack. Not entirely anyway."

"Then, tell me what's going on, Adelaide. No more platitudes. I mean it."

She doodled a *J* in the frost on her mug and erased it before he could see. "It's me," she admitted because she had nothing left to lose. "I'm disgusted with myself."

"Why?"

"Because I'm giving you the 'girlfriend experience.' "

"Ah." His eyes filled with realization and the slightest hint of regret. "I shouldn't have said that to you."

Adelaide folded her arms and stared down in her lap. She felt embarrassed and angry, but in the back of her head were those two little words he'd used—*insane, amazing*—bouncing around like her brain was a blow-up castle.

"Look," he said, leaning across the table and waiting for her to look up. His eyes seemed cornflower blue tonight. "I can't help you with the part where you're disgusted with yourself. That's your own deal to figure out, Adelaide. I apologize if that sounds cold to you, but frankly, I'm not your therapist. I could tell you a hundred times that you're beautiful and that using it to your advantage doesn't make you a bad person, but it won't matter if you don't believe it yourself."

"You didn't even ask me why," she responded, surprised when her voice trembled.

"We've gone over this before. *Why* doesn't matter to me. I'm not a benefactor, Adelaide. You're not a charity case. You're an adult who signed a contract. If you want out, say it. I'm going to try and negotiate the shit out of that twenty-five thousand dollars, but you *are* free to walk whenever you want. But I came up here to hash this out with you because I think you might actually start to enjoy this, if you can just get out of your own head."

Adelaide's eyes sank back to the table, where she found she had ripped up her napkin into little bits.

"How about this?" Jack said when they hadn't spoken for a full two minutes. "Just for tonight—and I mean, *just* tonight—you can ask me about the others, and I'll tell you what you want to know."

Her eyes snapped to his. "Seriously?"

He took a big swallow of his beer, resigned. "Sure. Why not? Don't say I never bled out a little for you, Adelaide."

She leaned forward, tucking her beer in her chest. There were a hundred things she wanted to ask him—for herself and for Declan. Deep background, she knew, was something all good journalists needed to do. It was the basis of Matthew Prior's sophomore-year midterm.

"How many have there been?"

"Don't ease me into it or anything." He rubbed a finger over his chin, thinking. "Six."

"Six," she repeated, trying to decide if this felt like a lot or a little. Declan had thought the number was closer to ten. "Six others. Okay. How did you find them?"

"I met them similarly to how I met you. Happenstance. Coincidence. Social circles interacting. We met; we connected. They were interested in the arrangement."

Unless they had manipulated him the same way she had.

"Has anyone ever said no?"

"Yes."

"More than one?"

He licked his lips, and she could tell he didn't want to answer that one for some reason. "Yes."

"And they were all older than me?"

"Closer to my age."

The waiter checked on them, and they each ordered another beer in unison. Was it possible Jack was nervous too?

"Did you sleep with all of them?"

"Is that really going to be helpful for you to know?"

Adelaide nodded.

Jack looked off, debating something before turning back to her. "Yes, I slept with all of them."

"Wow," she breathed, feeling a little taken aback. "I see."

"It's not like you're thinking."

"You don't know what I'm thinking."

"Yes, I do. You're thinking I only do this for the sex and that whatever I say, that's what it always comes down to. Glorified prostitution."

She started to argue, but he leaned forward abruptly, a wicked little twinkle suddenly in his eyes.

"But you're also wondering if the sex was as good as it was with us."

Her mouth parted.

"It wasn't," he answered quickly. "That was new for me too."

"It was a fluke."

"Only one way to find out." He leaned back properly in his chair. "If you want to, that is. If you never want to do it again, that's fine, but I would appreciate if we drew some boundaries because that thing with you at my apartment was—"

"I said I was sorry."

"Stop. Apologizing. You can stay. You can shower. You can put clothes in the drawers. It works better if we do this like friends and not like strangers."

She scoffed before she could stuff it back in. "Of course not. Strangers don't end up sleeping together for three months."

"I said I had sex with the others. I didn't say how much sex."

"So, it wasn't …" She trailed off awkwardly. *Insane, amazing, insane, amazing.* "A regular thing?"

"With two, yes, it was more like that. I mean, they wanted that, and so did I, and it didn't muddy the waters of our business relationship. With the first woman I ever had a contract with, we tried, and the chemistry just wasn't there. With Fiona—with number four, I mean—we sort of ended on bad terms, so it was only a handful of times."

The food came, interrupting the conversation for the time being. Jack dived in, but she ignored her plate altogether. "Do you still talk to them?"

"All, except one."

"Number four? Fiona?"

"Yes."

"Why?"

Jack shrugged. "She wanted our relationship to be something else."

"Why didn't you want the same thing? If you're always so on the same page."

"It started out well enough, although when I look back, I missed the signs that she was only going along with what I wanted. She thought it would lead to something more … permanent. And it can't." He put his burger down to focus on her completely. "I'm up front about that from the start. I've learned this is the type of thing you need brutal honesty for. Are you going to eat anything?"

"My eyes were bigger than my stomach." But really, she was too keyed up to eat. "Did they all, in your opinion, enjoy the relationship?"

"They were compensated well for it. They were able to take it for what it was, I think. Not everyone can."

She watched him eat for a few bites before he wiped his mouth with a napkin.

"Now, let's talk about the nitty-gritty. The night of the birthday party obviously took us both by surprise. I would be open to seeing if it was a fluke or not."

"Okay."

"Adelaide, you don't have to agree." He unexpectedly reached over and ran his thumb over her bottom lip, lowering his voice to a register that made her stomach squeeze. "Tell me what you want. Negotiate with me."

She thought about it for a long time and then folded her hands in front of her. "I would be willing to try again. But I'm not sure when. And I'm staying in the guest bedroom until further notice." This she knew for sure—whatever it cost her with Declan.

"Fine. I'll have Gerta set it up, so you're more comfortable."

She nervously jiggled her foot. "And the kissing in public. What about that?"

"What about *that*?" he challenged, raising his chin.

She wasn't sure if it was her or the beer that was making her bolder as the conversation went on, but she was becoming less petrified, more serious about the arrangement. "You have to ask."

"Fine. Ditto." His mouth twitched like he wanted to smile, but he didn't.

"Fine." She shrugged. And frowned. "No, it's too simple. You're trying to sell me butterflies and rainbows, but if I don't fuck you sometime soon, I'm sure my shelf life will decrease significantly."

Jack was undeterred. "If we don't fuck, I'll find someone else to do that with, same as you."

She gave him a doubtful look, but he remained unperturbed.

Instead, he motioned to her plate, effectively ending the conversation. "Eat."

When they left the restaurant, the temperature had dipped, and she could see their breath in the air. Autumn had arrived in Connecticut, yet tonight, she felt all warmed up inside.

Jack had called a car to take him back to the city and it was waiting for him outside her apartment when they arrived. The driver handed something off to him, and when she looked down, she realized he was holding her forgotten beanie between his hands.

Standing toe to toe with her, he worked it over her head. "I have an important business trip coming up I'll want you to accompany me on. My office will send over travel details." He was back in business mode, except his hands were still worrying at the hat, smoothing her hair down underneath it, away from her face.

"All right."

"You can't be late for this one. We'll be flying."

"I won't."

He squinted at her apartment building with slight revulsion. "You live here?"

"Yes."

"Alone?"

"I have two roommates."

"Roommates," he repeated, like she'd said she lived with cockroaches. "Do you have homework?"

"Yes, Jack."

"Is that what you'll do when you're holed up in the guest room all weekend?"

"Are you leading up to something or interrogating me for fun?"

He dropped his hands and gave her a disapproving look, turning toward the car.

"Jack."

When he turned around, she slowly moved toward him, so there could be no mistaking her intention. He was trying to be serious, but a beery, lazy smile fought through when her gaze fell on his mouth. She just needed to see …

"Ask me," he said when she was close enough that one more move would close the distance between their lips.

She paused, awkward, tempted to draw back. She hadn't realized he'd meant it so seriously, but then again, hadn't she? He must have felt her get a little stiff because he slid his hands into the sleeves of her coat, chafing her arms.

"Ask," he whispered again, bumping her nose.

"Can I kiss you?"

He looked smug as he soaked up the question. "Yes."

Gently, she did. His lips were the same and different—softer than she recalled, which made sense since she was moving slower now and her tongue was behind her teeth. She kissed his bottom lip and then his top lip before languidly moving on to the corners, keeping his face in her hands the whole time. Only after she was confident he wouldn't try and take over did she pull his lower lip into her mouth a little bit, catching it lightly and then letting it go. He murmured like he enjoyed it, and so she did it again, firmer this time. His hands left her sleeves and slid around her lower back, pulling her into him as she linked her arms around his neck.

Anyone could see them, but she didn't stop. They were kissing without trying to go anywhere else, and it felt like a novelty. She could test him however she wanted, discover what felt good, settle into him. They weren't even speaking, and yet she sensed he was still bleeding out for her, letting her take advantage before the night ended and they went back to their normal arrangement.

"Mmm," she hummed happily when he finally eased her away. She had no idea how much time had passed, but her toes had gone a little numb. She didn't care; she was floating somewhere, her head in the starry sky above them. "*That* we can definitely do again."

Jack smiled and kissed the tip of her nose. "Go inside now. Do your *homework*."

She reluctantly shuffled away, forcing her feet in the direction of her door, when all she wanted was to slide back into his embrace. He watched her until she was behind the doors to the complex and only turned in the direction of the car after they shut behind her. She waved to him through the glass after he ducked inside.

To her complete shock, Jack waved back.

The rest of the week went by in a bit of a daze. Adelaide tried to keep her mind on her schoolwork and midterms, but she couldn't deny her excitement about Jack's next event. She obsessively checked her phone, waiting for the email to come in with the details Jack had promised.

By Thursday, it hadn't, but what had come in were about half a dozen messages from Declan. All various versions of, *What have you learned?*

What *had* she learned? *I've learned that Jack's ass looks damn good in jeans. That he has a sense of humor once you pry him open. And above all, he can make a simple kiss sexy as hell.*

But no, she hadn't learned very much to help Declan. Not at all.

Deciding she couldn't put him off any longer, she typed in:

Hit a stall. Going to look at the gallery next weekend.

He responded with:

I'm having dinner with Hargrove next week. Find me something by then, or your time is up.

Groaning, she threw her phone down. Had she misjudged Declan's impulsiveness? She thought she was safe for a while, but with no leads on the paintings, he had no reason to believe she'd find them.

She had to give him something. Fast. But what?

Then, it hit her. She did have something. Nothing huge. But something.

She opened a message to him and typed in:

Fiona.

THIRTEEN

The next morning, Adelaide was greeted with a text from Tim Acker.

I texted you about a psych paper two days ago. You good?

She sighed and trudged out of her room for a morning coffee. No, she was not *good*, not since she'd sent Declan that message about Fiona. It felt like betrayal.

But who exactly was she betraying? Jack Nolan? Or herself?

Imogen and Katy were still sleeping, so she had the common area to herself. She poured a bowl of cereal and scanned through her emails, noting she'd gotten a B on that Modern Mysteries midterm and a B-minus in Eastern Philosophy. Not her best, thanks to her extracurricular activities with Jack. She was getting massively out of sorts.

Her heart stuttered in her chest when she saw the familiar esmith@jnolangallery.com email address with the subject, *Your presence required.*

She opened the email and read.

Mr. Nolan will require your presence at an exhibit in London this weekend. Please confirm your possession of an up-to-date passport. You'll need cocktail attire for one night and smart casual for the other. A car will pick you up at your apartment at five p.m. on Friday. Flight details attached. Please let me know if you have questions.

London.

She stared at the word until it blurred in her vision. Surely, his assistant had made a mistake. *London?* That was not what she thought Jack meant when he said business trip.

And, yes, she had a passport but a pathetic one without a single stamp. She'd gotten it on a whim when she turned eighteen, right before her parents' deaths, because it felt "adult" to do so. It'd been stuck in a drawer at the bottom of her dresser since then.

So much for getting her grades up next weekend. Didn't Jack expect she had a full course load?

No, she realized, and even if he did, he certainly wouldn't care. As long as she showed up on his arm—a reasonable facsimile of an attractive woman—that was all that mattered for their arrangement. She needed to remind herself of that when her conscience got to her, as it had with the Fiona thing.

As she mentally sorted through the papers she had due next week, another more pressing concern popped into her mind. *What am I going to wear?*

Whatever it was, she was pretty sure she didn't own it. She'd already worn all the clothes she'd purchased with Declan at the start of this whole thing, and she'd been trying to repeat as much as possible. Now, most floated at the bottom of her closet, unwashed because she'd discovered they needed to be dry-cleaned. Finding a cleaners near campus had never been high on her priorities list.

She had a mountain of studying to do, but it would have to wait. This was London.

This was an emergency.

She fired off a desperate text to Declan but was quickly met with a sick feeling in her gut. If she had Declan pick out her outfits, they'd probably be butt ugly, like the first dress he'd made her wear. Declan was *not* a solution to this problem.

But someone else she knew could be.

She rushed to Katy's door and banged on it. A second later, it opened, a sleepy eye staring back at her.

"Tell me you're dying. Otherwise, I don't want to hear it."

"Do you have any dresses? I know you have all those dresses from when you rushed Phi Sig—"

"Do I!" She grabbed Adelaide's hand and pulled her into her room.

Two years ago, Katy had made the big mistake of rushing a sorority. She often complained about how she'd nearly gone bankrupt, trying to buy enough little black dresses for their events, so she had a plethora to choose from. She sat Adelaide down on her unmade bed and marched to her closet.

"What do you need?"

"Two cocktail dresses. Not sexy, but not, *not* sexy either."

"Ooh ..." Her eyes went wide, and then a knowing smirk appeared on her lips. "You're going out with Declan, aren't you? You're totally together. Admit it."

Adelaide had run out of excuses. "Yeah," she caved, hating herself for lying. "We are."

Katy held up options, which she sorted through before picking what to try on.

"All of these are too formal. And it needs to be"—she thought of Jack's eyes on her legs—"shorter."

Katy pulled out a tight navy dress with cutouts along the side.

Adelaide touched the fabric. "Better." She wiggled out of her boxers and T-shirt to slip it over her head. She had a little gap in the chest, but she could fix that with a pin. "I think this will work."

Katy tilted her head as she inspected her reflection. "Hot. Are you going to a wedding?"

"Uh, yeah," she said, not meeting her eyes. She couldn't believe she wasn't going to tell Katy that she was leaving the *country*. "Just upstate. Some family member. A cousin, I think."

"Well, that'll work." Katy nodded, pulling out more clothes.

There were cashmere sweaters and pencil skirts and silk blouses—everything she needed. Thank goodness she and Katy were about the same size and that Katy actually cared about fashion.

"Any of this?"

"This one for sure." Adelaide nodded, pulling on a more conservative black dress over the navy one to model it just as someone knocked on the door.

Smoothing down her staticky hair, she ran and opened it to find Declan.

Paying no mind to her formal dress and sport socks combo, he said, "Seriously, this is good news. You must be doing something right if he's willing to—"

"Wait," she cut him off, glancing back toward the open door to Katy's room. She nudged him out into the hall and closed the door behind her. To his questioning look, she whispered, "My roommates are in there. And they've been asking questions."

"Ah." He finally took notice of her outfit. His eyes widened in horror. "What are you *wearing?*"

She rolled her eyes. "Look, forget I asked you for help. I figured it out."

"Are you sure?" His lips curled. "Because that looks hideous."

Her patience snapped. "Declan, for once, would you please just *shut up?*"

Bickering wasn't new for them, but she could tell he was taken aback at just how cold she'd gone.

A devious look that made her want to squirm crossed his face. "You sure you're ready for London, Addie? That's the big league."

"Yes." *Not a chance in hell.*

"Because you know what happened when I was in London with him. One foot out of place, and it was—" He made a slashing motion across his neck. "And you'll never know when it's coming. Bait and switch. He's famous for that."

"You're wrong," Adelaide answered, her voice shaky but her words confident.

She was surprised how firmly she believed this. Maybe Jack had manipulated Declan, but the man she knew had sought her out last week, asked her to stay when it would have been far easier for him to cut her loose. Whatever was between them personally, he'd kept his word to their business arrangement. And that was what she'd heard from Javier too.

Declan stepped closer, glaring at her with a disgusted little grin, until she could feel his breath landing on her face. "You would know, wouldn't you, Addie? You know him so well now that you're fucking him." He reached for the doorknob to her apartment. "Maybe we should go inside and role-play some scenarios in case—"

Without warning, the door behind her opened, and Katy poked her head out. "Hey you!" she said in the flirtatious, singsong voice she seemed to reserve only for attractive men. "What are you guys doing out here?"

Declan didn't break his gaze from Adelaide's, and he didn't back up. "I don't know. Addie?"

She began to say something about how she didn't want to disturb Imogen, but Katy said, "We were just trying to put together a wardrobe for your wedding weekend. That's so exciting! Where is it again? And do *not* worry; she won't be wearing"—she worriedly flicked her eyes to Adelaide—"*that.*"

Adelaide stiffened, but Declan didn't say a word.

Fumbling, she said, "Uh … Hartford. Which reminds me, we should get back to it. We don't have much time." She pushed back into the apartment. "Bye, Declan!"

She slammed the door and stalked into her bedroom, pushing away his words. Was she crazy, or had he talked like he was jealous?

Insane. Declan wasn't harboring feelings for her. He was angry she hadn't made any progress on the paintings.

I will, she promised herself. As soon as they got back from London, she would.

Adelaide pulled out her suitcase for the weekend, surprised when she felt an unexpected flutter in her stomach. That had been happening more frequently since her dinner with Jack a few days ago. She'd layered almost all her clothes inside when she realized what was causing it.

She was excited to see him.

Contrary to what she'd been expecting, Jack hadn't met Adelaide at JFK. Instead, his assistant had sent a terse email that said:

> *Mr. Nolan had to fly out early. He'll meet you upon your arrival.*

That was more than fine with Adelaide. All of this—leaving the country, the flight overseas, Europe—was new to her, so she knew she'd fumble around the airport like a naive idiot and probably draw impatient glares from him all the while. Not to mention that she had a paper to finish up for a sophomore named Janelle Roberts, which she promised herself would be the actual last one she did for *anyone*.

Probably.

So, it really was better that Jack had gone on ahead. His reaction to finding out she was in college had been bad enough; she didn't want to imagine what he'd be like if he found out about her little side hustle.

While the rest of the plane napped, she stayed awake, working. She finished the paper just as the captain announced that they were making their final descent into Heathrow. Packing up her things, she opened the shade on the window and scanned the landscape below for Big Ben. But the city was swathed in a fog that reduced visibility to nil.

I probably won't even get a chance to go sightseeing, she thought dismally.

The moment she stepped onto the escalator to the baggage claim concourse, she saw a man standing at the foot of the steps, holding a sign that said *Wright*.

"That's me," she greeted, yawning. Even wearing Katy's chic but comfortable travel outfit—a loose black dress, a leather jacket, and knee-high boots—she still felt as if she'd been twisted into a pretzel.

The man wordlessly took her carry-on and ushered her to a black town car.

As he helped her in, she paged through the travel papers Edith had given her. "It says here that I'm supposed to be staying in Mayfair? Is that far?"

The driver shook his head. "Sorry, miss, but the car was booked to take you directly to the gallery."

"The gallery?" She dragged out her ponytail and raked her fingers through her hair, panicking, as the driver nodded and pulled away from the curb.

Great. She grabbed her compact from her purse and powdered the shine from her nose, and then she added a little color to her lips. She looked down at her long, shapeless black dress. Jack would undoubtedly find something to criticize about it.

Then again, he'd also said, "It works better if we do this like friends."

Friends didn't criticize each other's wardrobe choices.

Of course, friends also didn't pay friends to fly halfway around the world when they needed to look good, and he'd seemed to have no problem doing that.

But something had shifted the last time they were together. *That* she was sure of. He'd seen her as more than just arm candy. He'd seen her as a person. She only hoped that now that his all-important work was once again involved, he wouldn't revert to the asshole version of himself she hated.

So busy was she, trying to make herself presentable with limited means, that she barely had any time to take in the sights of the city. Drizzly, cold, and crowded was as much as she knew when the driver stopped and opened the door for her. Adelaide stepped out and looked around, dazed.

"Which one is—" She stopped when she saw it, in elegant gold script—*J. Nolan Gallery.*

Among the other glass windows along the street, this one stood out. Somehow more understated and sophisticated than every other building on the street, it was an entirely black-painted storefront with a single neoclassical-style painting in the window. A sign beside it said *The Romilly Braxton Collection. By invitation only.*

Adelaide frowned, trying to process the scene before her. Jack's assistant had mentioned a gallery in one of the emails they'd exchanged earlier that week but hadn't said it was one of his own.

Which couldn't be right because Declan had said Jack Nolan closed this outpost down years ago. Hadn't he? Yes, she was sure of it. He'd closed it down the week before Declan's exhibit, with his paintings inside.

She was pulled from her thoughts when she caught sight of Jack's profile in the window. This gallery was smaller than the one in New York, yet it seemed more welcoming. He spied her and motioned to her to meet him at the door.

"And not even late this time," he mused, letting her in. He wore a dark suit with a light sweater underneath, the faint lines around his eyes and mouth relaxed in a smile. He helped her out of her coat, fixing her with a teasing grin as he draped it over his arm. "Can I kiss you hello?"

After she nodded, he snuck a kiss in the corner of her mouth, which made her stomach somersault.

To distract herself from the feeling, she motioned to her outfit. "I was going to go to the hotel to change, but the driver said—"

"You're fine, Adelaide." He handed her a drink that it appeared he'd been saving for her. There was something surprisingly informal about him tonight, though she couldn't put her finger on exactly what. "How was the flight?"

"Tiring," she sighed. "But I was surprised. Edith didn't send any long dossiers for me to brush up on. I won't have anything to say." From what she'd glimpsed on the way in, the exhibition was comprised of large acrylic triptychs featuring prostrate male figures. Kind of sexy, but a little off-putting at the same time.

"Because this one I think I have pretty much under control." His smile was mysterious, fraught with a meaning she didn't quite understand.

Before she could ask, he slipped to the side and took the arm of a rail-thin woman in a white button-down, open at the throat, and dark jeans. She had an ice-blonde pixie haircut and a nose ring, and if Adelaide had to place her age, it probably wasn't much older than her.

"Adelaide, this is Romilly Braxton, the artist."

She reached out to take the artist's bony hand and said automatically, "Nice to meet you. Your artwork is exquisite." Buttering up Jack's artists was becoming second nature.

Romilly's icy fingers only touched hers for a moment. "Thank you so much," she murmured as if she couldn't care less, her British accent clipped. Her eyes wandered to Jack, something unspoken in the air between them. "I have quite a muse."

Adelaide smiled politely. "What was your inspiration?"

Romilly winked at her in the way all women of a certain bone structure and attitude did when they deemed other females unimportant. It was something her sister did all the time. "You're looking at him."

"Huh—oh!" she stammered awkwardly.

There could be no mistaking the way the woman was gazing at Jack. It was the way Adelaide had caught many women looking at him before—hungrily, like they wanted to take a bite of him right there for everyone to see.

Rather than being embarrassed by this, Jack seemed absolutely unsurprised. This was not news to him. He watched Romilly with a vague smile, eyebrows raised.

As if to underscore her point, Romilly wrapped an arm through his, positioning her body like she was Jack's date instead. "Jack has been my representative since I started. And all I can say is, my work would suffer without him. Are you a buyer?"

"No," she started, looking over at Jack, still at a loss for words. "I'm actually—"

"An associate of mine," Jack filled in.

"Great to meet you, Adelaide." The gallery was beginning to fill with people, and Romilly headed off to greet her admiring fans with a wave.

Adelaide glared at Jack. "*Associate?*"

He gave an almost-imperceptible shrug. "Why dash a woman's dreams?"

"We'd never want to do that," Adelaide muttered under her breath.

Jack took her face in his hands. "Now, you know why I didn't tell you." He playfully tapped her nose. "I'm her muse. It's doing wonders for her creativity. She's producing some of her best work, and I am making a lot of money off of it. Why should I get in the way?"

She tugged out of his grip. "Why don't you just sleep with her then? Really get her *creativity* flowing?"

He'd turned to scrutinize one of the paintings, but now, he shifted his gaze back to her. Normally, by this time of the night, he'd dump her with some potential buyer's snobby date. "That's absurd."

"Why? Because Jack Nolan doesn't do meaningful relationships?"

"No. Because a relationship between a muse and an artist is a deep, sacred one and very tenuous. If the admiration were equal, it would ruin the entire dynamic. I'd wager that if I took her to bed, I'd change in her creative eye."

"Or maybe she'd just become more obsessed with you."

"Are you speaking from experience?" Something really *had* gotten into him tonight. He seemed to realize it, too, because his smirk receded into something less salacious. "Unfortunately, she'll have to settle for being inspired from afar."

"But she makes advances."

"Yes, and I've outright rejected them. I'm not that cruel."

"And yet I'm not your girlfriend. I'm an *associate*. Face it, Jack. You're leading her on."

He held up his hands in surrender, which was annoying and adorable in equal measure.

"She's pretty," Adelaide observed, watching Romilly laugh.

"Beautiful," he agreed.

"So, if she wasn't one of your artists, would you have offered—"

"Adelaide." His eyes met hers, warning her off the question before she could even ask it. Then, his expression shifted. "Are you jealous?"

"I'm just asking a question."

Unexpectedly, Jack dipped toward her, close enough that their cheeks were flush, when he whispered, "You know, the last time one of us got jealous, we ended up in bed together. So, by all means, keep it going. I'd love to see where this leads."

She blushed, hot all over, and drained the rest of her glass. "I'm not jealous. Excuse me." She walked off before he could see the lie that was written all over her face.

FOURTEEN

When Adelaide woke, she smiled at the bright morning dancing before her closed eyelids, the glorious feel of a goose down comforter, the simple beauty of heat that didn't make oddly human noises as it hissed through the pipes.

That contentedness only lasted a split second until awareness crept in.

Opening her eyes, she looked around a bright white room that looked like something out of a travel brochure. *When did I get here?*

She remembered the never-ending flight, her little embarrassing spat with Jack at the gallery, and Romilly. She remembered jealousy and getting tipsy on a single glass of champagne since she hadn't had anything to eat. She remembered telling herself she had to watch Romilly like a hawk, more champagne, and then …

She couldn't be sure. It was all a blur.

Throwing the fluffy comforter off, she found herself in her clothes from last night. She looked over at the spot on the bed next to her. There was an imprint of another head, right on the center of it. She ran a hand over the sheets. It was cold, and yet she had the sense someone else had been there.

Had she and Jack slept together? *Just* slept? Was that something they were doing now?

As she looked around, trying to sort the clues into some sensical order, even while a hangover started to throb, she noticed a piece of paper on the writing desk across from her. There was only one letter on it—*A*. She jumped to her knees and pounced on it.

Had a bit of work to catch up on.
Sleep. Shop. Enjoy London. It's on me.

—J

He'd left her his American Express card.

She traced her fingers along the edge of it and then let out a little squeal. Was this really her life right now? Two days ago, she'd been in a musty lecture hall, listening to Linker prattle on about the symbolism of 221B Baker Street, and now, she was actually *in* London, at one of the ritziest properties in the city, with a credit card to use as she pleased.

Shopping in London. Yeah, I could do worse.

Excitement bubbling in her veins, she quickly got dressed and set out, asking the valet to point her in the direction of the closest shopping district. He sent her to Bond Street, only a ten-minute walk from the hotel, by way of Grosvenor Square. She walked through all the iconic places she'd only read about and then found herself in a shopping wonderland—famous designers labeled every store, all brands that she'd heard of but never considered would be a part of her wardrobe.

Dazed, she walked about, admiring it all, but she was apprehensive of the idea of even *touching* the expensive items, much less trying them on. And purchasing them? She couldn't even bring herself to go into most of the stores with their pristine displays and snooty salespeople. Something about wanting these things made her feel guilty, though she couldn't understand why.

By noon, she'd only ventured into the nearest Starbucks to buy an overpriced latte, which she paid for with her own debit card. Standing there, staring into the high-gloss storefront window of a jeweler that gave off massive *you're not good enough* vibes, she took a sip of scalding liquid from her cup and gazed at a necklace with a single ruby in the center. Gorgeous, understated, her birthstone.

And probably more money than my yearly tuition at Cranst.

"You do know what shopping is, don't you?" a familiar voice asked behind her, making her spin around in surprise. "You actually go in and purchase the items, not just gaze at them through the window."

"How did you find me?"

Jack checked his heavy, high-tech wristwatch. "It's noon. I thought I'd find your arms laden with bags, having the time of your life. I was going to have the driver transport it all back to the hotel."

He was bundled in an expensive-looking coat, which seemed to perfectly frame the curve of his jawline. She had a fleeting temptation to snap a picture because she was sure she'd never be with a man this attractive again.

Adelaide turned back to the jewel. It wasn't possible to gaze at anything that beautiful without awe. But what would she even do with something like that? "I was just trying to decide— nothing. Never mind."

All morning spent wallowing in her inferiority, feeling terribly out of place, hadn't done much for her confidence. Unlike her, Jack fit in here. With his hands in the pockets of his coat, there was an easiness to his posture, as if he were sauntering across the living room of his own home.

He nodded at the window. "You like that?"

"It's my birthstone, but it's really not practical—"

Before she knew what was happening, he'd opened the door to the jeweler and swatted her inside. The prowling salespeople Adelaide had spied from the door, the ones she'd expected to eye her with derision the second she set foot inside, swarmed them with obsequious attention.

"Mr. Nolan!" one blonde greeted in excitement. Adelaide would wager the Queen couldn't have gotten a more favorable reaction. "You didn't say you were coming into town."

"Not here for me today. The ruby necklace in the window. We'd like to try that one on."

"Of course."

The woman scurried to remove it from the display case. Adelaide wandered about the other exquisite jewels, still feeling a bit like a newborn foal, and when she neared him, she whispered, "I think you've bought gifts for all the others here before."

"Not all. Not even many." He lifted his sleeve to show a tiny golden stud at his wrist, shaped like a spiral. "But I do get all my cuff links here."

"You fly all the way to London for cuff links?"

"I fly to London for art, don't I? Cuff links are just wearable art." He motioned to the saleswoman, who had placed the necklace on a velvet display for inspection. "Ah."

"This is an antique ruby and diamond pendant," the saleswoman explained in a posh British accent. "It came from an estate in Hampstead. Belonged to a baronetess."

"Oh." Adelaide cringed as the saleswoman handed it over to Jack. She hadn't noticed the diamonds before. This would *definitely* cost too much.

"It's her birthstone," he explained, turning her around by the shoulders. His fingers swept her skin as he fastened the piece on her neck. She tried very hard not to shiver. "Jewelry is so important, like the cherry on top of a sundae, Adelaide." Hands on her elbows, Jack twisted her toward a mirror.

The sight of the piece resting in the hollow of her throat, simple and delicate, made her suck in a breath.

That was all the confirmation he needed. "We'll take it."

Adelaide's eyes went wide. "Jack—"

He held up a hand. Her protest died in her throat. "My credit card?"

The necklace became hers with one quick swipe.

"It's perfect," the saleswoman assured her with a satisfied smile. "Shall I wrap it, or will the lady be wearing it?"

Jack's eyes traced her neck, her mouth, and finally met her eyes. "She'll wear it."

Adelaide had never worn anything so extravagant. It was *so* extra, smacking of all the things she'd professed she'd never care about. But now, she understood the thrill of wearing something like this. Of owning it. Of having a man, handsome and terrible and irresistible, buy it for her.

When he collected the receipt and they left, he took a deep breath of the bracing-cold London air and scanned the shopping district. "Where to now?"

"Back to the hotel. I don't need anything, and I don't want to—"

"You're right. You need a dress to go with it."

"Jack!" she complained, but she couldn't help smiling. "You've spent enough on me today, really."

He looked like he was going to overrule her.

She boldly threaded her hand through his. "But how about you buy me lunch?"

"So, who is it tonight?" she asked once they were settled at a table in a more expensive restaurant than she would have picked, but which Jack had beelined for. She'd forgotten he knew this city well, had once spent an extended amount of time here, back when he was representing Declan.

Was this how it had been for him? Expensive lunches and carte blanche with a credit card? She could see how easy it was to enjoy; her eyes kept drifting to a sliver of mirror across the restaurant, where she could catch the necklace's shine.

She shot him an expectant look. "Please tell me it's not someone else you've 'inspired.'"

"You'll be happy to know the people we're seeing tonight have been happily married to each other for the better part of forty years." Jack nodded at a waiter, who presented him a bottle of wine. "It's my mentor, Rene Saegner and his wife. They were friends with my parents, and I've known them since I was a kid. They're like my family."

"Is that how you got into art?"

"More or less. Nadine Allard—that's Rene's wife—owned a chain of department stores. She asked for my opinion on the artwork for a location one day, and it sort of all came together from there."

"As in—" She broke off to hum the corny jingle from their commercials. "That Allards?"

"Impressive," he remarked dryly, though she could sense his amusement.

"It was one of my mom's favorite commercials." She shook her head a little at the fact that she'd forgotten the way her mother used to sing the words under her breath.

"They put their daughter in charge of the business when they retired to London. I always visit when I'm in town. Rene is the reason I am where I am today. He taught me everything."

She studied him as he read the menu. "They must know all about you then?"

"Yes."

"*Everything?*"

"Not everything." He looked up at her curiously. "Did you have something in mind? I'm sure they could furnish you with baby pictures of me, if you're interested, but I'd rather not go down that road."

"About you. Your arrangements and how you don't like to get close to anyone …"

For a moment, there seemed to be a war going on in his head as he debated on how to react to her question. But finally he said, "Sometimes, things like this are best left to secrets, Adelaide. The second you start divulging details, everything becomes a lot more complicated. So, I don't. Won't. With anyone but the people who need to know. Now, can you please stop asking me about this and let me enjoy lunch?"

Adelaide relented. But she couldn't help wondering if she wasn't the only one with more secrets than she let on. He could've had his pick of willing girlfriends, and he'd chosen her. *Paid her.* He was rich, charming, hot, and magnetic, especially when he wasn't grouchy. He didn't have to pay women to do anything with him.

So, why did he?

She was still turning the thought over when they finished lunch, and Jack pulled her along to one final store, which she let him do because the glass of wine and the urbane, self-assured way he'd spoken at lunch had made her more pliable.

She stepped out in a low-cut V-neck sweater and leather pants to find him waiting. Watching. His eyes traveled carefully over her body, appraising her. He whirled a finger for her to turn around. She did, a puppet on a string. Today, she liked the position though. She liked it very much.

His eyes didn't leave her legs as he said, "I want you in pants more often."

If he meant it as her employer or as the man who had spent most of the day flirting with her, she wasn't sure. But the way he was looking at her …

Okay, so she'd let him get her two gifts. But that was it. No more.

Holding the shopping bag, he led her out onto the street, and she said, "Now, I'm serious. We're done."

"All right," he agreed, turning toward the hotel. "But I thought you'd enjoy shopping."

"I did. But you just blew I don't even know how many thousands of dollars without batting an eye. Most people would at least pause before making that kind of investment."

"I believe I did pause. You had my credit card." He laced his hand around her waist and guided her toward the crosswalk. "I've learned that when something beautiful speaks to me, I need to go after it. Hesitate, and it's gone." His fingertips floated over her necklace, making her heart stutter. "Did this not speak to you?"

"It did. It said, *You can't afford me.*" She reached up to touch the stone, brushing against his fingers in a surprisingly not-awkward way.

Jack still intimidated the hell out of her, but ever since their dinner at Cranst, she felt less timid with him. Someone alive was under the hard exterior, and he'd given her a glimpse. *Kept* giving them, like he had today.

"It just makes my stomach hurt to think of you spending so much money. Even if it is the cherry on my sundae."

Jack opened her car door and leaned against it as she climbed in. "Then, I probably shouldn't tell you this, Adelaide."

"What?"

"Not dollars. *Pounds.*"

Adelaide couldn't stop checking the necklace to make sure it was there. As she showered, she kept pulling back the curtain to be certain it was still on the counter. As she applied makeup, her eyes kept drifting to her neck, where the sparkle of the diamonds looked back at her. And as they left the hotel, her hand was constantly at her throat, pressing her thumb into the warm stone at her neck.

By the time they reached the townhouse, Jack noticed. He pried her hand from its spot under her chin and squeezed it as they were ushered into a small foyer.

Dinner was at the Saegners' home, so he'd told her to dress casually. But Jack had lived in his world a long time and didn't realize that dressing down for him was still dressing up for her. After a brief crisis over what said casual but not sloppy, she ended up in the leather pants he'd bought her today and an expensive sweater from Katy.

Rene Saegner and his wife were waiting in the massive kitchen, drinking wine and picking at a cheese plate. Under

Declan's tutelage, she'd learned that Rene had been the top art dealer in the world before his retirement several years ago. Jack had interned for him throughout college, gotten his start in Rene's galleries, and spent the better part of the last decade working his way to the same reputation Rene had. At only thirty-eight, he was already pretty damn close.

"Ah," Rene said, a smile cracking his face wide open. *"J'ai dit a Nadine que tu serais a l'heure."*

"English for her, please," Jack requested, motioning to Adelaide before being swept into a hug by Rene and then by Rene's wife, a beautiful sixty-something woman with raven-colored hair and sharp red glasses.

It was instantly obvious to her that they both adored Jack, especially Rene, who looked at him the way she remembered her dad looking at her brother, Michael. Proud but worried, amused but still worried. Like a father. It made her chest pinch so tight that it got hard to breathe.

Jack distracted her from it when he turned around and said, "Let me introduce you to Adelaide."

Not *my girlfriend*. Not *my friend*. Not anything. Just Adelaide. She tried not to read into it.

"This is my wife, Nadine," Rene introduced with a thick French accent. Jack had told her on the way over that they were both from France originally but had lived in many places since, thanks to his work.

Adelaide smiled and went to shake their hands, but both pulled her into a hug.

"It's so nice to meet you!" Nadine said in her ear, smelling of expensive perfume. "Let's sit down and eat. It's too cold to wait."

When they settled around a table filled with all sorts of delicious-looking food, they asked how she was enjoying London.

"Very much," she said honestly, taking a sip of the expensive French wine they'd uncorked. "It's my first time here."

The woman's eyes went wide. "Oh? Well, you must make sure Jack takes time out from the gallery to show you around." She cast a warning look over the table at him. "He can get so wrapped up in his work; it's like he becomes a different person. Rene taught him that way."

"Jack has *always* been that way," Rene interjected. "You know, when he was ten, it was baseball cards."

"Hey, I had a good collection," Jack said. "That Yastrzemski was autographed. It was worth something."

Rene rolled his eyes. "Sixty dollars maybe."

Adelaide glanced at Jack, trying to picture the ten-year-old he'd once been. The way he was slumping there, smiling and taking their gentle ribbing with a self-deprecating shrug, she could almost see it. He hadn't always been the man who'd spend six figures on jewelry for his untitled woman companion. Once upon a time, he'd been a boy who cared about making sixty dollars on a baseball card.

She had to laugh. "Is this true?"

"I guess." He polished off his drink, not meeting her eyes. Then, he looked at her and said, "Why don't you show Nadine your singing talent?"

She stared at him, confused. "What?"

He leaned over and jostled Nadine's arm. "Listen to her. She sang the Allards jingle when I told her we were coming here."

"Jack—"

But Nadine was already clapping her hands, eyes sparkling. "Oh? I wrote that song, you know!"

They'd been so nice to her, and she was so excited that Adelaide couldn't help but oblige, singing the jingle lightly and a little awkwardly under her breath. As she did, she imagined her mother in the kitchen on any old day of the week, doing the same. Like she had a hundred years left to sing the song.

Adelaide couldn't help it when her voice cracked at the end, the memories of her old house in Hamden flooding back strongly. Her mother in the kitchen and the book-cluttered living room; the smell of her father's aftershave and the tickle of his beard; Michael upstairs, looking for something; Samantha downstairs, on the phone; her life so insanely simple and full of the sort of love she didn't question she was coming home to every day.

Until she didn't.

Nadine was on the edge of her seat, practically bouncing up and down, but her face fell when she spotted the moisture pooling in her eyes. "Adelaide, are you all right?"

Perhaps it was because she looked so genuinely concerned that Adelaide felt like she couldn't lie. "My mother loved that commercial. She used to dance me around the living room whenever it came on, singing it to me." She cleared her throat, waving away the onslaught of emotion that made it feel like a boulder was lodged in her chest. She couldn't believe she'd lost it like that. "I'm sorry. They died four years ago."

Nadine gasped and reached over, taking her hand. "Poor dear! You must've been so young."

She gave her a tight smile and nodded, vaguely aware that Jack staring at her, but she kept her eyes on her wine.

"I didn't know that," he murmured, but she pretended like she hadn't heard.

Yes, Jack, she wished she could tell him, an errant flash of anger catching her off guard. *The people you use aren't just bodies that you can adorn with pretty things to keep them happy. They have histories and messy lives and feelings all on their own.*

Instead, she nodded at Nadine and said, "I was. But it's been a long time."

Nadine patted her hand. "I know what it's like to grow up without family. I was an orphan by ten. But then I met Rene, and my life changed forever."

Adelaide forced herself to peek over at Jack, who was still looking at her, eyes a little wide, like she'd just glamoured herself into someone entirely new.

The rest of dinner was less serious than the start, and after so many stuffy art engagements, Adelaide was grateful. Jack was relaxed and amicable and *human*, not the work-focused robot she'd come to dread. Rene and Nadine told them stories in tandem, like they shared a brain, completing each other's sentences as they spoke about the old days, when Jack was a kid.

From these stories, Adelaide learned things Declan could have never told her—that Jack had been born into money but had to work summer jobs for anything beyond the basic necessities of living; that he'd tried Yale for business but quickly transferred to UCLA when he realized the campus didn't have a recycling policy; that he detested Fauvism—whatever that was; and that long before she'd met him, he'd been a bit of a daredevil, enjoying things like scuba diving, bungee jumping, parasailing, and rock climbing at exotic locations all over the world.

Adelaide noticed how the mention of that seemed to embarrass him.

He simply shook his head and said, "Not anymore," with a small grimace on his face and then changed the subject.

If Adelaide had been curious about Jack before, the dinner, as enjoyable as it was, hadn't helped. Now that she'd been teased with a few details, she was burning with desire to know more about him. About everything.

But one thing stood out above the rest as they walked back to the hotel that evening, his arm securely around her, her head nestled firmly against his chest, like any ordinary couple.

"You really didn't need me for this trip." She lightly elbowed him in the ribs. "Romilly clearly loved you. So do Rene and Nadine. You didn't need me to impress them or keep any women at bay or amuse any bored dates."

"No," Jack said thoughtfully and didn't say anything else.

"And you're already paying me. You didn't have to buy me this." She fingered the necklace.

"No," he agreed again, guiding her into the elevator of the hotel lobby.

Adelaide licked her lips, searching the handsome face that wouldn't turn toward her. "Then, why am I here, Jack?"

The elevator arrived, and he pushed out without answering her.

When he entered the hotel room's small seating area, he roughly stripped off his jacket, scrubbing his face with the palm of his hand. His back was to her, and she watched his shoulders rise and fall in a sigh that seemed unexpectedly loaded.

"Please answer me."

That blue-eyed gaze was heavy on her shoulders when he turned around. It only got worse as he moved toward her. "You know why," he murmured breathlessly, pushing her up against the door, burying his face in her neck.

She wanted to surrender to his touch, but she forced herself to push on. "Is it …" He was at her throat, kissing her so softly that her legs threatened to give out. "Is it really just the sex?"

That seemed to wake him up.

He pulled away. "Is that so bad?"

Adelaide's voice was thick, her words ragged, when she said, "It just doesn't make any sense. You're confusing me, Jack. I don't know what to think."

He lightly traced her collarbone, and she arched into it. His touch was kindling to the fire inside her belly that had been building, building, building.

"So, don't think about it. Thinking about it ruins things."

"But—"

He let out a growl and turned away from her, tugging his sweater over his head as he headed for the bathroom. "I'm taking a shower, Adelaide. Join me or not."

Her pulse was hammering as she watched him, trying to determine what to do. She was two people in that moment—one woman who wanted the safety of going to bed and forgetting this had ever happened and one who wanted him to do what her body had been pining for since the night of the birthday party, consequences be damned.

As she stood there, debating, Declan's words came back to her. *You are not you.*

And Jack's—*thinking about it ruins things.*

Maybe they were both telling her the same thing in a different way.

Do whatever the hell you want.

Everyone else did.

In the bathroom, she stood in the doorway and removed her clothes. Steam had begun to fog up the mirrors and the air, casting everything in a hazy, dreamlike state. Jack was already in the shower, his naked form glorious and masculine beyond the water-spattered door. She hadn't looked at him enough the last time, and now, she saw his body was even stronger and more defined than she remembered.

Steam hovered around him, like it, too, didn't know if it wanted to stay or go, when he opened the door to let her pass through. She stepped inside, facing away from the spray and into his face, watching as his gaze followed the rivulets of water soaking her hair and skin, meeting her eyes with the unrelenting heat she remembered so well.

"You have me here," she said, steeling her voice. "And I'm not thinking."

It wasn't like last time. He went slow, working a bar of soap down her shoulders, over her stomach, and around her legs, purposefully avoiding all the spots she wanted him most. When he was done with that, he pushed her behind the spray of the shower and ducked under himself, watching her through the streams of water running off his eyelashes, hungry and patient in equal measure.

Impulsively, she reached up to run her fingers through his hair, pleased when the tension in his shoulders seemed to fall away. She washed it slowly with handfuls of citrus-scented shampoo, thrilled every time he purred happily, like a lazy, affectionate cat. When he was rinsed, she kissed her way over his collarbone and his chest, ran her hands over his hips and his back and his butt, smiling a little when he drifted languid kisses on her temple as a reward.

When she finally reached between them, Jack's fingers dug into her shoulders. He'd been half-hard when she stepped in the shower, and she'd watched him grow as she touched him, her throat dry, stomach knotted.

"Stop," he ordered, even as he leaned his forehead against her, breathing heavily in a way she couldn't get enough of.

"No," she whispered back. It was the only time she dared to outright refuse him.

Jack shuddered when her hand closed around him, sliding back until her knuckles were flush against his stomach. It was such a primal, distilled feeling from a man she'd seen as so emotionless that she realized with a sudden, intense clarity that she really *was* a different person after meeting him, not just playacting one.

Whatever she'd done and whatever happened next, she would never be the same.

Accept that, and you *could* stop thinking, stop worrying, stop ruining everything that wasn't this perfect moment with this wonderful, horrible man in your hand.

That, Adelaide realized now, was how all his others had done it.

"Enough," he rasped, dragging her off of him, trying to slip his own hand between her legs.

She begged him with her eyes, and somehow, he understood.

Jack backed her against the shower wall, watching her intently as he hiked her up and pulled her legs around his waist. His gaze fell to her neck, to the necklace still fastened there. "I want you to wear this whenever I see you," he ordered, voice so husky that a little noise left her chest. "So you'll think of this. Me. So I know you're mine."

"I will; I will," she promised, surprised at the intensity of her own voice.

He bent forward and kissed her, right over the stone resting against her throat, like he was soldering it to her skin. She pressed her head back into the tile and tried to breathe, but it was too much—too sexy, too sweet, too much like something that wasn't what *this* was supposed to be.

"Please, Jack," she whispered shamelessly. "I need you."

He gave her what she wanted, pressing inside her slowly but all at once. Jack caught her gasp in his mouth, kissing her for the first time in so, so long. And then it was like the first time all over again because just like then, she couldn't get enough of him.

Surrendering, she thought as he thrust into her hard and slow, over and over, until she pressed her palms flat against the shower wall behind her. Though who was surrendering to whom, she wasn't sure.

When she came, she dug her teeth in his shoulder, distantly aware of him doing the same a moment later, her name slipping out of his mouth in a broken rasp.

No thinking, she promised herself when he eased her down from the shower wall. *No thinking,* when he washed her again and wrapped them both in fluffy white towels, and laid her in bed, facedown, where he made her come one more time with his tongue.

Thinking ruined everything.

FIFTEEN

"So, can you write the paper or not?"

Jarred by the question, Adelaide blinked, almost surprised to find herself in her usual booth at the coffee shop at Cranst, where a potential client waited in front of her. After a late night with Jack—and those *never* involved sleeping anymore—she barely remembered dragging herself to her usual Sunday spot. She showed up solely to give Janelle Roberts her paper, but a few stragglers had shown up, looking for her services.

"You know, architecture really isn't my jam. Maybe you'd be better off with someone with more passion for the subject," she admitted to the girl in front of her.

"Seriously? Thanks for nothing," she muttered, picking herself up and slouching away.

It was strange. Before London, she would have been tempted to take that job, but now, she couldn't imagine how she'd even fit it in.

She hated to admit it, but as much as she tried *not* to think about Jack, it was quickly becoming a full-time job, eclipsing everything else she had going on. He demanded it. When she wasn't at class, she was with him ... and not just at his events. Actually, half the time, they didn't leave his apartment.

Adelaide hadn't known that sex could get better, the more you did it with the same person, but the past two weeks had proven to her that it did. Every time she thought he'd outdone himself, it felt like he had devised a new way to make her lose control. Jack did things to her, let her do things to him, that made her feel that she was an entirely different person, someone older and more confident, in tune with her own body in a way she hadn't been before.

Even now, as she sat in a coffee shop, innocently sipping her latte, she couldn't help but feel that need coiling in her belly.

She closed her green notebook, ready to brave the blustery cold so that she could grab a shower and get ready for Jack's event, this one right here at Cranst, when her phone buzzed with a text. She expected it to be Jack with a militant, *Be here at this time and don't be late, blah, blah, blah.*

But it was Declan.

This is taking too long. What else have you found out?

Her teeth clenched. She shouldn't have expected the half-tidbit about Fiona she'd provided would satisfy him for long. She hadn't spoken to him since she'd returned from London, but she really hadn't been around to talk. All her weekends were spent in the city now, and when she was there, it felt like being in a vortex. Sometimes, she felt like she was living two separate lives—her weekend reality and her day-to-day life—in stark contrast to each other.

She texted Declan back quickly.

I'll stop by in a few.

Adelaide headed to Declan's apartment, checking her phone every so often to see if he'd responded. He hadn't. Yet, somehow, she sensed he'd seen it and he was only trying to make the point that he wasn't happy with her. When she climbed up to his studio, she found the place littered with canvases, most simple, half-painted outlines. All were quite good—at least by her estimation. Jack had caught on to her lack of knowledge, she suspected, because he'd been giving her thinly veiled lessons.

In the center of the room, she found Declan standing in loose, low-slung jeans, shirtless and barefoot. Facing away from her, holding a paintbrush in midair, preparing to swipe it across the canvas. He seemed too absorbed in his work to have noticed her entrance.

But as she stood there, wondering how she should announce herself, he said, "Fiona was shit."

She blinked.

He turned. "So, thanks for nothing. I looked everywhere for her. And when I found her, she wouldn't answer my calls."

"Oh." Avoiding the hot malice in his eyes, she looked around. "You've been painting a lot. That's great."

"I don't need commentary on my art, Adelaide. What happened in London? Since I haven't heard from you, I'll assume you've not made progress. Again."

"That isn't true!" she opined, shifting in her heeled boots. Normally, she saved outfits like this for Jack, but more and more, she found herself reaching for her new, improved wardrobe instead of her old, drab one. These clothes made her feel good. Confident. "I looked. I practically tore his London office apart."

She wasn't lying either. Before they'd left the morning after their dinner with the Saegners, they'd stopped at the gallery so Jack could sign some paperwork and grab a few files. While he was gone, she'd rummaged through the drawers of his desk, looked in his closet, checked under the carpet, and even felt up the walls for any hidden compartments. No paintings and no hints about the paintings. Another dead end.

"You have to give him some time to start trusting me, all right? He's … private. It's not easy for him to open up."

"Spare me the psychoanalysis, Addie. You're fucking the guy, not making a wedding toast."

She huffed. But because she didn't want to fight with him, she picked up a dry painting of an arrow aiming for what she guessed was meant to be the sun, although it was green and blue, not yellow. "Did you know that he kept the London gallery open?" She tried to keep her voice inoffensive. "I thought you said he closed it down."

"Hmm?" Declan murmured and then spied her examining a picture. He grabbed it from her hands and groused, "This is terrible. Every one of them is shit. They remind me of everything I wish I could forget."

The reason she was supposed to be helping him. And she'd failed. For a moment, she felt guilty. "I don't think that's true."

He pulled at his hair, seemingly unaware his hands were covered in paint. It was streaked through with shades of purple when he tossed the picture back on its easel. "All I'm doing is trying to make sense of things. Painting is where I find out whatever it is I can't see in real life. But nothing gets clearer. And it's all shit." He stared into a half-painted canvas, as if seeing something that wasn't there. "I'm not making any sense to you."

"You're an extremely talented person. I don't think I can understand what it's like to see things through your eyes."

Without warning, he pushed the canvas off its easel, letting it clatter to the floor. She jumped back in surprise at the same time he tilted his head at her.

"Would you let me paint you again? Start all over from the beginning?"

She stared at him, speechless.

A flash of the dark basement on The Night of the Peach Schnapps came back to her. It *had* felt like magic that night when she saw her picture—he'd painted her but not her, similar in the facial features and yet somehow different. Brighter. He'd done her in shades of gold and green, a crown of white flowers on top of her head with the petals falling off like rain. She thought the picture depicted her secret self, like he'd somehow lived in her head and her body for the past sixteen years and could tell exactly the person she was when alone in her bedroom. Who she became when there was no one to watch.

"Autograph it, please," he'd asked before she left, holding out a pen. Back then, he'd had none of the swagger, but there had been an appealing youthful certainty. "I like my subjects to put their own names on their portraits."

She'd agreed, kissed his cheek, and left.

And then nothing until she'd run into him on campus.

Adelaide had no idea what to say to him now; his request felt loaded with implications.

Thankfully, his phone rang, rescuing her.

"Speak of the devil," Declan said, answering with a calculated grin. "Professor Hargrove, I was just talking about you."

Her eyes went wide.

"I have some very interesting information about one of your—"

He didn't get the rest of it out because by that time, she'd sprinted across the room, snatching the phone in desperation. When she had it in her hand, she looked at it and found that it had been nothing but a scam caller, a recorded voice still faintly audible through the phone.

She scowled at him. "You're an asshole."

Declan gave her one of his sharp, pointy grins that made him look almost elfin. "Get out of here, Adelaide. Get back to work. Because if you don't get me something—something real—and soon? I *will* make that call. You got that?"

She didn't bother to answer before she stormed out of his apartment, loudly slamming the door behind her.

But it was Declan's threat that echoed in her ears long after she left.

When Adelaide arrived at Jack's room at the Claremont two hours later, he answered the door in nothing but a towel. "You caught me on the way to the shower. Adelaide?"

"Hmm?" she murmured.

"You're staring."

She was, and she didn't care. Once her time was up, she'd probably never be with a man this chiseled again. After this, it was all postgrads with softening bellies and invisible jawlines.

He teased her with a chaste peck on the lips.

"I'd join you, but I spent an hour on my hair."

"Are you sure? You'd probably look adorable in a shower cap."

"Positive."

"Fine then," he sighed, pulling off his towel. He nodded toward the desk, where his laptop was set up. "Then, you'll just have to sit here like a good girl and wait for tonight."

Her toes curled in her shoes, a thrill skittering down her spine. Warmth built in the deepest parts of her, but she ignored it. Fresh off her conversation with Declan, she knew she had other things to do.

Jack flashed her a final smile and headed into the bathroom, closing the door slightly. Through the mirror, she saw him duck inside the shower. By then, she'd already headed across the room to the writing desk, and opened his laptop. Touching the trackpad, she woke it up, hoping for something. Anything. Any bit of evidence she could give Declan to keep him off her case for a while.

Listening for the water running, she sat down on the edge of the chair and wheeled it close. She opened up his email account, scrolling through to see if there was anything of interest. All of the subjects were about certain paintings and different gallery items. She hurriedly typed in Declan's name, and a flurry of old emails came up. The most recent ones from a year ago.

There had been a few buyers inquiring about his work, and in her very brief skim, it seemed like Jack had gone back and forth, entertaining it.

She texted Declan quickly.

Is it possible he sold the paintings and didn't tell you?

He responded lightning fast.

I'll look into it. What else?

She turned back to his email and scanned. One recent message in particular caught her eye. It said, *Re: Gabrielle.*
Is he already lining up his next girl?
She was just about to click on it when a voice boomed, "Adelaide."

Her stomach dropped. She turned to find Jack, hair wet and dripping on his shoulders, gazing at her, his eyes hard.

She rocketed out of the chair. "Oh! I'm … sorry. I just realized I'd forgotten to send my professor an email for my class. And I was wondering if I could—"

His brows came together. "You can't do it from your phone?"

"No. For some reason, I've never been able to get my school email to sync up," she fudged, sidestepping him as he swooped toward his laptop.

For a moment, she thought he might try to help her bring up her email.

Instead, he slammed the lid closed and said, "New rule. Actually, it's always been a rule. I just didn't think I needed to tell you. Don't touch my laptop. Ever."

Gnawing on the inside of her cheek, she nodded.

"Give me ten minutes, and I'll be ready," he muttered, pulling his suit from the closet.

After that, things soured. He walked three steps ahead of her on the way to the elevator and didn't say more than a few words on the trip down.

It was only when they walked into the crowded reception that he seemed to remember she existed, taking two flutes of champagne and offering her one. She sipped to ward off the tension and looked around. She'd been too flustered to read the briefing his assistant had sent over after her talk with Declan, but she knew it had something to do with the best artwork of the semester by Cranst students and that Jack was the featured speaker tonight.

"Was this a bad idea?" she whispered, shaking her hair in her face. "What if someone recognizes me?"

For some reason, that put a small smile on his face. He looked her up and down—she was in a slinky black dress and the necklace he'd bought her—and lifted an eyebrow. "You spend much time with the president of Cranst?"

"Sure, we go way back," she deadpanned, craning her neck.

She wouldn't have known him by sight, but it still made her jittery to think of being in the same vicinity as him and lord knew who else from the administration. She had no reason to feel suspicious, but if they knew about the papers …

Jack nodded a hello to a group of men. "I'll point him out. We play golf sometimes."

"Jack, if someone finds out I'm a student—"

"Shh," he quieted, brushing his thumb over her lip, fanning it down just slightly.

Her worry was replaced swiftly by longing. She cursed herself for not getting in the shower earlier. "You play golf?"

"Play, yes. Enjoy, no."

She wrinkled her nose. "Why waste your time then?"

"Cranst has one of the best art schools in the country. By keeping close to the talent, I get the first pick of it."

He was speaking to her, but he was a bit distracted, ready to shake hands with whomever he deemed important enough. She jumped at the opportunity to ask him questions. Though she'd need to be more subtle than she'd been with the laptop.

"Is that how you source your clients, primarily? Cranst?"

"I find them all over the world, but Cranst has a great program. I work best with young artists. Their talent might be rawer, but I find they're far less jaded."

"Until you corrupt them."

She'd been thinking of Declan, but there was no mistaking who *he* was thinking of when he turned to her, eyes sparkling.

"I only corrupt the ones who want to be corrupted."

As she stood there, eyes locked with him, the whole purpose of the conversation seemed to slip away, as it so often did with him. There were moments when he looked at her and she'd lose her train of thought completely, taken aback by the intense desire she found there.

They were interrupted by a woman Jack introduced as a dean in the art department, an impish little grin on his lips when he presented Adelaide.

"And what do you do?" the dean asked politely.

Adelaide's voice tripped over itself twice. "I'm, uh … a writer," she bluffed, trying to sound nonchalant.

Jack immediately steered the conversation toward other topics.

But when the dean wandered off and they were alone again, he guided her to the bar and asked, "Is that what you want? To be a writer?"

Adelaide shrugged. "It was just something I said."

"You're a senior. You must have thought about it."

"Why?" She laughed acerbically, wishing he'd stop asking her questions. *She* should be the one asking him. And anyway, it made her annoyed to talk about her future in a room full of the people who could control it. The conversations tonight struck her as snobbier than usual. "Are you offering me a job? A *real* job? The kind where I don't suck your—"

Jack grabbed her arm and gave her a sharp warning with his expression. His eyes were fiery. "You don't want to finish that sentence."

She was suddenly ornery, her voice a little loud. "Suck your di—"

He kissed her to shut her up, rough and annoyed, curling his tongue in her mouth for half a second, more to assert his own dominance than for anything else.

When he ripped his mouth away, they were both breathing hard. Whatever he saw in her made him fortify his hold on her arm. "Come with me."

Jack pulled her out of the reception hall, down hallways, trying doors until he found a room he was satisfied with. Shapes of furniture—a desk, a chair, bookcases—registered, but he slammed the door and pressed her against it, kissing her in that hungry, rough way she loved. There could be people right outside, but tonight, she didn't care, letting go of a long, desperate noise when he sucked on her tongue.

"What has gotten into you tonight?" Jack murmured against her mouth.

He could be such an asshole sometimes, and yet when it came to sex, he always treated her like a queen. When Jack had his arms around her, it was like every inch of her was something special, important. Like this, he'd give her anything she wanted.

Adelaide realized he was dropping to his knees in front of her before she realized it was her own hand pushing him down. She had no idea when she'd become this brazen, but it made Jack grin as he spread her legs apart.

"Holy shit," she gasped when he started French-kissing her through her underwear, making little starbursts of pleasure explode in her nerve endings.

Was the door even locked? Did she care when his mouth was separated from her body by a scrap of cloth? She was mad and horny, and her body felt like it was trying to crawl out of itself.

Jack stayed down until she was bowing at the waist. Then, he stood and kissed her again, lifting her up to wrap her legs around him. Her head swam at the angle, the bulge in his pants turning her on even more, making her agitated with need. Far away, she could hear the music and conversation of the reception, but it was slowly being replaced by her own heartbeat, which pumped loudly in her ears when Jack dragged her away from the wall and laid her across a desk.

In the dim light of a stranger's office, she could tell his jaw was like steel, his eyes glinting as he stood over her, angrily working off his belt. He glared at her as he freed himself from his pants and then dragged her panties around her knees. He was inside her a second later, shoving her up the desk so hard that she gripped the edges for leverage.

"Is this what you wanted?" he whispered, withdrawing before slamming back inside, making her grunt unattractively. "You wanted me to take you right here, with everyone downstairs?"

"Yes," she rasped, twisting her hot cheek into the cool surface of the desk.

They'd die if they knew what she was doing up here, if they knew what she did with half the students at this school. It made her feel powerful, alive, in control. Instead of hating what she did, she felt a swell of pride, of danger. She didn't know what was going on with her, but she almost felt like laughing.

Jack changed his angle, going deeper. So deep that she started crying out until he finally covered her mouth with his hand. "I didn't lock the door."

The sentiment was her undoing. Jack seemed to know instinctively what was about to happen, and the second before she came, he jammed his knuckle between her teeth to keep her from shouting. She bit down hard, moaning, distantly aware of Jack's head falling into her neck as his thrusts got harder—harder than she liked, but it didn't matter because a second later, he started to come inside her, and a deep, mysterious hunger she hadn't known existed was satiated.

"Did that settle you down?" he asked, pushing off of her after he caught his breath.

"These people are snobs—that's all," she replied, following him up. She came face-to-face with the framed seal on the wall that instantly identified who this office belonged to. "This is the president of the university's office!" she hissed at Jack, horrified. "It's his desk!"

"I don't think either of us would have cared if this was the Resolute desk," Jack answered calmly, swiping a wad of tissues off the end table. He handed her a fistful and used another to clean himself up. "Let's go. They're going to be looking for me to do the toast."

Of course. Now, it was time to focus on business. She would never get used to the way they sometimes seemed to be doing two parallel things at once—work and whatever was going on with them personally.

Right now, she wasn't entirely ready to let go of the personal. Adelaide swallowed. "Have you ever corrupted someone you shouldn't have?"

Jack was halfway to the door, but now, he turned all the way around to face her, hands on his hips. "Adelaide, you're beautiful, but if you start inventing issues between us, I'm going to have a problem with it."

"I'm not talking about myself."

Jack shook his head. "What is with you tonight? I can't tell if I'm turning you on or pissing you off." He crooked a finger at her. "Let's go."

She followed him, defeated, not realizing until afterward, when he lifted his glass in the toast, that his immediate answer to her question hadn't been no.

SIXTEEN

In the last weeks of November, everywhere at Cranst looked like an advertisement for fall in New England. It usually made the fact that Adelaide spent Thanksgiving alone tolerable, but this year, she was disappointed to see the final bursts of color before the leaves fell—it meant she was that much closer to the end of her time with Jack and to whatever would happen if she didn't find Declan's paintings.

For the first time, she considered the possibility that there simply weren't any paintings to find. Had Declan even thought that far ahead? She doubted it and certainly wasn't going to plant the seed in his head, but part of her wondered if Jack had even held on to the paintings like Declan thought. Was it possible he had gotten rid of them, either by selling them or destroying them, somewhere along the way?

Unfortunately, Thanksgiving in Aspen wasn't going to be the best place to try and find out.

It felt odd to spend the holiday with someone she hardly knew, but Jack had told her he spent Thanksgiving socializing with his contacts; therefore, he needed her there for work, and that was the end of the conversation.

Well, sort of.

After she accepted, she learned that the flight left on Wednesday afternoon, which meant that she'd be missing Imogen's big twenty-second birthday party. She and Katy had been planning it for weeks. When she called to ask Jack if she could take a flight on Thursday morning, he refused.

"The flights are already arranged," he'd said flatly. "I need you there for cocktails with Rene on Wednesday. He's introducing me to a huge collector from Berlin. Why am I even explaining this to you? The answer is no."

That officially made her the worst friend in the world.

Sitting at the window seat in the first-class cabin, she couldn't even look at Jack. That made for a very frosty four-hour flight. At first, he attempted to speak to her, telling her about what they'd be doing all weekend. The Saegners would be there, as they had a condo in the village, too, which all sounded annoyingly posh. They'd have Thanksgiving dinner with them. The rest of the time though, there would be various meetings and events with his associates.

"One, I hate the cold," she muttered to him when he asked why she was so cranky. "And, two, I don't ski."

Then, she grabbed her book and buried her nose in it until the flight touched down in Colorado.

The condo complex *was* charming. As crabby as Adelaide was over the whole situation, she had to give it that. It looked like a little gingerbread village, snow-covered, with lots of people in colorful parkas, heading to the slopes. She hadn't lied though. She didn't ski, had never wanted to. During their one family vacation to the mountains of Vermont, she'd spent most of the time in the lodge, in front of the fire.

Jack's condo was much like his apartment in the city— homey and comfortable yet modern too. Luckily, it had two bedrooms. While Jack headed toward the master, she swerved for the smaller guest.

"Hey," he said, looking back. He held up her suitcase. "In here."

"I'd rather be on my own, thank you."

He dropped her duffle and crossed his arms, a smile twisting his lips. "You can stay in there, but the curtains are being replaced. You'll be woken up by the sun at about five thirty."

Adelaide let out a big, dramatic sigh and stomped into the master bedroom. Ignoring Jack, she peered out the window at the mountains. Lovely, but in another few hours, Imogen would be having an insane birthday party, and she wouldn't be there.

"I'm going to shave," Jack informed her, pulling out his toiletry bag. "Why don't you get changed, and we can go down and meet Rene for drinks?"

"Whatever," she muttered.

He let out a short laugh. "How can you seem so old sometimes and so juvenile at others?"

"I'm extremely multifaceted."

He checked behind him to see if she was kidding. "You're mouthy tonight."

"I must have missed the silence clause in the contract."

He ate the distance between them in three strides, looming over her. "I could think of better things for you to do with that mouth."

"Pass," she grunted, flicking his chest. She slipped around him, groaning in frustration when he pulled her back, pressing his front against her back, and making them sway. She fidgeted for half a second, decided it was futile, then went dead in his arms.

That did the trick. He let her go, hands back at his sides. They'd stopped in front of the mirror, and she was momentarily distracted by what she found there. She'd never seen them together, from the outside. In the reflection, she saw that without shoes, he was tall enough to tuck her head under his chin, big enough that his arm would span the length of her hips. He was painfully handsome, and without a hint of makeup, she looked woefully plain. Not to mention, young. Their age difference would be obvious to anyone. Still, there was something that looked right about the two of them together. Something that made sense.

Jack must have noticed it too—or at least, he noticed her checking him out—because he smiled genuinely. Slowly, he put his hands on her shoulders and pulled her back toward him. "You're fun like this," he noted, breathing her in. "You're very honest when you're cranky. I like it."

"I hate when you're cranky."

"I know," he sighed, lifting her hair and running his mouth over the back of her neck. She shivered. "Give it back to me. I deserve it."

Adelaide leaned her head onto his shoulder and let him rock her, testing to see if it actually made her feel better. No one had ever held her like this, but with Jack, it seemed natural.

"Tell me what's wrong," he murmured into her ear, meeting her eyes in the mirror.

"Do you actually care? Or are you just worried I won't fuck you later?"

Jack's arms tightened around her, even as his head snapped up. She'd done it now; the anger stabbed into his expression like his smile had never even happened.

He nodded toward the window, where everything outside was blanketed in snow. "See out there, Adelaide? It's *Colorado*. Sorry you missed a frat party, but you. Are. Here."

"It wasn't a—"

"Whatever it is, get over it. And I don't want you pouting all night either."

"It's always what you want."

"Yes, it is," Jack agreed. "Because it's my money."

His money, his rules, his girlfriend experience. How could she forget?

He shook his head. "Jesus, you really are in a foul mood. Must have been one hell of a party to miss."

"It was," she snapped before she could stuff the sentence back in.

But Jack either didn't notice or truly didn't care.

She raised her chin defiantly. "Why are you still holding on to me then?"

"Because I'm a man and not a boy, Adelaide. I'm not going to run away with a bruised ego because you're a little pissed off at me."

"You're not being fair," she whispered, letting her forearms rest on top of his.

"No, I'm not."

This was what had made him so successful, she realized. He'd simply never give in to anyone, for any reason. Even though Jack had agreed with her that he was wrong, he wasn't going to change. He walked full speed into his decisions and backed them up relentlessly. It was one of his best qualities, she thought. And his worst.

Jack's gaze stayed on her, one eyebrow raised just slightly, but she didn't bother arguing. When it was clear he'd won, he kissed her temple and let her go, heading back into the bathroom.

He appeared in the doorway a minute later though. "Adelaide?" Shaving cream was rubbed over one side of his face, his jaw so defined underneath it that he could have been in a commercial for aftershave. "What would you do differently next time?"

She furrowed her brow, confused, before it dawned on her what he meant. "Negotiate."

Jack nodded. "Good girl. Don't ever take the first offer of anything. Please, if I teach you one thing, let it be that."

She had no idea why he cared, but she took the advice for what it was and filed it away for later.

Twenty minutes later, they were headed downstairs, to the lobby of the complex. She let him keep his arm around her even though she was still upset about missing the party. It was too much effort to pout, for too little result. Besides, Jack was right. She was in Colorado. There was no making it to the party now. It might have been the altitude, but she *did* feel slightly giddy and breathless when they stepped off the elevator.

"Ads?"

Adelaide's spine stiffened. She turned around slowly to face the voice, but there was only one person in her life who called her that.

Her brother, Michael, stood two yards away, eyebrows knit together as he took in her form, leaning against Jack. He wore a flannel shirt, dark-washed jeans, and a warm, obviously expensive jacket. His cheeks seemed a bit windburned, so he must have already been here for a day or two.

"Michael?" she croaked. "What are you doing here?"

"Client crisis." He approached, arms cautiously outstretched, letting out a small laugh at the strange serendipity as he hugged her. "What are *you* doing here? You don't ski."

"I'm … we're just …"

She'd learned to lie on her feet, but faced with her brother, her brain totally flatlined. He could see through her. She became suddenly, irrationally convinced that he knew everything.

Michael's eyes flicked to Jack for the briefest of moments. When they returned to her, there was undeniable concern in them as he intuited what was going on. Seeing exactly what she had earlier, in the mirror.

"Oh," he said finally. "Oh, I see."

Jack cleared his throat.

Adelaide shifted, snapped into action by him, as always. "Michael, this is Jack Nolan. Jack, this is Michael, my brother." As they shook hands, she added, "Jack is … my boyfriend."

Lord, strike me down, she prayed. There was no way she'd ever recover from this.

Michael's eyebrows shot up. "Really? Wow. Well, that's a … surprise. You never mentioned anything."

"Right, well, it's pretty new."

"And yet you're here. Together. For Thanksgiving. In Aspen?"

"It's been intense." She peeked up at Jack, who seemed impervious to the situation, except for the very slight clench of his jaw she'd learned meant he was dissatisfied with something. She'd noticed it over the weeks she spent next to him while he worked.

But why would he be unhappy right now? She was the one who had to explain to her brother what she was doing with a man almost twice her age.

Michael's eyes ping-ponged between them. Then, he grabbed Adelaide's arm. "Jack, do you mind if I talk to my sister alone for a minute?"

"By all means." He waved, strolling off.

The moment they were out of earshot, Michael fixed her with such a *big brother knows best* look that she rolled her eyes before he even started talking. "What the fuck, Ads?"

"What?" She knew exactly what he meant, but she thought it would benefit her to play dumb.

"That man is, like, twice your age."

"No, he's not. He might be a little older, but I'm a twenty-two-year-old woman. And he's not some dirty old man, playing sugar daddy. So, stop making it like that." Except, yes, that was exactly what it was.

Michael eyed Jack over Adelaide's shoulder. "Where'd you meet him?"

"An event at Cranst. He's a big donor to the school. We met a few months ago."

"And yet this is the first time I'm hearing about it?"

She sighed. "I didn't think you needed a play-by-play of my love life, Michael."

"No, I don't," he agreed. "But do you even know what you're—"

Michael cut off abruptly at something over her shoulder, which turned out to be Jack, approaching them in the same careful way he always approached potential clients.

"I have an idea. Adelaide's not fond of skiing, and I have that business meeting tomorrow on the slopes. Why don't the two of you spend the day together tomorrow? Catch up?"

She turned to stare at him, her mouth parting in surprise. Jack, who earlier this week wouldn't agree to let her show up eight *hours* later than him, was offering her a whole free afternoon?

"Oh, Ads hates skiing. She cried the first time we put her on the bunny slopes, and she's never been back."

Jack smiled as Adelaide shot an eye dagger in her brother's direction. "So she told me."

"We'll have lunch," Michael decided. "Meet you here tomorrow at noon?"

She had no choice but to agree.

He kissed her cheek again and nodded at Jack. "Nice meeting you."

When he was gone, Adelaide whirled on him and snapped, "That was awfully nice of you, considering you nearly bit my head off when I wanted to make one measly little flight change."

Jack's eyes darkened as he watched Michael walk away. "*Nice?* That was not me being nice. I'm letting you off the hook because you need to make sure your brother doesn't open his mouth about how old you actually are."

She snorted. "Please. He doesn't gossip."

"Make sure it stays that way, Adelaide. Everyone knows each other here, and I don't need anyone whispering about what we're doing together. Or figuring out how old you are. And I don't do family drama, so whatever he says, keep me away from it."

"My brother is not some moron. He's actually a very successful publicist in California. He's used to discretion."

"I don't care. Handle this, Adelaide. You understand?"

"Yes," she snapped, rolling her eyes to the rafters. "I'll make sure he doesn't say a word around the village."

And more importantly, to their sister.

The following day, Adelaide and her brother stopped at a café overlooking the slopes.

She couldn't remember the last time she'd been with family on Thanksgiving. But as much as she wanted to enjoy the novelty, she couldn't help glancing at the skiers, wondering how

Jack would look, cutting his way down the mountain. Something told her that he skied the way he did everything—with effortless elegance that made even seasoned pros look amateur.

After drinks with Rene and Nadine—who were as lovely as they had been in London—Jack had gone to bed without so much as trying to kiss her. It was still stinging.

Michael dispensed with the small talk and leaned forward, a businesslike expression on his face. "Now, tell me about this Jack guy. He's a donor at Cranst?"

"He's an art dealer, but I met him at Cranst," she explained, which wasn't technically untrue. "Honestly, it was really sudden, him asking me here." And because he still looked doubtful and possibly a little disgusted, she added, "It was better than spending my holiday *alone*."

A look bounced between them, riddled with words neither of them wanted to say to the other just then.

"But as for the relationship, there's nothing to talk about. It's probably not going anywhere. I don't even know if I like him."

Michael raised an eyebrow. "From the way you two looked, you could've fooled me."

She hated to think she wore her emotions on her sleeve, but in the case of yesterday, she was certain he was mistaken. She and Jack had just gotten done arguing.

"I promise, whatever it looked like … it's not serious."

He held out his hands in surrender. "All right, all right. Hey. Just watch out for yourself, Ads. You might not think so, but serious or not, guys like that have a tendency to run through women. Fast."

"I've been taking care of myself a long time, Michael."

Michael opened his mouth and closed it, opened and closed, until finally settling on, "I know."

Another loaded beat of silence passed between them, and she could tell, like she always could, that Michael was itching to bring up Samantha. She was actually shocked he wasn't with her now, for the holiday. From what she'd gleaned, her sister always threw a big party for Thanksgiving, gathering all of her fake friends around a lush table, basking in their compliments and showing off just how lovely and stable she'd turned out.

Perfect Samantha, perfect holiday. Perfect life.

Michael did want to talk about their sister, but instead of talking about making amends, he shocked her and said, "I talked to Samantha about Declan Jones."

She blinked. "What? Why would you—"

"You mentioned you saw him at Cranst."

She had. She'd almost forgotten. Her conversation with Michael at the beginning of the semester felt like years ago. "Why do you always have to tell her about my life, Michael? She's not in it for a reason."

"Because she's our *family*, Ads. And honestly, we don't have much left. You want to cut her out of your life, that's fine, but I'm not cutting her out of mine." His fingers circled his temples. "Look, that isn't why I'm bringing it up. Samantha kept in touch with his family—did you know that?"

She was pissed, but now, she was curious too.

Adelaide gave a small shake of her head.

"You remember how it was when he was young? Declan this, Declan that. First around town and then online. When he moved to London, I think everyone just assumed it would be the culmination of his hard work and didn't think anything else of it. But Samantha said that wasn't what happened at all."

Adelaide raised her eyebrows as their waiter put salads in front of them.

"Things went badly. He had some sort of mental breakdown. His parents got him home, but it didn't help. And then he attempted suicide."

"Suicide?" she repeated. She thought of the last time she had been at his studio, how he'd been painting like a man possessed, eyes wild and unfocused. His bitterness. His anger. She'd been aware of his oddities before, but now, she felt her palms grow clammy.

"He was always a little out there," Michael pointed out around a mouthful of greens. "Those creative types always are."

"I didn't know any of that," she said, her voice wooden. Did she need to have a talk with Declan? Try to rein him in? "He's just my TA."

"My point is, be careful around that guy, Ads. They got him help, but I've always had a weird feeling about him."

She knew his concern was genuine, but this was her third warning from him in two days. It was nice that he worried about her now, when it was convenient. But would they even be having this conversation if it wasn't for Samantha, who he routinely sided with, enabled, and defended? The whole thing felt obtuse.

But it was Thanksgiving, and she didn't want to fight. She wasn't even sure he'd understand her point anyway.

"I will. Just promise me you won't tell Samantha. About Jack, I mean."

He winced.

"Jesus! You already told her?"

"Sorry," he said with a shrug. "I told her I saw you and that you were with a guy, and the rest just came out."

"Oh my *God*," she muttered, grabbing her water, swallowing a gulp, and then setting the goblet down so hard that the silverware clattered. "What I do with my life isn't any of her business, Michael! It hasn't been since she cut me off."

"Well, she called me. We *call* each other, Ads."

"A good brother would've lied."

"What's done is done. Anyway, remember a few months ago, when I told you Samantha and Bear were engaged?"

She frowned and swallowed back a sour taste in her mouth. "How could I forget? It's the pinnacle of her entire existence."

Michael didn't speak for a long moment, and she braced herself for whatever bomb he was about to drop. "She says if you go to the wedding, she'll sign over your inheritance to you."

Adelaide gaped, wide-eyed. "No way."

"She seems pretty serious about it, Ads. Like, Samantha serious."

She hadn't thought her sister could sink that low. "She can't—Michael, she can't do that."

"I told her that. But she's desperate right now."

"Come on—"

"That's the deal. They moved up the wedding, and they're going to keep it simple. Have the ceremony in their backyard with a few friends. She said if you come, you get your share of the inheritance. No strings attached."

A sick feeling crawled into her stomach. Samantha had probably moved the date last night, just to force Adelaide's hand sooner. And backyard? Please. Samantha and Bear lived in a sprawling mansion in Beverly Hills. Their backyard looked more like the grounds of a five-star resort.

"There are always strings."

"She promised."

"Right," Adelaide grumbled, sipping her water. She wished she'd ordered something stronger. "And I suppose you think I should play her game and take the money?"

"I told her she needed to stop this shit. But it went in one ear and out the other. So"—he threw up his hands and shrugged—"I guess, yeah. I'd take it. And be done with it. One night of pain, and you'll get your inheritance."

Adelaide scrubbed her hands down her face. Did he realize how insane that sounded? "She hates me. I don't know why she'd even want me there."

"I think she's worried she's going to be cursed if you don't show up. That Mom and Dad will roll over in their graves if she doesn't smooth things over."

"If she wanted to smooth things over, she's had plenty of opportunities. The reason she brought it up now is because you told her about *him*." She motioned to the slopes, where Jack was right now. "She wants to check out the competition. Make sure she's still the only Wright with someone worthy on her arm. Can't have anyone outshine Queen Samantha." Adelaide stared at her plate full of food. Since when had it arrived? She didn't even remember ordering, and now, she wasn't hungry.

"Queen Samantha?" Michael chuckled. "Ads, you ever think your idea of the girl isn't entirely accurate?"

Adelaide shook her head. When she spoke, her voice was quiet. "Samantha still blames me for what happened."

"No, she only said that because—"

"It's true. She's right. It is my fault."

Michael stiffened, as he did every time she brought this particular point up. "Ads, come on now. Stop—"

"I've got to go," she said, standing abruptly.

He didn't stop her because he knew how this would play out. They'd done this drill enough. Once he brought Samantha up, it was almost guaranteed she'd run from him, from the whole ridiculous conversation. All it ever did was open up old wounds that made her want to crawl into bed and cry alone for a few hours. Which was exactly what she planned to do now.

She didn't get to be alone though. When she arrived at the condo and ran for the bedroom, she was surprised to find Jack standing there, pulling off his ski jacket.

"Oh, I—" She hovered in the door, unsure of what to do. "I didn't know you'd be here."

He frowned at her expression. "What's wrong?"

She battled back a sudden onslaught of memories—of her sister's frantic call, of Michael's wailing when he had come home to find his entire life upside down. The day her parents had died was the worst day of her entire life.

What's wrong?

Since that day, everything.

"Adelaide," he said when she didn't answer. "You're crying."

She touched her cheeks, surprised to find them wet.

"Come sit down." Jack crossed the room and put a careful arm around her, guiding her to the edge of the bed, where he sat right next to her. "Is it your brother? What did he do?"

"Nothing." She sniffled, trying to regain control of herself. "He didn't do anything. Holidays can be hard for me after …"

He gently touched the bottom of her chin. "You don't ever talk to me about your parents."

"What is there to say?"

Jack brushed a tear off her cheek. "Well, you've just come in crying, so I would guess quite a bit."

But she couldn't talk to him about all that. She'd barely spoken to anyone about it before, besides her roommates, in bits and pieces. And things like that didn't matter to him. Anything that went beyond surface level was more than the parameters of this arrangement allowed.

"No, I'm fine. Sorry for getting upset. How was skiing?"

"Don't apologize. Tell me how to fix it." He shook his head. "Do you want me to go beat the shit out of your brother?"

The offer made her laugh, even as it made her cry. "I thought you didn't do family drama."

Jack tsked as he wrapped his arms all the way around her, holding her in a tight circle against his chest. She could feel an almost-imperceptible shake of his head when another tiny sob broke free.

She'd get her tears under her control in a minute. She'd learned to compartmentalize a long time ago. But for a few seconds, she gave in and let him soothe her.

Basked in how good it felt when he acted like he cared.

SEVENTEEN

"I have a bone to pick with you," a voice said as Adelaide stumbled out of her bedroom the following Monday, in search of coffee.

They'd had a long flight back from Colorado, arriving after midnight, and she hadn't gotten to her bed until two in the morning. The jet lag was already killing her.

Imogen was curled up on the recliner in the living room, covered in an afghan and wearing her big glasses, a giant biology tome in front of her.

Adelaide pouted and stooped to give her a one-armed hug. "I'm sorry I missed your birthday. I really wanted to be there. Was it amazing?"

"Not that! Yes, it was amazing, and thank you for paying for half the booze. We drank it all and then went sledding with cafeteria trays on Brandt Hill." She smiled tiredly. "I still have a hangover. But that's not what I'm talking about."

Adelaide poured herself a cup of coffee and sat across from her friend. "All right, what then?"

"You're living a secret life!" Katy appeared in the bathroom door, wrapped in a towel and bathed in a cloud of steam. She skipped over to the recliner and sat on the arm. "Where were you this weekend?"

"*Because*," Imogen added pointedly, "we went to the Rathskellar for a drink, and your boyfriend was there."

"My boy—" Adelaide bit her tongue. The first person she'd thought of was Jack.

"Obviously, Declan did *not* take you home to his family's Thanksgiving, which is where you told us you were going when you left." Katy crossed her arms. "So. Where have you been all weekend?"

Adelaide sighed. Keeping up with her other lies was exhausting enough. Did she really need to keep Jack from them too?

"Fine," she relented. "But don't freak out, please."

Her roommates' eyes widened in anticipation.

"I've been seeing an older guy, and we went to Aspen for the weekend. I know it's crazy, and I'm sorry I didn't tell you, but I thought you might freak over the age difference."

Katy and Imogen opened their mouths and stared at one another, but they didn't speak for a good twenty seconds.

Finally, Imogen ventured, "How much older?"

The way she hesitated before answering said it all.

"Twice your age or"—Imogen's eyes went big—"three times?"

"He's thirty-eight."

"Wow," Katy breathed. "But at least we're not talking, like, sixty. I'd have a problem with sixty."

Imogen nodded. "And Aspen. That means he's rich?"

Adelaide shrugged. She'd hoped this would curtail the questions, but that had been foolish of her. Of course they'd want to know all about him. "Yes, but can we not talk about it anymore? It's not that serious, honestly."

"Why?" Katy prodded, wiggling her eyebrows. "Is he married?"

Imogen gasped, her hand flying to cover her mouth.

"No!" Adelaide barked, standing up so fast she nearly spilled her coffee. She didn't want to conjecture about Jack's reasons for dating her. Not least of all because she knew he'd never trust her enough to give them. "This is why I didn't want to tell you. I knew you'd make a production out of it."

"Considering you've been bullshitting us for the past few weeks," Katy laughed mirthlessly, "I think a little production is in order."

Imogen's face pinched. "Why wouldn't you just tell us, Addie?"

She could see the hurt and the judgment in both of their eyes. And she couldn't handle that, not right now.

"I'm not fighting about this," Adelaide snapped, heading for her bedroom. "Let's talk later."

She slammed the door and stared down at her steaming mug. Part of her wished that she could tell them the whole truth. They knew about the papers, so maybe they'd get it. But in her gut, she knew that there were some lines people just couldn't conceive of crossing, and for her roommates, this would be one.

The problem was, in Aspen, after she had come back to the condo in tears, Jack had been painfully sweet to her for the rest of the night. He'd drawn her a bath, rubbed her shoulders. Let her nap and concocted her a big cocktail when she woke up.

When they'd celebrated Thanksgiving at a restaurant overlooking the mountains, he had been more attentive than usual, holding her knee under the table, leaning over to tell her she looked beautiful, that he was happy she was there, wanting to know if she was okay.

At the time, she didn't honestly know. And she still didn't. Samantha's offer had rattled her. Was it possible her sister really wanted to make amends after all this time?

And if she did, was that something Adelaide was ready to do?

The history between them was so long, so messy; it was like a tangled ball of string. The effort it would take to unwind it negated the purpose of trying.

Yet as she lay in her narrow apartment bed that night, she couldn't help but feel a chink in the armored wall she'd built up around her heart. Samantha, Michael, and Bear had all remained close, remained *family*, without her. She always told herself it was because they were superficial people; because Michael and Bear kowtowed to overbearing Samantha in some misinformed definition of love. She'd told herself she could live with a distant relationship and make her own family some other way.

But now, her mind couldn't help returning, over and over again, to the moment at Thanksgiving dinner, when she'd realized that despite the beautiful surroundings and Jack's hand slipping into hers, she'd felt an acute awareness that something—someone—was missing.

Two days later, an insistent, full-fisted knock on the door startled her, as if someone was trying to break it down.

Adelaide was in her bathrobe, but after she peered through the peephole and swung the door open, Declan pushed past her without asking to be invited in.

"I found Fiona."

Since she'd returned from Colorado, the new information from Michael had been hanging heavy in her mind. Had Jack known Declan was that fragile? Had he cared? Or worse, had he *caused* it?

No. She'd been thinking and thinking, and even at his worst, she didn't believe Jack would take advantage of Declan like that. He was single-minded, ruthless at work, but the man who'd held her in Aspen, calming her and whispering the most soothing things, couldn't be the asshole Declan had said he was.

If Declan had found Fiona, that meant that they could be one step closer to the paintings. Except how could she betray Jack now? The lines of the arrangement were becoming so blurry that she could no longer distinguish between work and pleasure, real relationship or not.

"How?" she asked.

Declan looked around. "Your roommates home?"

She shook her head.

"I found her in the Main Line in Philly. She never returned my calls, so I wrote her a letter." He shook his head, like he couldn't believe his own luck. "And she finally called me back."

"Wow." Adelaide put her hand on the counter, needing something stable to lean on. "What was she like?"

"Hot, high maintenance. She looks nothing like you, so don't ask me what this guy's type is. She's technically still under a nondisclosure, but I think she got so burned by the guy that she was thrilled to have someone to bitch to."

She tried to keep her face neutral, though she was desperate to know more.

"I told her a bit about what he did to me, and she said she wasn't surprised. Between us, I think she was way into him and couldn't stand the fact that he didn't want her back. But that wasn't the interesting part. She says that Jack has a house in Maine that he never uses. And she doesn't think he takes any of his girls there either."

"Okay …"

Declan widened his eyes at her. "*Okay*? Addie, he could be keeping the paintings there!"

Adelaide nodded, but she was only half-listening. Mostly, she was wondering if Jack had been with Fiona the way he was with her, and also, she was gazing at Declan, trying to decode what was really going on in his head. There was a fine line between intense and obsessed. Had Declan crossed it? It felt as if he'd morphed into someone she didn't know. Or maybe he'd done that a long time ago, and she was only now figuring it out?

"I'll look into it," she promised, shooting him a smile she hoped appeased him. "Look, I have a really big exam to study for, Declan. Can we catch up tomorrow?"

She reached for the door, about to open it, when someone knocked.

She almost answered without looking. Katy was famous for forgetting her key whenever she went out. But at the last moment, she looked through the peephole, and her heart jammed in her throat.

"It's Jack!" she whispered hoarsely at Declan, wheeling around to brace the door with her body.

He stared at her, expressionless. "Oh."

When she motioned for him to hide in Imogen's bedroom, he did so slowly, taking a calm, measured stroll down the hall.

"Go, Declan!" she hissed. She hadn't been bloodthirsty over his Fiona news and it felt like payback that he was acting unaffected at Jack's appearance. "What the hell are you doing?"

He turned in the doorway, his eyes fixed over her shoulder, in the direction of the living room they'd just come from. "Maybe I should let him find me here."

"*What?*" She shook her head. He was talking nonsense. "Get inside!"

"What would he do?" he continued, resisting when she frantically pushed him back by the shoulder. "What would Jack do if he found us together?"

Adelaide shoved him in without answering and slammed the door behind her, nerves rattling. *What the hell was Declan thinking?*

On her way back through the living room, she noticed he had left his wallet on the table. She shoved it in the closest drawer. When she finally pulled the door open, she found Jack standing there, hands braced on the doorframe.

"Hi," she said breathlessly, smoothing back her hair. "Sorry, I was …" Seeing the surly smile on his face, she abandoned the bullshit excuse and stepped back. "What are you doing here?"

He pushed his way in, much like Declan had. He was wearing a black suit, and he had a hint of stubble dusting his jaw—two things that made her heart backflip despite the situation. "I have a meeting with some board members on campus."

"I wasn't expecting you—"

He hoisted her up onto the kitchen counter and captured her lips with his before letting her finish. His mouth was insistent, excited, and in an instant, all her protests died away. She would've loved this under any other circumstances—the impulsivity of it, the way he was grabbing her hard, like he wanted to inhabit her—but now, all she felt was slightly sick.

Declan was here.

In the next room.

"What are you doing?" she squeaked when his hands found the tie of her robe, unfastening it before roving over her naked body underneath.

Jack had the power to make her lose sight of everything, to forget her own name, but not now. Definitely not now. She wanted to make up some sort of excuse, but she wasn't sure if that was a better idea—the contract still stood, she hadn't helped Declan, and, God, his hands felt good.

"What does it look like I'm doing?"

"Jack," she gasped, heart hammering in her chest when he bent down to suck her nipple into his mouth, working his pants open as he did. Her mind still hadn't caught up to the fact that he was here. In her tiny apartment, surrounded by her very *real* life. The blending of his world and hers and Declan in the next room was almost too much to wrap her head around this fast.

"I wanted to make sure you were okay," he murmured against her body. "After Aspen."

"You could have just called."

"But then I couldn't have done this." Yanking her to the edge of the counter, he pushed inside her with shallow thrusts that made her groan. Loudly. Declan could probably hear everything.

Jack kissed her roughly, holding the back of her head with one hand as he pushed her legs wider with the other.

Despite the fact that Declan was right down the hall and that she was scared out of her mind at being found out, Adelaide still found herself clawing at Jack's suit in an attempt to hold on to something—*anything*—as his body slapped against hers over and over again. Her head was in a million other places, but her body was reacting to him on its own, and a quick, unsettling orgasm slammed into her like a freight train.

She buried her face in his neck, so Declan wouldn't hear her scream. That was one favor she still had enough wherewithal to do for him.

When Jack pulled out, he said, "I'd ask you for a shower, but I'd rather smell you on me."

Adelaide smiled sheepishly, closed her ratty robe, and let him ease her down from the counter. She watched him zip and buckle his pants, not trusting herself to meet his eyes.

"So, are you? Okay, I mean."

"Yeah." She crossed her arms. Back to scared. Willing him to go, even as she wished he would stay for a slower round two. "It was just a bad day."

He held her hand for the few steps it took to get back to the front door. Their fingers were still linked when he reached up to tap the necklace at her throat. She'd forgotten she had it on— she always did these days. "Seeing you wear this never gets old."

He kissed her forehead, whispered goodbye, and disappeared down the hallway. Adelaide waited for the butterflies in her stomach to pass.

Then, she braced herself for the firing squad.

Instead, Declan came out of Imogen's room wearing the best mask of calm she had ever seen. His expression gave away absolutely nothing.

"I'm sorry," Adelaide said quietly, watching as he collected his wallet from where she had stashed it with the forks and knives.

"It's not a problem." He didn't meet her eyes.

"Are you sure about that?"

Declan paused next to her. She was blocking the door.

He gave her a sideways glance. "Move, Addie."

She did, and he was out of there before she managed another word.

For some strange reason, Adelaide felt a pang in her stomach. What right did Declan have to be upset about Jack coming over? This was exactly what he wanted from her, what he had so carefully orchestrated. Why had he stormed out like a jealous boyfriend?

And what was going on with him when Jack had shown up, almost like he was trying to get caught? When they'd started all this, Declan hadn't wanted to be seen, yet now, he was acting cavalier about it? Antagonistic?

Almost like he was taunting her with his presence.

What would Jack do if he found us together?

End it with me, Adelaide realized unceremoniously. Break up with her. Hate her even.

Disturbingly, Declan had unearthed a new way to threaten her. Revealing her secret about the paper-writing might get her expelled, but Jack finding out about her deal with Declan?

That would do damage of an entirely different kind.

EIGHTEEN

Adelaide didn't think Jack had had much of a view of her small apartment while he was there. He'd been busy with *other* things. But when she told him she felt smothered by her roommates and needed to get away, hoping he'd mention something about the house in Maine, he instead told her he was going to see a collector in Chicago and invited her to spend the weekend at his place.

It wasn't what she'd intended, but she took him up on the offer anyway. She really did need to distance herself from the apartment and not only because things had been tense with her roommates ever since their tiff about Jack. That awkward event with Declan had been cycling through her mind nonstop. Declan had never been predictable, but she was unsettled by what had transpired.

So, getting away from Cranst for a weekend seemed like exactly what she needed. She packed up all of her books and got on the train, eager to spend the time studying in a comfortable place. Maybe a little more than comfortable, considering.

As promised, Jack left the key with the reception desk in the lobby. When she went inside, she couldn't help feeling like this was a new, important step in the relationship. Even if it was just sex, he trusted her enough to leave her alone with his private things.

Declan would be happy about that.

He would not be happy that she did absolutely no snooping and instead luxuriated in living in the kind of place most people could only dream about. She puttered around for a while, then headed to Jack's room, where she promptly sprawled out on his duvet for a nap.

She'd just started to rouse when Jack called to check on her a few hours later, her phone lighting up the now dark room.

"Where are you?" he asked when she answered.

"Your bed," she said and then laughed awkwardly. She wasn't sure if it was weird or not that she'd posted up in here instead of the guest bedroom, which still felt unequivocally like her domain, even though she'd stayed in his room every night since London.

There was silence on the end of the phone.

"Are you mad?"

"Mad?" he scoffed, voice low. "I'm fucking hard."

"Jack," she gasped and loosed an unexpected burst of laughter.

"You can't tell me things like that when I'm working."

She flipped onto her back, surprised to find pressure building between her legs. "I guess I shouldn't tell you I have on those silk pajamas you like either. Well, just the bottoms." Lie. She was also in his favorite gray T-shirt, which she'd put on because she was lonely earlier.

"Adelaide," he warned.

"You remember what you did last time I had them on?"

Who was she, flirting like this? She had no idea where this brazenness had come from. She'd spent too many hours in this apartment alone perhaps, surrounded by everything Jack. Or maybe it was just easier to pretend she was a different sort of person here, in the dark, with no one's eyes on her and his low, silky voice in her ear.

"You put me up on the bathroom counter …"

A car door slammed, and Jack barked at the driver to circle the block until he told him to stop. She heard the faint hum of the privacy divider going up. "I had to get back in the car. I can't go inside like this."

"Dirty Jack," she teased. "And with no relief."

And she didn't know what came over her, but she found her hand slipping under the waistband of her shorts, to the place that had begun to ache. She bit her lip when she found it, hips jerking up a little to meet her touch.

"You're killing me," he breathed petulantly. "You have no idea how badly I want to be with you right now. To taste you."

Her breath strangled in her chest. "What else?"

"I'd put you on your knees, so I could see all of you. Then, I'd fuck you like that until you begged me to make you come."

She slid one finger inside herself.

"Or maybe I'd make you ride me, so I could watch your hips move. Watch you slide down every single inch."

"Jack," she gasped, straining. "I'm touching myself."

He groaned like he was in physical pain. "In *my bed?* You're trying to kill me. Ruin me."

"It's worse for me," she promised, biting back a groan, aching for his hand instead of her own. She was so sensitive, and yet nothing she did was enough; nothing gave her the feeling she wanted because only he could do that. She needed him so much that her whole body throbbed.

"Are you on your front or your back?"

"Back," she whispered, throat dry. "But I want it to be you. It almost hurts how much."

"Which part of me?"

"Anything," she answered, rolling her hips, vaguely aware she sounded like she was begging. It felt so dirty to be doing this in his sheets, without him there. Like she was marking her territory or something. "I need you, Jack. I don't think—not without you …"

"Turn over."

"What?"

"Turn over. Pretend it's me under you."

"I can't."

"Yes, you can. Come on, Adelaide. Listen to me."

When she did, the noise that came out of her was inhuman. How could he know what she needed, halfway on the other side of the continent?

"There you go," he coached even though she hadn't even told him she'd done it. "Imagine what I would be doing if I were there. Where you'd want my hands. Where you'd want my mouth."

Her stomach clenched as her mind ran wild with possibilities. "I'm so close, Jack." Her hips twitched against her hand now, desperate, seeking.

"I can tell by your breath. Your legs start to shake. Your hips have a life of their own. You get so tight around me …" He sounded dismal, heartbroken. "I can only imagine how wet you are right now. And in my goddamn bed …"

She turned her face into his pillow, and the smell of him was so strong that it overwhelmed her, made her want to cry and laugh and come at the same time. "It's too much," she whined, though she wasn't even sure what she meant by that.

"Come for me, Adelaide," he ordered her, bossy and benevolent, all at the same time. "Like I'm there. Like I'm watching you. Like my hands are on your hips. Like my mouth is all over you. Don't stop."

And even though Jack was hundreds of miles away, she obeyed. After the orgasm rocked her body, she fell into a heap in the center of his bed, hand still buried between her legs, panting hard.

"Wow," she breathed, too satiated to be embarrassed or uncomfortable or anything she usually was after Jack talked to her like that.

"I can't believe you just got off in my bed, without me. And I had to listen to every damn second of it."

"You didn't …? I mean, you weren't …?"

"I'm sitting in dead-stop traffic, watching a family in a minivan share yogurt snacks, Adelaide."

She burst out laughing, which felt almost as good as the orgasm. How she could laugh so casually after he'd just heard her do *that* would have been incomprehensible with anyone else, but with Jack, it just felt like an extension of it. Like the moment could tumble easily from dirty to playful to—

"I miss you," he said simply.

To *that*.

Alarming since the second the words left his mouth, she realized she missed him too. Yes, physically—he'd practically had to talk her into an orgasm just now—anyone would miss that. But this was a different sort of longing, one that she felt in a deeper, harder-to-reach place.

But she wouldn't tell him that. That would be breaking the rules, for sure.

"And what will you do to me when you get here?" she asked coquettishly.

Jack didn't miss a beat. "Hug you."

She laughed again, but now, it was awkward, devoid of humor. She couldn't let what he said sink in too deep. "I lied to you before."

"I'll dole out your punishment when I get home. What was the lie?"

"I have a shirt on."

"This changes everything."

"It's the gray one you like."

"In my bed, in my favorite T-shirt, touching yourself. I'm fucked." Jack was smiling on the other end of the phone—she didn't know how she knew, but she was sure of it. "Do you sleep on my pillow too?"

"And shower in your bathroom. And use your toothbrush. And eat that expensive mint jam you always hide. And put my feet up on your desk and—"

"I have to go to my meeting now, Adelaide. I'm fifteen minutes late. And you know how intolerable I find lateness."

"Bye, Jack," she whispered, hanging up with a great big smile she had no business having on her face.

She made herself dinner, poured a big glass of wine, and had them both in his bed while she watched TV. Then, she took a bath in his massive tub and rubbed expensive-smelling lotion on her body, curling back up in bed to read the last twenty pages of a spy novel she'd found tucked among his art books. She couldn't remember ever being this indulgent with her time, but she didn't want to go downstairs, to her schoolwork sprawled across the coffee table, waiting for her. She felt cozier and more relaxed than she had in months—years maybe.

Home, he'd called this place on the phone. *When I get home.*

The word floated over her like a blanket. This wasn't her home—it could never be. But just for tonight, she'd curl up in Jack's bed and pretend. For one night, she'd imagine she deserved this, same as everyone else.

The weekend went by much too fast and not because of the three papers Adelaide had due on Monday. Living in such lovely conditions, taking walks in Central Park while the snow fell, enjoying Thai carryout in a massive bed that could've had its own zip code. Even without Jack there, it was exactly the change of pace she'd needed.

On Sunday morning, she poured herself an extra-large mug of coffee and spread out at the kitchen table, overlooking the park. Popping in earbuds with some of her favorite zone-out music, she got down to business, putting the finishing touches on what she promised herself was the *actual* last paper she'd do for anyone besides herself. Things were going well with Jack, and there was no reason to play with fire.

Adelaide was so intent on finishing, her eyes glued to her screen, that she didn't notice Jack's appearance until he was dragging the headphones out of her ears, staring at her.

No, staring at the papers next to her.

She followed his line of vision to her green notebook, where her list of clients lay faceup. She blinked down at his extended hand and realized that pinched between his fingers was the folded rough draft of Cecilia Heinle's six-page paper on *Clotel*, which she'd been editing on the couch.

He spoke through his teeth. "What is this?"

She prayed the floor would open and swallow her down. She'd practiced what she'd say to Professor Hargrove if Declan ever pulled the trigger. But the eyes of Jack Nolan, narrowed in shock and disappointment, was something she was completely unprepared for. She found herself speechless as she gathered the papers to her chest, as if she could hide them.

"History ... Economics ... who is Cecilia Heinle? These aren't yours," he murmured, prying them from her grip. "Are you writing papers for other people, Adelaide?"

"Jack," she began, her heart cramming itself in her throat. "I thought you were coming back tonight."

"Are you *insane*?" he hissed, his gaze darting from her face to the papers rapidly. "This is *illegal*. Not to mention stupid. You're going to get yourself expelled!"

"Hold on," she pleaded, trying to focus over the new roaring in her ears. "Just hold on. I only do it sometimes." But, God, she was sick of lying to him. Just like the essay writing, she didn't know how to stop. "It has nothing to do with us."

Jack still looked like he wanted to throttle her. "I'm on three different boards at Cranst, Adelaide. Jesus, I just brought you to a reception with the entire fucking administration there!" She could see his wheels turning, trying to figure out exactly how much this could fuck him over if it got out. "It's bad enough you're a damn kid, but this?"

She stared at him, hoping there was a punch line to that statement. None came.

His disbelieving eyes searched her own. "Why are you doing this?"

"It's not like I *wanted* to. I had no choice. The tuition at Cranst is—"

"The tuition?" he scoffed. "Really? If that was the issue, you should've told me. I'd pay you more."

"You haven't been paying me for that long."

She hadn't realized Jack had been moving, until he went stock still. "This has been going on since *before* you met me?"

The question surprised her so much that she didn't even think about lying when she answered, "It's been going on for three years."

She thought he'd been shocked before, but now, Jack tipped into something else entirely.

Normally, he was Mr. Calm, Cool, and Collected—unless she was pissing him off. Now, as he dropped the papers down on the table and rubbed the bridge of his nose with two hands, she saw those instances had been nothing compared to this. He was so furious he actually looked a little heartbroken. So much that she started to grow angry with *him*.

What right did he have to judge her choices? Wasn't it obvious, given the fact that she'd agreed to this deal with him, the kind of financial situation she was in? Did women who *weren't* generally desperate want to do something like this?

Her embarrassment waned to resentment. She didn't need to hear how reprehensible she was from his privileged ass. "I really don't see why you're being so dramatic," she said carefully, trying to control her voice. "You said *why* didn't matter."

If she thought she'd get him to back off again by using that old trick, she was sorely mistaken.

Jack advanced on her, seething all over again. "Any one of the names on that list could rat you out and you'd be in a mountain of trouble. You're risking your entire future, Adelaide! Don't you get that?"

"Yes, Jack!" The volume of her voice surprised them both. "Thank you for reminding me just how fucked up my life is—I had no idea until *you* pointed it out!"

That stopped him from yelling at her, as least.

Instead, he paced the floor, thinking. After a minute, he stopped abruptly, and turned to her. "Get dressed."

She froze. "What? Why?"

"You're going to see my lawyer."

Adelaide crossed her arms. "No."

"It's not up for discussion. You're going to need help if any of this ever gets out. This is a damn mess you're in, and we're going to be proactive about it." When she still didn't move, he pulled her out of her chair by the shoulders, like a stern schoolmaster. "Party's over, Adelaide."

Jack's attorney worked on the top floor of a Midtown high-rise, in a corner office overlooking the city skyline. The office was empty on a Sunday, but he'd made a call, and his lawyer had agreed to come in just for Adelaide.

Her name was Mariana Lopez, and she had every single hallmark of American success in her possession, right down to the Harvard Law School diploma on the wall and a row of glittering plaques with her name inscribed. She wore nice slacks and a blazer, which made Adelaide feel juvenile since she'd shown up in jeans and an oversize sweater.

To his credit, Jack had sent her there alone, as if he sensed that his presence would make things worse. She was glad on the way over, but as she sat down in the intimidatingly sleek office, she wished very much that she'd brought an adult.

Mariana took a seat across from her and opened a notebook. She was probably close to Jack's age and very pretty, with dark eyes that seemed like they never missed a detail. "Adelaide, I hear there's a potential legal situation you find yourself in?"

She swallowed.

Before she'd gotten in the car, Jack had pulled her back into his front and whispered, "Don't lie."

"I've been writing papers for cash in order to pay my college tuition," she admitted now. "And I need to stop, but I also need to finish my degree."

Jack's lawyer nodded, taking the information in stride. "That's not a trivial matter. When did you begin this?"

"Freshman year. It didn't start seriously. I just wrote a couple here and there for friends. But it snowballed. Fast. And then I'd built up a clientele. The money was good—better than some off-campus job, blending smoothies, at least—and I just kept going." Adelaide tried not to search too hard for judgment in her eyes, but she knew it was probably there anyway. "I know I had a choice," she conceded. "But this is the one I made."

"And you *do* want to stop?"

"Yes."

Mariana sighed and sat forward in her chair, her face serious. "It's going to be hard to quit this cold turkey. You now have a reputation on campus. You understand, it's really only a matter of time before word gets to the wrong people?"

"What do I do?"

"Well, you *do* quit. Cold turkey. I don't want you even talking to these people. Don't call them back or text them. If they hunt you down and ask you for help, tell them you're busy. The ones you've finished, give them out, but that's it. No more. Got it?"

Adelaide nodded.

"If anyone from the university contacts you about it, I want you to call me as soon as humanly possible and don't say a single word. To anyone. You're in a tricky situation, Adelaide, but if you stop now, you might be all right."

Mariana handed her a business card, and she placed it in her pocket.

"Okay. I will. Thank you."

"I'll do some research to see exactly what your exposure is, if this gets out. But let's hope your luck will hold a few more months until graduation."

Mariana asked her a few more questions and then walked her back to the elevators. Adelaide was surprised to feel relieved. Not better about it morally, but at least she had a plan now.

"Thank you for your help," she said sincerely. "I know it's not good, but I was desperate—"

"Hey," Mariana said, holding up a hand and offering her a smile. "We all do what we have to, to get by. I'm the only female partner at this firm, and you'd better believe I didn't like myself all the time on my way up." She grinned as the elevator arrived. "Jack threatened to leave the firm if they didn't put me on the masthead. So, I'm not surprised he freaked out about the papers. He's very loyal to the people he cares about. Wants the best for them, at all costs."

"Yeah," Adelaide muttered, just to be polite. She was still stinging about his reaction, even if she was glad she had come. "He's a real crusader for women's rights."

"You'd be surprised." Mariana winked as she stepped into the elevator. "Hang in there. He might bark at you awhile, but then he'll soften up. First few months are the worst."

The doors slid closed before she could say more.

Did that mean Mariana was …

No way, she thought.

Mariana was a high-powered attorney, who, from the looks of it, had no need for Jack's money.

She was still puzzling over the advice when she returned to the apartment, head down, feeling simultaneously grateful and pissed that Jack had put her through that.

He was just wrapping up a phone call, wearing glasses she'd never seen him in before, plus a T-shirt and jeans. She hated the way the mere sight of him made her heart pump with desire, so she skirted the area and went toward the stairs.

She made it no more than two steps before he called, "Well?"

Sighing, she paused. "I'm not doing it anymore. It's over. And she said if there's any trouble, I should call her."

"And you're *really* not going to do it anymore?"

She pressed her lips together. "That's what I said, didn't I?"

"I want you to forward your next tuition bill to me. And your rent. I'll take care of it."

"That's not neces—"

"I insist."

It wasn't about the money anymore though. Ever since she'd started writing those papers, she'd felt like a lesser person.

That was what she'd had to do to survive. Was having her sugar daddy paying her way any better?

"What?" He approached her, taking her hands. "Adelaide, look at me. What?"

She shook her head, unable to meet his eyes. "The money isn't the issue. It's … me. You talked to me like you thought I *liked* what I was doing. And I didn't, Jack. Ever. And I don't like myself very much either."

"Adelaide." His voice was gentle but firm. It seemed to command that she look up at him, which she did, even as she fought back the tears that were threatening to spill. "You sold papers. Not your soul."

She let out a shaky breath. "If that was everything, maybe I'd believe you. But it's not. Look at what I'm doing with you." She swallowed the hard lump in her throat. "None of it sits right with me. It's not who I am. And not the person I want to be."

"You're being too hard on yourself. I told you already, stop judging it. We all do what we need to, to get by."

"You sound like Mariana."

"Mariana is an extremely smart woman."

Adelaide jutted her chin up. "She was one of your others, wasn't she?"

Jack's eyes were inscrutable. "Would that shock you?"

"Yes," she told him honestly. "Why would she need your money?"

"Maybe she needed it at one time. Or maybe she just wanted it. This isn't always something people choose out of desperation."

"Spoken like a man in a man's world," Adelaide muttered.

He angled his head down, conceding. "Fair point. But a woman should be able to do what she wants, when she wants, and *why* she wants. If I didn't believe women should be able to profit off their desirability, I'd be an enormous hypocrite, wouldn't I?"

Adelaide tiredly shook her head. She didn't even know what they were talking about anymore. "But this isn't a philosophical debate, Jack. This is my life."

"You're right." He backed up a few steps and crossed his arms. "So, what are you trying to tell me, Adelaide? Are you leaving me?"

"No!" she snapped quickly. Then, more levelly, "No."

He was quiet for such a long time that she couldn't imagine what was going through his mind. Probably regret, for ever entering into this arrangement in the first place. She'd basically just told him it was a mistake, and now, he was likely realizing how terrible of one it was. She'd broken the cardinal rule after all—she'd gone and made this arrangement into more than what it was. Just sex. Theater. No emotions. No, she hadn't confessed her feelings for him, but wasn't this just as bad?

After a moment, he said very gently, "I think you should take the guest room tonight."

She did. She slinked into the room and closed the door behind her, wanting to never open it again. She could tell from his voice that the arrangement was over. She'd gone and spoiled things.

Wasn't that what she wanted? No more papers, no more arrangement?

Yes, it was.

Except as she curled up in the guest room, tears in her eyes, she realized that somewhere along the line, she still wanted Jack.

In the morning, the apartment was silent when her alarm went off. She quickly changed, hoping to slip out, unnoticed, but when she reached the door, something propped on a ledge nearby caught her attention.

It was a simple, folded white sheet of paper with her name written in slanted script on the front. As she unfolded it, she scanned the house that she'd once been so comfortable in, sure it was going to be the last time she ever laid eyes on any of it. Then, she read:

Adelaide,

I'm staring at one of your hair ties on the counter. The other day, I went into my briefcase for a pen and found your ChapStick there. Gerta washed three pairs of socks you'd left behind and put them in a bag for you, which I emptied into my own drawer so I would see them in the morning. I find myself looking forward to these little reminders of you—a book wedged in the corner of the couch, the smell of your shampoo on my pillow, those awful energy drinks in the fridge. When I came in late last weekend and you were already asleep, you turned over and held out your hand for me when I climbed into bed.

It hasn't been like this before. Why matters.

Jack

Adelaide hadn't ever received a love note before, but she was pretty sure this qualified as one. She read it three times and then went into his bedroom to inspect for herself. Her socks were indeed in his drawer, two pairs of hot pink and one pair of blue, mixed in with a sea of black and white.

She smiled the entire way back to Cranst, thumbing Jack's note in her pocket. He'd changed so much in her eyes since they'd first met, and she had clearly changed in his.

So, if she came clean with him about Declan, maybe he would understand. And even if he didn't …

Even if he didn't, she was still going to tell him. If she'd been unsure before, his letter had chosen for her.

Maybe once everything was out in the open, Declan would move on and give up the ghosts of the past. She hoped, perhaps naively, that he'd show her a little mercy.

Adelaide was beginning to see that when you tangled yourself up in as many lies as she had, when the truth came out, mercy was the most you could hope for.

NINETEEN

Two days later, Jack asked her to go on a long weekend with him.

As in *just* him. There was no event to attend, no client to schmooze. He just wanted to get away with her for fun.

It felt like he'd committed to breaking all the rules now.

"Are you going to tell me where we're going, or are you waiting for me to guess?" she asked that Friday night.

Once they'd left Boston proper, the tightly packed row homes had gradually given way to farmhouses and tall pines. Now, they were headed up the highway, snowflakes skittering across the windshield as the headlights cut through the darkness. He had been cryptic, telling her only that she should pack warm clothes and no underwear she cared about him ruining.

Jack finding out about the papers had been terrible, but somehow, this new dynamic between them had made all the angst worth it. Ever since she'd left the city, it felt like she'd been floating through the past few days, lighter than she'd been in months. Years even.

Even with the prospect of telling Jack about Declan hanging over her, for the first time in a long time, Adelaide had hope.

"A cottage I own," he answered her with an easy smile. "In Maine."

The bubble of hope popped and then fizzled.

No, she told herself. *You've made up your mind about this. You're telling him.*

But if what Fiona had said about Maine was true ... then what if she didn't have to tell him about Declan at all?

Adelaide cast a sidelong glance at Jack, his handsome profile so perfect that it made her chest ache, his mouth still carrying a lazy grin. The new intimacy between them was thrilling, but it was also delicate, fragile. He'd said it had never been this way before with any of the other women, but then why did the contract matter anymore? Why hadn't he told her to forget everything and just be with him, no arrangement necessary?

Adelaide gently brushed her fingers through his hair. "Jack?"

"Yes?" He slid hand over her thigh in a proprietary way that said, *I want you right here. You are precious to me.*

She swallowed down whatever she had planned to say before. "It doesn't sound like you get up there much."

"It's a far trip. I mostly go alone and only once or twice a year."

"But you have a house. Doesn't it stay empty the rest of the time?"

He nodded. "It's not really a house. More like a cottage. It's still a far trip. I used to come a lot more before. I love it up along the coast. You'll see why."

Before. Before what exactly? The question danced on her lips, unspoken.

When she took stock of what she knew about Jack's past, it wasn't much. He never brought it up willingly, and when he did, it was always about his career, his clients, his galleries. He had a way of evading personal details, she'd noticed.

They arrived at the house shortly after ten, when Adelaide had nearly nodded off, her head against the window. That was when the car bumped onto a dirt road and trailed off through a narrow passage with dark pine sentries guarding the way. The path curved on and on, bordered by a low stone wall, until the headlights illuminated a small white cedar-shake building. It was the traditional Maine farmhouse—by now, she was an expert on them because they'd passed hundreds on the drive. This one though was far nicer than she'd expected. From Jack's description of it, she'd expected a dilapidated hovel, a step up from camping outdoors.

"Total cottage," she noted wryly.

He shifted the car into park and pointed at a dark line of trees. "You can't see it now, but beyond that tree line is the dock to Eastern Bay. We can take a look tomorrow."

They gathered their weekender bags and headed through the crisp ocean air, and into the house. Though the place hadn't been lived in, the moment he turned on the lights, Adelaide felt as though she were in a home. Sure, the furniture and furnishings were more outdated than his apartment in New York, but everything still signaled the guests should feel at welcome here.

Literally. A huge sign in the kitchen asked her to *Be Warm, Be Welcome, Be Home!*

She'd been expecting a rustic, manly cabin with checkerboard and rough hewn logs. But this decor tripped the line into feminine and, even more interestingly, not rich. These were like the houses back in Hamden, well furnished, but with that obvious air of middle-class that she didn't think Jack knew anything about.

As her feet creaked along the wide-planed floor, she peered in a bathroom and saw a lovely claw-foot tub. Across the hall, there was a bed with a flowered comforter and lace canopy.

Lace. Jack. The two things, juxtaposed, did not compute.

"It's … very sweet."

Stopping at the farmhouse sink, shooting a confused look at the sponge holder shaped like a giant bee, she resisted the inevitable question fighting its way out. *Who the fuck decorated this place?*

"I get it." Jack chuckled. "You're freezing and starving." He dropped their bags at the bottom of the stairs. "I'll get the heat on and a fire going. We'll go into town tomorrow for lobster. Tonight, it's Gerta's sandwiches."

She nodded as he headed up the stairs. It wasn't beyond reason that a man like him could like bee sponge holders and other knickknacks, was it? Maybe since it wasn't in the city, he wanted those things here. Or there was a possibility he'd purchased the house with these things already included. She didn't have to read into everything he did.

Except, she realized as she looked around, there was no artwork anywhere. Which definitely wasn't like the apartment, or like his place in Aspen, or either of his offices, both New York and London.

Adelaide fiddled with her necklace as she looked around, a strange feeling she couldn't name coming over her. Suspicion? Worry?

She tried to push whatever it was away when they sat in front of the fireplace, sandwiches and a bottle of wine on the floor in front of them. Once she ate and had a few sips of alcohol, the feeling that something was off receded, and she started settling into their surroundings. The windows of the place gaped open, dark beyond, not a single light from any neighboring house seen. It felt as if they were in their own little insulated world.

"What are you thinking?" he asked after they finished eating and she settled back into his arms so they could both watch the fire.

Their hands twined and untwined lazily, his long legs bracketing her shorter ones. He brushed a kiss against her hair every so often.

"That it feels like we're all alone out here. Like I finally have you all to myself."

Jack pressed his nose into the crown of her head. "You can have me all to yourself whenever you want, Adelaide."

She preened at that, nestling even deeper into his arms. "How long have you had this place?"

"It's been in my family for years, but before me, no one used it. When my parents died and left it to me, I had it fixed up and started coming here more and more."

"*You* had it fixed up?"

He nodded. "Why?"

"It doesn't exactly scream Jack Nolan." She hoped that would prompt an explanation. When it didn't, she added, "Which one helped?"

He took a sip of his wine and slowly swallowed, then he set the glass down on the table.

Awkwardness crept in.

She quickly fumbled to fill it. "When did your parents pass away?"

"Long time ago. Typical story. My father had a bad heart, and his death broke my mother's. She died three months after he did. They were close. Too close to live apart."

"And you were close to them too." It wasn't a question. It was obvious by the pain in his voice.

She turned around to look at him. His jaw was set, his pupils reflecting the glow of the fire in a way that made him look almost otherworldly. He'd had perfect parents, who had set an example for him of what it meant to love one person and be loved for life. She had to wonder what had changed him into a man who couldn't freely offer himself to a woman. What had hurt him? *Who* had hurt him?

As if he anticipated she was gathering the courage to ask, he quickly broke in. "Your parents died suddenly too."

She could see the question on his face, but she knew he'd have too much tact to ask it.

"Car accident," she explained, turning back around. It was easier to tell him without him looking at her. Her voice had cracked a little, and Jack buried his face in her neck. "It was the middle of the night. Some drunk idiot ran a red light and they swerved into a ditch. The car rolled. I was seventeen."

Jack tightened around her. "Jesus, Adelaide. I'm so sorry. What did you do?"

"My older sister, Samantha, got custody of me until I turned eighteen. She sold the house and moved us out to California, to live with her boyfriend."

"You didn't like it there." A statement, not a question.

"No, I left as soon as I could, after my eighteenth birthday. I hadn't wanted to leave Connecticut in the first place. But my sister is … difficult."

"Yeah? Tell me about her."

This was different. As much time as they'd been spending with one another, they were always discussing their likes and dislikes, flirting about inconsequential things. But something had shifted, and now, she could feel his curiosity, trying to piece together all the parts of her life he hadn't cared about before.

"She's typical type A. Massively pretty but very vain and shallow in the worst way. She's about to marry an NFL player. Finally fulfilling her dream of becoming the perfect trophy wife." Adelaide took a sip of wine, distracting herself from the rising anger in her gut. "We've been at odds ever since my parents died. I think, somewhere deep down, she believes I'm the one responsible for what happened."

"That's insane. Why would you think that?"

Adelaide tried to breathe over the tears rising in her throat, but they gathered in her eyes anyway. She had to work up her voice to tell Jack what she had only ever told Michael, but he waited for her patiently, running his knuckles against her arm. "Because she told me she did. They were coming to pick me up from a party."

From there, the whole story poured out—even little details she had never told anyone. Like those days afterward, when Samantha had always looked at her like she wanted to deck her. How Samantha sold her parents' house just three weeks after they died. How she started her new life in California like the old one never even existed and expected Adelaide to do the same. How lonely she was, ripped away from the only life she'd known. How Samantha gave her the ultimatum. How she'd ended up broke at Cranst.

"My parents did leave me and my older siblings an inheritance. But their wills were a mess—they didn't think they would be important for a while, I guess. Samantha had power of appointment, so she could distribute their money however she chose. She wanted me to stay in California because she insisted that was what my parents would have wanted. All of us together. She used the money as a bargaining chip. Told me she wouldn't give me my share of inheritance money unless I stayed. I refused, obviously, and went back to Connecticut."

Jack's body held every bit of the indignation she'd felt at the time, even as he soothingly ran his hand over her hair.

She wiped her eyes on the sleeve of her sweater. "I guess I could have tried to find a lawyer to fight for it, but I had tuition and rent and—"

"You know I'll pay for one, Adelaide," he murmured lightly, though she could sense he was admonishing her. "Let Mariana handle it. You'd have the money in your bank account by next weekend."

She knew he'd say something like that. But she didn't want him to do more for her than he was already doing—not until he understood what was really going on.

"How come you never call me Addie?" she asked instead. "Everyone else does."

"I like your name." Jack kissed the back of her earlobe. "There's nothing I don't like about you, Adelaide. Except for your lateness." After he was sure she'd smiled, he nudged her to keep going.

She sighed. "Half of me knows I should fight for the money; the other half doesn't want to deal with her ever again. I haven't decided which is the right half."

"And your brother?"

"Michael is the peacekeeper. He's always trying to keep things from escalating from the Cold War to World War Three. He knows Samantha is being insane about the money, but he refuses to take sides. Easy for him since he moved out there after college. They're really just one big, happy family most of the time." She shrugged. "I'm the outsider."

"How long has it been since you've spoken to your sister?"

"Three years. I haven't been back there since. I get all my information through my brother. The latest is that she's getting married and she says if I come to the wedding, she'll give me my inheritance." She took a big gulp of her wine. "Not that I believe her."

"She's lied to you before?"

"Well, no. But I think she would. I don't think I need to tell you how little I want to go to that wedding. It's the principle of it, you know? They wanted me to have the money, and I should have it. Who is she to keep what they willed to me?"

"Which is why you resorted to writing papers and … this."

"Mostly," she said, keeping her eyes on her lap. At that moment, she *wished* she'd resorted to signing his contract simply for the money. What she was doing was so much worse. "The thing is—"

"When's the wedding?" he interrupted.

"What? Oh, it's in two weeks. There's probably going to be, like, three hundred people attending."

"I could be your plus-one," he suggested, curling a lock of her hair around his finger.

She turned to stare at him. "You'd do that?"

"Why not? I've been wanting to look at some gallery spaces in LA anyway." He winked in a playful way she'd never have believed him capable of in their first meeting. "You'll be doing me a favor really."

"After everything I said about Samantha? You can be pretty intimidating, Jack, but trust me, she has fangs."

"I'll wear my garlic." He chuckled and motioned her to move back into his embrace. "I'd protect you from anyone, Adelaide."

She smiled, and for a moment, she felt all the unease she'd had about the event drain away. Yes, of course, Samantha would probably be a bitch, but having Jack there as her own shield *would* be more of a good thing than a bad one. Definitely.

But she couldn't ask him to act as her savior just yet.

She'd told him everything, except the most important part. "Jack," she started for the second time that night, sitting up. "I need to—"

But when she twisted around to face him, he reached over and smoothed out a line on her forehead, smiling in a way that was so utterly charming, the fire's heat doubled on her face. "You always get a crinkle right here when you're worried." He said it so tenderly that she couldn't help but lean into his touch, swinging her body and legs around so that she was straddling him. When she threaded her hands behind his neck, he pressed a kiss between her eyes.

"Do you want me to take you up to bed?" he whispered, rubbing his hands up her back. "You must be tired."

Adelaide shook her head and then sat back to pull her sweater off. His breath left him in a satisfied *whoosh* when she discarded it next to them. "I want to stay here awhile longer."

Whatever waited for them on the other side of this, tonight was too perfect. *They* were perfect.

One more night, she told herself. *Just one more night.*

TWENTY

The following morning, when Adelaide woke, she found herself alone in bed with the late morning sunshine streaming through the sliding doors to the outside, painting white waves on the hardwood floor. Scrambling out of bed, she pushed aside the lace curtains to find majestic, tall pines and, beyond that, a dark blue sea, sunlight glittering on its surface like a blanket of diamonds. Small green islands popped from the water in the distance, fading into the haze on the horizon. Jack had said she'd see why he loved this place, and instantly, she did. It was breathtaking.

Spinning, she caught the note on the dresser, beneath his wristwatch.

Went for a run. Coffee's on. Be back soon.

—J

She pulled on his T-shirt and found a pair of heavy wool socks from her bag. As she sat on the edge of the bed, her eyes volleyed around the place, as if she'd never seen it before. The daylight simply confirmed her earlier suspicions. Lace curtains. A flowered canopy. Doilies underneath the lamps. The place *did* have an oddly feminine touch.

Standing, she opened a drawer of the dresser, only to be hit by a thousand memories.

The space was empty, but a scent lingered—a scent that was distinctly her mother. Adelaide had bought that perfume for her mother once, for Christmas, and she'd worn it every day, without fail, even when they'd gone camping. It was expensive but pretty, with notes of lavender and vanilla.

Closing it, she went to the night table and pulled that drawer open, bracing herself for more déjà vu. Instead, she found a few old paperback romances. She lifted one out and turned the pages, and a bookmark fell out—part of a receipt for a café in town. Two salads, two glasses of wine.

He'd brought other women here.

It was no longer a question, hovering somewhere in the back of her mind. It was truth. Fiona might not have made it, but others had. And now, Adelaide was here, the latest in the parade.

Feeling a bit like a voyeur, as if she were peeping into someone else's private life, she went to the closet door. Opening it, she found a walk-in closet, filled with clothes. *Women's* clothes. The smell was more cedar than perfume, but there were dozens of pieces. But it was not a mishmash, a scattered assortment of left-behinds from the numerous women who'd held a place in Jack's bed. No, these were all silk blouses, blazers, sweaters with expensive designer names. Size six, size six, size six. Not the latest style though. These clothes had belonged to a woman of substance, one who valued quality and timelessness over flash, yet something about them seemed old. As Adelaide lifted the sleeve on one, running her fingers through the soft cashmere of a cardigan, a strange sense came over her. She felt like a stand-in for someone else.

One other person. These clothes had all belonged to the same woman.

Feeling dizzy with the sudden realization, as if the walls were closing in on her, she headed out of the closet. Still, the walls pressed in. As she picked up the pace, her socks slipped on the hardwood as she made it to the kitchen, where the strong aroma of coffee did nothing to block out the scent of the perfume that seemed to have inked itself inside her.

She opened a few drawers here and there, not sure what she was looking for. Pulled on another door to either a closet or a basement. Locked. That only seemed to make her feel more frantic. She'd known what he'd presented to her. What Declan had said. Jack was the typical man, who was too infatuated with his bachelorhood to commit. Who liked to play the field. Who'd maybe been hurt before and decided not to get close to that fire again.

She hadn't thought …

Before the thought could form, she found another closed door. This time, when she tried the doorknob, to her surprise, it opened. She found a dark, unadorned office, like a communal visitor's space in a place of business, with a simple desk and bookcase. No decor at all. The only thing on the desk, other than a thick layer of dust, was an old landline phone.

She lifted the receiver from its cradle and listened. Dead air. Then, she realized that the phone wasn't plugged in. She reached down and put the plug back into the outlet. Immediately, a light on the base of the phone began to blink, right beneath a button that said *Messages*.

Her finger shook as she pressed the button.

"You have eighteen messages," a computerized voice said.

There was a click, and it announced the date. A date that was from ten years earlier. Another click.

Then, suddenly, an energetic, sunny female voice said, "Hi, babe. It's me. Listen. Your cell must've died, so I'm leaving you a message here, assuming you'll get it in a little bit, when you're home. We're about to head out, and I'm going to lose service, so I just wanted to say I miss you, I love you, and I'll talk to you tonight! Wish me luck, Jackles!"

Another click.

She stared at the machine after the message ended, as if it had spontaneously burst into flames. *Jackles*. That woman, whoever she was, had loved him. Been familiar with him. Had a *nickname* for him. Was she the woman who'd owned the paperback romances, who had worn those clothes and perfume, whom he'd treated to salad and wine at the café?

She thought of Katy wiggling her eyebrows and asking if her older man was married.

There was another message after that, the tone drastically different. It was from a year later.

"This message is for Jack Nolan. It's Liz from Topeka Heights, calling with an update. Please call me back at your earliest convenience."

And the next, "Hi, Jack. It's Liz. Status quo today. Talk to you tomorrow."

She listened to message after message of Liz reporting no status change until she was hunched over the desk, nausea swirling in her stomach. When she heard a noise outside, she quickly unplugged the phone, stepped into the hallway, and closed the door behind her.

Jack appeared at the back patio a moment later. He slid the door open, his cheeks red from the cold air and a thin sheen of sweat on his forehead. The sea air had definitely done wonders for him; he looked ruddy and vital this morning.

She, on the other hand, felt so much worse, and it must've been obvious because Jack clasped her shoulder and said, "Hey, what's wrong?"

She shook her head and pointed at the coffeemaker. "Nothing. Just woke up."

He brought a mug down from a hook under the cabinet for her. "It's not too cold out. Get dressed. We'll go for a walk."

"Actually, I was going through my bag, and I realized I forgot some things."

She kept her back to him, hugging her body to ward off the sudden chill in every limb. She had a feeling it had less to do with the wind that had blown him in and more to do with *him*. But it was still too early. Maybe this was all … nothing. Maybe there was some reasonable explanation why parts of this house were like a shrine to a woman.

"There's a drugstore down the hill. I was going to suggest we go to town anyway for lunch."

She shook her head, her stomach lurching at the thought. Had Jack thought of this woman last night when she was in his arms?

"Why don't you stay here and take a shower?" she forced herself to say calmly. "If you point me in the right direction, I'll go myself."

Adelaide could feel him wrestling with the right thing to do. "You sure?"

"Of course. It's really no problem."

She managed a smile as he fished his keys out of his pocket, deposited them in her palm, and kissed her cheek.

He pointed outside. "Right down that way. Harbor Drugs, in the center of town. Can't miss it."

She got dressed and pulled out of the drive, and ten minutes later, she stopped at the corner and entered the address into her phone's GPS. Topeka Heights, whatever it was, was a few miles back up Route Three, on the mainland, near Ellsworth.

When Adelaide pulled up to the address, she stayed in the car for ten minutes before she could convince herself to get out. Her legs were stiff from the ride, but what made her unsteady was the sign on the front of the building, wholly unexpected yet as obvious as it could get. Standing out among the rustic farmhouses and crumbling mobile homes that lined the highway, the Topeka Heights Long-Term Care Facility was a modern-style building with sliding glass doors and windows that were actually walls.

She found her feet moving toward the entrance on their own.

It didn't smell like a hospital inside. In fact, it looked almost like a hotel with a plush seating area and a reception desk with smiling workers in neatly pressed blazers. It was quiet, and there was only one person checking in before her, who seemed familiar with the routine and greeted the receptionist warmly.

Adelaide looked around curiously, trying to figure out what Jack came here for—or rather, *who* he came here for.

"Can I help you?" The receptionist smiled.

It was her turn.

"Yes," she decided slowly, stepping forward. "I'm here to, um, visit someone."

"What's the last name, honey?"

Adelaide's mouth opened, but no words came out at first, her tongue hovering over her teeth like it had become frozen in time. "Nolan," she said finally. "The last name is Nolan."

"Oh, sure. Yes, she's here." The receptionist typed in a few things on her keyboard. "Can I see your ID?"

She took her wallet out and robotically handed over her license.

"All right, Adelaide, thank you. Head down this hallway and take the elevator to the fifth floor. She's the fourth room on the right."

She followed the directions all the way to a nameplate that read *Gabrielle Nolan*. Adelaide skimmed a fingertip across it, shaking. *Gabrielle*. She'd seen that name in his emails.

When she opened the door, she heard the machines beeping first. She carefully inched inside, sweeping her eyes over the scene in case there was anything gory she didn't want to see. The room was large with two big couches pushed by a window and a long row of cabinets against one wall, ending in a refrigerator. It was dim in the room, so much so that it took her a moment to realize there was a hospital bed nestled in a corner.

Tucked inside, a frail-looking woman with streaming red hair and a ventilator attached to her face lay silent and unmoving. Her hands were folded over her chest.

Adelaide stood there, looking around, unsure of what to do. No one else was here, except the woman, and she wasn't going to question Adelaide. From the looks of it, she wasn't going to question anything ever again.

She took a step closer, her breath rattling as it escaped her, thrown off by her slamming heartbeat.

Photographs surrounded the woman on the side tables next to the bed, and Adelaide lifted one to assess. In it, a young woman with red hair stood between two older people, all three with hands outstretched toward the sky. Her parents, Adelaide guessed since the features on her face matched that of the older woman's. In the background was a mountain range somewhere unidentifiable. She picked up another. This one featured the redhead in a clubby-looking dress, surrounded by a group of glammed-up women, waving sparklers in the air. There was a cake on the table in front of her, which read *Happy 25th Gabby!*, and several bottles of champagne.

In the next picture, Gabby was a bride, grinning at her father, mid-twirl.

She was a bride in the next one, too, posing with her groom. His eyes were so blue that they leaped out of the frame, his megawatt smile taunting her with its joy. She had never seen him look like that in real life—all excitement and anticipation and indulgence.

Jack was married. To her.

Adelaide about-faced. "I am so sorry."

But of course, Gabrielle Nolan didn't respond. Studying her now, Adelaide could see gray strands woven into the hair near her forehead, a sharper jawline than the soft, almost-teenage one in the pictures. There was a slim gold band encircling her left ring finger.

Adelaide backed away, trying to get her mind around what she was seeing. Jack had committed himself to this woman. He'd had a life with this woman. *Loved* this woman.

No, not past tense. If the condition of the cottage was any indication, he still loved her. He was still holding out hope that she would wake up, that they would be able to continue the lives that they had looked forward to in that photograph. As man and wife.

That explained the contract. The emotional distance. The secrets. He was waiting for her to wake up.

When that realization settled in, she backed out of the room and ran for the exit.

As she reached the glass doors of the lobby, she saw Jack charging inside.

She froze when his eyes found hers. He didn't need to say a word. His posture, the look on his face, told her everything. Jack from last night was gone, and the old version had slipped easily into his place.

"They notify me of every visitor."

She didn't care *how* he'd found her. All she cared about was getting as far away from Jack as possible. Sidestepping him, she beelined for the car, ignoring him when he called her name sharply. She opened the door, hurled herself inside, and stuck the keys in the ignition. By then, he was at her window.

"Adelaide." He wasn't pleading. He was pissed. "Get out of the car." When she didn't, he tried the handle. "Don't act like a child. Where are you going to go?"

She didn't know. She needed to be alone, to think. Somewhere in her mind, she thought to drive home in his car, leave him stranded up here. Put distance between them. But the thought made her physically ill. She stared at the console, wrapped her fingers around the wheel.

"I need to get out of here," she said to no one but herself.

He gestured to the building, his motions jerky with anger, voice muffled through the window. She still caught every word. "This place was not for you! This isn't any of your business."

That had her kicking out of the car, incredulous.

"Not my business?!" she shouted, her voice rising at least three octaves above normal. "Last night, when you were fucking me on my hands and knees, it wasn't my business that you have a *wife?*"

"Keep your voice down," he gritted, looking around for anyone listening.

Adelaide yanked the car door back open. "I'm out of here."

Her mind was spinning, sharp bursts of realization shooting out from her brain at all angles. This was why he was obsessed with having no strings. Not because he didn't want more, but because he *couldn't* have more. And yet last night...

Jack's hand landed on her shoulder. "Adelaide."

She'd stopped short of getting in the car, and she was now just standing there, staring at the dark leather inside.

"You're right. Okay? You're right. But let me explain this to you. You deserve that." When she didn't move one way or the other, his grip tightened. "Dammit, Adelaide, I've never had to do this before. Show me a little grace." His voice got low, closer to her ear. She could feel his body an inch from hers. "Please."

Despite everything, the plaintive tone of his voice turned her to putty. His voice were rough, desperate, and it wore her resolve down so much more easily than she expected.

Above them, a seagull cried mournfully.

She lifted the keys over her shoulder.

He took her to a little coffee shop on the water. They were seated in the enclosed patio, where the sky and water turned varying shades of gray, threatening a snow. Adelaide hugged herself and shivered. She hadn't stopped shivering since she'd pulled up to the facility.

Jack rose wordlessly to drape his jacket around her shoulders, leaving her swaddled in his smell and the lingering warmth from his body.

When he resumed his spot across from her, she watched him wrestle with his own instincts until the guard behind his eyes finally lowered. "Gabrielle and I married young. Mutual friends had introduced us when I was in grad school at UCLA. She taught high school art in New York. Said it was her passion even though she was a beautiful artist in her own right. My unofficial first client, I used to say."

The small smile that touched his mouth nearly broke her.

"I won't say it was perfect, but it was good. We had our ups and downs, like any couple. We were long distance most of the time because of grad school, and then my work took me all over." He paused when the waitress came over and deposited steaming coffees in front of them. "We were very different from each other, honestly. She was a careful person. When I wanted to go charging into adventure, rafting or rock climbing or whatever, she'd always insist on staying home. She wanted that domestic kind of life for herself. For us."

Jack was anything but domestic in her eyes, but she kept quiet.

"Gabby wanted us to live here, in Maine, permanently. She hated the fact that I wanted to be an art dealer, hated anything having to do with the business at all. I used to tease her about it. Tell her she should have married a man without a passport. But then, on her twenty-seventh birthday, she got it in her head that she was getting older, hadn't done enough." He shook his head. "She wanted to go parasailing, but she could only get an appointment during a gallery show I was doing with Rene in New York. And, well … you know the way I am."

Yes, she did. For Jack, it was work first, play second. Always. She pulled his jacket tighter around her shoulders.

"I told her I'd meet her up here later." His voice had been hollow, as if he were speaking about someone else, but now it grew unnaturally hard, as if he was trying to make it that way so it wouldn't break. "Something went wrong. The line broke, and she crashed. When I got to the hospital, she was like you just saw her. It happened on impact, they said." Jack wouldn't—or couldn't—meet her eyes. "She's been that way ever since. Ten years."

Adelaide blinked and realized moisture had pooled in her eyes. She remembered that breathless horror after she'd found out about her parents, the way time had slowed down and sped up simultaneously, her mind spiraling out nonsensically in all directions. The feeling was just as fresh now as it had been then.

"I made a vow on my wedding day, Adelaide. To love and cherish. Sickness and health. And I had been raised by people who believed in that very strongly." His voice caught, and she knew he was thinking of his parents, of all the loss he'd been through in his life. Like her. He was so much more like her than she'd ever imagined. "I meant it when I said, 'Till death do us part.'"

Adelaide hadn't said a word since they'd sat down. But now, she found her eyebrows creasing. "Then, why are you paying me? Why did you ever pay *anyone?*"

"I've always thrown myself into my work, but I doubled down after the accident. That's why I got the reputation, I suppose. But I liked it at the same time—being the ruthless asshole who didn't show a ripple. It scared people off. Kept me insulated. Kept everyone from looking too close at what I didn't want them to see." Jack's eyes wandered out to the water. The sky was mirrored in his irises, turning them from navy to denim. "I couldn't be the person I needed to be with this following me. It wasn't because I didn't love Gabrielle or because I stopped caring about her."

Adelaide forced herself to swallow over the thickness in her throat.

When Jack's eyes slid back to her, his mouth twisted in a thin, sad smile. "We all have to do a bit of shapeshifting to get to where we want. As you very well know."

"So, the reason you pay women is to keep the attention off of this?"

"Primarily, yes. My work is social—you know that. I kept having all these events to go to, and when I showed up alone, it felt so … obvious. And like I said, I enjoyed how insulated it made me. I don't mind scaring people, Adelaide." He gave her a look filled with a hundred different meanings. "But it's been ten years, and my wife isn't coming back. So, what started as something I did for my image became something I did for selfish reasons. I couldn't leave her, but I couldn't be with anyone else either. Paying women let me be … a single man and still keep my word to Gabby." His head dipped, and for the first time in the whole time she'd known him, he seemed embarrassed. "And I can see by the way you're looking at me, that disgusts you. But I didn't know another way."

"Will she ever recover?"

"No. She's gone." He raised his eyebrows at the unasked question in her eyes. "I couldn't bring myself to let her go. She was so young, so vibrant. It just wasn't possible that, one day, I was just going to tell them to take her off the machines—"

She could sense the tears in his throat when he cut off abruptly.

"Why did you bring me here, Jack?"

He lifted a hand like he was going to touch her face, but then, thinking better of it, he brought it back down. "Because I wanted to be with you. Just you, no distractions. I haven't been up here in two years, and I honestly didn't know how the cleaners had left everything. I'm sorry if it felt like … like I brought you to *her* house."

His palms flipped up, as if he was hoping she'd slide a hand in his. She didn't.

"I thought about telling you last night, when we were talking about your parents. But I didn't know how you'd react. Obviously, this didn't go much better."

"If I hadn't found out, would we be having this conversation now?"

"Yes." And now, his hands did slide across the table to cover both of hers, even as she tensed with surprise at his resolve. "When we met, you were so beautiful and frustrating and unsure. I wanted you the first time I saw you. And you seemed so unaffected by me, which didn't help."

"I was affected," she admitted in a whisper, thinking back to the moment in the ballroom when she'd first seen him, his energy reaching out to her like an invisible string.

He pressed his cold lips against her knuckles. "You were the first woman I'd met in years who I thought about just *trying* with. Without the paperwork. Without the rules."

"Jack …" She wanted him to stop telling her this. She shouldn't be letting him talk like this when she was—

"No, you need to hear this." He took a deep breath and looked her straight in the eye. Straight in the soul. "My wife is not coming back. I miss her, but I don't pine for her. I loved her, but I can love someone else. I know you probably see me as heartless, Adelaide, but I promise"—he drew her arm across the table and pressed her palm against his chest, and underneath his sweater, his heart was pumping fast and hard—"it's there. It's beating. And ever since I met you, it feels like you are the reason it still does."

She drew back from the touch because she wasn't sure what to do with something that sounded like *I love you* but wasn't. With a story that could either end as a tragedy or a fairy tale, depending on what she said next. With her own pounding heart. With her own lies.

Jack was waiting for her to say something. She could see the hope in his eyes. But nothing made sense anymore, and she didn't know what to do. How she felt.

"I want to leave," she finally answered.

TWENTY-ONE

The calls started coming as they pulled up to the house and didn't let up. Declan, Declan, Declan. Over and over, his name bubbled on the screen, which she shielded from Jack, who kept cutting his eyes over to her, his expression shifting between worry and longing.

She sent Declan to voice mail again as Jack shut off the car. They sat in silence, except for her phone buzzing almost noiselessly in her hand.

"All I can ask you to remember," Jack said slowly, his hands still on the wheel, "is that I didn't have a road map for what to do. Some decisions I made, and some I was pushed into, and the more time that goes on, the harder it is to remember which was which."

She'd never heard the way she'd felt for the past four years distilled so well. She turned to him, wide-eyed. He *would* understand.

"Jack, I really need to tell you—"

"Who keeps calling you?"

She faltered. "What?"

He pointed to her phone. "It won't stop. You should get it."

"I don't want to."

"It could be an emergency."

"No, would you just listen—"

"Give it to me." His hand came toward her lap.

A panicked sort of muscle memory kicked in, and Adelaide pushed her door open, hopping down onto the gravel, safely out of his reach. She couldn't let him find out about Declan like *that*.

"I'm taking a walk," she announced abruptly. She had to follow through on her jumpiness somehow, even though she had no intention of answering Declan's calls.

"I'll join you. Some of the trails are a little steep. I don't want you getting—"

"I want to be alone." She said it a little more harshly than she'd intended, digging her hands in her pockets and marching away.

She headed down to the bayside, taking the dirt path along the pebble-lined coast.

Maybe she couldn't blame Jack for lying when she was no better, slinking off to deal with her lies. After he'd found out about the paper writing and stood by her, she'd begun to believe that if she told him about Declan blackmailing her, he'd eventually forgive her. She could almost see a future between them, one that extended past the contract.

Now, what future did they have? He was married.

It started to get dark as Adelaide walked, the sky turning a deep indigo, melting into the color of the calm, quiet bay. She was trying to use it to soothe herself when her phone buzzed again.

She was going to give in and answer, but when she opened the screen, she stared down in disbelief. She had over twelve missed calls from Declan. And twenty texts, which got progressively more frantic.

Where are you?

Adelaide?

Hello???

Call me back!

What the fuck? Where are you???

You'd better not be doing anything stupid.

You know he'll never think of you as anything but his whore.

She quickly scrolled through the rest, versions of the same, until she got to the last two, which made her breath hitch. First:

You're on his side now, aren't you?

And second:

It would be a shame if he found out you're lying to him.

A branch cracked behind her, and she nearly jumped out of her skin.

"Adelaide, it's getting dark," Jack huffed, his tall form making its way down the embankment. "And I don't want to keep hiding behind this tree, watching you like a creep."

She pressed a hand against her chest, where her heart slammed in double-time. "You scared me!"

When Jack arrived in front of her, he tugged off his own scarf and wrapped it around her neck. "Be angry with me in a warm house. Unless you'd rather me take you home now?"

Did she want to leave like this? She couldn't decide. She felt stung by his secrets and awkward around him. But she had no idea what Declan was waiting to do at home, and right now, she felt relieved that he didn't know where she was. His threats worried her more than usual. "We can stay tonight."

Jack kept a warm hand between her shoulder blades as they walked, which she didn't fight. She was still shivering.

Inside the cottage, he nudged her upstairs for a hot shower and said he'd wait in the kitchen. Before she climbed into the water, she fired off a quick text to Declan before shutting off her phone completely.

It simply said, *I'm always on your side, Declan. We're friends.*

Let him go to Professor Hargrove with that. Let him call the dean, the president, whoever he wanted. He'd gone round the bend of suspicious and into full-on paranoid, and she was out of her depth. Before, she'd understood the need for justice, but now, Declan seemed to be near compulsive about the paintings. Or was it hurting Jack? Or hurting *her*? Somewhere along the line, all three had seemed to become conflated.

She resolved that as soon as she got back to Cranst, she was going to try and convince him to get some help. Her brother's story still troubled her, and she was worried about how far Declan would go to get what he wanted.

After her shower, she pulled on her pajamas and peeked her head out of the bedroom door to the smell of what she thought was probably roast chicken below. Her stomach, which had been empty all day except for the coffee, rumbled.

She found Jack sitting in the kitchen, working.

Adelaide wasn't offended. Jack had spent the whole of their relationship with work as a priority, and she realized there would be no sense in trying to change him. Plus, it had always made the rare moments when he switched his focus solely to her that much better.

Tonight though, when he met her eyes, she wished he were distracted. His gaze was intense, drinking her in as she stood in the doorway, hair wet and face bare. She could see pain in his eyes, and it made her ache. She wanted to go to him, but she didn't know how. She felt like an intruder in every way.

He stood and held out his hand. "I want to show you something."

Jack motioned her into the chair he'd just vacated. While she sat, he moved across the kitchen, standing in front of the sink with a sliver of his profile and most of his back toward her.

He gazed out the window blankly, waiting.

Of all the things she was expecting, it wasn't an email.

It was between him and Mariana, and a few other lawyers at her firm.

Subject: Nolan v. Nolan

Please start the paperwork for the divorce. Custody to her parents, but all expenses will be handled by me. I'm ready to sign as soon as it's drafted.

—Jack

The rest of the chain was legalese until it got to the last one, which included divorce papers, ready for Jack's signature. It didn't appear he had acted on them yet.

"Look at the date on the email," he directed without moving a muscle.

She scanned back to the initial email he'd sent Mariana and sucked in a surprised breath.

"Right after we got back from London," he clarified. "I knew then, Adelaide. I swear to you, I wasn't planning to hide it forever. I just didn't know how to tell you. And I worried if I told you too soon, I'd lose you. Which worked out spectacularly," he added under his breath.

"You're doing this for me?"

He turned around, leaning back against the counter as he met her eyes. "For you. For me. For Gabby, because her parents are ready to do what I can't bring myself to. What I should have done for her a long, long time ago."

She had too much tact to make him say it outright, and she didn't want to see him struggle more. Even though she still felt the hot rush of betrayal, it was slowly being leeched away by his words, by the way his gaze had turned soft and longing. She knew he wanted something from her, but she wasn't sure what she had to give.

So, instead, she said, "Did you cook?"

They ate at the kitchen table, the cozy fire from last night a memory now. She'd felt so safe and settled under his hands, but now, everything felt different. She'd thought then that it was the start of something, but tonight, it seemed like it was actually the crescendo of something else.

Maybe what she'd done with Declan didn't even matter anymore. Maybe she and Jack were simply too fucked up to make an honest go of it.

Jack said he'd sleep in the guest bedroom.

She thought that was for the best. But she tossed and turned for hours, her mind in a hundred places, each more confusing than the last.

In the velvety part of the night, she crept down the hall to his door. Jack looked at her from his pillow, awake.

At the foot of his bed, she stripped off her clothes and climbed over him, her hair falling like a thick curtain around their faces. When she kissed him, it was deep, so deep that she felt it in every single nerve in her body. She poured everything she couldn't say in words in the kiss, claiming him in a possessive way she hadn't been aware she was capable of feeling. It was more than jealousy. More than fear. He belonged to her now too.

When he finally dragged her hips off of his so she could tumble in the bed next to him, she expected to see the sun coming up.

But it wasn't. Not yet. For now, they still had the murky night to hide themselves in as they molded together to sleep. Soon, daylight would ask all the questions they didn't want to answer, but for now, there was just this.

Them.

TWENTY-TWO

Adelaide woke up to her head on her own pillow and Jack's on his, their hands tangled together in the small gap between them. He was still asleep, so she had uninterrupted time to study the strong features of his face, the steady breath in his chest.

It hit her with no warning and very little fanfare—she loved this man. She'd loved him before the events of yesterday, and she loved him now.

She'd done the very thing the arrangement was supposed to ward against.

Like she'd called his name, Jack's eyes opened and focused on her. They stared at each other for a few heartbeats, watching the other. Testing.

Then, his hand locked around the back of her neck and drew her toward him, so he could kiss her. Hard. When she moaned, his tongue darted between her lips, catching hers and dragging it into his mouth as he rolled her on her back, crowding her body possessively.

They were both still naked from the night before, so when her legs opened around him, they were skin to skin, electric and effortless in the same moment.

"I want you," Jack whispered, nudging her thighs wider. He brought his forehead to hers and added, "To forgive me."

I want you to forgive me.

Stupid, stupid man.

"I already have," she insisted when he tilted her head back to kiss her throat. "Please, Jack. I already have."

He slid inside her gently. So gently that it scared her. A tear leaked down her cheek, which he caught with his mouth.

"Stop it," he murmured, moving to kiss another that had slipped out of the opposite eye. "Stop that, sweet girl."

Adelaide buried her face in his neck and clung to him when he started swiveling his hips, whimpering when he went too fast, begging when he went too slow. She sucked at his neck, inhaled him, until it was all too much, and she broke apart, crying his name into his chest over and over until something released in him too.

They fell asleep again, tangled up in each other.

When she opened her eyes, it was afternoon. Jack was in the shower, and she joined him there, sticking her face directly into the spray, letting the hot water soothe her tired skin. He laughed and did the same, and then they were taking turns, playing a silly game that had no rules, except *make the other person laugh.*

When they tired of it, he pulled her into his arms. "Want to hear some good news?"

She nodded.

"I know how to make pancakes."

He mixed the batter while she sat on the counter next to him, dangling her feet. She'd put on one of his shirts and a sweater; he was in sweatpants and no shirt. Adelaide loved him like this. She was sure Gabby had too. She knew nothing about the woman, yet this felt like a strange net cast between the two, connecting them.

"My sister never wanted to talk about my parents," she told Jack quietly, eyes on his hands. "After they were gone, she wouldn't even say their names." When he stopped stirring and looked her, she impulsively reached up to brush his cheekbone. "You should stop pretending like she doesn't exist."

"I don't know how to do that and make you feel like you aren't playing second fiddle."

"I don't feel like that," Adelaide answered honestly. "Right now, I'm mostly wishing I could have met her."

Jack smiled. "You would have liked Gabby. She was insanely funny. And quite a good artist. I probably have some of it around."

"See?" She nudged him. "It's nice talking about her."

He nodded as he doled out a ladle of batter, which sizzled in the pan.

"Show me her work."

"After breakfast."

Conversation made its way back to normal as they ate, the emotional drama of the day before feeling like a bad memory now. Yes, he was married, but what could she do? Walk away from him forever because of the shit in his past? Because he hadn't been completely forthright with something that was obviously deeply painful for him?

She couldn't play judge and jury with this when she herself still had a few things to clear up. Which she decided to do once and for all right when they got back to Cranst. Things were too shaky right now. They were just making their way back to each other. She needed another few hours to make sure they were solid before she told him everything.

She'd just finished packing her duffel when Jack appeared in the bedroom doorway.

"Come with me. I'll show you Gabby's work before we go."

He led her downstairs to a locked door in a hallway off the kitchen she remembered trying yesterday. Producing a key, he opened it, letting a surprising gust of cool air slip out.

She followed him downstairs into a place that she expected to look like a basement, but was surprisingly high-tech. There were dozens of floor-to-ceiling storage racks lining the walls, each housing several paintings encased in clear acrylic.

"Whoa," she breathed.

"Yeah," Jack agreed. "It's temperature-controlled to preserve the artwork. I had all this installed a while ago for my personal collections."

She watched closely as he slid one drawer open and rifled through various plastic-coated folios.

"For a long time after Gabrielle's injury, I couldn't look at anything she'd painted. It was too raw. But maybe that was wrong," he said thoughtfully, pinching his eyebrows at the items moving through his fingers. "I was scared to tell anyone about her, like she was some kind of dirty secret. But it hurt me, too, because I never got to talk about her. Remember all the good parts of her. I don't want to do to myself what your sister did to you."

Adelaide nodded, trailing her own fingers across one of the racks. "There are so many," she remarked.

Declan's warning came back to her. *He could be keeping the paintings there.*

"Are they all Gabby's?"

Jack pulled out a large canvas done in what she thought was watercolor, which depicted a spot she recognized from her walk last night. Except this was taken in the summertime. Flowers and trees were bursting around the shoreline and in the water, someone was swimming, waving at the artist.

"It's me." He chuckled, holding it at arm's length. "She did this shortly before her accident." He nodded and put the picture next to him. "I think I'd like to take one back with me. Would it bother you if I did that?"

"Huh?" She'd begun scanning the labels. "Uh, no. Jack, are all of these pictures Gabby's?"

"Hmm?" he murmured absently. "No, there are others from my collection here." He pulled out another box, buried deeper. "I'm looking for one she did in New Mexico. At some point, I mixed up a box of hers and someone else's. Yes, see, this is a collection called—"

Jack went silent. He pulled out a large canvas from the box, dragging the plastic off as he did.

"Adelaide."

She couldn't see what it was at first, and then he shifted, his face oddly blank.

"What the hell are you doing in my basement?"

When she saw the painting, her face fell. It had been six years, but she could still recognize the lines, the colors, the texture of the canvas. The basement and the schnapps, the way Declan's complicated eyes had gazed at her with such intensity as his pencil sketched out her shape. She was younger, quieter, naiver, but undoubtedly, this was her own reflection.

Her breath hitched as she attempted to wrap her mind around what was in front of her. She'd had no idea Declan had even kept it.

"It's you." Jack turned around to face her fully, staring at her like she was a ghost.

"No, it isn't," she lied automatically. Then cringed.

Jack's eyes narrowed. "Then, why does it say your name?"

Their eyes simultaneously drifted to her signature, barely a smudge of charcoal pencil on the old canvas, but legible nonetheless.

Adelaide Wright.

She'd forgotten Declan had made her sign her own damn name.

Jack's eyes tore into her, as if they could already read everything in her head. "Why are you lying to me, Adelaide?"

Her mouth opened and then closed. In that single instant, everything became clear. She wasn't just obsessed with Jack's good looks, his bossiness, his wealth, or even the sex. No, she loved this man—*really* loved him. She fell deeper by the second every time she was with him. He was terrible and frustrating and complicated, and then something would crack open, and he'd reveal a different, softer self underneath. Everything about the way they'd happened was fucked up, but she didn't care anymore. None of it mattered because she felt this way about him now.

So, she had to tell him the truth. No more secrets, no more lies.

"I can explain."

He kept his hands on the painting, waiting, his face revealing nothing, save for his clenched jaw.

"I knew him, the artist who painted that. I grew up next door to him. His name is Declan—"

"I know who did the painting, Adelaide." His voice was deadly cold.

She forged ahead. "I hadn't seen him in years, and then one day, he showed up at Cranst. He was a teaching assistant there, and he—" Her voice faltered. The way he was looking at her was making her fumble over her words. "He found out I was writing papers for other people. He told me that the only way he wouldn't turn me into the school was if I helped him." She'd been so sure yesterday that Jack would understand, and yet now, she felt fear creeping in. "He blackmailed me, Jack. He—he wanted me to seduce you. He wanted me to get you to pay me so that I could get close to you and find out where you kept the paintings you'd stolen from him—"

"He told you I *stole* paintings from him?" Shock cracked his face wide open. "And you *believed* him?"

"I didn't know what to believe!" Adelaide insisted, her voice climbing. "He knew about the papers, and he was threatening me, and it wasn't like you were treating me very nicely," she blubbered, speaking faster than her mind could keep up with, desperate to make him understand. "I just wanted to graduate, Jack. I wanted to get away from him without getting expelled. But then I got to know you, and things are so different with us now. I've never told anyone the things I've told you. Trusted anyone the way I trust you. And I don't even care that you took the paintings because Declan is—"

"Stop. Talking." Jack's jaw was set, eyes fiery. He set her portrait down gently, but came back up vibrating. "You lied to me for *months*, Adelaide. Over and over again. Were you just rummaging through my life behind my back?"

"No, Jack, I didn't—"

"Who are you?" he demanded, repulsed.

She cowered, her heart shattering at his response. Before indignation swelled in her chest. She'd been willing to see past his deceit, his secrets. But he wasn't able to do her the same courtesy?

"How can you say that?" she snapped back. "You kept your wife a secret from the world—from *me*—for how long? I didn't hold that against you."

"I kept a personal secret, Adelaide. You lied straight to my fucking face! You *manipulated* me. And the fact that you believed *him*—"

"Manipulated you?" she repeated, incredulous. "You want to talk about manipulation, Jack? Go ahead. You are the master."

"What is that supposed to mean?"

"It means, you didn't come to me, contract in hand. You worked me up to it nice and slow. You made me want you first, and then you made me your whore. *That* was manipulation."

"Adelaide." He shook his head, a dark smile coming into the corner of his mouth. She hated it. "I told you exactly how I felt about you in the beginning. And if we're really talking manipulation, it's Declan who's screwing with you. I never stole any of his paintings."

"Then, why are they *here*?"

But Jack wasn't going to be drawn into an explanation. "What were you going to do, hmm? Find the paintings and steal them out from under me? Tell him where they were, so he could break in and get them?"

"No," she protested, but her voice was weak. "I was going to tell him to forget it. I was going to tell you everything when we got back and—"

"Like you told me about the paper-writing?"

"Jack."

He paced in a circle, hands raking through his hair. "You did a good job, Adelaide—I'll give you that. Seriously, what a performance. Last night? This morning? You had me eating out of your fucking hand."

Impulsively, he turned around and dragged a large acrylic box out from a shelf. With a grunt, he shot it across the floor, where it skidded to a stop at her feet. In big black marker, someone had labeled it—*Jones, Declan. Abscission Collection.*

Her picture was a part of the fucking collection.

"Take it," he snarled through clenched teeth. "Take it back to him then, if that's where your loyalty is."

"Please, Jack."

But he was already shaking his head. "We're done here."

She could sense him withdrawing, his features pulling back and molding into that cold, cold man she knew well.

He pointed to the door. "That's where this story ends."

"So, now that you say it's over, it's over?" Tears started to leak from the corners of her eyes, but unlike this morning, there was no Jack to kiss them away. This man—who'd held her in her lowest moments; who, minutes ago, she'd imagined a life with—was staring at her like a stranger. Betrayal mixed with pain. "I was right about you, you know," she spat. "All those weeks ago. You *are* a hypocrite."

It didn't dent him. "Your final payment will be in your account next week."

Before she could say anything else, he turned his back on her and walked slowly up the stairs. The silence in the room was deafening. The conversation was over.

Everything was over.

She backed away from the paintings, the eyes in her own portrait following her, casting judgment. Turning away from them, she went to the stairs, wondering how one so easily surrendered something they cared about.

Maybe it just proved they never cared at all.

By the time they arrived back at Cranst, Adelaide could barely breathe.

She'd spent the entire car ride feeling as though she was being suffocated, torn between wanting to pour her heart out to him again and feeling too prideful to say a single damn word. In the end, they'd made the entire drive in silence.

When they pulled onto the campus, the sky had turned gray, and a hard, icy rain was falling. The windshield wipers, on full blast, weren't doing enough, and the windows were frosting over.

Her apartment looked dark. Uninviting. Katy usually worked nights, and Imogen was away with friends. Not that either would have much sympathy for her at this point.

Dread pooled in her stomach as she thought about going up there, into that cold, empty apartment. She wanted his arms around her; she wanted to sink against his chest and let him hold her. Desperately. Even if it was just for a moment. She felt starved for it, terrified at the loss.

"Jack …"

"I'll return any of your effects left at the apartment."

He looked beyond her, at the door—her signal to get out. It was that easy for him to say good-bye. Maybe Declan was right. Maybe he'd never think of her as anything but a whore.

When she slipped out of his car, he still didn't react.

She turned to him, letting the icy rain pelt her face. "I just want you to know, what happened this weekend doesn't change things for me. I'm sorry if it does for you."

He stared straight ahead, his hands wrapped tight around the steering wheel. "Good-bye, Adelaide."

"Good-bye," she whispered, but he was already pulling away from the curb, his taillights disappearing into the distance.

She went up to her room, picked up her phone, and did the only thing left to do. She called Declan.

"I know where your paintings are," she informed him, her voice toneless.

"You saw them? You're sure? Where? Which ones?"

Adelaide skipped over all of those questions. "You didn't tell me you'd put me in the collection."

Declan was silent for a beat. "Your picture *started* the collection, Adelaide."

She waited for him to catch on to her meaning. She could sense the understanding when it happened.

"He realized it was a picture of you."

"Yes," she whispered, stomach rolling.

Declan processed that, then snorted. "That's too bad. You'll still need to find a way to get those paintings, though. That was part of the deal. Not that you find them, but that you bring them to me."

"That was not our deal, Declan. And besides, that's impossible."

"It's not impossible."

She closed her eyes. "Yes, it is. I can never go there again."

There was another long silence on his end. "Because you're in love with him."

She didn't confirm or deny. She was, and she wasn't. Could she love someone who had left her like this?

"I did everything I could. It's over, Declan. Tell Hargrove or don't. I'm done."

If they expelled her, if they dragged her name through the mud, so what? Her life was already in shambles. Maybe this would just be her karma coming back to her after everything she'd done—at Cranst and with Jack. She'd played the system, and perhaps it was just her time to get caught.

"Stupid," Declan muttered. Then, he started laughing. "You are so stupid."

She ended the call, climbed into her bed, and sobbed.

TWENTY-THREE

California welcomed her with beautiful weather and the smoothest flight she'd ever taken.

It figured that everything revolving around Samantha's wedding would be perfect, even for the guests. It was as if her sister's iron will had been cast over the very universe, ensuring no one would have a single blemished memory of the weekend.

Even the traffic, which she remembered as generally horrendous, wasn't that bad. She arrived at Samantha and Bear's Beverly Hills mansion right on time.

As she got out of the car and looked up at what was once her interim home, her heart, which had grown permanently heavy in her chest, felt like it'd gained ten pounds.

Two Jack-less weeks had passed since the cataclysmic weekend in Maine, and if possible, everything that had happened stung more than before. At first, she had some sort of hope the situation was temporary, but with every silent day that passed, she fell deeper into despair.

The only indication she'd had that Jack thought of her at all was a final check deposited into her account. Then, silence.

As for Declan, she'd never gotten a call from the administration telling her she was getting kicked out of Cranst, so that was a good sign. She had no idea what he was going to do about the paintings now, and she honestly preferred it that way. She didn't want any part of his scheming. And if he was going to turn her in, she'd rather not see it coming. Ignorance, she'd seen, was truly bliss.

Cut off from Jack though, she wasn't exactly flush with cash anymore. Her once-comfortable finances had begun to dwindle. She wasn't desperate yet, but she would be, come graduation, when her school loans came due.

She wouldn't let herself go back to paper writing—ever. The stakes were too high now; she was too close to the finish line. Beyond that, her choices for moneymaking were slim. Except for the possibility of her inheritance.

So, here she was. She'd show up, get the money, and get out.

But looking up at the ostentatious home, crawling with caterers and florists and party planners, she felt her resolve waver.

The large double doors shot open and revealed her soon-to-be brother-in-law, Bear Wilcox, grinning at her around a spoonful of ice cream. "Adel-le-he-whooo!" he called, opening up his arms.

Bear was six feet six inches of pure muscle with dark blond hair and hazel eyes. He played tight end for the Los Angeles Goldens, and while his face was boyish, his imposing frame was anything but. He was even more buff than she remembered. Today, he wore a henley shirt and jeans, no shoes, and a backward fitted cap.

She slowly moved up the front steps and into his embrace, careful not to get her hair in his open container of Ben & Jerry's.

"Look at you, kiddo. I like your hair. Shit, I'm so happy you're here, *sister-in-law*."

She couldn't *not* smile.

Of all the things Samantha had gotten lucky with, Adelaide would rank Bear close to the top of the list. He was rich, hot, and treated Samantha's outbursts like an odd quirk and not a fatal flaw.

Only once in the entire six months she'd lived with them had she actually seen him yell, and it was the night Adelaide had packed her bags and left for Cranst, two weeks early and with tears leaking down her cheeks. The decision to go had been made swiftly, after a cataclysmic fight in which her sister had finally admitted she blamed Adelaide for their parents' death.

Samantha had locked herself in her bedroom and refused to come out to say good-bye. Bear stood outside the door for an hour, bellowing at her to get her ass downstairs and talk to her sister. To fix things.

Samantha didn't listen, and Adelaide's cab arrived.

Bear walked her out and pressed a thousand dollars cash and a credit card into her hand. "Please use this, Addie," he'd pleaded. "I'll pay it, no questions asked. And call me when you get there. I want to know what's going on."

She kept the cash but snapped the card. The money got her to Connecticut and put her up in a shitty motel for a week until she finally convinced someone at the Cranst housing office to let her into her dorm early. She called Bear once she got there.

They'd kept in sporadic touch, mostly because Bear was a busy person with an incredibly rigorous training schedule. But he always called her on her birthday and any major holiday, reminding her she was welcome to come back at any time. She'd never had the heart to ask if Samantha knew he'd told her that.

"I'm happy I'm here too," she lied.

"It's gonna be a sick party. Wait until you see the grotto. Samantha turned it upside down. Come on. Let's go say hi."

Adelaide wouldn't expect anything less. When Samantha threw herself into a project, she went all in. She'd been a perfectionist her entire life, and her wedding would undoubtedly be the most perfect of all.

As they walked through the foyer, there came a sound from outside, like something crashing or maybe even shattering. A high-pitched voice launched into a diatribe. She didn't need to see the speaker to know who it belonged to.

Bear chewed on his lip and said, "You know what? Let's get your bag upstairs first. We'll see Samzilla later."

He motioned for her to follow him upstairs. She looked around as they climbed. Her sister had obviously gotten her hands on most of the furnishings because when they'd first moved in, everything about the place had screamed *bachelor pad*. Back then, Bear had been living like a total party boy. She had no idea why he'd ever wanted Samantha and her teenage sister to move in, but he never treated her like a nuisance. Most days, he'd been more family to her than her own sister.

"We put you in your room, obviously," he told her as they rounded the corner to the hallway.

"Oh, I'm fine with any spot."

Bear peeked over his shoulder, a bewildered smile on his face. "Addie, we didn't just, like, pack up your room. It's the same as it always was."

He wasn't kidding. It was as if her eighteen-year-old self only left for a weekend, not three and a half years. The bedspread was different, and there was a bouquet of fresh flowers on the desk, but they'd left it as she had that night she left for Cranst. There was even an old pair of her slippers lined up by the bed.

"Get settled. I'll tell your sister you're here. We have everyone coming in an hour for the luncheon. Michael is already on his way." Before he left, Bear pulled her into a massive hug that nearly dented her lungs. "Thank you for coming. Seriously, Addie. It means everything to us."

"Of course." She forced a smile, trying to be polite. No one had hugged her since Jack and an unfamiliar set of arms felt irksome.

She'd told herself that she would focus on the inheritance this weekend, but thoughts of him slipped back into her brain the second she was alone. It was always that way nowadays. Every look, every kiss, those precious final days with him, turbulent as they'd been. Her mind went over and over those moments, reliving them, searching them.

Trying to trace the logic made her unhappy on a regular day. Today, alongside the extended wave of déjà vu being back in this room produced, she was downright miserable. This place had been her hell and haven for the six months she lived here, witness to some of her darkest days. It felt like she'd made it back, only for the walls to witness a few more.

Adelaide braced herself with every step as she made her way to the luncheon one hour later.

The money, she repeated silently. *Shut up and take the money.*

Lunch was cocktail-style, held around the sparkling in-ground pool, which she noticed had also been upgraded. An intricate tile design had been added to the floor and walls, and there were rocks building out the grotto, plus a new waterfall. Trees and plants bloomed around the edges like they'd sprouted up naturally. As for the rest of the landscaping, it was lush and divine, the sloping lawn surrounded by mountains with slight views of the city below. All the way at the opposite end, Adelaide could make out a giant tent.

As a teenager, she'd hated being around the kinds of well-heeled people currently roaming the lawn. They'd always made her feel awkward and inept. But being with Jack had taught her what to say and how to act. Cruelly, she'd grown into an adult during the arrangement, as if acting like another version of herself had actually pushed her into being one. Now, she didn't know how to go back to the old version.

Just as she was getting lost in the crowd, a hand wrapped around her elbow, turning her around.

Michael was smiling behind his sunglasses. "You missing someone?"

Knowing he meant Jack, she slowly shook her head.

Michael gave her a sad smile and a quick hug. "I'm sorry, Ads. Let's get a drink."

In the time it took to get two glasses of wine, the party doubled in size.

"So, what happened? You two get into a fight?" Michael asked when they wandered to a quiet spot at the fringes of the crowd.

She glared at him. She'd hoped that the sunny, warm weather, so removed from the frigid temperatures and gloomy gray sky of Cranst, would help her mood. But it hadn't. And it was making her bitter. "Why would I subject him to this?"

"I think you would, if only to have a buffer between you and her. You know Samantha would have to be on her best behavior then."

"Right," she scoffed, tilting her face toward the sun. She took a deep breath. "The truth is, we're not together anymore. We haven't been."

"Ah. Well, you were very different." Michael didn't need to say *told you so*; she knew him well enough that it was implied. "How about school? That must be a good distraction. Graduation and all."

She took a surly sip of her wine, which was crisp and delicious on her tongue. She was positive Samantha had had a sommelier pick it out. "I have finals first. Next week. Then, I have to wait until May if I want to walk in a ceremony, but I really don't care. I'll get the diploma in the mail." *It's not like anyone else would be there to cheer me on.*

"And then what?"

Her chest tightened. She really didn't want to have the *what are you going to do with your life* conversation right now. "Look for a job in the city, I guess."

By then, she'd have her inheritance.

"Well, if you need any help networking—"

"Michael," she said, holding up a firm hand. Guests were pressing in closer now, forcing them to move shoulder to shoulder. "I'm not here for the fun of it. I'm here to collect my money. As soon as Samantha signs it over to me, I'm out of here. And I don't plan on coming back."

"Ads," he said gently, "that's harsh. It's her wedding. Can't we all just get along for once?"

"No, we can't. And don't look at me like I'm some obstinate child, Michael, because this is on her."

"Look, you of all people know how she is. She's good with taking control. She's not good with emotions. Some people play tough. She plays perfect. She doesn't want anyone to see her looking less than that. Even you. *Especially* you."

Adelaide gave him a doubtful look. "Why would she care?"

"Think of it this way. Did you ever see Mom have any emotion other than *perfectly fine?* No. Because she was your guardian. That's who Samantha was trying to be. For you. For us. Stability. But you had other ideas, and she couldn't deal with it. So"—he shrugged—"she made mistakes. But I still think you each need to cut the other a little slack. We were all devastated. We just dealt with it in different ways."

Adelaide shook her head at his little speech and watched her sister across the lawn, moving easily through the crowds, hamming it up with whoever stopped her. She was frighteningly pretty, as always. She'd opted for a trendy white pantsuit today, her hair slicked back in a perfect platinum bun, her feet nearly vertical in her heels. Dressed to ensure people would envy her.

Yet, shallow or not, Samantha seemed happy. Maybe it was because she was finally becoming the trophy wife she'd always wanted to be, but Adelaide knew her sister, and it seemed more genuine than that. Samantha had managed to form a life out here.

She felt the slightest bit jealous.

As if she felt her watching, Samantha cut her eyes over to her siblings. She beamed at Michael, tugging Bear from his conversation to fight their way over to them.

"You can be a part of it, you know," Michael murmured, like he was reading her thoughts. "You're going to have to accept her for what she is though."

When Samantha and Bear stopped in front of them, her sister gave no hint that she felt awkward about Adelaide's presence. "Addie," she chirped, putting a hand on her shoulder and giving her a kiss that barely brushed her cheek. Samantha's perfume surrounded her like her own personal cloud. "You look cute."

"Thanks," Adelaide said stiffly. She was having a hard time meeting Samantha's eye. "Place looks different."

"Upgrades," she sighed absently, at the same time someone called her name from across the lawn. "We have to go mingle, but we'll all have dinner together tonight and talk. Glad you made it."

And that was it.

Three and a half years of buildup for fifteen seconds.

"I expected worse," Adelaide ceded when Michael turned up his chin at her.

"You expected *the* worst," he corrected. "Give her a chance this weekend, Ads. For me. For ..." His voice cracked unexpectedly. "For them."

But with everything else shredding her insides, she couldn't have him tug at that thread too. So she did what would shut him up.

She smiled.

As quickly as the luncheon was cleared away, another setup began to take its place.

Once the guests departed, a fresh crew started assembling tomorrow's layout, hauling in tables and chairs and massive chandeliers that they began stringing up over the pool. *Some backyard wedding.*

The opulence ticked her off all over again.

Dinner for the family was being served in the dining room—another spot they'd redone since her last visit. Now, it looked like something out of a design magazine with its creamy tones and mismatched patterns. Then again, Samantha didn't work. What else did she have to do all day?

As Adelaide sat down, she could feel her sister scrutinizing her through her fake eyelashes. Adelaide's extensions had fallen off in proportion to the amount she'd cried, which, in the past few weeks, had been quite a lot.

She stared at her plate as everyone settled in.

"So, Adelaide," Samantha said once Bear poured them all wine, "tell me about this mystery man you're with. Is he arriving tomorrow?"

Adelaide glared at Michael, but he and Bear were pretending to discuss some sporting event. She could feel their ears on the conversation though—neither were that subtle. "Actually, there's nothing to tell. We broke up."

Her eyes narrowed. "That's a shame."

"Not really."

"I'm sure it was for the best. Michael said he was quite a bit older than you. Men that age, who haven't settled down yet ... you have to wonder about them. They're usually perpetual playboys. Try not to take it too hard. He was probably using you."

"Samantha," Michael warned, his head turning an inch.

A hot knife of pain stabbed straight through her chest. Jack *had* used her. Used her and left her like it was nothing.

"I'm just saying it because I know you didn't date much when you were younger. And you really have to look out for men like that. I'd hate to see your heart get stomped over."

Adelaide fisted her napkin under the table. No mention of how Samantha had already stomped all over her heart by wrenching her away from her home. And for what? This glitz, this glamour, this illusion of a perfect life? Who was it perfect for? Because it'd felt like a prison at seventeen, and it felt like one now too. "I can take care of myself. After all, I have been for the past three and a half years."

Samantha didn't break her stare. "That was your choice."

"I don't know," Adelaide drawled, casually sipping her drink, though her knuckles were white around the glass. "It wouldn't have been a choice if we'd just stayed in Connecticut."

"We had to move here." Samantha kept her voice intentionally calm. "You know that."

"Guys," Michael warned again, giving Bear a look as if to say, *Do something about your fiancée.*

But Adelaide knew he wouldn't. Bear wasn't like that; he only opened his mouth when he felt Samantha's actions were truly indefensible. At least in public. She was pretty sure that behind closed doors, they could duke it out with the best of them.

"Did we?" Adelaide snapped, leaning across the table. "You did it to escape. You left everything about them behind. Except their money … which you still refuse to give me my fair share of."

Samantha's lips curled. "Is the money all that matters to you?"

"It's the only reason I'm here. Once I get it, I'm gone. Forever. I'll never see you again."

"Addie," Samantha scoffed, shaking her head. "You don't care about your family? Not about being here—*together*—after we lost so much?"

"No!" she shouted in response. But the second it came out of her mouth, she flashed to Thanksgiving in Aspen, to that lonely feeling that had come over her. She'd missed them that night.

"Adelaide!" Michael cried, hurt all over his face. "How can you say that?"

"Because you all treat me like I'm some angry little orphan instead of looking at *her*, the entire reason I *am* angry. But that's okay, really. Just give me the money, and you can all go back to your pretty, perfect lives without the complication of your little sister."

"You think our lives have been perfect?" her brother retorted. "You have no idea what's happened here since you've been gone." He looked at Samantha and Bear for backup, but they both shot him a look that very clearly said, *Leave it alone.* Michael shook his head. "We might have been together, Ads, but we haven't been a family since you left. And you," he said, now turning to Samantha, "you owe her an apology."

Their sister's features pinched. "I'm not apologizing for wanting to keep our family together."

"That's not what I mean, and you know it."

Samantha licked her lips and glared at Michael for a beat. Then, dismissively, she waved her hand.

"I'm going," Adelaide announced, pushing back from the table.

She couldn't take another minute of this. The money wasn't worth opening up old wounds with her family. They'd never heal; they'd only get worse. She'd never been so disgusted with her sister as she was right then.

"You leave now, and you will *never* get the money," Samantha hissed.

Adelaide laughed darkly. "Maybe so. But at least I don't have to live every day, knowing how fucking disappointed Mom and Dad would be in me. Not the way you do. And they would be, Samantha. They'd be so damn disappointed to see you now."

Samantha recoiled, as if she'd been slapped.

With the bitter satisfaction of those words buoying her, Adelaide spun on her heel and stormed out the front door, down the massive driveway, and out the front gates. She called an Uber that slid to an easy stop in front of her on the street and climbed inside. They could ship her luggage back to her or burn it. She was too angry to care.

By the time they hit the highway though, something crawled into Adelaide's stomach in justice's place. It was cold and clammy, even worse than she'd felt before.

She knew she'd done enough damage to push her family away for good.

Except now, she had no Jack. Her roommates thought she was a liar. She didn't even have Declan.

Adelaide was completely on her own.

TWENTY-FOUR

The flight home was terrible. Too much turbulence, a long delay, and the plane had shuttled to different airports because of inclement weather. Rain was *still* pummeling the windshield when the taxi pulled up to her apartment, fat, cold drops that chilled her as she stepped out of the backseat.

The campus was unnaturally quiet for the middle of the night, when tipsy partygoers usually peppered the streets, so it jarred her more than usual when her phone screeched a second after she entered her apartment.

It was Declan. She hadn't spoken to him in two weeks, and she was angry with him for avoiding her. Angry with the world for a million other things too.

She answered, ready to tell him off. "Declan," she snarled, her temper taking over, "I don't want to be involved in whatever it is—"

"Addie." His voice didn't sound like him. It was distant, far away, like it was being transmitted through cotton wool.

For a second, she thought someone had hijacked his phone.

She had no idea what quality in his voice provoked it, but a flash of fear shot through her. Something was off. "Declan? What's wrong?"

"Nothing. Everything. Nothing anymore."

She could hear what sounded like wind around him. Was he outside? In *this*?

"I just wanted to tell you I'm sorry. Sorry about everything that I did to you. I didn't mean it. I didn't mean to drag you into this." His voice trembled.

Was he crying?

Shit. That sounded like a good-bye. A permanent one.

She looked around, helpless. "Declan, what are you talking about?"

"I've hurt a lot of people, Addie. You more than anyone. And I didn't mean to. I just don't have anything left. Not even my art. And ..." There was a long pause. "And I just need to end it."

She froze. Somehow, she was halfway to her apartment door, as if her instincts had moved her feet by themselves. "End what? Declan, what are you saying?"

"I just wanted to say good-bye," he said, but his voice was interrupted by the very loud sound of a bell clanging.

"Declan!"

But the line went dead.

He attempted suicide, Michael's voice rang in her ears.

He'd been unhinged, desperate. Not himself.

No, no, no, no, no.

Frantic, Adelaide flew out of her apartment building, rushing outside, only to be pelted with freezing cold rain. *Where the hell would he be?*

The bell in the old Cranst clock tower chimed the hour.

The bell. The clock tower. Right by his office.

Shit.

She raced down the street, toward the campus square. The clock tower was behind it, tucked in by a long stretch of campus green. She sprinted past houses and buildings that were quiet, dark because of the hour. Even fraternity row was suspiciously inactive. She splashed through puddles on her way, and by the time she reached the green and caught the old tower in the distance, she was thoroughly drenched.

The clock tower had never been of much interest to Adelaide in all of her years at Cranst. It was the requisite old, ivy-covered stone architecture that made a school like Cranst look collegiate. For maybe the first time since that stupid ghost tour freshman year, she gazed up at the illuminated, moon-like clock face, shielding her eyes from the rain. Squinting, she tried to spot Declan, but a new deluge had started, and it was far too dark.

Someone had fallen by accident once, she remembered.

Or was it?

Grabbing her phone, she punched in 911, barking orders to whoever answered to come to the tower as she raced across the lawn. Every moment was of the essence. She flew so fast that she could barely feel her feet, touching the pavement and then the grass.

When she got to the base of the tower, a jagged edge of lightning split the sky, and she spotted him, standing on the ledge of the roof, arms outstretched, like he was preparing to fly.

"Declan!" she screamed, still clutching the phone to her ear. "No!"

He didn't even look down. She waved her arms, but he seemed focused on something in the sky.

The rain was falling even harder now, mixing with thick, giant snowflakes. She desperately looked around, but the campus was empty. No ambulance, no security guards. Who knew how far off the police were? There was no one else to help her.

Circling the base of the tower, she dived forward, grabbing hold of the door handle and wrenching it open. It gave with a creak. Throwing herself through the door, she raced up the stairs, her muscles burning with effort.

When she reached the top, she flung open the door to the roof. Declan was standing with his back to her, balancing precariously. She gasped at the sight of it. He heard and whipped around, and for a moment, she thought he might lose his balance and topple off. Her heart lurched.

Hair hanging in wet ropes upon his face, he grabbed ahold of one of the rafters instead. A flannel shirt and dark jeans hung, waterlogged, on his now painfully slim frame.

"Don't, Adelaide," he yelled, desperate and woeful at the same time. "Don't try to convince me. I didn't call you because I wanted you to come here."

"Please, Declan. Let's just talk. Come down from there," she begged.

Thunder boomed overhead, and he turned away. "Talk about what? I've lost everything."

She crept closer, struggling to hear him over the storm. Or was it the roaring in her ears? "Maybe you don't have the paintings, but you're so talented, Declan. Everyone thinks it. You have so much to live for, and this *will* get better."

"I'm a fucking TA," he snarled, whipping his head towards her so fast he swayed.

"It doesn't matter to me what you are," she continued, coming closer. "*Please*. I care about you, Declan."

He blinked, leaning forward, as if he hadn't heard. "You *care* about me? I ruined your fucking life."

"Maybe so, but I'm trying to fix it! I'm making it better!" She was pleading now. "Please, Declan. I've lost too many people. I don't want to lose you too."

His features seemed to soften just slightly as the first sirens screamed through the night. Rain spattered against his face, but she couldn't miss the look of absolute betrayal that clouded his features. "You called the cops?"

"Because I care about you. Because you need help—"

"I needed *your* help, Addie. I needed you, and you went and fell in love with him instead. You turned on me. Why did you do that, Addie?" he shouted at her, his right foot sliding halfway off the ledge. "How could you fucking do that?"

She'd only wanted to help, and now, all reason was abandoned. She'd made things worse. He turned his gaze back towards the ground, his fingers loosening their grip on the rafter.

In a split second, Adelaide made a desperate decision.

Flinging herself toward him, she grabbed the back of his flannel shirt with both hands and yanked him as hard as she could. She felt it as he lost his balance, his shoes slipping from the ledge, careening this way and that before finally falling backward, onto her. As he fell, he delivered a hard elbow to her collarbone, and her head flew back against something iron. The resulting clang made her see stars. She was dizzy and under Declan's full weight, and her knees gave out like a house of cards.

They fell together, a tangle of limbs on the floor.

She thought that was it. Hoped he'd come back to himself or had gotten knocked unconscious or something. She didn't have any more strength left in her.

But Declan wasn't done. He peeled away from her, reaching for the ledge.

"No!" she shouted, gripping his arm.

He wrenched himself away, nudged her down. She grabbed again, only managing to get ahold of the hem of his shirt. The resulting rip was drowned out by the sound of the relentless rain.

"Declan!"

He shrugged out of his flannel and stood there in a dripping black T-shirt, gazing at her with an expression that brought terror into her throat. This time, he slowly approached the ledge, determination in his gait.

"Please!" she cried, scrambling to her feet. Too slow, too slow.

He already had a leg over.

"You can paint me again!" she screamed desperately. "You might not have the pictures, but you can start over with me."

He peeked behind his shoulder. "Addie ..."

"Please." And now, she was crying, crying so hard that she didn't know what was rain and what was tears. "We can start over."

Two policemen burst through the doors, one instantly at her side, the other approaching Declan with his palms up.

To her surprise, Declan didn't move. He just stared and stared at her, even as the policeman coaxed his leg back over. She turned away to assure the cop next to her that she was all right—mostly all right.

When she looked back at him, Declan was crying.

TWENTY-FIVE

After the police came to the clock tower, an ambulance quickly followed. The EMTs wheeled Declan off as he murmured incomprehensibly about how sorry he was. To Adelaide? To his art? To Jack? She wasn't sure.

Because she'd been so banged up in the tussle, the nurses shuttled her through several X-rays and had a doctor come in to check her out. In the interim, she had to give the police a statement and explain how she knew Declan. It took hours.

When these things were finally finished, the sun had broken over the clouds, and she was bone tired and aching.

Declan had been sedated and was resting.

The doctor said they thought the event was likely the result of exhaustion, and with his previous history of depression, they wanted to keep a close eye on him. His parents had been notified.

She passed on the chance to see him. Not because she didn't care—she knew, logically, he had an illness—but she was angry with him, shell-shocked at the events of last night. And she hurt—physically and emotionally—in ways she never had before. She couldn't have grace for him right now.

They discharged her with instructions to rest and ice her bruises, which had sprung up on her skin over the past few hours. Her body felt like it weighed about a thousand pounds.

Declan had nearly died tonight, and for what? What had been the point of any of it if it ended this way—with both of them broken and alone?

She was shaken up, injured, and yet as she made her way through the sterile corridors, she realized she still had no one to call. She held all the people in her life at arm's length, even her roommates. And when someone new tried to make inroads, she fought it. Jack was the first person she'd let in maybe ever, and she'd ruined it. Somehow, all along, she had known she would.

"Oh good," a nurse said as she approached her station. She buzzed open the doors. "He's been waiting for you."

Her heart fluttered into her throat, mouth parting, expecting—

"Addie!" Bear cried, rising. His arms swallowed her a second later, burying her in his chest so hard that all the fluorescent lights above them were blinked out. "I never prayed in my life until last night."

"How did you—" she started, trying to pull back to look at him, but a second later, another set of arms snapped around her, so now, she was stuck between two people, being slowly depleted of oxygen.

"Ads," Michael breathed into her hair. His hands were shaking. "Thank fucking God."

Wiggling her head out of their arms, she spied Samantha at the other end of the hallway, barking into her cell phone. When she caught Adelaide's gaze, she stopped talking and ended the call, her expression indecipherable as she moved toward their huddle. She was wearing blue jeans and a wrinkled T-shirt, like she'd gotten dressed in a hurry.

Bear and Michael pulled apart when she got there, though Bear kept his hand on Adelaide's back, like he was scared she'd tip over.

Samantha took in the cuts and bruises on her arms, mouth pinched. She wouldn't stop looking, clocking every detail in that way she always did.

"You're supposed to be at your wedding," Adelaide said finally, when she'd had enough scrutiny. "Aren't you?"

Her sister crossed her arms. "We're your family, Addie. We're supposed to be right here."

Michael hugged her again, a little too hard, pressing on the tender spots that seemed to be all over her body.

"I'm okay, I promise." She shot a pleading look at her sister. "My head hurts, but I'm okay."

"Michael, enough," Samantha snapped, and Michael straightened, eyes a little glassy.

"Sam," Bear nudged, widening his eyes in Adelaide's direction.

She hadn't hugged her sister in years. Maybe since their parents had died. Actually, she couldn't remember if they'd even hugged then. Now, her sister came at her carefully, softly wrapping her arms around Adelaide, so much more softly than the boys had. It took them a few seconds to orient themselves, but finally, Adelaide lifted her hands to Samantha's back, taking in the familiar smell of her perfumes and lotions and hair sprays. Samantha smoothed Adelaide's hair against her back, the way her mother used to, and she didn't pull away until Adelaide did.

They stared at each other for a few seconds afterward. Were Samantha's eyes red? Had she been crying? It was so hard to tell after being awake this long. Her sister was here but as much of a mystery as ever. For once though, Adelaide was content to leave it there, because her brain couldn't go further than that right now.

When Samantha stepped back she said, "You look like shit."

Adelaide nodded. She felt that way too.

"Come on." She walked Adelaide back toward the reception area and aggressively flagged down a nurse. "Hello? Can we get this girl some Xanax, please?"

The nurse sprang to attention, as people usually did when Samantha talked. Adelaide let her lead, grateful she was like this, for the first time ever. All she could think about was a pillow and whatever the doctors had prescribed, followed by a blissful fade into nothingness.

When Adelaide woke up, there was buttery morning sunlight filtering into the room, which meant she'd slept through an entire day. She shut her eyes again, trying to figure out what hurt. Her tailbone mostly and her elbow. Her scalp stung where she'd cut it, but she resisted the urge to prod at the stitches. Instead, she slowly raised her head, looking around the hotel room where they'd stored her overnight. And blinked.

A tall, broad-shouldered figure stood with his back to her, arms crossed, staring out the window.

Something combusted inside her chest.

Jack turned, his face shadowed by the sun. She squinted as he came closer, trying to see his expression, trying to figure out if this was a dream.

When he got to the foot of her bed, she saw his eyes were red, exhausted, and there was scruff on his jaw. The shirt he had on had probably been neatly pressed at one point, but now, it was creased with a hundred wrinkles, and his hair had been raked through at least as many times. He looked so real, so damn alive. If she was dreaming this, she didn't want to wake up.

What was he doing here?

"You got hurt," Jack said simply, answering a question she hadn't even asked.

She was up and kneeing her way across the bed to him in a second, flinging her arms around his shoulders, going limp when he caught her around the waist. She was crying before her head landed on his chest, full-on sobs that racked her deeply, memories of last night flooding without end—the phone call; the rain; Declan's tortured, wild eyes. She didn't even try to contain it. She laid it all on Jack, and he took it in stride.

"It's all right," he soothed, tangling a hand in her hair. "None of this was your fault. You stopped him, Adelaide. That was all you could do. That's everything." His lips brushed her forehead. "It's okay. I'm here now."

After some time, her knees started to give. She sank down onto the bed but kept her arms around his waist, burying her face in Jack's stomach, devouring the scent and feel of him so close to her again. Relief flooded her body, dulling the pain. Jack let her stay just like that for a minute, stroking her head, getting her used to him again, until he finally tilted her face to his and gave her a gentle smile.

"Let's get you cleaned up."

She'd vaguely registered her family's suite at the Claremont Hotel last night, but now, she realized it was probably the biggest in the place—with a living room, a kitchen, and two bedrooms, one of which they'd put her in. Jack led her into its en suite bathroom and held a tissue to her nose, waiting for her to blow. Then, he turned on the shower and pulled some towels off the shelf, and found her some shampoo, plus a washcloth. He lined these things up with a practical efficiency she had never seen him use before.

"Who called you?" she asked, her voice small and hoarse, when he leaned in to test the water temperature.

"Michael. The university's publicist. Michael again. Your family is in the living room. They're still panicking, I think."

Adelaide froze. "You met Samantha."

"I had that distinct honor, yes. Arms up."

She didn't move. "What did she do to you?"

Jack's head dipped to check her expression, chuckling when he saw her features painted with horror. "Nothing I couldn't handle, sweet girl."

"That's what everyone thinks." Adelaide winced at the soreness in her shoulder as he pulled her sweater over her head, leaving her in the same T-shirt and leggings she'd worn when leaving LA … when? Yesterday? She could only guess how long she'd been asleep, thanks to the pills the doctors had given her. "She was supposed to get married."

"I thought that was this weekend. She didn't say anything. Mostly, she's been calling various doctors, reciting your injuries and asking them if you need another brain scan." He looked around for a place to put her ripped-up sweater and decided on the trash. Then, his thumbs hooked in the waistband of her leggings, but he stopped, meeting her eyes.

"It's okay," she assured him, her voice giving out at the end like she'd come down with laryngitis.

He winced at the sound, worry etched around his mouth, his eyes like he'd just taken an arrow to the chest. He was making a good attempt at hiding it, but his gaze kept skirting over her like he was going to find an injury the doctors had missed.

Jack brought his forehead to hers at the same time his hands found her hips, and he let out a heavy, exhausted sigh. "I never wanted to get a call like that again, Adelaide."

"I'm right here."

"What the hell were you thinking, going up there alone?" he demanded. "You should have called the police and stayed put. Or the university. You should have called *me*, for God's sake!"

"You're yelling at me," she pointed out.

"Of course I'm yelling at you," he hissed. "I didn't warn you about him. When you told me what he was doing, I should've said something. I knew he was unstable. I should have fucking—"

"Shh," she quieted, bumping his nose with her own. "Let's beat ourselves up later, okay?" Her hands curled in his shirt, and she breathed in the smell of him until it was the only thing in her brain.

Jack was here, after everything. It didn't matter what had happened between them or what would happen in the future; she just needed him now.

He gingerly worked her T-shirt over her head. There were red welts on her ribs, promising more ugly bruises tomorrow. He walked around her in a slow circle, appraising the damage, and sucked in a breath. Most of the bruises weren't so bad, but altogether, she looked like she'd gone twelve rounds in a prizefighting match.

After he helped her out of her pants, he pulled back the shower curtain and waved her in.

"Are you coming?" she asked shyly, not entirely sure what she wanted his answer to be.

"No. Do you want me to?"

She shifted the sore muscles of her back and grimaced. "I might need help, washing my hair."

He still didn't climb in, but when it was time to do that part, he reached past the curtain to massage shampoo into her scalp, being careful around the cut just past her hairline. He started at the top, lathering it up before running it down the length of her long hair. She responded with small moans of appreciation.

"I didn't realize that you had such a way with hair."

"Well, I'm no stranger to this. I have my own."

"Word gets out that the best shampoo in the city is right here, all the other salons will close down."

"The only difference is, I wouldn't do this for just anyone."

She smiled into the spray of the shower.

When she was done, he held out a towel for her to step into and wrapped it around her tightly. Then, with another, he dried off her shoulders and her arms before kneeling in front of her to do her legs and feet as she held his shoulder for balance. When he rose again, he wrapped the towel around her hair, wringing excess moisture from the ends.

"Thank you," she whispered sheepishly, unable to meet his eyes. "For coming here."

"Adelaide." He pressed a thumb against her lips, quieting her. "There is no other place I should be."

He turned her around and nudged her butt back toward the bedroom.

"What did you tell my family about us?" she asked, looking around. Someone had left a change of clothes on the end of the bed—sweatpants and her favorite Cranst sweatshirt. *Good*, she thought. *At least someone called my roommates.* Though she couldn't imagine how they'd explained what had happened.

"From what I gather, the same as you. But Michael said it seemed like things were still unfinished with us and he figured

I'd want to know. I'd have been at the hospital with them, but I was in Paris. It took me longer to get back."

She didn't let herself imagine who he'd been there with, as she slipped the sweatshirt over her head. "How's Declan?"

"Alive, probably to his disappointment." Jack was unable to keep the bitter edge out of his voice. "He'll need to spend a week or so in the hospital, leveling out. I got his parents a flight out as soon as I could."

"You did?" She wrinkled her forehead as Jack sat on the bed and held her pants open by the waistband, waiting for her to step inside.

"I feel responsible for all of this," he admitted without meeting her eyes.

"Jack." She tilted his face up. "Declan's sick. It's no one's fault."

"He wasn't well when I knew him, and when you said I stole his paintings, I should have known things had gotten bad again." It was hard to place the angry, pained look in his eyes, but the closest she could come was shame. "Dammit, I'll never forgive myself for leaving you. I was just mad, Adelaide. I wasn't thinking."

"I'm okay," she insisted.

He flipped up the hem of her sweatshirt, exposing a quick flash of a bruise. "Sure, you look just fine."

She bit her lip. "What do you mean, you knew it had gotten bad again?"

But Jack waved her off. "Let's talk about him later. Your family will want to know you're awake."

"They can wait," she responded firmly and not entirely nicely. "And I think I deserve an explanation."

He met her eyes, and seeing her adamancy, he nodded. He tugged her down onto the bed next to him. "Declan probably told you I pursued him. That's true. He was young, unpolished. I could see his career so clearly in front of me. I brought him over to London—I was spending a lot of time there that year— as soon as I could." Jack brushed a yellowing spot on her forearm. "You know by now, the lengths I have to go to, to woo a client. Declan was eighteen, so I gave him what anyone would give an eighteen-year-old. Parties. Girls. Alcohol. A huge studio at the gallery. I probably promised him too much. But I never expected what it would do to him."

"It didn't go well," she guessed.

"Early on, it became clear there was something off about him. At first, I attributed it to his age. Unfamiliar city. Someone powerful taking an interest. No expenses spared. He would stay up for days, painting, partying, painting again. Then, he'd crash, and I wouldn't see him for a week. I thought it was just his way, his genius. But after a while, I realized it was more than that."

Jack pushed off the bed and began pacing in front of her. "Declan started acting paranoid. He was drunk all the time, ranting that he was sure someone was going to steal or sabotage his work. Then, he thought *I* was sabotaging his work. He'd gotten some incoherent scheme in his head that I wanted to take his money from him. But his art …" Jack paused and stared out the window, like he was seeing an entirely different scene below. "It was amazing. I knew he was going to be big. I told Declan to get sober, show up for his opening, and I'd handle the rest. But he couldn't even do that. He showed up two hours late, drunk, babbling. Screaming."

Jack pressed the heels of his palms to his eyes. "He pulled out a lighter. Went at his own pictures like I've never seen. I mean, people actually thought that was the exhibit for a few minutes—him burning his own pictures.

"Security wrestled him to the ground but not before he destroyed a couple of his best pieces. We got him to the hospital, but I was worried about what he'd do to the rest, so I took the paintings for safekeeping. I closed the gallery while they repaired the fire damage, stored the collection, and told Declan and his family that I'd hold on to them until he was well."

He turned back to her, dejected and guilty. "I thought it was *genius*, Adelaide. That I'd just never been in the presence of it before. But I was wrong."

"What was it really?"

"Oh, it *was* genius. But it was also something dark. Something that requires doctors. Therapy. Medication. I'm not sure exactly, but it's not *just* genius. Maybe you don't get one without the other." He moved back to sitting next to her and took her hands between his. "I've had his paintings ever since. I just did what I thought was right—and that is the truth, I swear to you. I kept them, thinking, eventually, he'd get help, and I'd manage him to the fame he deserved. If he told you it was something else ..."

"He wanted them back. He said he couldn't paint without them."

Jack snorted. "Then, why did he try and destroy them?" Adelaide couldn't give an answer, but he nodded like she had. "He's just ... sick."

"I'm sorry," she said quietly.

"You have nothing to apologize for," he scolded, an edge in his voice. "I should be apologizing to *you*. I should have protected you from him."

"I'm still sorry for lying. You didn't deserve it."

"You did what Declan forced you to do."

"He wouldn't have forced me if I hadn't been doing the wrong thing to begin with."

Jack blew out a big breath and dropped his head between his shoulders. She wanted to massage the back of his neck, tangle her fingers in his hair as easily as she used to. She settled for touching his hand, stroking the empty space of his ring finger.

They looked down at the touch together.

"You deserve so much more than me, Adelaide," Jack said softly. He covered her hand with his and moved it off. "Come on. We really should let your family know you're awake."

TWENTY-SIX

They must have ordered from every restaurant on Main Street. There wasn't a food group unrepresented, and Michael loaded her plate with a little bit of everything even though the painkillers had made her slightly nauseous.

"Killer pasta salad," Michael said, spooning her some. "Sorry, was that insensitive?"

"We've gotta eat." Bear shrugged, biting into a burger. Well, he definitely did. She remembered Bear's eating schedule was pretty strict to keep up with the amount of calories he burned. Half the food here was probably for him.

"I didn't even know they had this big of a suite here," Adelaide murmured, mostly to Jack.

He turned up a casual palm at her, hanging back from the table, vaguely like the older teacher on a school field trip. He wasn't sure of his role here, and neither was she. But he wasn't leaving either, and for that, she was grateful.

"What about the wedding?" she asked Bear after she choked down a few bites of pasta salad.

"Oh, we still had the wedding. The bride and groom just weren't there."

"You mean, everyone still went?"

Bear nodded and pulled out his phone. "Not to a ceremony, obviously, but the reception was ready to go. We figured, whatever, let everyone enjoy. Looked like a crazy party too."

Her eyes widened as he scrolled through pictures of elaborately dressed wedding guests in Samantha and Bear's grotto. They featured more and more debauchery as they went on.

"I can't believe that Samantha just dropped everything to be here."

Bear took the phone back. "Believe it."

"You probably convinced her."

"Not even remotely," he said, popping the last half of a burger into his mouth. "She was up and moving the second we got the call about you from the university."

Adelaide let that simmer. "So, you're not married?"

"Nope, still very much engaged." He wiggled his eyebrows. "You think all this is a sign I should back out?"

Adelaide pretended to think about it.

Bear laughed and pulled her in for a half-armed hug. "I was scared as shit, you know. When they told us what happened. When they said you were going to the hospital. And your sister—you can imagine what the plane ride was like. I think her life flashed before her eyes."

Adelaide tried to smile, but it ended up as disbelieving as it felt.

"I mean it—she was petrified." When she still didn't budge, Bear elbowed her lightly. "She's not like she used to be, Addie. She's so different now."

"You sound like Michael."

When he turned to face her head-on, Bear's eyes got serious, more serious than she'd ever seen him look before. "Look, you can be mad at her for what she did forever. Hell, there were days I thought I would be too. But eventually, you'll dig yourself so far into a pit that you can't climb out of it, and no one will be able to pull you out either." He wrapped a big hand around her forearm and squeezed. "You and your brother and your sister are my family, Adelaide. I'd throw myself in front of a bus to keep one of you safe. Shit, I'd throw *Samantha* in front of a bus to keep you or Michael safe. But you know what? I don't think I'd have to. She'd jump first. For both of you."

Adelaide looked at her lap, turning that over. She didn't deny that her sister had seemed ... different in California. But they'd fought the same as always. Of course, then she'd shown up here, leaving her own wedding at the drop of a hat. Which was not at all like the sister she knew.

"You should talk to her." He nodded to the second bedroom across the suite, where her sister presumably was.

"What is she doing?"

"Trying to make new wedding arrangements. You know her."

"I've already ruined her wedding once!" Adelaide protested, only half-joking.

"Nah." Bear gave her a gentle, playful punch on the shoulder. "Go in there. She said she wanted to talk to you too."

She cut her eyes to Jack, who gave her a single nod. Michael looked at her so hopefully that her heart squeezed.

Adelaide drew in a deep breath and stood. One pro of feeling like she'd just gotten majorly beat up, was that she was hurting too much to have the energy for a fight.

She knocked on the closed door once, and when her sister said, "Come in," she pressed the brass door handle and stepped inside.

Samantha sat in the middle of the bed, laughing into her phone. "It's all right, Katrina," she insisted, her eyes sparkling. "No, I'm glad you're using the pool. How many people actually slept—oh my *God.*" She held up one finger to Adelaide. "Listen, I have to go, but tell the caterers the reschedule is the twenty-fifth. And if they give the date away, I'm going to lose it. *Lose it*, lose it."

"Rescheduling?" Adelaide asked when she hung up.

Samantha nodded, a trace of vulnerability in her voice when she spoke. "The caterer probably won't have the date open for me, so I've got to try and work some magic on him. But if the Goldens are in the playoffs … then I really don't know what we're going to do."

"I'm sorry I screwed it all up."

Samantha dramatically rolled her eyes. "Addie."

"Right," Adelaide murmured. "I'm going."

"No, that's not what I meant." She slid to the edge of the bed and patted the spot next to her. "Sit here. Please."

Adelaide went hesitantly, settling herself beside her sister, far enough so they weren't touching.

Samantha took a deep breath. "You never understood it, after Mom and Dad died."

"That's ridiculous. I was still a kid—"

"Wait. Just listen." Samantha flattened a palm against her forehead, like she was trying to slow down her thoughts, and took a deep breath. "I'm going about this all wrong. What I mean is, for me and for Michael, it didn't matter where we were. At the old house or even in Connecticut. It just mattered that we were together. Wherever all of us were, that was where our home was."

She pushed a lock of blonde hair behind her shoulder, hiking one knee up on the bed as she faced Adelaide. "But just because I felt that way didn't mean you did. You were younger, Addie; you needed to be where you were comfortable. A place you could adjust to being an …" Her sister trailed off, unable to say the word *orphan*. "And I should have seen that. I should have given you what you needed instead of being so focused on what I *thought* you needed. That was my job as your older sister, and I failed. And I'm sorry."

Adelaide stared, trying to figure out how the woman in front of her could look so much like her sister and yet act in her exact opposite manner. Because surely, this couldn't be Samantha Wright, the queen of no apologies, apologizing. Understanding—for perhaps the first time in her entire life—

that when her actions hurt people, it wasn't just an unfortunate consequence they needed to accept.

"After Mom and Dad died, everything was just thrown into my lap. You and Michael and the house and the future. All our futures. I was barely older than you are now. I had a whole life, and then … it was a new life."

Adelaide was too shocked to respond. Samantha, for as long as Adelaide could remember, had been the least self-aware person on the planet. Now, she was talking like she'd spent the past three and a half years soul-searching.

"I just crumbled. I was trying to take care of you, but all I could think of was, *Who is going to take care of me?*" Samantha sheepishly looked down into her lap. "Sounds stupid to you, I know. But I'm not as strong as you, Addie. You're so independent, so capable."

For a moment, Adelaide dared to think that her sister might cry. It made the heavy feeling in her chest recede.

"I didn't think going out there would solve everything, but I thought moving in with Bear would give us all the best shot at moving on. He could take care of us. Of me. I'm not saying I don't love him because I do, so much that it makes me want to hurl." She cleared her throat. "But I was selfish. I didn't think enough about what *you* needed. But it was only because I wanted you with me." She sniffled, and now, tears did form in her eyes. "But I shouldn't have done it at the expense of pushing you away."

Adelaide could feel something cracking around her heart. She didn't forgive Samantha—at least, not entirely—but a window had appeared and let something else in. Something warm and not prickly at all.

She tried to hand Samantha a tissue, but she pushed it away and took Adelaide's hand instead. "I know it was a bad thing, what I did with the inheritance. Holding that over you. I want you to have it, and Mom and Dad wanted you to have it. I just … I couldn't help thinking that if I gave you the money, you'd leave, and I'd never see you again."

Adelaide bit her lip. Samantha was right. That had been her plan when she was eighteen, looking for any way to escape. But in the end, it would've been a tragedy because what Michael had said was right—her parents would've hated knowing that they weren't all together. If they'd had to leave the world the way they had, then all Adelaide was left with was ways to honor them. And knowing their children stuck together was one.

"But I see now," Samantha continued, putting on a brave smile, "if you'd stayed around just for the money, it wouldn't have meant anything anyway. I want a relationship with you just because you're my sister. Not for any other reasons."

When Adelaide didn't respond right away, Samantha's face fell just slightly.

"I get it if you think I'm full of shit." She stood up and started rifling through her purse. "I'll just give you the papers now."

"Samantha," Adelaide said, speaking for the first time since Samantha had started. She leaned forward to touch her sister's cashmere-covered elbow. "I want that too." She hadn't thought before she said it, but she realized she did mean it. Things with her sister wouldn't heal overnight, but she wanted to start here. Now.

"You do?"

Adelaide nodded. "I just miss them so much."

"I know," Samantha answered, her voice raspy. A tear slipped down her porcelain cheek. "I do too. Every minute." She swallowed and met Adelaide's eyes. "I didn't mean what I said. It wasn't your fault, what happened to them. I never thought it was. I was just so angry at everything." She held out a manicured hand. "I'm sorry, Addie."

The crack in Adelaide's chest split open now, and tears brimmed in her eyes. There was no ulterior motive she could come up with for Samantha to say all these things, no reason beyond what was stated.

Adelaide clasped her hand in return and squeezed.

"God." Samantha laughed, brushing away her tears. "What is wrong with me today? Bear has turned me so fucking soft."

After a few deep breaths, her eyes went sharp again, tears cleared away like they'd never happened. "Now, for the juicy stuff. What's up with Jack? He's here, so things are obviously *not* as over as you thought."

"No, we are. You were probably right. He's too old for me."

"I'm always right," Samantha corrected, shooting Adelaide a teasing wink. "That said, he clearly cares about you. You should have seen him when he got here. It was like ..." She rearranged her face into a mask that was equal parts panic and fury, even mimicking that little jaw tic Jack got when he was focusing really hard.

"He's very intense," Adelaide agreed, trying to push away the image of Jack as her knight in shining armor, coming to her rescue. She'd written a paper for a junior named Abigail Diccicio on why the trope was so pervasive and detrimental, yet today, she'd found herself as desperate for him as any damsel in distress. "And things are ... complicated."

"Did it have to do with Declan? I *told* Michael to tell you what I knew about him—" Her jaw suddenly dropped. "Were you doing both of them?"

"No!" She smacked her sister's knee and laughed despite the fact that doing so hurt her sore ribs. Only Samantha, her sister, could be so direct. Adelaide had forgotten how much she missed that. Samantha had always been straight up with her about everything, without mincing words. "It's a long story," she said finally.

And one she had no intentions of telling Samantha *ever*, reconciled or not.

"A lot has happened. We've both been pretty shitty to each other. It was nice of him to come here, but he's older, and he's"—*married*—"difficult. And I'm ... Me."

"Yeah, you're you. So what? He should die to have someone like you." Samantha dipped her face, so they were eye-level. "And Addie? No hyperbole now, okay? He knows it."

"Jack doesn't think about me like that."

Yes, he'd come to her, taken care of her like she was fragile, but he felt guilty about Declan. That didn't mean he suddenly wanted to start things over.

"Don't be an idiot, Adelaide. Talk to him. Figure it out. He's here, and I don't think he plans to leave your side anytime soon."

But he *had* left her. Probably to hop in bed with his next hired woman. His next *her.*

When she didn't answer, Samantha threw up her hands. "Then, I guess you don't care about him that much after all. Look, everyone makes it sound like love is this secret little key to unlock everything, and if you have it, things will be fine. But they're wrong. It's just step one. The rest is work. Compromise. Forgiveness."

"Easy for you to say. You have, like, the American dream man."

Adelaide was surprised when her sister's eyes grew unexpectedly wistful. "You saw us as perfect because that's what I wanted you to see, Addie. But we've gone through our shit, like anyone else." Samantha's eyes traced the door, on the other side of which was her fiancé. "We had a lot of growing up to do, together. We hurt each other plenty. But we came back and fixed it. Over and over until we figured out how to stop doing it. Now, he's like ..."

"Your best friend."

Samantha pressed her lips together and nodded. "So, you have to ask yourself, are you ready to do the work?"

Adelaide thought that over. Fixing things with Jack felt enormous. How did she know what kind of relationship they could have, outside of the arrangement? Even when things had been good, they'd always been bound by a contract.

When they finally made their way outside to rejoin the group, Jack was at the table with Bear and Michael, having what looked like a congenial enough conversation.

"Can you get out of the playoffs?" Samantha asked, flicking the back of Bear's head when she came to stand behind him.

Michael looked at Adelaide for an indication as to how the talk had gone. Adelaide smiled at him, so he knew that nothing had exploded.

When her eyes moved to Jack, he lowered his chin, as if to say, *Whatever you want, I'll back you up.*

Bear said between bites, "No new dates?"

"None that I'm confident in. At this rate, we might as well wait until after the Super Bowl."

"Hey, you know what?" Michael started, looking around. "Why wait? We're all here. Addie is here. Let's just do the wedding right now." He pointed to his chest. "I bet we can find an officiant to get registered online."

Adelaide scoffed. "Yeah, right. Samantha wants to have her dream wedding. She's been planning it since she was—" But she broke off when she looked over at her sister, expecting to find her glaring. She was actually narrowing her eyes at Bear, who was hiding a smile behind his hand. "Unless … you want to?"

"Sam?" Bear nudged. "You wanna marry me today?"

All eyes turned to Samantha, waiting.

To everyone's surprise—mostly Adelaide's—she said, "Yes, I do."

TWENTY-SEVEN

In the end, Samantha and Bear's wedding took place in the bar of the Claremont, in front of a big stone fireplace they'd turned on just for the occasion. Thanks to Jack's clout at the hotel, they closed off the bar for the night and brought in a full dinner spread afterward. Samantha wore jeans and a white T-shirt, and Bear gave her a pinkie ring that had been floating at the bottom of Adelaide's purse.

It was nothing like they'd thought, but when the vows were done and the bride and groom shared their first kiss, Samantha put her arms around Adelaide and whispered, "This was so much better than what I'd planned."

The celebratory mood kept things breezy between her and Jack, which was a relief since she wasn't sure what she'd say once they were alone. If he even wanted to be alone. Where did they stand now? Their apologies from earlier had settled some things, but others still floated in the air around them, unfinished.

"No lawyers necessary then?" Jack asked quietly, pushing away his plate of dessert.

Samantha, Michael, and Bear were excitedly video-calling someone in Los Angeles on the other side of the table, rehashing the whole story.

"Your inheritance," he clarified when she frowned.

"Oh." She cleared her throat. "No. None for now."

Jack brought his head an inch closer. "I'm proud of you, you know. For forgiving her. Or at least trying to. Family is very precious."

She nodded, the compliment making her stomach flutter. "Thanks for staying today."

Under the table, his hand covered hers. "Looks like I was your plus-one after all."

But the joke hurt, and she bother to didn't hide it when she met his eyes. Their heads were closer than she'd realized, his breath landing on her cheek. Talking in voices like they were sharing secrets.

He threaded his hand through hers fully.

"I fucked everything up," she murmured, voice thick with unshed tears.

"Shh," he quieted, stroking the back of her hand with his thumb. "Not possible. You're smart. You're beautiful. You're about to graduate and make your mark on the world."

"I meant, with us."

Jack leaned in until his nose brushed her cheek. "According to my calendar, you have two weeks left on the contract. So, no, you haven't." He pulled back to shoot her a questioning look. "If you're willing to come back, that is."

Her heart pounded a wild drumbeat. "Is that what you want?"

"If that's all I can have, yes. Absolutely. I'm going to milk this time for every second I have left."

Adelaide's lips parted in surprise. Back to the arrangement, except now, they had no more secrets. They could just be themselves, completely.

"Yes," she breathed without hesitating.

"Good."

Jack approached her mouth with his, but at the last second, he shifted and dropped a quick kiss on her cheek instead. As he did, his fingers touched the bare spot on her throat, where his necklace usually sat. She'd taken it off after Maine. It had felt like it belonged to someone else.

"Put it back on for me, please."

Adelaide nodded, a blush climbing up her cheeks when her sister looked over and smiled at them, huddled together.

Two weeks.

She'd make them count.

TWENTY-EIGHT

Jack hadn't been exaggerating when he said he planned to milk this time for every second he had left. He asked Adelaide to accompany him everywhere—exhibitions and business meetings, dinners and drinks, even on quick trips to see his high-maintenance clients. They spent Christmas in Miami, New Year's Eve in Boston, and the sleepy days in between doing nothing at all.

It turned out that doing nothing with Jack, was a hundred times better than doing anything without him.

After she finished up her finals, she separated almost completely from the Cranst campus, except for the few nights she spent hanging out with her roommates, filling them in on everything she'd kept from them the past three months. Besides Jack, they were the only people in her life who knew the whole truth, and it felt good to be honest with them again. Their relationship wasn't entirely back to normal after her deception, but now, at least they understood her reasons. They'd get back there eventually.

The rest of the time, she spent at Jack's. They didn't have sex, but they slept tangled around each other at night and showered together in the morning, watching the other with hungry expressions as they dressed.

It wasn't that she didn't want him—she felt like she was going mad some nights, pressed up against him—but after everything that had transpired, sex felt like it would start something new instead of ending this. Which was what she was really there for anyway.

They were the happiest two weeks of her life.

Her final night with him included an event at his flagship gallery in Chelsea, for an up-and-coming artist Jack found in Cincinnati a few months prior. It was a big event with write-ups in all the major magazines and newspapers. The art world, which oftentimes agreed on nothing, seemed to have come together for once, and the room was filled with major players from all over, clamoring to get a look. Even Rene and Nadine had come to town.

It made Adelaide feel a little sad, walking around the pictures, because she couldn't help thinking of Declan. Declan, who, years ago, had had the same aspirations as every budding artist. Who'd shown up at Jack's gallery, hoping for an illustrious career. Who'd perceived things in a way that made people think differently and wanted nothing more than to share that vision with others. He deserved to have this too.

Now, that dream was on hold. Maybe forever, but some things were more important.

Though Adelaide had tried to see him, she'd received a simple answer in response—no. Declan didn't want to see her. At first, she hadn't known whether he was angry with her for stopping him or bitter he'd been hospitalized because of it.

But now, she understood.

True to his word, Jack had mailed every last painting he'd kept back to Declan's parents. If Declan wanted him to represent him one day when he was well, Jack would be glad to take them back. If not, he'd seemed to realize they were no longer his to keep, no matter how noble his intentions had been.

A few days after he'd returned them, she received a letter in her mailbox at Cranst. It was postmarked from Upstate New York with no return address, written on a piece of torn scrap paper.

Addie,

The doctors tell me I need to stop being so hard on myself.

But I can't do that until I make things right with you, so let me say up front, I'm sorry for everything. I put you through hell, and I don't deserve forgiveness for it. I took away your choices—from the start and right up until the night you pulled me back from the ledge. The truth is, when I painted that picture of you in Hamden, what you couldn't see was that I ripped open an artery for it. That day, I started bleeding, and until now, I haven't been able to stop.

The doctors here are helping me figure that out too.

They're also helping me figure out why I spiraled so hard in London and then again when I met you. Talking helps. Painting is better. I've been working on a picture of a big tree on the grounds, which is bare right now, but which I paint to look as if it were blooming with flowers. I like thinking of it that way more—what it can be, not what it is.

Did you know that in botany, the process by which plants shed their leaves is called abscission? They're genetically wired to do it. We watch it happen every autumn, and we say the leaves have died. But in actuality, they've just made way for new, budding life come spring. It's an ending and a beginning at the same time. I keep thinking about that while I paint. For the first time, I feel like I am at the beginning of something.

Like there's hope.

I'm not ready for visitors right now, but maybe when I'm out of here, we can catch up.

In the meantime, let me say again how sorry I am about what I did. Every day, I feel like I took something from you, and I wish I could give it back.

Thank you for saving my life. And thanks to Jack for keeping my work safe.

Declan

Adelaide found herself in front of a beautiful portrait, painted by Jack's new artist, a wide-eyed girl named Morgan. It was indeed something special. And thankfully, the artist herself, though as young as Declan had been when he began his career, was personable, the life of the party. Jack had made it his mission to handle her with kid gloves, but she was a natural. Most of the gallery was gathered around her as she explained her inspiration for a picture she'd done last year.

Adelaide glanced over and caught Jack staring at her. He bridged the distance, grabbing two glasses of champagne on the way, and handed her one.

"She doesn't even need me," he muttered a little mournfully.

"Give it time. She will. I've heard that you really know what you're doing when it comes to these things."

He gave her a self-deprecating shrug. "Maybe."

"Well," she began because she'd been genuinely curious about this all evening, "tonight's the end of the contract. How do you plan to say good-bye? A cordial shake of the hand?"

"Is that what you want?" he asked, giving her a sideways glance.

"I believe, as you made it pretty clear in the beginning, that it's not about what *I* want. Remember? *Do this. Do that. Blend in. Don't embarrass me …*"

"Well, since this is your last official night, I suppose I can let you have a little leeway. If a cordial shake of the hand is what you want, that's what you'll get."

Her heart sank even though she knew he was playing with her. But this event was it. The end. Contract fulfilled. After this, there was no reason to stay together. Every reason to separate. He could continue on, making arrangements with random women, and she'd throw herself into her postgraduate career. Thanks to her inheritance, she had enough money now to keep herself afloat while she searched for a job.

But when she looked at Jack, she couldn't help but see her future. Maybe not a perfect one, but was anything really perfect? Even the most legendary works of art had their flaws. And maybe that was the best they could hope for.

But she wanted him to acknowledge it, too, and without her prodding him to do it. Without that, it felt like he really was ready to let her go, leave their arrangement for what it was.

When they pulled up to his apartment after the showing, she reached out her hand. "Good-bye then."

He looked at his watch. "I still have forty-five minutes."

"Oh?" She smiled. "What should we do?"

Creases appeared around his eyes as he pretended to think. "You can come in?"

"All right."

When they were through the door of his apartment, she tried to kiss him, but he shook his head and stepped back. Grin on his face, he held out his hand for a handshake.

Instead, she pressed her mouth against his palm, watching him closely, memorizing every minute reaction. The way it made him smile and then the way it made him look a little sad. Then the way his eyes hooded when she moved her mouth up to the sensitive skin on the inside of his wrist.

He pushed her back until she was leaning on the arm of his couch, roughly kissing her, lifting her dress. She'd been waiting long—too long—for this, and her movements were excited, clumsy. She advanced her hands up his chest, past his shoulders, to a full-on offensive campaign through the thickness of his hair. She kissed him harder, urging him closer. Never satisfied.

Jack moved to the couch and pulled her onto his lap, leaning his head back while she unbuttoned his shirt, kissing the column of his throat and the warm, bare skin of his shoulder as she pushed it down his well-defined arms. Slowly, tenderly, she skimmed his hot flesh with the feathered touch of one finger and then bent low to press her lips against his collarbone.

"I missed you so much," she whispered.

"You have no idea how much I missed you, Adelaide."

She rocked against him, heat spiraling through her body at the touch. Her hips moved instinctually, her movements growing more exaggerated when his eyes shut and his breathing became rough.

When her hand drifted between them, he sucked in a breath, buckling with need. "We're wearing too many clothes."

She took hers off for him, right there in the living room, letting him watch without feeling self-conscious at all. Gazing at her with appreciation, he tugged her closer and kissed her bare stomach. "Gorgeous," he whispered against her skin. "You're so gorgeous."

"Why are you still dressed?"

"You were the one who pulled my shirt off." He dropped his hands and sat back, fixing her with a lascivious smirk. "Finish what you started, Adelaide."

She undid the button of his pants, losing her breath when he reached out to stroke her cheek at the same time she dragged his zipper down. He let her tug them off, but the second they were discarded he hauled her back into his lap, like he couldn't stand to have her away that long.

"Good girl," he murmured when she settled back on top of him, no separation between them now.

The praise made her whimper. At the sound, he sat up, cradling her by the small of her back, his tongue grazing its way down her jaw. He licked his way down to her collarbone. Pulling her near, he set out on a trail of exploration. Her breathing got more desperate, the closer he dragged the hot moisture of his lips to her breasts. He snaked his tongue toward her left nipple, closer, closer, nearly to its peak. Instinctively, she pressed toward him.

Jack smiled against her, skimmed it along his bottom lip and then pulled it inside his mouth.

Her hands fisted his hair in a no-mercy grip. She'd needed him for weeks, and she was terrified to let him go. Terrified this would be the last time she'd ever have him this close.

As if sensing her worry, he moved up to kiss her chin, her cheeks, her mouth. She shuddered against him, wrapping her arms around his shoulders to hold him for a second, before they went too far.

"I can't believe you're here," he whispered into her ear. He pushed her hair aside, and his eyes traveled from her eyes, to her nose, to her mouth, and back again, as if he was trying to commit each and every one of her features to memory. "I feel like I've dreamed you back into my life."

"No," she said breathlessly, as he gathered her body up against his. "I'm right here with you. Flesh and—oh my God." As she talked, he'd slowly lowered her down, her body molding around him like it had never stopped. It drew a curse out of him.

Adelaide rocked slowly, stars dancing in her vision until she squeezed her eyes shut, overwhelmed. Being away from him— from *this*—had been like missing a piece of herself.

Jack bit her shoulder, and then he soothed the ache with his tongue. "And you wanted to say good-bye."

"This isn't good-bye," she rasped, trembling. She started moving in desperate little waves, breathing hard. "It can't be."

He raked his hands through her hair, tugging her head back to expose her throat. Then he leaned forward and kissed her neck so reverently that something unspooled inside her, making her body feel like it was melting.

"Again," she pleaded.

He complied, kissing her just as gently as before, like he knew anything else would throw her off. Jack could make her lose her mind in a hundred different ways, but when he was tender like this, it was like he was reaching in and stroking her very soul.

The second she tensed and gripped his back, he pushed her down further in his lap, his every muscle vibrating and tightening, clenching and releasing, as she let out soft whimpers above him.

When they both returned to earth sometime later, their eyes locked on one another.

Jack tipped forward to kiss her jaw. "I can't remember the last time I did that without signing a damn contract first."

She pulled away to see his whole face, her body still languid. "We did sign one. You made me."

"No." He reached a long arm out and twisted the clock on the end table toward them. "Our contract expired at midnight."

Sure enough, it was twelve fifteen. Her heart lurched.

"The deal is over. We're both here because we want to be." He met her eyes. "Right?"

She kissed him as an answer. Slowly, taking her time. There was no deadline now. She kept at him until they both grew tired, and he carried her up to bed with her legs locked around his waist, their mouths still moving against each other's. There was nothing holding her here, except that it was the place where she knew she belonged.

Leaning over her, still kissing, Jack started to smile.

"What?" she demanded, laughing for no good reason.

He sighed and pressed his forehead to hers. "I'm in love with you, is all."

Her eyes went wide. "You are?"

"Been here for a while."

"Me too," she whispered, keeping her eyes on him.

"Why didn't you tell me?"

"I wanted you to go first."

"Honest." He chuckled. "Thank God."

Side by side, they lay in bed, talking well into the morning about anything and everything. Eventually though, sleep won out, and Jack was lured off to dreamland. She watched as his eyelids fluttered shut, and then he was gone, his breathing calm, relaxed, like the slumber of a man who didn't have a care in the world.

Adelaide rolled out of bed and then padded to the window. The sun was just coming up over the city skyline, the clouds dappled with pink and orange hues. It was a gorgeous scene, full of the kind of effortless beauty that couldn't be replicated on a canvas. Good art transported, she knew, but there were some things you had to experience for yourself.

She turned back to Jack's sleeping form, his torso and face bathed in the rising pink light.

So perfect, she thought. *It could almost be a picture.*

If you or someone you know is in crisis, please contact the
Suicide Prevention Lifeline.

1-800-273-8255 or https://suicidepreventionlifeline.org/

ACKNOWLEDGMENTS

If our art is a reflection of ourselves, then this book is a mosaic of the people I am indebted to for their help in creating it. Thank you to Cyn Balog, Kristen Weber, Jovana Shirley, and all of the beta readers—your expertise and guidance were invaluable.

Thank you also to the family and friends who have supported me, lent an ear, or inspired something in these pages. I won't tell if you won't.

The journey of publishing a book is long and winding and often feels more important than the destination. So, finally, thank you to the readers, for meeting me when I arrived.

ABOUT THE AUTHOR

Maren Mackenzie is a graduate of Rutgers University and a New Jersey native. She spent the early part of her career working in the literary department of a mega-talent agency, wondering why she was helping everyone else with their books instead of writing a few of her own. Maren has since traded publishing for the legal industry and New Jersey for Miami Beach. *Rules of Arrangement* is her first novel.